"Ellison is not only a first-rate novelist and a highly skilled screenwriter, but a man of passion and, consequently, his book . . . is less journalese than informal literature (the difference, an old newspaperman once told me, is like the difference between bricklaying and architecture). Unlike a lot of quack critics that abound these days, Ellison can be enthusiastic . . . he can attack his typewriter with both fists in white anger . . ."

Cecil Smith, *Los Angeles Times*

"THE GLASS TEAT can be called nothing less than a memorable book . . ."

Walter Cronkite

"Ellison has been a writer for both television and the movies and is in an advantageous spot to see both sides of the screen. His view is an engaging one. His book offers a fresh look at the tube and the people who people it."

Bob Woessner, *Green Bay Press-Gazette*

"The pieces are refreshingly frank (if four-lettered) and acutely critical. This book is not for those who dig the King Family or Green Acres."

Publishers Weekly

"Harlan Ellison, better known to most as an award-winning science fiction writer, has proved himself one of the most lucid television critics in the country with his articles entitled THE GLASS TEAT. Ellison is an effective gadfly. He presents the anti-Establishment view with a flair . . ."

San Jose Mercury-News

BOOKS BY HARLAN ELLISON

- ■ Web of the City (1958)
- ● The Deadly Streets (1958)
- The Sound of a Scythe (1960)
- A Touch of Infinity (1960)
- Children of the Streets (1961)
- ■ Gentleman Junkie *and other stories of the hung-up generation* (1961)
- ● Memos from Purgatory (1961)
- ■ Spider Kiss (1961)
- Ellison Wonderland (1962)
- ● Paingod *and other delusions* (1965)
- ● I Have No Mouth & I Must Scream (1967)
- Doomsman (1967)
- Dangerous Visions [Editor] (1967)
- From the Land of Fear (1967)
- Nightshade & Damnations: *the finest stories of Gerald Kersh* [Editor] (1968)
- ■ Love Ain't Nothing but Sex Misspelled (1968)
- The Beast that Shouted Love at the Heart of the World (1969)
- ■ The Glass Teat *essays of opinion on television* (1970)
- Over the Edge (1970)
- ■ Partners in Wonder *sf collaborations with 14 other wild talents* (1971)
- Alone Against Tomorrow *stories of alienation in speculative fiction* (1971)
- Again, Dangerous Visions [Editor] (1972)
- All the Sounds of Fear [British publication only] (1973)
- The Time of the Eye [British publication only] (1974)
- Approaching Oblivion (1974)
- The Starlost #1: Phoenix Without Ashes [with Edward Bryant] (1975)
- Deathbird Stories (1975)
- ● The Other Glass Teat *further essays of opinion on television* (1975)
- ● No Doors, No Windows (1975)
- Strange Wine (1978)
- The Book of Ellison [Edited by Andrew Porter] (1978)
- The Illustrated Harlan Ellison [Edited by Byron Preiss] (1978)
- The Fantasies of Harlan Ellison (1979)
- All the Lies That Are My Life (1980)
- Shatterday (1980)
- Stalking the Nightmare (1982)

- ■ Available in Ace Books editions.
- ● Forthcoming in Ace Books editions.

HARLAN ELLISON
THE GLASS TEAT

Essays of opinion on the subject of television

ACE BOOKS, NEW YORK

THE GLASS TEAT

These columns appeared originally in the
Los Angeles Free Press.

An Ace Book/published by arrangement with
the Author

PRINTING HISTORY
Ace edition / May 1973

ISBN: 0-441-28988-6

Ace Books are published by Charter Communications, Inc.
200 Madison Avenue, New York, New York 10016.
PRINTED IN THE UNITED STATES OF AMERICA

This collection of random thoughts and strident alarums is dedicated, with gratitude, respect, but mostly love to the affectionately named

CRAZY JUNE BURAKOFF

and to ART & VAL KUNKIN, JACK BURGESS, TED ZATLYN, MARY REINHOLZ, CHRIS BUNCH, RON COBB, FRAN TROY, ALEX APOSTOLIDES, ALISON KAUFMAN and to JOHN O'HARA, whose "conservative" columns, "My Turn," in the Establishment newspapers convinced me of the need for some hyperthyroid gadflying.

The author wishes to thank the following persons for their assistance and support in the preparation of these columns and this book: Lynn Lehrhaupt, Leslie Kay Swigart, Terry Carr, Norman Goldfind, William Rotsler, Tom Smothers, Allen Rivkin, Louise Farr, Mary Reinholz, Norman Spinrad, Barbara Benham, John Baskin, Nat Freedland, Mary Freedland, Ed Bryant, Lucy Seaman, Sandra Rymer, James Sutherland, Joseph Stefano, Ray Bradbury, Cecil Smith, Laurence Laurent, Robert Blake, Stan Freberg, John Jakes, Joyce and Robert and Jeff Angus, Digby Diehl, Sue Cameron and the late Spiro T. Agnew.

NEW INTRODUCTION

The Glass Teat Revisited: A Supplementary Introduction / 1983

Now that Dick and Spiro and all their ghoul errand-boys are gone, you can read this book again.

I'm not much one for conspiracy theories—I'm not that paranoid yet but I'm getting there, I'm getting there—and so you'll understand that I'm telling you nothing but the flat truth when I explain that Agnew and his minions scuttled this book the first time around, in 1970. I'll even tell you how it happened, who to ask for verification that I'm not making it all up, and how it happens that THE GLASS TEAT got a second chance . . . thereby proving I've been storing up some good karma.

As you'll read in the introduction to the original edition of this collection of essays (it follows immediately hereafter), I started writing my television column for the *Los Angeles Free Press* in late 1968. I wrote the column every week for two and a half years; enough copy to fill two books of essays. The first was this one, originally published by Ace Books in 1970 as THE GLASS TEAT, reprinted by Pyramid in 1975. The other book, with the balance of the columns, was to be published by Ace in 1971 as THE OTHER GLASS TEAT. Second book never got born; and in *that* story lie the seeds of verification for everything I've set down in *this* book . . . everything about the rapacity and need to stifle criticism of Nixon's reign, that is. I'm wrong about a few things—like the nobility of youth, f'rinstance—but then, even God made a few mistakes. Otherwise how do you explain poison ivy, *tsunamis* and Donald Segretti?

As best I can make it (and getting cold-fact substantiation of the sequence of events was like trying to screw fog), here's what happened:

Ace released the original version of this book in March of 1970. It was their leader. Nice promotion, nice package, a lightweight PR trip during which I covered the major markets in the West and on the East Coast. The column was still running in the *Free Press* and I was hyping the book through that medium, as well. Reviews started coming in. Excellent reviews. Several hundred of them, not a downer in the batch. Cronkite mentioned the book, Cecil Smith in the LA *Times* did an entire column on it, college newspapers picked up on it and said it was the best down-home look at tv ever published; lotta that kind of ego-buildup.

The publisher was overjoyed. Terry Carr, then an editor at Ace, the man who'd first decided to publish the book, felt vindicated; John Waxman (now a v-p at another New York publishing house, but at the time Ace's head of publicity and promotion) kept a box of the books under his office desk so he could fill special requests on the spot; several colleges ordered large quantities and adopted the book for their "media" classes.

Preliminary reports from the field, after two months, showed an incredible seventy per cent sale on the first print run of 88,565 copies. Ace started talking about going back to press for another one hundred thousand copies, just in case we had hold of something that was taking off. Terry approached me for a second book, on instructions from the Ace higher-ups: "Sign him up for the sequel before the book hits so big he demands more money."

On August 10, 1970, I signed the contracts for THE OTHER GLASS TEAT, for four thousand dollars advance, same as I'd gotten on THE GLASS TEAT. And I kept on writing my columns, saying what I had to say about the condition of life in these here now United States, as viewed through the lens of television. Merely waiting till I hit column number 104 so the second book would be the same size as the first.

Then, suddenly, everything turned into a nightmare!

A friend called from Sacramento to tell me I'd been placed on then-California Governor Ronald Reagan's "subversives list." This was four years before we were to learn of "enemies lists" via the Watergate route, though such lists undoubtedly existed at that time. My name was one of several hundred on a semi-public document being circulated out of the California state capitol, ostensibly setting out guidelines for colleges and universities who hired guest lecturers. There I was with Abbie Hoffman and Dave Dellinger and Jane Fonda and other Commie-Symp radicals like John Ciardi and Dick Gregory. People our dear Unca' Ronnie would frown upon being solicited to come and talk; the hook was, of course, that state funds might be withheld at budget time the following year, from institutions that chose to ignore this friendly suggestion. It wasn't *exactly* a blacklist, just don't breathe too deeply, y'know what I mean?

That was the first indication I had that maybe my big fat typewriter had gotten me in deep stuff with the shadowy Them who took as a concomitant of power sneaky panther games we've come to know and love so well as brought to a fine Machiavellian art by King Richard the Phlebitten. What I *didn't* know at that moment was that Spiro had been shown a copy of a column I'd written, by someone on his staff, and had taken direct offense at a wayward line I'd written about him. What line? Uh, er . . .

"Spiro Agnew masturbates with copies of *The Reader's Digest.*"

Uh, heh heh. All in, er, uh, good fun, Spiro . . . see, I was just trying to make a smartass reference to your oneness with the Common Man in America during that period, your homey-ness, your commonality of roots with Middle America, your utter sexlessness, your purity, your squeaky cleanliness. Not a mean thought in my bones, Spiro, honest to God.

Would you believe, gentle readers, Spiro took that line as a personal slur. Simply no pleasing some people!

I should have gotten the wind up when the rotten letters started coming in. From the Kiwanis in Florissant, Missouri. From the American Nazi party in El Monte, California. From the American Legion in Harrodsburg, Kansas. From a bailing wire salesman in a motel in Talihina, Oklahoma. From my mother in Miami Beach, Florida.

And Ace's running ads for the book in college newspapers, with the banner headline AGNEW'S ANSWER! didn't do much to help.

So there I sat with a two grand advance of Ace's money, just shucking and jiving, writing my columns, heading toward the 104th installment of "The Glass Teat" column, at which point I'd Xerox up the lot from installment #53 to installment #104, fire it off to Terry Carr in New York, and collect my remaining two grand advance money. But it didn't work that way.

One day Terry called me. Now I've known Terry for close on thirty years, ever since we were both sf fans. He's a tall, mostly quiet guy with an impeccable sense of decorum and restraint. Good editor, nice man, patience of Job. Can't even remember seeing him angry or demonstrably troubled, even when he was. Called me. Troubled. Heard it in his voice.

"Hi, Terry, what's up?"

"Got some bad news for you."

"Krakatoa *isn't* 'East of Java'?!"

"Serious."

"Okay, sorry. What is it?"

"We're not doing THE OTHER GLASS TEAT."

(Long silence.) (Fighting for breath.) (Battle won.)

"Don't fuck around with me, man; it's been a meat-grinder of a day."

"I'm not kidding."

"Well, *shit*, Terry! You've *gotta* be kidding because the damned book is selling seventy per cent of its print run, so what the hell is the story?"

"I don't know. I got the word from the front office. The returns are starting to come in. By the carloads. Some of the distributors aren't even just tearing off the covers and sending *them* back; they're sending back the whole damned book, boxes of them, most of them unopened, more every day, like they were plague carriers."

I sat stunned. What the effulgent hell was *happening*!?!

Well, it was true. John Waxman called a week or so later and advised me the warehouse was filling up with returns of THE GLASS TEAT. No explanations, no whys&wherefores, just thousands of copies bouncing back from all over America faster than the Night of the Lepus. By December 30th, 1970, what had looked like a sellout of the 88,565 copy print run turned out to be a total sale of 36,304. Don't ask me what per cent that was; I was too stunned to know or care.

It didn't make sense. I'd gotten a call from a friend who worked in the offices of Marboro, one of the biggest chain booksellers in New York. THE GLASS TEAT had been their non-fiction leader for three solid weeks; they couldn't get enough copies to stay in stock. And I knew for a fact that here in Los Angeles the damned book was moving faster than a Tijuana breakfast.

Terry called back a few days later and said Ace had told him to tell me I could keep the two thousand dollars I'd already received as first half of the advance. Just let them out of the contract for THE OTHER GLASS TEAT. Book was mine, no claims, I could do what I wanted with it. Now, if you have ever had any dealings with New York paperback publishers—known to hang onto a property unto the ninth generation—you will perceive my shock and stunned disbelief. They just wanted *rid* of me and that sequel.

So. What had happened, as best I've been able to piece it together since 1970, by asking discreet questions of people now years' removed from the situation and somewhat less under pressure, was that the word had come down from what John Dean liked to call "the highest offices in the land" that THE GLASS TEAT was a seditious, Communistic, mind-polluting snare of verbiage promulgated by elements bent on the violent overthrow of the Miss America Pageant, Let's Make a Deal, Monday Night Football, MacDonald's toadburgers and, not incidentally, the United States of America as personified by the mouth that walked like a man, Spiro T. Agnew.

Distributors, newsdealers, wholesalers and retailers, all got the clear but surreptitious message: this book ain't for sale. Not nowhere, not nohow, not no way!

And Ace took a bath on the book.

And when they found out what was behind it, they jumped out of the contract for THE OTHER GLASS TEAT with sighs of relief that they'd only lost two grand, and not their lives.

So for the next four years THE GLASS TEAT— which had sold enormously well on either Coast, where all you radical swine congregate, polluting the precious bodily fluids of Amurrrica—began to acquire something of an underground reputation. I received hundreds of letters from college students and teachers who were using the book in their classes, handing around one dog-eared copy because they couldn't find others, dog-eared or otherwise. Reviews continued appearing, all of them admiring. And here's a little

photo-extract from the *Journal of Popular Culture* just
to prove I haven't been dreaming all of this.

Excerpted from:
892   JOURNAL OF POPULAR CULTURE
_____v. 7, no. 4, Spring 1974._____
TELEVISION AND TELEVISION CRITICISM:
A SELECTED BIBLIOGRAPHY

Compiled by John L. Wright

Arlen, Michael J. *Living Room War*. New York: Viking, 1969.
Arnheim, Rudolf. *Film as Art*. See pp. 188-198, "A Forecast of Television."
   Berkeley: University of California, 1957.

Berelson, Bernard. *Content Analysis in Communication Research*. Glencoe:
   Free Press, 1952.
Bluem, A. William and Roger Manvell, eds. *Television: The Creative Experience*.
   New York: Hastings House, 1967.
Brown, Les. *Television: The Business Behind the Box*. New York: Harcourt
   Brace Jovanovich, 1971.
Burgheim, Richard. "Television Reviewing." *Harper's* (August 1969), 98-101.

Carney, Thomas F. *Content Analysis*. Winnipeg: University of Manitoba, 1972.
Carpenter, Richard. "Ritual, Aesthetics, and TV," *Journal of Popular Culture*
   (Fall 1969), 251.
CBS. *The Eighth Art*. New York: Holt, Rinehart and Winston, 1962.
Chester, Giraud, and others. *Television and Radio*. 4th Edition. New York:
   Appleton Century Crofts, 1971.
Cole, Barry G., ed. *Television: A Selection of Readings from TV Guide
   Magazine*. New York: Free Press, 1970.
Compton, Neil. "Television and Reality," *Commentary* (September 1968), 82-
   86.
Currie, Rolf Hector. "The Stylization of the Dramatic Television Image." Un-
   published Ph.D. dissertation, Stanford University, 1962.

Daedalus (Spring 1960). Symposium on "Mass Culture and Mass Media."
DeFleur, Melvin L. *Theories of Mass Communication*. 2nd Edition. New York:
   David McKay, 1970.
Donner, Stanley T., ed. *The Meaning of Commercial Television*. Austin: Uni-
   versity of Texas, 1967.

Elliott, Philip. *The Making of a Television Series*. London: Constable, 1972.
Ellison, Harlan. *The Glass Teat*. New York: Ace, 1970.
Ephron, Nora. *And Now . . . Here's Johnny*. New York: Avon, 1968.

Greenberg, Daniel A. "Television—Its Critics and Criticism (A Survey and
   Analysis)." Unpublished Ph.D. dissertation, Wayne State University,
   1965.
Gumpert, Gary. "Television Theatre as an Art Form." Unpublished Ph.D. dissertation, Wayne State University, 1963.

And now, 1983, THE GLASS TEAT is back. As the sixth in Ace Books's series of Ellison reissues and new titles. The sixth in the series of twelve because the letters still keep coming from people who want to know where they can buy a copy. Because the things said in this book, even though ostensibly concerned with tv programs most of which have been off-the-air for the last ten-plus years, still pertain. The subtexts are still current. Doesn't matter if we're talking about *Mission: Impossible* or *Magnum, P.I.*, *The Beverly Hillbillies* or *The Little House on the Prairie*, *The Brady Bunch* or *Too Close for Comfort*. The names change, but the banality remains. If you've caught samples of this season's fare, you know damned well I could be writing about network slops from the early Devonian Age and *still* have it all dead-on.

Only it's fifteen years since I started writing those first fumbling *Free Press* observations about television and nothing much has happened. Nothing much except:

● Agnew and Nixon proved all the warnings I trumpeted about their evil were accurate.

● Agnew and Nixon succeeded in crushing the spirit of the rebellious Sixties, smoothing the way for the deadhead Seventies.

● The networks have grown more frightened and restrictive.

● The audience-testing methods and de facto black-lists of actors, directors and writers have become firmly entrenched.

● Almost all genuine creative talents have fled the medium.

● Middle-class mediocrity and law'n'order programming have become the rule.

● We're all fifteen years older and not one scintilla wiser.

So here comes THE GLASS TEAT again. To be read as a slice of your recent past. To serve as a stock-taker. And if it doesn't suffice, get ready for next month when Ace will risk the wrath of the Gods and republish—in glorious black and white, 52 wonderful columns 52—THE OTHER GLASS TEAT!

I suggest you buy it and hide it. Because, unless something strange and wonderful happens between the time I write this (5:54 P.M., 6 January 83) and the time you buy this book, and Nixon kicks off, he'll still be alive and can always make a comeback. Don't laugh. We thought the crazy sonofabitch was politically dead when we wouldn't elect him Governor of California in 1962.

Which brings me to a freaky idea. A weekly situation comedy about a nutso politician who actually committed suicide in 1960, resuscitated by voodoo, who keeps coming back to life every four years, a zombie, and keeps getting elected by all the nerds and gits who forget how creepy he was *last* time around. Now let's see, who'll we get to play the politician?

How about Reagan?

Nah. Type-casting never works.

Anyhow, I'll see you next month. Maybe.

—Harlan Ellison

23″ WORTH OF INTRODUCTION

If you believe that "all the news that's fit to print" is what you'll find in *The New York Times,* and if you *believe* all the news they find fit to print, chances run good you've never stumbled across my column of television criticism. "The Glass Teat" appears weekly (when I'm not off in the Great American Heartland gathering source material) in the liveliest underground newspaper in the United States, *The Los Angeles Free Press.* (Known to friends and bomb-throwing right-wingers alike as "The Freep.")

It has been running for a year and a half, approximately, as you buy this book. It has netted for me piles of abusive, threatening letters, some critical praise from men in the Industry whom I respect—such as Walter Cronkite, Joseph Stefano, Christopher Knopf, and several other familiar newscasters who'd rather I didn't use their names—damned little financial return, an assurance from ABC that my scripts are no longer welcome at that network, two attempts on my life that didn't come nearly close enough, an ill-deserved reputation in the subculture as a guy over thirty who can be trusted, and a forum from which to express my fears and sorrows about the way we're fucking up this country.

Oh, yes, by the way: I occasionally use profanity.

But,.you see, that's one of the lovely things about the Freep. You can say what you want to say, in the way you want to say it. That's sort of *de rigueur* with the underground press. Despite its frequent lapses into bad taste and paranoia, it has become the last bastion of genuinely free journalistic speech in America. Though frequently denied press credentials accorded to any

17

other legitimate news medium (which sometimes makes for muddiness in the reportage due to subcutaneous sources of information), the underground press persists in presenting the other side of the news we are daily fed through TV, radio and newspapers via "official sources" and the spokesmen of the Establishment.

How this column came to be is a short story to tell, and I do not think you will revile me overmuch for taking the time here to tell it.

In 1962 (or was it '63?) I first met Arthur Kunkin, who is the publisher of the Freep. He was at that time trying to get the paper started, using as its model the now-terribly-straight *Village Voice*. He asked me to contribute to the paper, and along in that first year I did a drama review. But the pressures of other writing kept me from becoming a regular contributor.

Years passed. In late September of 1968, both in attendance at a dull Hollywood party, Art and I bumped into each other and the conversation went *exactly* like this:

KUNKIN: Hey, Harlan, how are you?

ELLISON: Great, Art. How's the paper doing?

KUNKIN: Fine. Why don't you do something for us?

ELLISON: Why don't I do a TV column?

KUNKIN: Okay.

ELLISON: I can say what I want to say, and nobody edits it? Not a period, not a comma, strictly untouched?

KUNKIN: Of course.

ELLISON: Great. I'll do it.

KUNKIN: Your first deadline is day after tomorrow.

And he walked away from me. I went home that night and sat down and wrote the first installment of "The Glass Teat" (which you will find herein, slightly rewritten at the request of Ace's splendid editor, Mr. Terry Carr, who quite rightly felt that in fumbling out a first try I had not approximated either the tone or quality of what was to follow; the rewrite was done by myself, and aside from dropping repetitive references to other columns in this book, which speak for them-

18

selves, the installments appear exactly as they were written and first published ... though typographically more articulate ... until recently the Freep's typesetters apparently had never heard of *italics*).

During the year and a half of the column's existence, the tenor of the times has changed radically, and the horrors that now hold sway over us have grown more malignant. This column was conceived to fulfill the role of social gadfly. It was born out of a need to examine what comes to us across the channel waves and to extrapolate from its smallness to the bigness of the trends or concepts to which it speaks. A situation comedy is not merely a situation comedy. It means something. Why do we—who know *The Beverly Hillbillies* is bullshit—sit and watch such banality? What does the acceptance of death but not sex on network TV tell us about ourselves and the broadcaster's image of us? How accurate is TV news reportage? Why is there so much bad TV and who is responsible for it?

These and other unanswerables I've attempted to answer in the pages of the Freep each week, through the frequently transparent device of working over the cultural whipping-boy, the medium of television.

But make no mistake. I am not *really* talking about TV here. I am talking about dissidence, repression, censorship, the brutality and stupidity of much of our culture, the threat of the Common Man, the dangers of being passive in a time when the individual is merely cannon-fodder, the lying and cheating and killing our "patriots" do in the sweet name of the American Way.

As for my credentials, I am thirty-five, a writer by profession with 22 books, over 700 magazine stories and articles, several dozen TV scripts and half a dozen motion pictures to my credit. I am not a Communist, a drunkard, a doper, a lunatic, a straight, a hippie, a Democrat, a Republican, an astrology freak, a macrobiotic nut, a subscriber to *The National Review,* or even a member of the staff of the Freep. I am all alone out here, setting down what I've seen and what it means to me.

If that has some worth, then this is a good book. If I'm an idiot with only peripheral vision, then at least maybe the writing was amusing.

There are warnings herein. I hope some of you get their message before it's too late. 'Cause, baby, time is running out.

HARLAN ELLISON
Hollywood, California
26 December 1969

1: 4 OCTOBER 68

Hello. You ought to be frightened. You ought to be scared witless. You think you're safe, all snuggled down in front of your picture tube, don't you? They've got you believing all you're seeing is shadow play, phosphordot lunacies sprinkled out of a clever scenarist's imagination. Clever of them. They've lulled you. McLuhan was right: give me your young every Saturday morning from eight till noon, and they're mine till I send them off to die in a new war (don't ask me which one, Mommy and Daddy, I haven't checked my schedule for this week; but I'll consult *TV Guide* and see what prime-time they have open next year and *that's* where I'll send your bouncing baby boy).

They've taken the most incredibly potent medium of imparting information the world has ever known, and they've turned it against you. To burn out your brains. To lull you with pretty pictures. To convince you nothing's going on out there, nothing really important. To convince you throwing garbage in the river after your picnic is okay, as long as the factories can do it, too. To convince you all those bearded, longhair freaks are murderers and dumb Communist dupes. To convince you that Viet Nam is more a "struggle for Democracy" than a necessity for selling American goods. To convince you that certain things should not be said because it will warp the minds of the young. To convince you that this country is still locked into a 1901-Midwestern stasis, and anyone who tries to propel us beyond that chauvinism and bigotry is a criminal.

I want to start gently, with this first column, to ease you into the world as-it-is with some questions and

21

some observations. For instance: I want to talk for a few seconds about the war on dissent, as manifested on that big momma mammary we call The Tube. (Marvel, gentle readers, at the cultural shorthand: *The* Pill, *The* Man, *The* Tube. You can only use that kind of shorthand when you've got one, only one of each, and everyone knows it. Yeah: *The* Establishment.)

I want to ask the right questions, because every time I leap into learned discussion with my straight-shooting, clear-thinking contemporaries or adversaries, they whip it on me that there is no concerted war against dissent in this country, and sure as hell not on television. (That most public of possessions given into the trust of the networks. And God knows no one named *General* Sarnoff would use that public trust to back up *The* Establishment! Men of honor, all!)

I'd like to ask why Mayor Daley, the Butcher to the Hog Butcher of the World (as Sandburg called Chicago), expended all those dollars preparing a clever cop-out TV show of 60 solid minutes of socko entertainment, to prove that his cossacks didn't *really* bust any heads in the streets of the Windy City? I want to ask why nobody offered the Yippies a bundle of loot to prepare *their* side of it? Where were the Guggenheim or Rockefeller grants? There were certainly enough filmmakers in that monster crowd who could have done something equally as artful as Daley's Lady Macbeth routine. ("My hands are clean!" she wept, wiping away the blood.)

I want to ask, most humble and scuff-kicking, if that all-American Channel 5 would have scheduled such a documentary as quickly? And showed it as often? But why bother asking rhetorical questions. Mark Twain it was, when once asked why such awful things went on in the world, who confided with sincerity to the woman who had inquired, that it was because the Universe is run by God and God (so saith Clemens) "is a malign thug."

So let me ask a much simpler one. If there is no war

on dissent, no illiterate conspiracy to discredit anyone and everyone who speaks out against *The* System, why did the following happen last Sunday, September 29th, at approximately 5:15 on our esteemed NBC outlet here in LA, the equal-time Channel 4?:

Robert Abernathy was chairing a show called *News Conference*. The guest at whom the panel was firing questions was Dr. Benjamin Spock, well-known aging gut-fighter, baby doctor and peacenik/jailbird (as he is known in Orange County). The first half of the show dealt with the fact that (obviously) because Spock's baby book had advised parents to be permissive with their kids, we were now reaping the harvest of that submissive attitude by harboring a generation of cranky, rebellious kids who didn't know what was good for them or the country. Spock fielded it all with great dignity and articulation. Spock is an impressive dude. He isn't one of them redolent, longhaired, cross-eyed hippie freaks. He is a gentle man of prepossessing demeanor, international reputation and obvious common sense. Hard to discredit a man like that.

Yet NBC managed. With Machiavellian ease.

At the half-time commercial break, we were treated to a "public service announcement." It was ostensibly on buying savings bonds. It was headlined: "Buy Bonds Where You Work ... They Do" and of course the workman shown was a 24-year army vet, sweating in Viet Nam. He did his little number about how he'd bought a bond a month for eighteen dollars and change, every month for 24 years, and one of these days he was going to get R&R'd out of VC-territory, start cashing in some of that twenty-five grand he had stashed away, and blow it in Bangkok having—in his words—"a ball." Then the vet vanished, and the screen went black, and the headline appeared again. Now in the usual run-of-the-commercial style, the headline would have held, without sound, to let the message sink in. But *this* time there was a soundtrack overdubbed (obviously cut at a later date than the video segment) in

23

which he added, "Oh, and by the way, I just extended my tour over here in Viet Nam for another six months, because all of us guys believe in what we're fighting for over here."

Then Spock came back and they popped their first question at him: "Why do you feel we should be out of Viet Nam?"

Pow! That man was dead. With his mouth he dug his grave. Into a pre-recorded interview had been inserted that one special "public service announcement" out of the millions every network runs—concerned with multiple sclerosis, drunkenness, help the blind, drive carefully and help save our water birds—that could invalidate everything Spock said.

So I want to ask: no war on dissent?

And having asked so many questions, I herewith promise that as long as I am allowed to continue writing this column, I will continue to ask questions, and report some personal answers arrived-at from seeing what they set before us on the screen every day.

(I say *allowed,* for unbidden, the dead eyes of Martin Luther King and Lenny Bruce and Bobby Kennedy and Malcolm X swim before me. And behind them Peter Zenger and Galileo and Thomas More and poor Jesus Christ, all of whom were too stupid to know the only way the assassins overlook you is if you keep your head down and your mouth shut. This all smacks of melodrama, for which I have an unnatural love, and yet I feel the stormy stirrings of madness in the land, and even though I don't seek the role of spokesman, any more than Lenny did, the time has come to speak out, to hold back the Visigoths, and that sure as hell makes the spokesman ripe for a bullet in the brain. So while you can enjoy me, gentle readers, I urge you do so, and ask the questions along with me.)

Who knows: we may even locate a few correct answers. And don't be so scared. The worst they can do is kill us.

2: 11 OCTOBER 68

Each new television season is marked by a trend which the general run-of-the-extrapolation critics choose to examine in terms of what is most prevalent: twenty-three new westerns or ten new private eye shticks or two series about gynecological gropers. (Mr. Amory, of *TV Guide,* did a brief turn on the abominable Joey Bishop bash a week or so ago, and he characterized this season as the Year of the Widow—citing Hope Lange in *The Ghost And Mrs. Muir,* Diahann Carroll in *Julia* and Doris Day in *Doris Day.* Tune in, Cleveland baby, and I'll lay a few alternative titles on you.)

What with idiot shows like *Blondie* and *The Good Guys* rearing their microcephalic heads, we could call it The Year of the Asshole. Or that disaster called *The Ugliest Girl In Town* might make this season eligible as The Year Of The Closet Queen. Or the unseemly spate of pro-John Law shows—*Hawaii Five-O, Adam-12, Mod Squad, N.Y.P.D., The F.B.I., Dragnet 1969* and *Ironside*—might easily tag this The Year Of The Cuddly Cop.

But those are merely staples in a diet guaranteed to cause scurvey of the mind. The two shows that really tell us where it's at are *The Outcasts* and *Mod Squad.* These are the shows that *dare* to take the enormous risk of utilizing black folk as heroes. These are the shows that win the title hands-down for this being The Year Of The Shuck.

The year the mickeymice inherited the public airwaves.

The year they used Nat Turner as the mouthpiece of

the honky. Stuff him and stand him up and pull his ringstring, and the do-it-yourself Mattel Nat Turner doll will gibber about equality.

Oh, it is seamy stuff to watch.

In the event you have been busy in the streets doing what it is these shows talk about, but don't understand, let me hip you to what's coming down on Channel 7, Monday nights at 9:00 and Tuesday nights at 7:30 in living black and white.

On Monday, *The Outcasts* ride. Don Murray, who is so white he makes Ultra-Brite dull by comparison, and Otis Young, an Afro-American of uncommon surliness, are bounty hunters. One is an ex-Virginia Confederate soldier, the other is an escaped plantation slave. Through one of the great syntactical gymnastics in the history of plot-cramming, they wind up being trail buddies. They mooch around together, preying on their fellow man and snarling at one another for sixty minutes of self-conscious ethnic drama. There are half a dozen obligatory interchanges each show, in which Young calls Murray "boss" and Murray responds with a churlish "boy." They do it over and over till you feel the urge to tell them to kiss and make up. (But the networks aren't ready for interracial faggotry yet; that's next year.)

In the September 30th segment, viewers were treated to a scene in which Young and Murray—trail-weary after God knows how long—break jail and stop off after much eating of dust and pounding of ponies at a run-down way-station for express riders. The wife of the owner is a bit horny; and comes out in the moonlight to grab a little air, and anything else the boys have to offer. Now pay close attention: Murray and Young see this broad by the well, doing a lot of heavy breathing. They exchange a few *bon mots* about the state of their not-getting-any, and Murray sashays off to give the little lady a fiesta in the tackle and harness shed. Young watches.

Now I'll even grant the producers of *The Outcasts*

26

the benefit of historical verisimilitude. In them days a black man knew better than to try cozzening up to a white chick. The question does present itself, however, why didn't Young drop a gentle hand on Murray's shoulder and say something like, "Hey, hold up a minute, boss. Y'know, we both been on the trail eight weeks, and I seen the rushes of the next sixteen shows, and uh er, y'know not once in any of them sixteen shows do I get a piece, so why not let *me* go on out and further the plot a wee bit with that there fine little fox?" Granted, we couldn't let Young *do* anything like that, I mean, actually get down with a white woman—but how much more like *real* men they would seem than the posturing prototypes they now play! Murray gets uptight when they won't let Young sleep in the house—it's the barn for the black boy, natcherly—but I wonder how tough he'd get if they refused Young service in a whore house? The point is, will Otis Young be given any more natural manifestation of manhood in this series than the wielding of phallic substitutes like horse and six-gun? Or will all the boy/girl jive be confined to the "acceptable" (i.e., white) Murray? Until separate but equal sack-time is established, this remains just another example of the shuck: the great American TV Boondoggle that seeing a black man make it sexually is too steamy and sordid for the fine-tuned sensitivities of the Great Unwashed.

Which brings us, with gorge rising, to *Mod Squad*. It has to be seen and heard to be believed. Take last Tuesday's offering, a script I have it on good authority was rewritten by the Executive Producer. Now get this, because we travel fast and tricky:

These three overage Now Generation types, once free spirits but now straight-arrow types working as undercover narks for the L.A.P.D. (how they justify their gig is never really dealt with; one assumes that even the most militant Strip type would be converted to Redden's Folly were he only to be exposed to the logic of the billy club and mace can), return under aliases to

27

high school, to break the back of a car-boosting syndicate. Through incredible stupidity and ineptitude, the three Mod Squadders get their one witness shot through the gut. After 56 minutes of idiot plot the case is cracked, and in the final scene one of the three undercover cops, Clarence Williams III, goes to try and explain to the girl friend of the slain boy why he's sorry she lost her man. The chick is busy cleaning out her school locker. Despite being an "A" student, the chick is going to drop out and "get a gig somewhere."

Then follows one of the most incredible banalities ever concocted on network TV.

Mr. Williams III first demeans the dead boy friend (who was trying to avenge his murdered teacher) by telling his bird that "Doc blew his chance." (He sure did; he should have stayed clear of the fuzz as he had done all through the first half of the show; at least he was alive.) Then he tells her the school is where it's at. It's where it's happening, baby. And then he starts to cry, for no damn reason save possibly to demonstrate an aptitude for Glycerine Bawling 102. And *then* he tosses her the clincher: he quotes from Ted Kennedy's eulogy of RFK and says (approximately), "Some men look at the way things are, and ask why . . . I dream of things that could be and ask why not?" Then he asks the broken-up chick if she knows who said that. She, being no dud, knows this is a test that will count for ⅔ of her grade, and she replies, "A very great man."

With the two of them thus bound together in banality, the mod cop splits, leaving the chick—we can only presume—to the tender mercies of higher education.

Did I mention that Mr. Williams and Judy Pace, the actress who played the girl friend, were black? I didn't? Perhaps it was because they didn't sound like any blacks I ever heard. They sounded like The System, and The System is white, so there must have been something wrong with my set's color control.

What does all of this say? It says that those series are bastardizations. They relegate the black community once again to proselytizing the party line. They are a shuck.

They are ostensibly intended to show the black man and woman as normal, functioning members of the society, yet in actuality they are warped views of what's going on by the aging mickeymice who put these shadow plays together. The producers in their Italian silk kerchiefs and wide belts need more than groovy gear from deVoss to get them into the heart of truth in the streets today. Or even the streets of Laredo, 1883.

In one series the black man is allowed to vent his frustration and loneliness and hostility only through the use of the gun. We know what jingo propaganda *that* parallels. In the other series a black man speaks in such an uncool, unhip, untruthful manner that even the dumbest *white* chick would laugh in his face and call him a sellout.

The mickeymice rule. They don't know what the burning gut of the problem is all about, and so they try to shuck us by taking a palm-feel of a high temperature.

If this is integration on TV, it makes the days of Steppin Fetchit look almost cerebral by contrast.

3: 18 OCTOBER 68

Nothing pleases me more than that the major networks had a few of their newsmen dribbled around the streets of Chicago like basketballs. Nothing delights me more than that a few of those arrogant swine with their creepie-peepies got their heads and Arriflexes busted by Daley's kulaks. The only thing that would have pleasured me more would have been Cronkite or Huntley/Brinkley being beaten to guava jelly in full view of the cameras, in the gutter right outside the International Amphitheatre. There is a Yiddish word—quite untranslateable into English—*kvell;* it means, like, to feel as if the sun were glowing in your tummy; you rock back and forth with contained happiness. I would have *kvelled* to see "Good night, Chet," and "Good night, David" said through puffy lips, around Band-Aid Sheer Strips.

No deep-seated hostility prompts these blood-curdled pronouncements. Though I'm not what might be considered a nonviolent person, I have no animus for the gentlemen of the Video Fourth Estate. My feelings are prompted out of a gut-level desire for justice. The Universe is run in a sloppy manner, I'll grant you, but overall it has a dandy check-and-balance system, and for justice to be meted out in full, what the newsvideo boys got was not nearly what they deserved. I'll try to explain.

In a roundabout way.

I know a girl who was at the Century City free-for-all. She wasn't in the area where I was tumbling, but she was there. She's a third-grade teacher in a local grammar school. She went to the demonstration with a doctor of her acquaintance, and two attorneys. They were all dressed in acceptable Establishment garb: little white gloves and a pretty dress for her, suits and ties for the gentlemen. They dressed that way on purpose. They knew that a large segment of the demonstrating crowd would be in battle garb—sandals, hard hats, clothes that could stand sidewalk-scraping—and they wanted to show that all segments of the population were against WW2½. She told me, with a touching show of naïveté, that it seemed as though the television cameras, when panning across the throng, always avoided her little clot of squarely dressed dissenters, in favor of loving closeups on the scruffiest, most hirsute protesters. I smiled. Of course, baby.

The news media invariably slant it. Whether it's anything as flagrant as the prepared protest placards one of the local outlets took to a Valley men's college for a debate, or as subtle as the proper defamatory word in a seven-minute radio newscast, the reportage is *always* corrupted so the dissenters look like fuzzy-minded commiesymp idiots (at best).

There seems to be no question of ethic or morality in the minds of those who write the news, those who program the news, or those who deliver the news. Several friends of mine who work for CBS News here in Los Angeles have confided off-the-cuff that it appalls them, the manner in which the outrage of the minorities is presented. In private they'll say it, but they haven't the balls to actually *do* anything about it. They won't make protestations to their superiors, they won't make statements to the newspapers, they won't back up their hideous parlor-liberalism with anything but muted whispers to activists they milk for inside information.

So then the hypocrites get a little bloodied, and they shout "police brutality!" You could hear the outrage to the bottom of the Maracot Deep. Well, I'm afraid I can't feel too upset about it.

Where were they when the cops turned their bikes into the crowd outside the Century City Hotel? Where were they when fifteen-year-old girls were getting their heads busted on the Strip? Where were they at Columbia and University of Chicago and Berkeley? Where was their outrage then? Ask not for whom the bell tolls, brother reporters: it tolls for every one of you who sell out the people looking to you for truth. And when you reap a little of what you've helped sow, don't come crying back and expect the field troops to feel sorry. It doesn't work that way. You called the rules of the game, and now you're uptight because the trolls with their mace and clubs decided it wasn't how you played the game, it was whether or not you won.

Which violent thought brings me to the topic of violence—or the lack of same—on prime-time TV. Everyone and his Doberman has had his say on this little topic, and having been a man who lost two grand when a segment of a show he wrote was canceled for re-run because it was too violent, I feel I'm as equipped as *any* dog to comment.

It would be simple to make an artistic case for violence. All great art from Beowulf to Faulkner's *Intruder In The Dust* has demonstrated that violence is often what results in moments of stress, when people under tension must seek release. Conrad, Shakespeare, Twain, Dickens, John D. MacDonald, Arthur Miller—all of them bring their characters to the point of no return, and then follows violence. It is the way the machine works. (Note this: physiologically speaking, while Man's forebrain, where he does his formulating, has grown larger as the eras passed, his medulla, where the emotions click, has remained the same size as his Neanderthal ancestors'. In effect what we have is a highly complex thinking machine, able to extrapolate and cogitate and parse, still ruled by the emotions of something little more godlike than a killer ape. Deny this, and you deny the facts. Ignore it, and what emerges artistically is a shuck.)

A critic in *Story Magazine* recently ventured, in an article on the literary precedents for violence, that there

32

is an "illiterate vocabulary of violence." That when all reason fails, there is always the sock on the jaw. It says precisely what it means. There is no arguing with it. It makes a clearly defined dramatic point. And as the most valid argument for that theory the author cited Melville's *Billy Budd*. When Billy, harried and chivvied by the detestable Claggart, finds himself literally unable to vocalize his frustration, or to deny the charges brought against him, the injustice being done to him in all its monstrousness, his futile attempt to speak finds voice in only one possible way—he lashes out and strikes the First Mate, killing him with one punch. Any other solution to the problem would have been illogical, untruthful, fraudulent.

So then, if violence is *necessary* to the freedom of creating art, what is it about TV violence that has all the tippy-toe types running scared? What is it that has usually sane and responsible writers, producers and directors signing idiotic advertisements that they will *never* write violence again? (And thereby castrating themselves, and leaving the door wide-open for more and better network censorship; and proving what liars they are, for we all know if it comes down nitty-gritty to shooting that fight scene or writing that blood bath, who among them will walk away from the money?)

What it is, of course, is what George Clayton Johnson, the videowriter, said it was, at a recent brouhaha thrown by the Writers Guild of America, West. He said it was "gratuitous" violence. Let me hit that again: *gratuitous* violence. And what is that, gentle readers? It is a death onscreen that no one cares about.

If you've traveled through forty minutes of teleplay with a kindly old man who helps crippled children, and you see him shot to death on the steps of the altar where he is telling his beads, you *care*. You cry for that death. You feel you have lost someone.

If, on the other hand, Little Joe Cartwright shoots down seventeen faceless hardcases trying to prevent him from snipping that bob'wire on the South Forty, you don't give a shit. They were extras. They fell and they lay there and that's that. (And the grossest debasement of the human condition of all, practiced regularly in TV series, is the scene in which someone has been murdered and lies there all through the shot while the remaining actors talk over what they'll do next. Have you ever been in the same room with a corpse? No? Try it some time, and try carrying on polite conversation while the stiff's blood and brains seep into the carpet.)

It is the difference between our being stunned as though struck by a ball-peen hammer when we saw Bobby Kennedy get hit on-camera, or continuing to munch our potato chips through all those newsreel footages of massacres in the Congo. We *knew* him; whether we dug him or not, he was *real,* he mattered.

So the blame, and the solution, lies in the hands of my fellow screenwriters. Most of them couldn't write their way out of a pay toilet for openers, and they simply don't have the craft or the heart to write what matters, what counts, what we can feel and care about. The solution to the question of violence stems from the insanity of the times, of course, but in interpretation it is filtered through the artfulness—or lack of it—of the writers. And then the producers. And then the directors.

If the shackles of series format were removed from the writing hands of the creators, we would be many long steps toward solving the problem. Dispensing with violence on TV is tantamount to dropping a Bufferin and thinking it'll cure your cancer.

And if they decide that all violence must go, I suggest they start not with the innocuous banalities of combat demonstrated on half-wit series like *The Outsider* or *Mannix* but with the affectionate handling of freeway decapitations, sniper slayings, race riots and random brutalities delivered blow-by-blow in close close CLOSEUP by the ghouls on the Channel 7 news every night.

Or doesn't it disturb anyone to see a video newsman shoving his hand-mike down the gullet of a grieving widow on her knees before the burned body of her seven-year-old son?

4: 25 OCTOBER 68

Several things perplexed me this last week. The first
was the Mitzi Gaynor special on Channel 4, Monday
night the 14th. The second was the CBS Playhouse special, J.P. Miller's 90-minute drama *The People Next
Door,* on Channel 2, Tuesday the 15th. The third was
a segment of the Channel 11 Donald O'Connor variety
show—Thursday's offering, the 17th, specifically. They
befuddled me, unsettled me, and defied analysis ... until something crummy happened later Thursday night,
something that really zapped me and dropped everything into place.

May I tell you about it? Thank you.

The Daisy is quiet these nights, since all the lem-
mings followed the spoor to the Factory and Arthur
and the Candy Store. So it's a good place to go late at
night for a cup of coffee and a few dances. After the
O'Connor show had been on a while, and my mind had
been extruded out through my nostrils, a young lady
and I motored down. It was quiet, nice.

We sat and talked for a while, and then a small podium was set up, and two young men who call themselves "The New Wave" came out. They each carried
an unamplified guitar, their hair was stylishly long, they
were nice-looking guys, and they mounted the stools on
the podium, and they prepared to play.

At that moment, into the small but polite audience
came a table-load of stretch-black knee socks/dark lint-
free suits/midnight beard-stippled/powdered and co-
logned/cigar cellophane crinkling/pure Hollywood
types. With their ladies of the evening. They were

noisy. That is the most polite way to put it. They were noisy.

They took a table at the edge of the dance floor, within arms' length of The New Wave. As the two boys started playing—with great skill and beauty—the egg-suckers began gibbering. Talking, laughing, doing all the square old *shticks* that old squares pull in the presence of the terror generated in them by youth. (And I finally learned what a tramp is, incidentally. Their chicks were in their twenties—naturally: old impotent squares need fresh meat to reassure them the world isn't *entirely* against them, that they aren't *completely* turning to ashes in their husks—and the chicks laughed right along at such brilliant *bon mots* as "Is that a girl or a boy with all that hair?" A tramp is a chick who will laugh at a swine's gaucheries because she wants something from him, even if it's only another stinger.)

The New Wave played eight or nine songs of genuine beauty, most of which they'd written themselves, many of which said something fresh and searching about life in our times, the struggles of the young for identity, in general a fine and lovely set, concerned with what is coming down these days. The old farts could have learned something if they'd listened. But they wouldn't. As those sweet guitars worked, the crustaceans of the Alcholic Generation screamed louder, made more impolite remarks, jeered, goosed their whores and went to decay and garbage before the eyes of The New Wave—who were beautifully cool and ignored them without dropping a measure—and everyone else in the room.

I left the Daisy confused by what I'd seen, and deeply troubled. Oh sure, I'd seen this kind of ridiculous behavior before, many times, in many night clubs, at many concerts, in movies. But why, I asked myself, couldn't they have at least taken a table at the rear of the room if they wanted to talk, if they didn't want to hear a live performance? Why did they sit right in front; and sitting right in front, why couldn't they open their gourds and maybe learn what these kids had to say.

These were the kind of swine, I thought, who groove on those hincty, square, bible belt-style Las Vegas lounge acts, all screamhorn and sweaty thighs. Trini Lopez and Shirley Bassey and Sam Butera and Robert Goulet and a big sequined finale where everybody exudes phony enthusiasm marching around singing *When The Saints Go Marching In.* The Judy Garland lovers. The ones who dig . . . and it all dropped into place . . . Mitzi Gaynor and Donald O'Connor and what *The People Next Door* were putting out.

The linkage was there, plainly. And though I shied away from the cliche, it was dear God help us, the Generation Gap. Those were the most *gapped* people I'd ever seen. And I knew why those three TV shows had unsettled me.

The Mitzi Gaynor special was old. It was cornball. It was all that *papier-mache* elegance, all the highkicking chorusboy shit that goes big in Vegas, and goes down smooth as honey in redneck territory, because it feeds the unrealistic images all those rustics have of glamour and showbiz. It was the essence of the-show-must-go-on-ism. (And let's put a hole in *that* one right now: what the hell would it matter if the show *didn't* go on? Is the arrogance of the showbiz type so monumental that he thinks the course of Western Civilization would somewhichway be slowed if the Osmond Bros. *didn't* make the midnight show on New Year's Eve at the Sahara?)

The same holds true for the O'Connor show. Night after weeknight we are treated to a dull, dreary hegira of Vegas lounge acts, slouching like some rough beasts toward a Bethlehem that looks like nothing so much as the interior of the Stage Deli. It is outdated entertainment. It is an atavistic throwback to the cornball of the Thirties and Forties, without the saving grace of being nostalgic or even camp. They take it seriously. Henny

Youngman still works as though he were a fresh, apple-cheeked act. The days of belting, busty chanteuses and vaguely off-color comics with cuffs that shoot automatically is past. They are on the other side of the Gap. They are as far from *The Smothers Brothers Comedy Hour and Laugh-In* as Little Orphan Annie is from the Mona Lisa.

Sure the septuagenarians should have equal time in the networks' programming. Sure they should. But when will the powers-that-do realize that being *au courant,* achieving that across-the-board viewership they revere more than the blood of Christ or their mother's gefilte fish, means more than adding Harper's Bizarre to an Ed Sullivan bill featuring Kate Smith, the Sons of the Pioneers and Betty Hutton doing her road-show rendition of *Hello Dolly?*

Time is passing them by, and they obstinately remain gapped.

Even as J.P. Miller, author of *The People Next Door,* is gapped. Demonstrably obvious from his 90 minutes of hysterical reaction-formation to his own son's dropping out and becoming a hippie, *The People Next Door* was as dishonest and stacked-deck as a drama could be.

I won't go into the plot. If you missed it, you didn't miss much but an object lesson. It was an exercise in hypocrisy. It started with cliche characters and espoused a view of the generation of revolution as imperfect and disembodied as the uninformed opinions of the most militant and frightened Orange County Bircher.

It was the vocal statement of a man who is confused and terrified by the things young people are doing today, a statement that did not comprehend the blame lies in the venality and alienation of the older generations. It was as dense and studiedly unknowing as the grave-fears of a little old lady dying away her moments in a Beverly Boulevard convalescent home.

One can only conjecture what effect Miller's play had

on the errant son. Were I he, it would have solidified once and finally my feelings that Dad was a phony intellectual, and a man to distrust simply because he knows not where it's at. Nor where it's going to be.

5:   1 NOVEMBER 68

Wags at a recent craft forum meeting of the Writers Guild suggested that the reason for the recent bombing of the *Free Press* was this column. I pshawed them, naturally. It's true I received an irate call from an irate producer, whose series I'd bummed in these pages, assuring me that I was a toad and that I would never work on that series. (This, gentle readers, is a threat roughly as imposing as telling a man who has just crawled out of the Gobi Desert on hands and knees that he cannot have a peanut butter sandwich.)

It is also true that I received a communication from CBS News here in Los Angeles, demanding to know the names of the confidantes who had freely discussed the hypocrisy of their network and its news staff. There were implied threats. Dark and devious references to Judge Crater and Amelia Earhart and Ambrose Bierce. (I didn't nark on my sources, gang. Bamboo shoots under the fingernails could not drag that privileged communication from me. Which brings us to an interesting sidelight that came down this week: a representative of ABC-TV, facing the Senate investigating committee on television violence, copped-out that not only was ABC clean clean clean, but that because of the effulgent brilliance of ABC's *Mod Squad*—a disaster area I dealt with several weeks ago here—a teen-aged girl, a "user," had "kicked," and "split her scene," and had joined forces with the L.A.P.D.—like the kids in the series—to work as an undercover informer, a "stoolie." This network rep was really h-e-p, he used all the jargon . . . user, kicked, split, where it's at . . . unfortunately, he doesn't smell out the horror of what he'd said: that the ethical corruption of the series had miasmically drifted off the tube, and clouded that poor little chick's mind, thereby causing her to turn on/in her contemporaries. And if it be demonstrably true that this nitwit show can cause one person to turn from "evil" to "good," then it should conversely be true that it could turn them from "good" to "evil," and so it probably follows that seeing violence on *Mod Squad* could get thousands of little teenie-boppers to run amuck and send their parents through meatgrinders. God save us from network representatives so chickenshit frightened for their jobs that they feed the witch-hunters the raw meat they need to batten and fatten.)

So ... anyhow ... back to the point, whatever it was, originally. Oh yeah, threats, displeasure. I remember.

This column has attracted some small attention, and not all of it dedicated to the concept that the author is a pussycat. So, before the impression is too strongly implanted that I am a bitter, cynical, rude and violent critic with a heart as mellow as a chunk of anthracite, I am sliding this column in among the contributions I make weekly in which I explain the Ethical Structure of the Universe and help Keep America Strong! A column of fun, folks. Get set for funtime! A direct appeal to your funnybone, in an effort to prove that I am a man of mellow habits and gentleness. And how do I set about proving this to all my critics? By listing those current shows that I recommend unqualifiedly as excellent TV fare, and then by making a few thoughtful suggestions as to potential series that might make it big on prime-time.

First: the shows I recommend:

> *Rowan & Martin's Laugh-In*
> *The Smothers Bros. Comedy Hour*
> *The Ghost And Mrs. Muir*
> *Mission: Impossible*
> *Ted Mack's Original Amateur Hour*

(I also recommend the new ½-hour police series *Adam-12,* on Saturday evenings. Very nice, very realistic, and almost too damned good to believe from gung-ho Jack Webb.)

Now there may be those among you who think I'm kidding when I recommend Ted Mack and Dan Smoot and the prayer just before the station signs off. Nothing could be further from the truth. I'm dead serious. For sheer sustained bald humor, nothing is funnier than Mr. Smoot awakening us to the dangers of the International Communist Freako-Devo-Pervo-Sickie World Conspiracy. And if you think *Laugh-In* is funny, fall down on Ted Mack's show. You don't know what humor *is* till you've seen a boilermaker from Moline making music by rapping his skull with his knuckles. (And remind me some time to tell you about the freakout existentialist experience I had one Sunday morning with the *Original Amateur Hour.* Uh!)

And if one chooses to worship Ba'al or Zoroaster, the late night psalm is refreshing, stimulating, uplifting and hysterically convulsing.

But it must be obvious to everyone that TV has nowhere nearly approached its potentialities for comedy series. So in a constructive attempt to hip them to what *can* be done, I offer the following proposed series concepts, some of which are mine, some of which come from other TV writers who wish their names unknown and their homes unbombed.

BERKOWITZ OF BELSEN! With the success of funny POW camp shows like *Hogan's Heroes,* the next natural step is a funny series about a Nazi extermination camp. Our hero is Morris Berkowitz, an engaging scoundrel of the Phil Silvers-Sgt. Bilko stripe, whose hilarious exploits among the quicklime pits and gas chambers of Belsen are calculated to send you into paroxysms of joy. I can see a typical segment now:

Berkowitz has flummoxed the cuddly Kommandant of Belsen into selling him half a dozen ovens for purposes of setting Berkowitz up in the pizza business. Conservative, Orthodox and Reform pizzas, all with meat.

JOHNNY BASKET-CASE! A two-fisted western about a trouble-shooting multiple amputee who rides his great white stallion Trumbo side-saddle, in a wicker basket. He is a sensational shot, firing the six-gun with his mouth.

FREAKOUT! A weekly series of music and blackouts featuring kids who've been committed to the UCLA Intensive Care ward, acid-victims all. Their hilarious nightmares and problems being fed intravenously while in shock should help establish a necessary rapport between the generations.

A MAN CALLED REX! A situation comedy about Oedipus and his Mom. Heartwarming social comment and unaffected comedy for the Love Generation.

CHICAGO SIGNAL 39! A true-to-life police show starring those two great Americans Fess Parker and Buddy Ebsen, as a pair of Chicago flying squad cops assigned to the Special Riot Detail. Homespun comedy about mace and mad dogs. Will play big in the Midwest.

This is only a sampling of the wonders modern TV could provide, if they would only carry to logical extremes what is already being delivered to the public.

And this sampling should once and for all put an end to the base canards leveled against this column and this columnist that we view with disgust and horror what comes out of the glass teat each week.

See, I told you. I'm a pussycat.

44

6:   8 NOVEMBER 68

As slanted and inept as television's handling of the
news may be, it is light-years away in integrity and lucidity from *Time Magazine,* a phenomenon of 20th
Century life I put on a level with dog catchers, summer
colds, organ music at skating rinks and the comedy of
Phyllis Diller: in short, items I can well do without.

I don't read *Time.* Except to check them against
Ramparts and gauge the degree of paranoia Mr. Luce
is currently proffering. Yet the other day my secretary,
Crazy June, in an attempt to destroy my mind, wafted
a copy of *Time* under my snout (she was hellbent on
reading me an item about snake-handling ministers of
the Holiness Church of God in Jesus's Name, somewhere in Virginia; don't ask me why) and I caught a
glimpse of *Time's* television page.

I was pinned to a listing of the Nielsen ratings released last week. I have to reproduce that list for you.
The mind flounders.

1) *Rowan and Martin's Laugh-In* (NBC)
2) *Mayberry R. F. D.* (CBS)
3) *Gomer Pyle—U.S.M.C.* (CBS) and *Julia*
(NBC)
5) *Family Affair* (CBS)
6) *Bonanza* (NBC)
7) *Here's Lucy* (CBS) and *The CBS Thursday
Night Movie* (Doris Day in *The Glass Bottom
Boat*)
9) *The Beverly Hillbillies* (CBS)
10) *Ironside* (NBC)

Now I have to confess that I have never seen a segment of the Lucille Ball show (*I Love Lucy* back when I was in high school was more than enough for me), or the *Mayberry R.F.D.* thing (which I gather is an offshoot of *Gomer Pyle* which is an offshoot of the original Andy Griffith Show), or *Julia*, which I understand is deeply sensitive and touching. In line of work I have caught all the others—at least when they were onscreen for the first season. It's been years since I've considered the peregrinations and problems of Hoss Cartwright or Ellie Mae Clampett, or wept sadly that an actor as fine as Brian Keith has to play second banana to a couple of saccharine cutesy moppets just to make a good living, but I consider myself reasonably *au courant* with what's available on prime-time, and aside from thoroughly enjoying *Laugh-In* (you see, I love Goldie Hawn and I lust after Judy Carne), I am frozen into immobility at what the bulk of the nation is choosing to watch.

Six of the ten leading items are wafer-thin, inane, excruciatingly banal situation comedies dealing with a view of American home life that simply does not exist save in the minds of polyannas and outpatients from the Menninger Foundation. All six of those items run only 20-some-odd minutes (minus commercials), which indicates how deeply the plot goes into any problem jury-rigged for the actors. Two more of the top ten are light comedy, the Doris Day film and *Laugh-In*. Miss Day fits neatly in with our first six winners, and *Laugh-In* manages to become consistent with the others by its escapist elements—laughter and silliness. Of the ten top shows, only two even remotely resemble drama. And both of them are—psychologically speaking— "family" shows. The Cartwright strength is in the family unit, and "Ironside" has his little family of assistants, the two white kids and the obligatory black kid.

While their world gets ripped along the dotted line, the average middle-class consumer-slaphappy American opts for escapist entertainment of the most vapid sort.

No wonder motion pictures grow wilder and further out in subject matter: audiences are getting their fill of pap on the glass teat. No wonder such umbrage and outrage by the masscult mind at the doings of the Revolution: they sit night in and night out sucking up fantasy that tells them even hillbilly idiots with billions living in Beverly Hills, are just plain folks. No wonder the country is divided down the middle; TV mythology causes polarization.

Walking the streets these days and nights are members of the Television Generation. Kids who were born with TV, were babysat by TV, were weaned on TV, dug TV and finally rejected TV. These kids are also, oddly enough, members of the first Peace Generation in history, members of the Revolution Generation that refuses to accept the possibility that if you don't use Nair on your legs you'll never get laid.

But their parents, the older folks, the ones who brought the world down whatever road it is that's put us in this place at this time—they sit and watch situation comedies. Does this tell us something? Particularly in a week when prime-time was pre-empted for major political addresses by the gag-and-vomit boys, Humphrey and Nixon? It tells us that even in a year when the situation facing us is so politically bleak that optimists are readying their passports for Lichtenstein and pessimists are contemplating opening their veins, that the mass is still denying the facts of life. The mass is still living in a fairyland where occasionally a gripe or discouraging word is heard. The mass has packed its head with cotton. The mass has allowed its brains to be turned to lime jello. The mass sits and sucks its thumb and watches Lucy and Doris and Granny Clampett and the world burns around them.

It goes to something stronger than merely one's personal taste in television shows. It goes straight to the heart of an inescapable truth: if the world is going to be changed, gang, if we're going to find out where the eternal verities have gone, if we're going to rescue ourselves before the swine mass sends us unfeelingly and uncaringly down the trough to be slaughtered, we have to face it: *they* will not help us. They will applaud now that LBJ has stopped the bombing, but they see no inconsistency in having beaten and arrested all the clear-sighted protesters who said it three years ago, before how many thousands of innocent cats got their brains spilled? And now that what those protesters protested for has come to pass, will they rise up and say free them, reinstate them, honor them?

We know the answer to that.

The answer is: they're too busy watching Gomer Pyle cavort around in a Marine Corps that never gets anywhere near jellied gasoline and burning babies.

Dear God, we must face the truth: for the mass in America today, the most powerful medium of education and information has become a surrogate of Linus's blue blanket.

A ghastly glass teat!

7: 15 NOVEMBER 68

The week was a veritable cornucopia of television-oriented goodies. It was a time when we were exposed to the incredible tunnel-vision of our public officials (or those *seeking* to be same) as regards the potentialities of the medium.

Instead of recognizing that television, in its McLuhanesque fantasy/reality, can spot a phony and pin a liar, Humphrey persisted in mouthing jingoism and concealing his true personality, and lost an election.

To our everlasting gratitude, however, the other side of the coin was exhibited by Max Rafferty, one of the few truly *evil* men I have encountered. He is a liar, a cunning ghoul with a nature that has apparently never been sullied by the presence of a scruple. On Wednesday morning, when he lumbered before the cameras in his campaign headquarters to concede the election to Cranston, he was asked what it was in particular that he thought cost him the race. Though I'm sure he didn't mean it in the way *I* interpret it, he said it was obviously because the people dug Cranston more than him. And he was correct. Though Cranston is by no means a Great White Hope (and certainly no Great Black Hope) he was demonstrably not an insipid man, nor a brute, nor a mudslinger, nor a phony ... all of which are charges than can be laid at the feet of Rafferty with some success. The tube revealed Rafferty for what he was. And so, in a year when he had everything going for him, he lost. As he deserved to lose.

Rafferty, thank God, failed to understand the ways in which the medium could expose him. His guru,

Nixon (I gag at having to call him *President* Nixon), finally came to understand the nature of the beast, after the licking he took at its hands in 1960. But the word never drifted down to Rafferty. For which small thanks can be given. Would that Humphrey had been as hip to TV as was JFK.

It became obvious this last week, inundated as we were with political "specials," that the days of the fraud in politics are numbered. Or, more correctly, the inept fraud. The baby-kissing, slogan-mouthing hypocrite: the machine politician. TV's eye is much too merciless, and the generations raised on TV are wise to the fraudulent; they've seen too many commercials to ever again be taken in by demagogues and political used car salesmen. (In this respect, I suppose we owe a helluva debt to Ralph Williams, whose hardsell parallels that of the office-seekers. Once having had one's skull napalmed by the Ralph Williams scene, one need never fear having the wool pulled over one's eyes by a Wallace or a Rafferty.)

Yet the demise of the one postulates the rise of another. The Show Biz Politician. Reagan is a classic example, of course. In a way, the Kennedys are another. I think the element is *charisma*. If a man can *look* sincere on the tube, if he can *seem* to be honest and forthright and courageous, he can sweep an election merely by employing the visual media.

In which case, the term "bad actor" would come to have a new, more ominous meaning.

Another goodie from the week that was: one of the pollsters, in conjunction with one of the major networks, promulgated a survey of feeling on the part of the American Public about Johnson's bombing halt of North Viet Nam. Seventy-three per cent said it was a groove, they were nuts about the idea, oh boy, gosh-wow, simply peachy keen. Now I don't know what boils *your* blood, gentle reader, but that is the same 73mother% that was out in the streets shouting "Lynch! Lynch!" at the kids who showed up at Century City, who chased the Dow recruiters, who burned their draft cards, who sat-in at a dozen universities, who marched to Washington, who got their skulls crushed in Chicago streets by the all-powerful John Laws. They are the same hypocritical 73% who refuse now to draw a line between all of that dissent, through Johnson's vanished popularity, past Johnson's decision (forced on him) not to run, ending with the bomb halt. Do you think there is no connection? Are they that incredibly unaware that they *still* think all those people with indictments against them, all those kids and old men lying-up in slammers across the country, all those girls and boys who've been fined or thrown out of school, are Communists? Where is the sense that we hear Nixon and Humphrey and Wallace rattle on about? Where is the awakening? At what point do those 73TVoriented% say, "Hey, wait a minute! If we agree with the bomb halt, and all those kids were *demanding* a bomb halt, then those kids were the same as us, only they saw it before *we* did! Then that means they're okay, they're real Americans, too. So let's spring 'em ... let's erase those charges ... let's hand them back their fines . . . let's reinstate them in college . . . let's let Spock off the hook!" At what stage of cultural adolescence do the people assume responsibility for their mistakes? At what point does the shuck cease?

And if the people refuse to face up to what they've done, where is the responsibility of our video conscience? Which network will take the initiative?

I hurl a challenge.

History has now proved the years of dissenting anent Viet Nam were intelligently directed. History has now shown that those who suffered, suffered for all of us, carrying a banner that only the bravest could carry. As Thoreau has put it: "He serves the state best who opposes it most." Those who chose to go to jail rather than cop-out on their morality and their country, they are patriots. And so I hurl the challenge to the major networks:

51

Which of you will take a stand on this truth? Which of you will prepare a special in which you set forth this obviousness? Which of you will serve us, the people . . . and us, the country . . . as you say you do?

Which of you will point out what the dissenters have done for America, and the world?

Specials on traffic safety and Stonehenge and Miss America and the mating habits of the Great Arctic Tern are marvelous. But they cannot compare in importance to a special in which the value of the dissenters is finally acknowledged.

A country that needs to know the depth of its guilt unconsciously awaits this special.

Which of you will perform this service? At this stage it isn't even an act of bravery, so that ought to make it well within the reach of your talents.

8:   22 NOVEMBER 68

Having just emerged from the Valley of the Shadow, I've got to admit it, gang. I blew it. I had my chance, and I blew it.

Watched myself on the *Joe Pyne Show* last Saturday night. There I was, called on to defend my belief that we are getting managed, slanted, corrupted right-wing news as a matter of course, called on as a spokesman for all of you, and even for *The Free Press,* and I blew it.

I even tried to play it cagey. Came the day that Steve Kane, Pyne's coordinater, called, my secretary Crazy June came into my office and said, "It's the Pyne Show. Should I tell them Excuse A or Excuse B?" Excuse A is the one in which Crazy June returns to the phone weeping, and advises the pain in the ass on the other end that Harlan is dying of cancer of the lymph glands and can't come to the phone. Excuse B is the one where she tells them I've just left to conduct a guided tour through the heart of Mt. Vesuvius. It usually works. They usually get the idea. Go away.

But I'd done the Pyne Show once before, and had had a ball destroying Pyne's replacement, Tom Duggan, by threatening him during the commercial break that if he didn't act like a pussycat and talk nice to me and stop the jerko remarks about the length of my hair, I would hip the video audience to the fact that there was a fugitive warrant out for him in the city of Chicago. Needless to say, Mr. Duggan purred for the rest of the hour.

So I figured the Pyne People were gluttons for punishment and why the hell not. I took the call and Kane said he'd been reading my columns in these pages and why didn't I come on and espouse Truth and Beauty and Wisdom to all the snake pit freaks who watch Joe.

(Now we all know that is a hype. Those people are sado-masochists of the purest stripe. They watch Pyne only because the Roman Arena was shut down, and they have nowhere else to go where they can turn thumbsdown and see some poor slob get a trident through his chest. The redneck *schlepps* who dig Pyne's brand of hypocrisy and brutishness are the ones who can be convinced only by demagogues and rabble-rousers.)

But he said that Joe wasn't feeling too well (I'd heard Pyne was about to cash in his chips via the carcinoma route ... and in fact, when I'd done the show previously, and a woman in the audience had asked Duggan how Joe was doing, Duggan had replied that Joe had been discharged from the hospital; to which my friend Brian Kirby, in the audience, had replied, "Yeah, dishonorably.") and he would probably just moderate while I debated with someone from some video network news staff, like Jerry Dunphy. Well, the thought of being able to ask Dunphy when the last time was that he'd actually been out on the firing line covering a story appealed to me so much, I accepted. I was told to be at the studio on Monday night, the 11th, at 6:00, to tape the show for the following Saturday's airing.

Came a week ago Monday, I was cagey, as I said. I wore clothes that were just square enough so the boobs who view the show wouldn't discount what I had to say even before I said it on the grounds that I was obviously one of those long-haired, unreliable, dope-drenched, crummy hippies. But clothes that were just groovy enough so The People would know I was an *agent provocateur* gadflying the Establishment. (It was so successful a disguise that a goodlooking chick waiting backstage, out of her jug on somethingorother, told someone that I looked much straighter than my columns would indicate. Sorry about that, baby, I'm just one of those damned souls with a foot in either world.)

To my sadness, I wasn't matched with Dunphy, but with a very nice, ultra-straight cat named David Crane, head of the news department at KLAC; in effect, though Pyne makes many times what *he* makes, Crane is Pyne's boss.

And we went on the air—in case you missed it, I hope—and Pyne opened up with, "Well, Harlan Ellison, you say we aren't getting honest news. Tell us about it?"

"Just like that?" I asked.

"No, I can prompt you," Pyne came back.

"That's okay," I recovered. "I think I can tough it out." And I launched into a recap of my column four or five weeks ago in which I said the cameras always focus on the barefooted members of every dissenting rally, but never the Doctors or Teachers or Squares in suits.

Crane came back reasonably by saying that what I was asking for was bias. That Daley in Chicago was upset because all the newsmen had shown was kids getting beat, but not cops . . . and what I wanted was the complete other view. He said what newsmen had to do was be impartial.

Well, that seemed sensible to me, so I didn't argue. Here I was, sitting there with my best indicting Synanon Games technique, ready to rip these two guys up the middle, and they outfoxed me. They both came on so gentle, so sweet, so honest, so sensible, that I was forced to agree with them.

When Pyne asked me what way *I* would have it, I responded, "I'd like to see a few more TV newsmen on the firing line." And Crane then tossed back the old analogy about a soldier learning more about the war from headquarters than from his little piece of the battle. I had to agree with that, too.

It went that way for a long time.

Crane asked if I thought a newsman would get a better story if he'd been clobbered on the head by a cop's baton. I said no, but it might give him a helluva insight.

One woman clapped.

I suggested that, for instance, the reportage of the Selma-Montgomery march had been slanted because there were 450,000 people marching but no network coverage I'd ever seen indicated there'd been more than 100,000. Crane jumped back that I was obviously deluded merely because I'd *been* on the march and so had not seen all the coverage *he'd* seen, which had showed just oodles and oodles of people.

The audience clapped for Crane.

I sat there like a good little boy and tried to work up enough of a mad through the fifteen-minute segment to call both of them lackeys of the Wall Street Imperialist Conspiracy, but Crane was more often right than not, Pyne laid back and let Crane do the work, and I found myself sounding like a cranky tot.

So I blew it, gang.

They convinced me. It's a great world we're living in. The news isn't managed. We're getting the straight scoop on everything. When idiot Bob Wright does a "documentary" on hippies and stands on the Strip with his cameras ordering kids to walk up and down so he can shoot dirty feet, when newscasters report only that "rioting" students at San Fernando State used "dirty words associated with the Free Speech Movement," when Nixon spots are inserted in prime time before and after the most popular shows as opposed to Humphrey spots that bracket such heavyweight programs as *Land of the Giants* and re-runs of the Roller Derby . . . they are oversights that can be discounted.

Crane is a good man. I don't doubt it. He very probably considers himself a liberal. He probably is, which tells you all you need to know about liberalism in Our Times. Pyne is a good man. No, let me retract that. The milk of human kindness isn't running *that* syruply in my veins. Pyne is sharp. He is by no means the lout

56

he appears to be on-camera. He is, without even knowing it, a major mouth in the illiterate, silent conspiracy against dissent in this country. He is a reactionary—by avocation; there are those who remember him when he was a poor liberal—and the election has proved that we are a reactionary nation. So be it. I'm willing to go along with it.

Fuck'm. It's like Jefferson said: "People get pretty much the kind of government they deserve," and this state *deserves* Reagan, and this country *deserves* Nixon. I'm convinced. It's a good life. It is, it really really is. I was wrong. Nothing's happening. Nothing's amiss.

It's as Joe, good sweet dear golden Joe, said to me, as his closing shot. Crane had just ended with the line that the American People ought to thank God for their Freedom of the Press, and wonderful twinkling Joe looked at me and said, "I think you ought to remember that, Harlan Ellison . . . now go . . . and sin no more."

Yes, Daddy.

9: 29 NOVEMBER 68

Two years ago I was asked by *Esquire* to do a lead article on the new kind of woman emerging from Los Angeles and environs. After extensive research and interviews of several hundred women from all stratas of Clown Town society, ranging from teeny-boppers and goo-goo girls to stewardesses, high school teachers, housewives, secretaries, starlets and post-debs, I amassed a longish piece which I titled "Kiss Me And You'll Live Forever—You'll Be A Frog, But You'll Live Forever." *Esquire* called it "The New American Woman," butchered it mercilessly, used a bad taste cover, and compelled me to remove my name from the piece. But the word leaked out that I'd done the article, and very soon I was being inundated with assignments from magazines to "write opinions about women." I was even forced (a peculiar word for a writer, but perfectly appropriate in this case) to do a series of columns on women for *Confidential*. Then, last year, *Cosmopolitan* rigged some phony number about the most eligible bachelors in Hollywood, and threw me into the list, I presume as a sop to the working classes. All of this is pre-stated as sorta credentials for what is to follow in this column, with the staunchly made declaration that I happen to dig girls very much. I am by no means a misogynist.

Which brings me to the subject of this week's revelation of Truth in Our Times: a little blonde cupcake named Kam Nelson, who disports herself weekdays 5:30 to 6:00 on KHJ Channel 9's *The Groovy Show*. In case any of you reading this are over the age of seventeen and don't catch *The Groovy Show,* let me hip you

58

that it is a high school-oriented tribal ritual in which an aging elf named Sam Riddle hosts Top Thirty records for dancing.

But it is not Mr. Riddle—a gentleman who manifests all the paranoia about growing old that terrors those who make their living off the young—with whom I'll deal here. It is Miss Nelson.

Describing her is like cataloguing mist. She is more vacuity than substance. Her appearance is what my secretary Crazy June calls "the Chinese waiter look": they all look alike, and it's difficult to figure out which one stiffed you for the Moo Goo Gai Pan. Miss Nelson has that look; the look of no-look at all. Her face is one of those pretty little girl shots that, having vanished from your sight, vanishes from your mind. The reference point being that there is no character in the face. At 17, Miss Nelson has long blonde hair, nice legs and a baby-fat face with cheeks like a hamster storing nuts for winter. But it is not her appearance, truly, that comes under attention here. I mention it only to establish her as a *visual, physical* role-model for all the girls presumably watching *The Groovy Show*.

Now, the question asks itself unbidden, why devote a column of discussion to a seventeen-year-old co-host of a rock-dance program? It certainly isn't the kind of subject with which this column has dealt in the past— topics of political import, subcutaneous slanting of news, violence and its effect on the mass, or any of the other relatively "heavy" material the television medium offers for comment. Why?

The answer is tied up in a news item released over television last week. The National Scholastic Reading Aptitude scores were published, and for the third straight year California's school children placed not only in the lowest fifty percentile, as they had for several years previously, but in the lowest *eighteen* percentile. The school children of the state of California are emerging from our much-vaunted school system little better than illiterates. Young people, as we all know,

59

obtain their images of themselves from what is commonly called "role models," those from whom they derive their manners, their morals, people they look up to. We have seen how these role-models have broken down in terms of parents and clergy and teachers, and so where do teens and pre-teens go to find their role-models? One can only assume, since we are in fact dealing with the TV Generation, that they get at least a substantial part of their self-image from television. From all areas of the television educational spectrum. From, among other sources, *The Groovy Show*.

Which brings us back to Miss Kam Nelson.

(In preparing this column, I spoke to Miss Judy Price, producer of the show, and Mr. Milt Hoffman, the executive producer for KHJ. They informed me that Miss Nelson is "a good, clean kid that other kids like a great deal," that she is deeply involved in charitable good works because she digs it, that she is a straight-A student, that she is an accomplished horsewoman with many trophies, has raced dragsters at 112 mph, that she flies her own plane, and that she is a track star—having competed in the AAU track & field competitions—and could have gone to the Olympics, had she so desired. Mr. Hoffman referred to her as a very honest, extremely complex girl. I am much impressed by all of this—data I would never have expected to be in Miss Nelson's background, from her manner on-camera—and I take all of it as gospel, while chalking up such virtues in her favor. Yet if this all be true, it only makes stronger the point of this column, and reinforces my conclusions about Miss Nelson's stated—as opposed to *actual*—impact for viewers.)

Let's take her stint on last Thursday's show. Mr. Riddle called her out and she emerged suitably micro-mini'd. He asked her what she'd been doing lately. She stared at him for several beats with wide, innocent eyes and then mumbled something about having gone to "the liberry" (sic) for research on marriage in Scandinavia. Riddle seemed to think that was pretty exciting, and asked her what she'd found out. Then emerged from Miss Nelson's mouth a syntactical jumble of half-sentences drenched with "yeahs," "uh huhs" and ending lamely with "I don't really know." (*Everything* she comments on ends with "I don't really know.") Riddle looked bewildered and segued into the first record.

Later, in an effort to get her to haul her own weight, he cleverly tried to introduce the second record by asking her something about French, I believe it was the word for bicycle. Once again there were mumblings and mouthings and Riddle, now floundering, went to the record. Yet just before it cut in, he could be heard asking her with something akin to bemused impatience, "What do you mean, *you don't know?*"

Still later, the audience was treated to a daily feature of the show, "Kam's Korner," in which the accomplished horsewoman and drag racer answered lovelorn questions from other (we must assume) "typical" teenagers. The first question was from a girl who sucked her thumb, wondering how she could stop. Miss Nelson suggested a baby's pacifier. I can see that correspondent in her chemistry class now, sucking on a rubber nipple.

The second problem came from a girl who was dating two guys at the same time and wanted to know how to put one of them down. I cannot even relate with any degree of coherence Miss Nelson's answer. It was *non sequitur* from first "yeah" to last "uh huh." The third problem was read from a school newspaper by Mr. Riddle. It concerned whether or not sideburns and mustaches should be allowed in school, if they were kept neat and clean—one of the burning topics of our generation. Miss Nelson's answer provided an insight into another aspect of her TV manner that I think significant. She said she "rillee" liked sideburns "cuz" they were groovy and "jist" because some people had messy sideburns "an'" mustaches she didn't see why they shouldn't be "'lowed" in school.

Now perhaps it is because I make my living from the

English language that I have a certain reverence for it; even so, I am very big on the People's English as opposed to the King's English. What people speak should be what is right, even if it ain't so pretty. But Miss Nelson's constant and flagrant disembowelment of the spoken word seems to me to tie in with the alarming lowest eighteen percentile of which I spoke a moment ago.

So we now come to what Miss Nelson represents in terms of image. Mr. Hoffman calls her "an average type girl" and says "the kids seem to identify with her."

If this is so, it is a sad comment. On the kids who will be inheriting the incredibly complex, constantly more-bludgeoning world in which we live. And on the people whose impressions of the viewing audience—notably in this case, the plastic formative minds of the young—are reflected in what they present for their pleasure.

Miss Nelson represents the deification of banality. She is the vapid, elevated to godhood. Young girls watching this show, and deriving from it an impression of what it takes to "make it" (rock music and its world being the most glamorous scene going these days), can only conclude that if a girl is cute and doesn't act "uppity," she can attend Beatles premieres and swing with the mighty. For teen-age girls whose larval stage was informed by the Barbie doll (that classic tool of preparing the young as daters and consumers), this cocoon stage with Kam Nelson as the role-model can only prepare them for emergence into adulthood not as butterflies, but as moths, fit for little better than dull lives of crabgrass, Blue Chip Stamps and quiet desperation. Miss Nelson's image is one that denies intelligence, genuine wit, the accumulation of information, the expansion of one's personality as a woman, and leaves her representing only material gain and surface beauty.

Kam Nelson lives in dream images. Her response to Riddle's question about how she reacted to a male singer who had just done his turn was to say that the guy should have been in a gladiator movie. Her perceptions of the world around her seem to be limited to those that form what high school kids call a "sosh," the complete cheerleader type. All fluff and giddiness, with a head wherein a cogent thought would find itself in Coventry.

A young lady of my acquaintance, who sat beside me during one of these shows, found my intention of devoting this column to Kam Nelson akin to killing a gnat with the battleship *Missouri*. I responded that Kam Nelson obviously got and has held her position as a role-model on this show because she was what the producers felt was most easily identifiable to other teen-agers, and that in that capacity she was a spokeswoman for illiteracy, vacuity, banality and transient values of life.

What would I have asked this young lady, a smart-ass girl who had an answer to everything? After all, it was only a dance program.

Precisely my point. On this sort of show, because it is the one kids relate to, there is an obligation on the part of possibly Miss Nelson, but certainly the producers, to offer something more golden with which kids can identify.

Television is too potent a medium, too exacting an educational force, for anyone to dismiss even a boondock area such as *The Groovy Show* and its ability to shape and mold manners or morals.

No, I would not have a 17-year-old girl genius on *The Groovy Show;* but neither would I have Susie Sparkle set up as the end-all and be-all for emerging personalities. What is wrong with Miss Nelson as a Force in our times is what is wrong about the Miss America contests and all the other shallow, phony shucks put over on kids too young to separate the wheat from the chaff.

And in conclusion, I trust Miss Nelson and her attorneys will understand that while I may have nothing

63

but the highest regard for her as a human being, it is the slapstick number she proffers six times a week on television that needs some examination. I think women are, uh, *groovier* than that.

10: 5 DECEMBER 68

Conspicuous by its absence: sanity in the machinations of television logic and programming. Dichotomies abound like a plague of the Seven Year Locust.

Point: Just at the end of last season, CBS prexy Mike Dann was confronted by a decision that had to be made. It came down to either the brilliant situation comedy *He & She* with Paula Prentiss and Dick Benjamin, or the pilot for *Blondie* with Patricia Harty and Will Hutchins. Only one of the two could be scheduled. Dann made the statement that in his decision his "job was on the line." So he canceled a show notable for its inventiveness and sophisticated humor, *He & She,* and scheduled an abomination of stupidity and cliches that were weary in 1943 when Penny Singleton and Arthur Lake were portraying the dippy Blondie and her castrated husband Dagwood. Now Blondie has been axed, after a rating disaster surpassed only by the all-time debacle, *The Tammy Grimes Show* (to which *Blondie* bears a marked resemblance). It has been said, with kindness, of *Blondie* that rather than putting it on CBS, we should have dropped it on Haiphong. But the dichotomies ride high: Mike Dann, great decision-maker and seer of the rating wars, is still firmly ensconced in his job, mucking things up with regularity.

Point: Robert Montgomery appeared as a guest on Dick Cavett's show, Thanksgiving day, and made the observation that from tax monies we can ill-afford to squander, political candidates had spent between forty and fifty million dollars for air-time during the presidential race. He reminded viewers that *they* owned the airwaves, and why the hell was all this money being wasted when free air-time should be provided for the major candidates, as a saving to us all. Why indeed?

Point: The FCC, ostensibly appointed to protect and defend our publicly owned airwaves, is little more than a toothless tiger, serving first the needs of the politicians who own television stations (LBJ and his bird are classic examples), and next the profit-bloated networks. Their effectiveness is nil, and their voice is seldom heard save when they are chivvying the creators. Newton Minow, who dared to suggest that TV was a corrupt pyramid from apex to base, needing most severely a razing and rebuilding, was rapidly canned. So who, we must ask, does the FCC represent, in the final analysis?

Point: With the horde of talented young writers pounding the Hollywood sidewalks in search of TV assignments, with the incredible number of excellent original scripts that go a-begging every year, with talent as vital as any currently working in the medium, helplessly dancing for dimes on Wilshire Boulevard, why do we continue to be "treated" to rehash remakes of clinkers like *Heidi, Arsenic and Old Lace, Dial M For Murder* and such outstanding lye pits as Princess Lee Radziwill as *Laura* and Max von Sydow in *The Diary of Anne Frank?*

One can only conclude that television is a snake without a head, a mindless creation that has run amuck since the moment a network executive with the soul of a ribbon clerk discovered there were enormous profits to be made by paying heed to Henry Ford's old adage that "No one ever lost money underestimating the taste of the American people."

So, in an effort to impart some little-known facts of television's realities, the better to inform you, and thereby make you harder to underestimate, the following random potpourri of stray intelligences.

1. There are twelve hours of prime-time movies this year. Next year there will be 14 hours. The shows that can compete with old movies are becoming fewer and fewer. Movies are proliferating because they are a bar-

gain: the average cost of something scintillant like last week's *Something For A Lonely Man* with the excellent Dan Blocker is 2½ to 3 million dollars. It runs for two hours, and can be re-run at least twice more during a season. Six hours worth of air-time for that kind of money is a stone bargain. But it also means that much less creativity.

2. *Any* series must be on the air at least two or three years to make dime-one of profit, and since syndication of a series affords an opportunity to recoup deficit financing, it has to go 2-3 years before it can be syndicated.

3. Networks seldom develop shows of their own. They are merely partners with the independent producers. And since studios develop 75% of the shows, and networks are the *only* buyers of shows, and since the networks go on what the Autometer rating in 1155 American homes say, we—the majority—wind up with fear-designed creations.

4. Pre-season previews in New York for "random audiences" work like so: when the tourists hit NYC, and make reservations for, say, the *Johnny Carson Show,* a certain number of them are shunted over to the pilot screening section, and are informed, "Gee, we're sorry, but Johnny's booked solid tonight. We can work you into the audience *tomorrow* night, and tonight, to show you what good guys we are, we'll show you the pilot of a new series." So they take these unhappy, angry, disgruntled yokels (whose mentalities were trained to a Carson level for openers, which should tell you what *their* imagination quotient is) and toss them into a screening room, and are surprised when even the *best* pilots rate somewhere down in the sewer.

5. Without a script, you have nothing. You can have the finest director, the most brilliant actors, the most imaginative production staff—without a story, you are clinging to driftwood and sinking from the start. What do they pay a writer for a pilot script? Between ten

thousand and (tops) twenty-five thousand dollars. What does the production itself cost? Between $450,000 and $700,000. I'm lousy at math. You figure out what the percentage of above-the-line cost that is, and then you'll know why so many shitty scripts are written.

Well, it's been fun going through all of this with you, and frankly I'm grateful it was such a dead-ass week on television so we *could* get into it. But let's hope next week provides something worth discussing that's current; we can, after all, always hope.

This week, we do it in tones of black.

Last Monday night, Diana Ross. Black. The beauty of blackness; God, how gorgeous. And the truest moment with no singing at all: the opening bars of *Reflections*, and then some inspired intercutting between stills of Miss Ross in native African garb and Herself, moving sensually to a black beat, dressed in that same clothing. It was the sole lone instant of a sixty minute spectacular that was not sold-out to Hollywood sequins and Vegas orchestrations. It was supposed to be Motown, babies; Motown, that's Inner City beyond the Boulevard, that's Woodward Avenue and 12th Street; that's John R. and Brush Streets, and the House of Blue Lights. That's black, babies, not them hincty Johnny Green smashbang Vegas lounge Timex flag-waving Saints Go Marchin' In horseshit orchestrations. Don't talk pride in black, joy in negritude, then sell-out to Mistuh Cholly because he spells his name with an N, a B, and a C . . . because he's got his hands full of bread. Even so, there was that one moment of black, with Diana Ross turned out in her heritage, moving like a dusky flamingo, all arms and legs and natural hairstyle, jabbing moving swaying stamping, proving that "they got natural rhythm" is not necessarily an invidious remark. That was beautiful. Even if she did muck it up by doing a tear-jerk immediately after, taking the name Martin Luther King, Jr. in vain. For one moment the screen and the world were black, and that was fine, just fine.

This week, in tones of black.

Tomorrow night, Friday night, 8:30 P.M., Channel

4, *The Name of The Game* goes black. (Have you noticed, soul brother, how uptight us honkies have got, that we don't use the words colored man or Negro or nigger or suede or spade no more; black is the only safe one. Black this and black that. You'll let us know when it goes out of fashion, okay?) The show is 90 minutes called *The Black Answer*. It is a special show, and I urge you not to miss it. Not because it is such a world-shakingly artistic offering, but because it goes a lot further toward reality in the TV-view of race relations than anything we've had since the networks became terrified of black militancy. (Oh, sure, Xerox will sponsor a series on black heritage, but when was the last time you saw a series segment with any clout behind it?)

The show is black. It is about the fire-bomb death of the outspoken publisher of a ghetto newspaper, *The Black Answer*. Tony Franciosa is the star, and if you can get past his nice even teeth you'll find a show that is very black. Ivan Dixon (simply excellent, as usual) and Raymond St. Jaques and Abbey Lincoln and a kid named D'Urville Martin who has enough starpower in him to run a small city's electrical system straight through Christmas.

I saw it on Tuesday. How it happened was this: the man who wrote, directed and produced the segment, Leslie Stevens, caught the final paragraph of last week's column. It said the week preceding had been dead on TV and here's hoping something hot comes up next week. So he called and said he had a winner, would I care to see a special screening. So I called *The Free Press* and asked the Powers to hold up my column—already written, already dummied, all ready for the printer—in lieu of what you are now reading, in order to hip you in time for tomorrow night's show. They ran it for me at Universal, that big ebony tower in the Valley, where they hold Childe Harold a prisoner, Wasserman's Folly. Leslie Stevens ran it—it was his baby—

and I told him I'd tell you to see it. In fact, I'll tell you three times: see it, see it, see it.

Not, as I said, because it's such a creative triumph, but because it is so improbable that Universal Studios, whose colophon on a production has systematically come to mean the acme of mediocrity on the television worm farm, *permitted* this show to be made; because the motives behind its conception and execution are in the truest sense of decency and (though I hesitate to use the word since the show uses it so liberally) brotherhood. Stevens is a good man; he is a talented man; and he has taken one of those rare holes in the defense line of Establishment timidity and run with the ball. He has by no means made a touchdown, but he has gained yardage, and for the broken-field plunging of Stevens we must applaud and pay attention. So see it.

But, having said that, now I must deal with the show and the realities to which it pays service.

(When I discussed the film with you, after the screening, Leslie, my statements had an implied "but" in them. I didn't vocalize the "but" at that time. This is it.)

But . . .

Though the show deals with the desire of a segment of the black community for a national state of its own, though it plays changes on all manner of current events (LeRoi Jones's having once been accused of peaching on a brother, Cleaver's fugitive status, bombings of dissent newspapers), though it portrays a wide spectrum of black feelings all the way from the search for African roots in clothes and manners to the perfectly logical fear of the heat, still the show emerges as a heavy-handed sermon. And denies reality in the most vulnerable areas, seeking to present itself as white liberal.

Franciosa plays a swashbuckling version of every guilt-ridden paddy parlor liberal, mouthing inane platitudes about brotherhood and integration, even at one point turning away from a conversation in badly acted frustration at "all the violence and destruction." He

71

says he's sick of it. Well, shit, baby, *everybody's* sick of it . . . most of all the blacks who've been hammered by the worst of it.

The drama jabs at some delicate sores on the body of racial strife in America, but never really draws blood. It backs off. I'll give you an example: the killing and fire-bombing have been blamed on Joe X, the leader of a militant group called the Black Battery. He has been cornered in a warehouse, and the laws are in the process of smoking him out, with the plainly stated probability that he will be killed in the embroglio. Franciosa has uncovered the real culprit, and has gone to Joe X's sister, to get her to tell him where Joe is hiding out (he doesn't know the cops have found him, but knows time is growing short). She won't tell him. The tension is building. It is one of those moments of genuine conflict during which *anything* can be said and be gotten away with. Franciosa pleads with her; she is adamant; he gets furious, frustrated. He says trust me, and she says why should I, and he gibbers some more about her knowing him well enough by now to blah blah blah (plotwise, there's no doubting why she's holding back; she *doesn't* know him well enough to gauge him as anything more than a nosey Whitey). Finally, a third party convinces Claudia to tell him. A cop-out. What should have happened was Franciosa leaning over and saying, in as rotten a tone as he could muster, "Listen, you dumb black bitch, I'm trying to save your stupid brother's life! Now if you can't find the smarts to help me help *him,* we'll forget the whole damned thing and you can count the riot gun holes in him at the funeral!"

But that would have been going too far. That would have been forcing both Mr. Stevens, the writer, and Mr. Franciosa, the actor, to relate as *human beings,* the way *real* people would have reacted. But the white liberal reaction took hold, and the thought of calling a black bitch a black bitch was too dangerous.

Understand something: I am being presumptuous in

telling Stevens how to rewrite his show. I am very likely overstepping the bounds of good criticism and letting the writer in me hold sway. But I explain it (though don't excuse it) by contending that, as Stevens put it, "this is an opportunity to use the Establishment's own instrument to disseminate a little information," and opportunities like this arise too seldom—on a medium where *Julia* is the new image of the black totality—to back off even a little. The responsibility for Stevens was far greater than usual. No one expects *Family Affair* or *Bonanza* to open any eyes, to say anything fresh and daring about the horrors that surround us; Stevens had that opportunity, and in his own words, all he added was "tabasco to the pudding." A stick of dynamite in that tapioca might have been harder to get down the censors' gullets, but the responsibility was there!

I've urged you to see *The Black Answer* tomorrow night on *Name Of The Game,* and I do not think you will treat me unkindly for the urging, but it is almost entirely for the portrayal of the proud black woman by Abbey Lincoln, for the adeptly carried preachment of black militant position by Ivan Dixon, and the noteworthy talent of D'Urville Martin that you should so expend ninety minutes of your time.

Stevens contends that this show will hit hardest at the "silent majority" of which Nixon prattled, not the hip minority that is aware of what's coming down. I hope he's right. We so desperately *need* him to be right.

12: 28 DECEMBER 68

Now the truth is revealed. My guilty secret. I am a
devout Saturday morning cartoon watcher. I could
cop-out and explain it all by saying a TV critic has to
watch *everything*, but there would probably be a fink
in the crowd who would point out that if such was the
case, why did I miss the much-lauded Michelangelo
special last week, not to mention the Elvis, Brigitte and
Ann-Margret bashes? Or I could bring mist and tears
to the eyes of my readers by reconstructing my hideous
childhood when, as a result of being one of the shittiest
kids in Painesville, Ohio, I was unable to make friends,
and was thus (fortunately for me and the World of
Literature) shunted off into a land of dreams, inhabited
by the denizens of horror movies, comic books, pulp
magazines and Golden Age radio. (It was a wild world
where my companions were Doc Savage, the Shadow,
Plastic Man, Sheena of the Jungle, Kharis the mummy,
Simone Simon, Capt. Midnight, Jack/Doc/& Reggie,
The Spectre and Lawrence Talbot the Wolf Man; you
can readily understand why I get along so well with
film producers and hippies.)

But none of this would actually, strictly be the truth.
And since I have begun the unseemly habit of dealing
in honesty with you, gentle readers, I must confess
boldly that I watch the Saturday morning cartoon
shows because they are a consummate groove. I dig
them; that simple.

You can sympathize, accordingly, with my upset at
the major networks' fear&trembling as regards what
they show the little no-neck monsters every Saturday
ayem. Last season, there was such a hue and cry raised

74

by paranoid parents (who can't cop to being responsible for their kids' traumas, so have to blame it on everything from Hong Kong Flu to masturbation, with comic books and TV getting a big blast), that the kiddie shows—notably the animateds—were warping their urchins' minds, that radical changes were proposed in Saturday morning programming. The nitwit parents were aided in their Holy War by that perennial doomcrier, Dr. Fredric Wertham, the man almost solely responsible for the institution in the Fifties of the Comics Code Authority, a bluenose regulatory apparatus dedicated to keeping the world as pure as the driven snow.

Refuting Wertham and the running-scared set is no difficult problem. Arrayed against the Wertham philosophy that TV (and comic book) violence cause children to use meat-cleavers on their mummies are hundreds of psychologists and psychiatrists who contend that filmed horror and terror are *good* for kids, that they offer a purgative, a release for adolescent tensions and hostilities. On a personal level, I can vouch for the accuracy of that theory. Every guy I know who grooved behind horror movies and comic books when he was a tot is today a productive, beautiful person, with imagination and a sense of wonder. The few I know who were only allowed to read Albert Payson Terhune and see movies where the virtues of God and Dogs were extolled are square, hidebound, bigoted, short-sighted schlepps who sport SUPPORT YOUR LOCAL COSSACK bumper stickers.

There is a thing called "tolerable terror" that kids derive from seeing Superman battling the Giant Tapioca Pudding That Swallowed Pittsburgh. There is a sense of wakening mysteries in the soul that kids derive from seeing Frankenstein stalk the moors. There is a keying-in to exaggeration of the human condition in following the battle against ee-vil waged by the Lone Ranger and Spider Man. To deprive kids of these simplifications of the complex world of good and bad, when they are at an intellectual stage where they cannot grasp the subtleties of inter-personal relationships and global politics, is to deprive them of the one genuine training ground for their thinking, on a level to which they can relate.

But I carp needlessly. Kids will still find their outlets, even if Saturday morning is turned over to cute gophers and harmless old men in clown suits. (What *I'm* concerned about is what *I'll* do for amusement on Saturday mornings; the chick is still asleep, and nudging her first thing on a Saturday morning can only serve to ruin a warm and growing relationship.)

Yet the days of the super-heroes may be numbered, and for those of you who have not as yet fallen down on what joys present themselves pre-noon every Saturday, let me clue you to several shows of worth.

Nine o'clock, Channel 7, the adventures of the Incredible Spider Man. Peter Palmer, who is, in reality, the dreaded nemesis of evil-doers everywhere, Spider-Man, while a high school science student, was bitten by a radioactive spider (don't boggle, read on); he acquired the super-powers of a spider, as a result. Wall-climbing agility, gymnastic excellence, clear-thinking ... and his acne cleared up overnight. Considered to be an outcast and a menace by the Establishment (as portrayed by J. Jonah Jameson, publisher of a great metropolitan daily—faintly reminiscent of Mr. Luce at his crankiest), Spider-Man goes his lone, revolutionary way, socking it to malefactors and bumbling cops with a nice impartiality. His struggles every Saturday morning to implement the revolution would bring tears of joy to the most hardbitten placard-carrier.

Nine-thirty on Saturday mornings is a toss-up. You can either dig Channel 7 and catch the adventures of a team of micro-reduced secret agents in their *Fantastic Voyage* (based on the s-f film of the same name) or turn to Channel 4 and groove with an insane rock group called The Banana Splits. In favor of the former is a team member named Guru who is a Hindu shaman of no mean talents. He can perform all manner of won-

76

derful shticks while having been reduced to the size of a white corpuscle, and speeding along inside someone's urine tract. Now, you gotta admit, a show that has a mystic microscopically moving midst miniscule matrixes manhandling maladjusted menaces means much mystery. How can you pass it up?

(But if you have to, the Banana Splits is the way to go. There are these four lunatics in funny suits, see. One of them is a big dog, and another is a ball of hair with a long snout, see. And they play Fender bass and rhythm guitar and drums, see. And they knock each other around, and they're live, not animated, like these other shows, see. And they've got some cartoons on the show, too, see. Like *The Arabian Knights* and *The Three Musketeers* and this live-action adventure called *Danger Island,* see, where there's this buncha people trapped on an island fulla cannibals and other unsocial types, see. And the whole show is a wild, insane take-out, with some very nice rock music on top of everything. See?)

Then at 10:30 on Channel 2 there's the animated Batman/Superman Hour of Adventure, and need I say more? The Riddler is there, and the Penguin, and the Catwoman, and the Joker, and Robin, and Batgirl, and Superboy with his wonder dog Krypto, and it is some of the best animation on network TV, and if you dug the comics, you'll love the films.

(Did you ever wonder if Superman wore a jockstrap under that long underwear?)

But the best, the very best, is a Jay Ward entry called *George Of The Jungle.* It usually gets usurped by a football game (as with the Army-Navy game a couple of weeks ago), but ABC puts it on sometime around four or five-ish. Check your local listings, as they say.

On the *George Of The Jungle* show there is this extra-lovely fuckup Tarzan named George, who can't swing on a vine without he bashes his *punim* on a banyan tree. He's not too bright, this George, and he's got a girl friend named Ursula that he calls Fella, cause he

77

don't know the difference. There's an ape named Ape who speaks with a Ronald Colman accent, and an elephant George thinks is a big dog: his name is Shep . . .

(Ably assisting George in the supplementary segments of the show are Super Chicken—alias Henry Cabot Henhouse III—and a racer named Tom Slick.

There is nothing on prime-time to compare with the social comment and satire being purveyed weekly on *George Of The Jungle*.)

And so, having hipped you to all the wonders extant on the kiddie terrain, I sign off, having written this on a Friday, knowing that tomorrow morning I'll be able to tune in on my favorite crime fighters and nutsos . . . and only wishing I knew a deranged chick who dug them, too, who wouldn't get uptight when I kiss the back of her neck and whisper romantically, "Hey, honey, guess what? *The Fantastic Four* is on. Y'wanna watch, or y'wanna make it again?"

13: 3 JANUARY 69

Comes a moment of truth.

Several weeks ago, in these pages, another *Free Press* columnist invoked the wrath of the readers by siding with The Establishment. Before what I am about to set down is construed as a like cop-out (pulling a mintz, as it has come to be called, he said innocently), let me inform my readers that acquaintances of mine in the nine-to-five scene handily castigate me for (as they put it) pandering to the muddy thinking of the "anarchists, hippies, unwashed degenerates and corrupt eggheads." Apparently, I am neither fish nor fowl, sorta twixt and tween, neither of one camp nor the other, a chickenshit to both sides. Well, friends and rock-toters, I like to think of myself as an honest man, mayhap even a seeker after Truth. (Stop that giggling right now, wiseacre, or I'll use phrases like "I tell it like it is.")

And this pathological concern with Truth leads me into areas where I'm forced to deny some of the things my gut tells me are groovy, simply because my head says they're full of nonsense. All of the preceding, naturally, is geared to set you in the proper frame of mind for a denunciation of the Holy.

But first, a word from my sponsor, the Great American Viewing Animal, which has asked me to remark on the following:

As beautiful as Stevie Wonder may be on records, it was horrifying to see him on the Ed Sullivan Show several Sundays ago. There are blind musicians whose mannerisms on stage don't make you feel like a descendant of Custer at a Buffy Sainte-Marie concert (Ray Charles, Feliciano, Shearing). But Stevie Wonder ain't one of them. And if venal peddlers of the Sound like Sullivan have to slip in acts like Wonder between the trained dogs and acrobats, for .Christ's sake the least they can do is camera-shoot him in such a way that he doesn't come off looking like a spastic.

The Apollo moonshot was the biggest washout, dramawise, since Mama Cass opened in Vegas. Here it was, for all of us science fiction buffs, the most incredible step away from this war-crushed mudball since Columbus said, "C'mon you guys, knock off the mutiny shit; we'll be in Cuba in a few days!" and the most exhilarating thing about it was Cronkite informing us that the English Flat Earth Society was prepared to reevaluate. Sure, okay, I'm woolgathering, but I just wish to God we'd get an astronaut with a sense of the dramatic. A guy who'd broadcast back from the darkside: "Jeezus, Houston, you ain't gonna believe this, but as we passed over the Mare Imbrium, we saw this little pink-and-white gingerbread house, with smoke coming out of the chimney, and there was a tiny gray-haired lady out in front waving a banner that said Lemonade, 5¢ a glass . . ."

And now, back to my main thesis this week, the Great Denunciation. Have I gotten you jollied enough?

Well, I've carped repeatedly in these pages that one of the networks should air a rebuttal to Daley's panegyric on Chicago (Wonderland of the Midwest). Two weeks ago, on Channel 11, one Sunday night, I saw it. The American Civil Liberties Union and the Yippies had an hour to state their case. It was telecast on the same channel that had aired Daley's propaganda, with typical disclaimers that the opinions herewith set forth were not those of the blah blah blah. The ACLU had 45 minutes, the Yippies had 15 minutes.

While the ACLU portion was nowhere nearly as artfully executed as the Daley film, a matter of money is all, it made its point with strength and conviction. Over and over we heard the now-classic Daley utterance, "The police are not there to create disorder, they're there to *preserve* disorder." There were touching and convincing interviews with college-age nursing students, McCarthy delegates, newsreel cameramen, straight types who could get the message across to the squares.

When the ACLU forty-five minutes was ended, one had the feeling that while it might not convince the 74% of the Great Unwashed who applauded the actions of the Chicago police (even *after* the release of the Walker Report) that the dissenters were not Communist-inspired anarchists bent on the assassination of the Hump, still it might put a nubbin of doubt in their dense skulls. Hurrah! Gold stars for a job well done.

Then came the Yippies' 15 minutes.

In just 15 short minutes, the Yippies managed to negate everything that had gone before.

Let me make a point: I quite agree that there is a need for humor and satire and ridicule in the Dissent Movement (if that's what it's called). The Establishment and its lies are what novelist John D. MacDonald once referred to as "a thing. Heart empty as a paper bag, eyes of clever glass." Any possible way at our command to make the piranha look ridiculous and jabberwockly should be taken.

But when it becomes (apparently) impossible for the strategists to realize they are in a war, and that war may well be hell but certainly ain't funny, then they must be labeled irresponsible. Not irresponsible to those nebulous jingoisms of Our Times—Law&Order, Civic Conscience, Human Rights, Respect For Our Appointed Leaders—none of that jello, friends, because those are the slogans the piranhas use to keep everyone in line. But irresponsible to the Cause and, more important, down in the nitty-gritty, to the troops. To the foot-soldiers in the war who are getting expelled from high schools and colleges all over this Cheyne-Stokes country. Irresponsible to the thousands who used their odd-job money to get to Chicago to protest, and for their concern got busted heads and police records. Irresponsible to all of (them, us, me, you, all of the above) who have spent endless hours in doctors' offices getting repaired after Our Appointed Leaders used heavy clout against us. Irresponsible to those of us who don't conceive of the war as a love-in or a gambol or a frolic. There's nothing funny about three John Laws stomping on your arm till they break it.

So. Funny. Yeah, the Yippie segment of that TV documentary was funny. It opened with a scantily clad chick standing in front of a gong with Daley's face in the center of it. As a voice proclaimed, "And now . . . here's *Yippie!*" the chick swung her striker and the gong rang hollowly. Funny. I laughed. I laughed because I thought Hoffman and Rubin and Krassner were going to zing the mothers as they deserved to be zinged.

But I stopped laughing very quickly. The fifteen minutes was taken up with self-indulgent, irresponsible private jokes and adolescent jabber.

Interspersed with badly selected newsreel footage of the riots and truncheon-swinging cops, the Yippies intercut footage from a silent Cecil B. DeMille bible orgy . . . I think it was *Sodom And Gomorrah*. Sure, I got the point: Chicago was an orgy of violence as opposed to an orgy of sex and depravity, both culminating in the fall of the metropolis. I got it, fellahs, I got it.

But the Yippies didn't just play that note once. They hit it again and again and again, and there was the porcine presidential candidate, Pigasus, and there were scuffy dudes making faces and sticking out their tongues, and there were kids running around shrieking insanely. And *no* point was made. No convincing argument was made.

Well, then, one of you out there offended by my seeming turncoat attitude will say, "So what? Who the hell were they supposed to be impressing? Surely not the squares!"

Yes, you jerk, the squares!

Otherwise, why go on TV, a mass medium for the dissemination of information? Those of us who *know* what came down in Chicago, *know* it. We don't *have* to

82

be convinced. We're there already. That television production was intended to show the other side, to let a little light into the catacombs. If not, what purpose was it to have served? Assuage the wounded egos of the Yippie leaders? Pull a shuck on the boobs? Commit a great put-on to posterity?

Nonsense. This was the only opportunity all the dues-payers who went to Chicago had to have their side of it heard. And the opportunity got blown.

Because by the time that fifteen minutes was ended, it had invalidated everything the ACLU had labored to put together; it made the Yippies look like the clowns they must be; it firmly solidified the prejudices and fears of the Great Unwashed. And by me, friends, that is stinking irresponsibility.

Credits were not run for the show. I don't know who actually conceived and executed that disaster, but I suspect it must have been the acknowledged Yippie leaders, and that makes me sad, because I know some of them, and dig them personally.

But if they can't separate their own ego-needs for childish demonstration (on a level with the romper tot who emerges in the living room of his parents during a party and pees on the floor to get attention), they damned well ought to admit that they don't care about what's *really* happening in this country in terms of dissent, and start a night club act like The Fugs, where they can pick their noses in front of the jerks who'll pay to be insulted, and stop paying lip-service to the Cause.

If this makes me a humorless bastard who can't understand the necessity for ridicule and satire in a world going mad, so be it. But I merely suggest that if there be any in the Yippie camp who think war is a ha-ha, sort of a refined *Hogan's Heroes,* have somebody run newsclips of the camps at Belsen and Dachau.

Life ain't a TV spectacular. And if it is, if God is truly mad and it is, then the only way these comedians are going to get their show renewed for next season is with the blood and pulped faces of kids who think they're into something dead serious.

That's a helluva price to pay for a good rating.

14: 10 JANUARY 69

As I sit down to write this column it is the day after New Year's, and not being a drinker I have no hangover, so my lucidity is firmly intact. It is also seven years since I arrived here in Clown Town from New York, as I write this. Seven years ago, when I informed my friends back East that I was heading for Cloud Coocoo Land, they predicted the direst consequences. I would sell my soul to the devil out here, I would cease writing, or if I continued writing it would be the sheerest hackwork. Well, it's seven years later and though I've had my soul up at remainder prices for the longest while, none of the accepted devils have ever tried to take an option on it; I'm still writing . . . more, and I think even better than when I was in New York.

But still my friends back East cry despair at my being out here where the phony tinsel only covers a true surface of genuine tinsel. (In a letter I received, from a promising young writer living in Wyoming, who is planning to come out here to set up shop, he says, "Jody has evaluated my basic crass materialism and maintains that I'll likely lose whatever artistic integrity I've painfully built up here in the unsullied Wyoming wilds if I spend any extended time amid the tinsel of L.A. . . . but I maintain that I've got the capability to survive in the jungle.") Crazy June, my secretary, constantly reports on the bleatings of her mother, back East, who *nudzhes* her with warnings of the messy finishes awaiting folk who commit to Los Angeles. And I must confess that I had the same myths rattling in my gourd before I began to dig Los Angeles and decided to stay on. But are they correct? Is L.A. truly Disaster City?

85

The enormous gap between the reality of what life is like here—artistically—and what they *think* it is, back there, has often confused and dismayed me. I could not pin a conclusion to thoughts about this inaccuracy.

But TV on New Year's Day answered the question for me, and I take this solemn opportunity to share my findings with you. To wit: it is the studied merchandising of lies and outmoded glamour and what Crazy June calls "glorious hokum."

I watched the Bowl games and the Tournament of Roses Parade.

I'll dwell only momentarily on the gagging saccharine mealymouthness of the half-time shenanigans, in which Mom, Democracy, Apple Pie and The American Way were extolled with enormous Uncle Sam figures that stared mongoloidally at a national TV audience, and eight million Munchkins who scampered around the 50-yard line forming replicas of the Mayflower while a sententious voice assured us this was A Great Moment for All Of Us. (The *greatest* moment, we were told a few minutes later, was the moment we all became A*M*E*R*I*C*A*N*S. I suppose they meant the moment of birth but if that was the case, the midfield replica would have much more appropriately been an enormous womb, rather than a star-and-barred shield with eagle a-crouch thereon.)

They loosed doves of peace, and they turned their placards in the grandstands to form a waving American flag, and all I could think of was the incredible hypocrisy: to maintain a pose of 1901 Middle-Class Midwestern flag-waving during a period in which college students are finally examining the nature of patriotism, and finding it wanting, is so blatantly a divorcement from reality, that to belabor the point only makes it more depressing. I'll go on to the Rose Parade, with clenched teeth.

The 80th Annual Tournament of Roses Parade in beautiful ticky-tacky downtown Pasadena is America's annual orgy of bad taste. A two-hour spasm of insen-

86

sate spending, flaunting the bloated ego of a country that can *waste* between twelve and twenty thousand dollars in the shape of a showboat or a giant glass slipper while children are dying of starvation in Georgia and Biafra. It is a strident note in a song of stupidity intended to lull the already dulled senses of yahoos and boobs who are not incensed at the outrage of flushing uncounted hundreds of thousands of dollars better spent on charities down an exploitation toilet whose sole *raison d'etre* is the selling of more color TV sets in time to snag the very yupyups who suffer most by the gaudy senselessness, the grossness of this testament to conspicuous waste.

(Before you get the impression that I am trying to slay a gnat with an elephant gun, let me hip you that I feel this same wrath at Miss America pageants, ostentatious weddings and lavish funerals.)

And I understood what it was about California that made all the intelligent ones back East feel this was the ass-end of reality. Why shouldn't they, when TV markets this public relations man's hash-dream of glory and grandeur? Why shouldn't they think we are all insipid dolts out here, when we proffer as our magnum opus a tasteless hegira of vapidly grinning non-entities on floats built from the corpses of flowers? The damned silly parade has all the style and class of an ex-hooker decked out in a Lily Ann prom gown, two dabs of rouge on her pale cheeks, strutting her weary wares before jaded mud-dwellers.

What are they to think in the shanties of Selma and the rat-traps of Chicago's ghetto, when they see the way we shovel money into the sewer? What are they to make of a George Putnam, prancing about on his palomino wearing a silver lamé fag cowboy suit priced at forty grand, and what must they think of a man who would pay that much to be so outlandishly overdressed?

What are they to make of a 55-foot long float in honor of Bob Hope, gorged with pink roses, and entered in the parade by the Chrysler Corporation? Does it make them wonder why Chrysler didn't save the money, shake Bob's hand to show him they loved him, and deduct the savings from the cost of new Chryslers?

And what segment of America goes for this jejune dullery? Do the Iowans and Kansans really sit before their sets drooling over the endless horse-groups and out-of-tune school bands? Are they uplifted by the USC Trojan band clanging out a medley of classics by Max Steiner, Miklos Rosza and Alfred Newman? Do they wonder at the seemingly bottomless cornucopia that spews forth those grinning scrubbed-clean chicks, sweating in furs as they are trundled down the avenue?

And what of the black community? Do they notice that there are barely any Afro-Americans on the floats; do they take note that once again the Rose Queen was white, as were all her Princesses? (It is as if no black face ever shone in the All-American light of all-American Pasadena.) (And when we saw a black chick, it was on the float of some Deep South city . . . and lord how the TV camera lingered on that ebony countenance . . . as if trying to stave off a riot.)

It was a day at once both dreary and infuriating. And it will go on next year, and the year after, and the year after that. And we will once again hear Steve Allen trying to get a word in edgewise with his flap-jawed missus, Jayne Meadows. (Steve Allen is my nominee for the husband most to be pitied in 1969. And he used to be such a good man.) And we will once again hear the virtues of Americana extolled.

And on the theory of bread and circuses, I suppose only rabble-rousers such as myself will carp.

But I tell you this: the extravanganza was so sad-making to me, that the only bright spot in the day occurred when Mr. Nixon crossed the field at the Rose Bowl, and was met by Wretched Ronald Reagan, and they were standing cheek-by-jowl with one another, and I began screaming for some Divinity to provide me with a helicopter mounted with machine guns.

But then, the thought of Spiro Agnew as the Rose Queen next year sobered me, and I flipped channels to 5, where I regained my sanity watching Dennis O'Keefe and Ruth Hussey in *The Lady Wants Mink*.

Next New Year's Eve, I think I'll take up drinking.

15:   17 JANUARY 69

Even as the sixty-seven foot carnivorous plant aphid advances on Mona Freeman, somewhere to the north of her in the intricate subway system of Hokkaido, Rod Cameron and his specially hand-picked assault force of shock troops, equipped with chemical spray-throwers filled with the last of the pyrohexachlorinate-dyalumi-naoxysulphazynamine formula created by John Beal at the cost of his life, hurry to her rescue. As they emerge from the stinking dank ooze of the feeder tunnels, they hear the high keening whine of the radioactive monster as its mandibles click a deadly song of menace. They know they only have moments to save her from a ghastly disembowelment. Will the formula work? Will the beast be stopped? Will the Japanese shock troops understand Rod Cameron's English? Suddenly, there is a terrifying scream . . .

"Hi, friends, this is Raf Wiyummz, Raf Wiyummz Ford, 98022 Ventura Buh'vard, inna siddyuv Encino; hanny to any point inna grayder Losanneles air-ya, simply take your nearest freeway tuh'thu Sanee-aye-go Freeway, take the Sanee-aye-go Freeway tuh'thu San Bernuhdeeno Freeway, take the San Bernuhdeeno Freeway tuh'thu Howood Freeway, Howood Freeway tuh'thu Goln State Freeway, Goln State Freeway tuh'thu Sannamoniga Freeway, Sannamoniga Freeway tuh'thu Harb'r Freeway, Harb'r Freeway tuh'thu Ventura Freeway, take the Ventura Freeway tuh'thu Glendale innerchange, take the Vannize eggzit, go a hunnerd an' seven miles portage overrland and there we are, seventeen full blocks of the fiyness newenuzecars inna Southern Californyuh air-ya, adda largess Ford deal'rshib WEST of Chicago, you don' haveta buhleev me, yuh c'n check out 'a records of the Ford Moder Comp'ny, that's Raf Wiyummz, Raf Wiyummz Ford, 98022 Ventura Buh'vard inna siddyuv . . ."

John Payne knows that the storm building up over the Andes makes the chances for success nil, but there are six cases of the new miracle drug, pyrohexachlorinatedyaluminaoxysulphazynamine, in the old beat-up Spad, and a colony of *Cholos* beyond these mountains dying of the dread Dutch Elm Blight. As Payne's comical grease monkey, Patsy Kelly, rolls the Spad out on the runway, Frances Gifford dashes out of the hangar, wearing her voguish new windsock. "John, John," she pleads, flinging herself into his arms, "Lloyd Corrigan says the updrafts over the Valley of Montezuma's Revenge will spiral you into the gorge. Please, please, pleeeeeez, I beg you, let them crummy *Indios* die! Don't throw away our love!" But John shrugs her off, noting with pique that her tears and the slanting rain have run the colors of his new Madras flight-suit. In the shadows he sees the one he *truly* loves, Susan Cabot, fearful for his life, but knowing he must do this good thing. "Knock out the chocks, Patsy!" John yells, over the roar of the wind and dashes for the Spad . . .

"Hi, frenz, thissis Raf Wiyummz agen, an' ritenow at my hunnerd an' seventy locations allover Ventura Bulvard we're ennering the final month of our big eighteen month cleerunz sale, movin' these li'l cupcakes outta here at an 'mazing pace. Everything gotta go . . . the Edsels, the Morris Minors, the Cords, the Spads, the new nineen sissty-nine Muzdang with the audomadic faggdorry air conditioning, par winnows, par braygz, par steering, par antenna, par ashtray, onny three thawzan' nine hunnerd an siggzdee three dollars . . . shop an' compare . . ."

George Zucco has ordered that Richard Jaeckel must die, for squealing, little realizing that Richard is the brother of his most trusted aide in the mob, Willard Parker, who is, in reality, a T-Man. Willard has followed Marc Lawrence, Ted De Corsia and Neville Brand to the cheap rooming house where Richard lives while working in the grease pit of the garage, trying to make a new life for himself after the hellish three years he served in Dannemora. Willard sees them enter the rooming house, and dashes around to the alley. Leaping up, he grabs the dropladder of the fire escape and with panic clutching his heart races up the five flights of fire escape steps to Richard's bedroom window. He knows that Richard has the information on him that will prove Zucco is behind the traffic in pyrohexachlorinate-dyaluminaoxysulphazynamine. As he reaches Richard's floor, he hears a fussilade of shots . . .

"Hi frenz, thizzis Raf Wiyummz, Rafwiyummz Ford, anthissusthelastdayyoucancomedownanzupzupzupzupzupblahblahblahblahblahgurgleslurpfloop. Urp!"

Mostly, this week, I watched the all-night movies. In times past, the worst you could get from insomnia was dark circles under your eyes; these days the penalty is brain rot.

16: 24 JANUARY 69

Bad manners should not, strictly speaking, be grist for this particular mill. Especially because the flagrant flouting of decorum and propriety on television is so ingrained after almost twenty years that it seems to be the accepted manner. But an incident that saw airtime on the Merv Griffin variety show, Channel 11, Wednesday the 15th (5:30 P.M.), is *so* appalling, *so* degrading, *so* demanding of comment—in that it brings to focus some things long needing to be said—that this week my column will bend the rule.

Generically, Griffin's show is a "talk show." There is some singing, and some comedy, but the mainstay of the program is conversation with various entertainment types, and that new breed of human being called "the TV personality," which means they are either unsuccessful novelists or advocates of some offbeat cause. It is one with the Joe Pyne Show, The Les Crane Show, the Tonight Show, Joey Bishop, Donald O'Connor, Steve Allen, Joan Rivers, Alan Burke, and all the local imitations in every major American city.

The show to which we address ourselves here was hosted by comedian John Barbour, standing in for Griffin. And in specific I refer to an interview with Jean-Claude Killy, the world-famous ski champion and all-around groovy man of our times.

To call Barbour's treatment of Killy cavalier, rude, degrading, shocking, uninformed, horrifying, humiliating, gauche, debased, obnoxious, reprehensible, vicious and in the ultimate of bad taste, would be to ennoble it. Barbour's approach was typical of that no-class, no-taste breed of Yankee who makes the Grand Tour of

93

Europe and endears himself with Stetson-wearing, backslapping, dirty-joke-telling rudeness and endless complaints about "them foreigners who ain't civilized enough to speak English; they have lousy plumbing; they don't appreciate us great wonderful Americans pouring all that foreign aid into their crummy little kingdom." He is the complete boor.

For openers, Killy is a soft-spoken man, a gentleman of controlled Continental manner. It is vastly appealing on a medium surfeited with stylistic descendents of Pinky Lee, all florid and bombastic, reveling in their own stupidities and crassness. When Killy came out and was greeted by Barbour, the host's first shot—exquisitely gross, and a portent of horrors to come—was something like, "When I announced you were coming on the show, all the women screamed, Killy. What's the story on that? What's this big sex image you have?" The inference, of course, was that Barbour (impelled by the twinges of his own undernourished ego) saw nothing outstanding in an athlete who is known as "the fastest man on skis in the world," has fought bulls without a cape, has worked at skydiving, sports car racing, skindiving, and is the holder of more Olympic medals for sports like slalom (which Barbour probably can't even spell) than any other man in Olympic history. Of course we should see nothing attractive to women in this: we should only find the king of the smartmouths erotically compelling.

Killy tried to answer this unanswerable gaucherie with class. He spoke softly. Barbour leaped in, saying, "What're you speaking so softly for? Are you trying to make love to me?! Are you gonna romance me, or answer my question?"

Then he asked the audience, "Can you people hear him out there? Huh? Huh? Huh?" It would have been a simple matter of courtesy for Barbour to have moved the microphone closer to Killy, or advise him that his voice might not be carrying. But he didn't. "Huh? Huh? Huh?" The audience indicated they could hear Killy without difficulty, and Barbour, with a classic proof that he not only doesn't know how to *talk* to people, but certainly doesn't *listen* to them, jubilantly shouted, "See, they can't hear you. Speak up, don't try to romance me!" Killy moved over toward the mike.

One expected Barbour's paranoia to interpret this as another homosexual advance.

But Barbour was too preoccupied with readying his next salients. The first was politely put as follows: "What's all this I read about you being involved in a scandal during the Olympics? Huh? Huh? Huh?"

The "scandal" to which the semi-literate Barbour referred was the question of Killy's having been paid by the Head Ski Company for wearing their product. The charges had been limp-wristed at the outset, and shortly after they were voiced, were blown away. There was no scandal.

Killy's response was reasoned, and brief. "There was a question about my showing the Head mark on my skis. They did not pay me. The matter was disposed of quickly."

Barbour was totally at sea. "Mark? Mark? Whaddaya mean, mark? I don't understand you? Can't you speak English? Whaddaya mean mark?"

Only a consummate dullard could be unaware—if not from *a priori* knowledge, then certainly from the context of Killy's response—that a "mark" is the company trademark, its colophon, the little decal found on almost every commercial product, from Chryslers to creosote. Killy tried, unsuccessfully, three times to explain to Barbour what a mark was. But the Swine King was already off on his next searching, penetrating question.

"What's this about you dating two French actresses at the same time? Huh? Huh? Huh?"

(Apparently the concept of going out with more than one girl is alien to Barbour. With a personality such as his, midway between maggot and masher, one does not doubt such a probability.)

Killy was a gentleman. He refused to answer. "That is my personal life, and I do not wish to discuss the ladies I know."

Barbour pressed him, in the coarsest possible way. It was expected momentarily that he would dig an elbow in Killy's ribs and leer, and ask him if they were good lays. Killy finally admitted that he was *not* making it with a pair of them lewd and lascivious frog flick stars, and was keeping fairly steady company with one young woman whose name Barbour would not recognize. Barbour broke up cackling, jibing at Killy with, "Ahhh, all you Frenchmen are alike!"

It went on in that vein for what seemed an eternity. Viewers encountering this horror show cringed in their seats. Only the most insensitive asshole, whose total conception of Europe is of a wasteland wherein one must not touch the water, could have conceived of this as anything but in calamitous, poisonous bad taste.

My Secretary, Crazy June, remarked on it with absolute chagrin the next day. She could only think what effect this kind of treatment of an outstanding emissary from overseas would have on his opinion of America, and by extension, what others overseas would make of us.

It was another example of the rampant bad manners of the so-called hosts of these talk marathons. There are far too many Joe Pyne and Alan Burke models on television. There are too few Les Cranes. In Chicago, a creep named Jack Eigen has been doing this number for years. In New York there are a host of them, led by Burke. I've appeared on this sort of show in almost every city in the States, and their model is Pyne. They use the word "controversy," but what they employ is the same sort of rough-trade cheapjack yellow animosity that Mike Wallace pioneered in 1956. It is deplorable, and one can only assume that its sole reason for being are the hordes of debased scuttlefish out there in the Great Unwashed who don't get their fill of personal vilification and hostility from the news reports. Obvi-

96

ously, until this kind of show, with its garbage can odor, no longer appeals to the atrophied tastes of the millions, it will continue.

And we will continue to be treated to such *adagios* of decorum as Barbour's parting shots to Killy:

After a film of Killy running the slalom, in which Killy pointed out that he was concentrating so hard missing the pitons that his tongue was protruding from his mouth, Barbour became positively raucous, repeating the word "tongue" and leering, till his implied references to *soixante-neuf* were teeth-grittingly obvious.

And when Killy said he had to leave—probably having taken more than enough abuse from this pygmy—Barbour's farewell was a charming, "Yeah, well, I know ya gotta go. So goodbye . . . and good riddance."

And they killed Martin Luther King.

17: 31 JANUARY 69

As some of you who read this column may know, among the many types of writing that flow off this typewriter there are occasional television scripts. I've written for shows as diverse as *Star Trek, Man From U.N.C.L.E., Flying Nun, Cimarron Strip* and *Outer Limits.* A couple of times my fellow videowriters have advised me that I may consider myself one of the more talented in their ranks, through the joys of twice awarding me the Writers Guild Award. Once for best anthology script of the '64-65 season, and last year for best dramatic-episodic script of the '66-67 season. I mention this in front, not only to puff my own shaky ego, but to prepare you for a sort of running diary I intend to introduce into this column.

From time to time I'm asked by friends, fans of this column, and aspiring TV writers, what the System is like. What it takes to sell a TV script. What the working conditions are like. How heavy the censorship gets to be. A myriad of questions it would take a week to answer. Or the contents of a running diary.

This week I got a job. I'll be scripting a ninety-minute segment of *The Name Of The Game*, the big Universal/NBC showcase starring Robert Stack, Anthony Franciosa and Gene Barry in alternating roles. The series hooks itself on a publishing empire, run by Barry, with Franciosa the hotshot reporter for *Fame Magazine* and Stack the ex-FBI man who runs the empire's crime magazine. The series is based on the Universal film-for-TV *Fame Is The Name Of The Game.*

Last year, I was called in by David Victor, Executive Producer of the series, before its debut. We discussed my doing a script for the series. When I found I would be working with Doug Benton, a Producer for whom I'd done a *Cimarron Strip,* I agreed. Victor and Benton are two of the most honest, reliable gentlemen I've met in this game, and their type is so hard to come by that I will work for them anywhere, anytime, for any amount of money they offer. But, as things turned out, we never did the segment, for reasons that had nothing to do with them, me, or the series. (I got a job writing a movie; more money . . . immediate deadline.)

On Friday, January 17th, my agent, Marty Shapiro of the Shapiro-Lichtman Agency, called to tell me George Eckstein wanted to see me. I remembered Eckstein as having been on *The Untouchables* as Producer, but had no idea what he was doing currently. Marty said he was going to produce the eight Robert Stack segments of *The Name Of The Game* for the 1968-69 season. A meeting had been set up for me at Universal City Studios for Wednesday the 22nd.

On Wednesday, I drove out to the black tower in the Valley, and went up to the ninth floor to see Eckstein.

A pleasant man with a direct manner, Eckstein told me that while the series had been popular, it had lacked some dimensions in its first season that he was going to try and correct. (I smiled. He was being charitable. Most of the segments of *Name* had been surfeited with the inane gloss Universal and NBC usually feel is necessary to impress the scuttlefish out in The Great American Heartland. It is the disease of creativity known as Overcompensation: everyone in the show has to be Beautiful, don't shoot any scene in Bringdown Locations such as slums, let the Stars carry the show.)

We discussed the Stack segments in particular, and while Eckstein never bum-rapped anyone, I got the distinct impression that he felt most of the shows had been strained; that Stack's (admittedly) proscribed range of abilities had segmented the shows so they lacked pace and clout.

Neither of us felt that Stack had been used as well as

he could be. Eckstein then informed me that Stack had final say over the scripts. I was momentarily alarmed. Bob Stack is a pleasant man, a wealthy man, and a face known to millions of Americans. He has an image to protect. I knew personally that his politics placed him slightly to the right of Mr. Reagan, another actor who made good, and I had the distinct impression I was going to suggest some topics for scripts that would get me politely ushered from Mr. Eckstein's office.

I was to be crossed-up. My first suggestion was a show that might strike somewhere closer to the nitty-gritty on the subject of college student dissent than what we had been seeing of late.

The postulated story went like this: A San Francisco State-type campus. An acting president a la Hayakawa. A state government pressing for "law and order" of the mace and truncheon variety. The Acting President, in an effort to stave off more confrontations, has called a series of seminars. At these seminars speakers of all political persuasions will participate. Cleavers, Karengas, Chavezes, Reddens, and because he represents the Establishment view of these goings-on via the mass media, Robert Stack. So Stack speaks. During the seminar, at which he espouses the time-honored philosophies of abiding by the law, using due process to achieve one's end, the evil of violence, the value of working for what one gets, etc., he is challenged from the floor by a young white boy who is the editor of the underground campus newspaper, *The Pig*.

That night, the Acting President is murdered. All the clues point to the editor of the paper, a militant of the most persuasive sort. He is arrested and the gears of the law begin to grind. From his cell he writes one after another pronunciamento, à la the *Ramparts* series by Cleaver. He is rallying a strong coterie around his cause, accusing the Establishment of railroading him to keep him quiet.

Stack gets into it. The clues are too pat, the case too sturdily constructed. He goes to the boy. The boys says

100

fuck off, I don't need any help. But Stack gets deeper into it. He is suddenly questioning some of the dead-certain beliefs he's had about anarchy on campus. If this boy is willing to die for his Movement, then there is something here to be more seriously considered.

Stack's two young aides are on the side of the militants. They nudge and chivvy their boss, trying to get him to open his mind to what the kids are about.

In the denouement, we find out that not only is the boy not guilty, he has had his girl out planting clues so he *will* be prosecuted for the crime. But he's a shuck. He knows he'll never go to the gas chamber. What with appeals and all the time-dragging mechanism of prosecution in America today, he can be of value to the Movement with copy-from-prison for some time. And if worse comes to worse, if the killer isn't found, his girl can always cop to having dummied up the evidence. But if the killer *is* found, he has tremendous clout against the Establishment for their harassment. It is a power play. The unfortunate element of the situation is that while *this* phony bastard won't really lay it on the line, he is surrounded by other kids who will, and are.

Thus, Stack comes to a more rational and reasoned view of the evils on campuses today. He knows all the things he believed in as gospel are not so, but neither is the random violence of the Movement right. He intends to work for reform.

I laid all of this on Eckstein. It was not as strong as I might have liked to make it, but it was considerably stronger than anything I'd yet seen. No cop-out on my part: I'm a militant, granted, and what I'd proposed as plot was exceedingly ameliorative . . . from where *my* head is at. But by doing it softer, I had a chance to get it on the air. Taking the hard line never would.

Even at that, I thought Eckstein would shake his head and say Stack would never go for it, or Universal would never go for it, or NBC would never go for it. But he didn't. He said it was a very exciting idea, with plenty of room to stretch out.

So he called the Universal negotiators, and they called my agent, and they made a deal for $7500 for me to script the show, tentatively titled *Corridor Without Mirrors*.

(One catch. There is what is called a "cut off" after the treatment portion of the deal. A script is written in three stages: the story, or "treatment," a present-tense straight-line of the plot, in about fifteen pages, to let the network continuity people and sponsors and Stack know what I'm going to do with the script; then a first draft; then a final draft. If they don't like what has been done in the "treatment," the writer gets cut off, and paid about a grand for what he's already done. If they dig it, the deal progresses, and there are no further blocks to finishing the script.)

That is where the history of this project rests right now. Today, the 24th, as I write this, I am about to go out to Universal to sit in on a screening of several segments of the *Name* series, to get the characterizations of the principals down pat. I will start writing on Monday.

While this column will not concern itself with the "Corridor Project" every week, from time to time I will bring you up to date, and we can follow, together, the progress of the dream. Will the starry-eyed Ellison get to write an honest script? Will the true word be given? Will the Blue Meanies at the network chop him off at the scruples? Will George Eckstein turn into a ghoul and gut the script? Will Robert Stack have Ellison investigated by Hoover's Lads?

Stay tuned to this column for the thrilling next installment.

And keep your fingers crossed, troops. Here we go again.

18: 14 FEBRUARY 69

Hey, Ken, I know I promised to do this week's installment of *The Smothers Brothers Comedy Hour,* and I know you're worried about them getting canceled because of bum-rap letters from the scuttlefish out there in the Heartland who are uptighted by denigrations of God, Motherhood and the American Way, and I promise honest to Ba'al that the column I started at your party will appear next week . . . but *this* week has been some other kinda crazy, man, and I have *got* to talk about it now; I think you'll agree this is of more immediate and dangerous importance. Okay, baby?

First Tuesday is NBC's entry in the big anthology documentary sweepstakes; their answer to CBS's *60 Minutes.* (And wouldn't you know the sonsofbitches would put it on directly opposite *60 Minutes* so you have to get cheated whichever one you watch. Would kill the mothers to put it on opposite something like *Green Acres* so we could have *two* nights of worthwhile viewing, wouldn't it!)

NBC calls the show "a monthly, two-hour journal of news, public affairs and today's living—leavened with occasional whimsy" and it airs the first Tuesday of the month, at 9:00, on Channel 4. A week ago Tuesday (as you read this) was the second edition, and what I choose to talk about this week does not, I think, fall under the heading of whimsy . . . unless the humor be as black as the heart of a torso killer. Is it news? Perhaps. But if it is, it is news that has been withheld from the American viewing public for many years. It is certainly a public affair—and one about which we must

103

instantly take action! For it speaks directly to "today's living" and the sudden, gruesome cessation of same.

First Tuesday did a documentary segment on chemical-biological warfare in experimental stages, being conducted all across the United States . . .

. . . and a more horrifying, cold-bloodedly insane declaration of disrespect for the basics of life and decency I have never encountered. It was more terrifying than all the Hammer Films horror shows ever conceived. In its pedestrian preparation for the eradication of sentient life on this planet through the use of botulism, anthrax and tularemia, it shrieked of the last extreme of human derangement. Its viciousness makes Jack the Ripper, Richard Speck, Charles Starkweather, Burke & Hare, Bluebeard and Madame Defarge shine as models of rational behavior. Beside the emotionless, rationalizing madmen who are preparing the aerosol sprays of nerve gas and plague, the Boston Strangler becomes a minor character disorder.

But . . . I gibber.

Let me try and relate it rationally, though the mind reels and the teeth chatter and the senses go numb at the consequences of what NBC presented calmly, quietly, seemingly without canard, certainly without editorialization.

CBW means Chemical-Biological Warfare. It means the use of "vectors"—animals bearing disease germs. It means seeding the atmosphere with anthrax the way US bombers seed the jungles of Viet Nam with defoliating weed-killers. It means spreading plague by aerosol spray. It means winds and air currents carrying the most virulent diseases known to man, killing guilty and innocent alike, indiscriminately. It means, dear God, the sheerest lunacy the concept of overkill has yet produced. It means that by its existence it can be utilized. It means there are actually men on this green good earth—and we saw them on that show—who can gather in conclave and discuss like ribbon clerks pricing bolts of cloth, how many megadeaths one seeding of turaremia

104

equals. It means we have certainly come as far as we can rightfully hope to come without the wrath of all the Gods, dead and alive, the universe has ever known, descending on us.

I cannot bear to think that I live in a country where this kind of *serious* experimentation goes on, all in the name of defense against an enemy who is merely human. What a pallid justification for mass murder: the Commies are doing similar research. What do we become if we unleash this most hideous of the Four Horsemen? Do we ennoble ourselves by working our hands in the black death, all to preserve ourselves from the specter of another social system? How can we realistically lay claim to any decency in our "democracy" if we adopt methods of destruction that would make a Genghis Khan blanch?

Again . . . I tremble and shudder and disgress.

Fear does that to me.

Would that the crew-cut, lupine-faced architects of that damnable nightmare felt a like fear. But apparently they do not.

As we saw on that documentary, they do not shudder at cramming kangaroo mice in metal containers, spraying them with nerve gas, and watching them die 44 seconds later. They do not cry at the piteous squeals of their lab animals as they jam needles into their underbellies, injecting death into their bloodstreams. They do not pause and consider their humanity as they urge human volunteers to breathe deeply of the disease germs sprayed through the mouthpieces.

First Tuesday's CBW segment was a seemingly endless compendium of nightmare images. We saw a film made some years ago—and only now released—of school children who had been given over with their parents' consent (!) for experimentation with germ warfare. Tiny figures, gas-masked and overcoated, hustled into a contamination chamber. We saw a lecturer describing the life-masks we would have to wear . . . masks that come in enough sizes to fit persons from the

105

ages of four to eighty. And a basket-carrier affair for tykes under the age of four. All done with aplomb and stately sincerity, as though the lunacy of what they were talking about did not exist.

And about that word "vector" . . .

One CBW experimenter, who had worked on a pilot project for disseminating disease germs via animal carriers, talked quietly and sensibly about having gone to an island in the Hawaiian chain, an uninhabited island, and turning loose a "vector" studded with diseased ticks. He talked of the "vector" doing this, and the "vector" doing that. And it became the key to understanding the level of debasement to which these "scientists" had descended. Not once did he say "dog" or "rabbit" or "hamster." He called the creature a "vector."

They have encapsulated themselves, denied their gut feelings, for whatever motives they consider good and sufficient. And by dehumanizing the experiments, by using "vectors" instead of "rabbits" or "mice," they can sleep nights.

But can we? Knowing our lives are held in the hands of men who may one day refer to a human plague-carrier as a "vector"?

And more horrors! more horrors! We saw rabbits used in an experiment to establish what only a tiny dose of nerve gas would do. A rabbit received merely a *drop* of some deadly fluid in his eye, and instantly the pupil contracted to a point where the creature was virtually blind. It took three weeks before the pupil returned to normal size. And that was with one infinitesimal drop.

We saw sheep in a pen, injected or sprayed with the virulence. Their heads hung pathetically, like cerebral palsy victims, all muscle-tone gone. We saw a cat in a cage; he was fed a mouse; he pounced and grabbed the mouse, and disemboweled him, as cats will do, then we saw the cat injected with a nameless fluid (Sander Vanocur suggested it might be LSD of a particularly nasty

106

formula) and another mouse sent into his cage. The cat's fur literally stood up and he cowered in fear of the mouse. At one and the same moment it was hilarious—like a bad MGM cartoon—and terrifying to see the ingrained instinctual behavior of an animal, fixed since the species came into existence, suddenly reversed. And it made me wonder what kind of perpetual bummer a human being would suffer if such a weapon was used.

But we were told repeatedly that these weapons were only experimental, that they were not "within our strike capabilities" at the moment. At the moment. But if that was so, how did NBC expect us to react to:

The filmed report of US Air Force bombers that had seeded the clouds near Salt Lake City, in a supposedly "uninhabited" area, with anthrax . . . a seeding that had been miscalculated . . . and 600,000 sheep died horribly. True? Yes, we know it was true, for the Air Force has already paid the sheepherders in the area over $400,000 in restitution monies. The Air Force rep who was asked to comment on this admitted that the bombers had been a little "off course," but he said only sheep had died. Yet we saw films of rabbits dying from the same disease, in the same area. And though the Air Force has never formally admitted culpability in the matter, the AF rep admitted that if those bombers had been only slightly more off-course, they would have hit the central reservoir that serves Salt Lake City. He mumbled a few words to the effect that the death toll would have been staggering.

If they can do *this* . . . *Now* . . . with such little concern for their acts . . . what must they be prepared to do in the event of a genuine threat?

It was an eye-opening presentation. For much of the nation. For those of us who were already aware of the chamber of horrors bacteriophage labs in New Jersey, Arkansas and Utah, it was only further documentation that they are proceeding apace, with little or no deterrent.

And suddenly, blindingly, all the student dissent for control of this and a voice in that became ludicrous. Screw it, troops! Stop fucking around taking over Sproul Hall . . . start picketing those goddam CBW labs on the campuses of the University of Texas, University of Pennsylvania, University of Washington, Stanford and Illinois Institute of Technology! Black, white, Mexican, Oriental, what the hell does *any* of it matter if we go blind and gag and feel the flesh ooze from our bones with running sores and agonizing death? One man, J. Robert Oppenheimer, stood up and said, "My God, what am I doing!?!" and the morality of the Bomb came under scrutiny. Oppenheimer was branded a traitor because he refused to accept the American Dream of killkillkill. History will call him a saint. If there *is* any history after this! Can the thinking young people of today do any less? What effect would concerted strikes at these labs have on the men who do the work? Perhaps none, but perhaps they might have to start examining what they are about!

Karate and akida and kung-fu are self-defense systems that proclaim they are only to be used as deterrents; but the other half of that proclamation is that once having committed, you go to kill. The Bomb was created, and no one wanted to use it . . . but one man said the need is great enough, so use it. Now we have CBW and they tell us again we won't ever use it.

Liars! The bullshitters are with us again! The demons in lab smocks are there, filling their vials and depressing the plungers on their hypodermics! Use it . . . you bet your ass they'll use it. For *this* is the result of all the stupid American Right Or Wrong patriotism that has so corrupted our country that we would wipe out the entire population of the Earth rather than see some other system of government in power. Pyrrhic victory, you imminent murderers!

NBC didn't editorialize. They ended on a note of justification. After all, wasn't Russia into the same bag? Killkillkill. The great American Dream. On the First

Tuesday of February NBC showed us the true face of that Dream. It was a death's-head vision.

After all that, Ken, I couldn't laugh too hard at what the Smothers Brothers or *Laugh-In* had to offer.

Frankly, I'm terrified.

19: 21 FEBRUARY 69

A few weeks ago, on the opening night of Sal Mineo's directorial debut with *Fortune And Men's Eyes,* I found myself sitting in the same row of the Coronet Theater as Doug McClure, a very nice guy and an actor of some quality who has been sadly misused by Universal Studios. We looked at each other, not having seen each other in several years, and instantly recognized a look of terror in each other. "Hey, Doug," I whispered down the row, "make a deal with you: you leave town when NBC shows *The King's Pirate,* and I'll leave town when ABC runs *The Oscar.* He laughed. We both laughed. But we both lived in terror of the evenings when our youthful indiscretions would catch up with us. I don't know how Doug handled it, but a week ago Wednesday I simply took the phone off the hook. (Not soon enough. They got it three hours earlier in New York and a friend called to cheer me up, damn him!)

I've apologized publicly, elsewhere, for having had a hand in writing that film; a film so embarrassingly bad why any producer would give me a chance to write another one is beyond my understanding. So I won't do a mea culpa here. All I'll say, to those of you who may wonder where I get the *chutzpah* to denigrate other people's failures when I have a veritable Krakatoa of failure to my own credit, is that having been through the shit, friends, I recognize the taste when I encounter it. Or, as Hymie Kelly says in *The Oscar:* "If you lie down with pigs, you get up smelling like garbage." Expiation is *so* refreshing!

Onward!

Ken, this guy I know, braced me a couple of weeks ago as to why I didn't actively support *Laugh-In* and *The Smothers Brothers Comedy Hour*. I told him that with the ratings *Laugh-In* has been getting I didn't think it needed any special boosting from me. Those ratings, incidentally, can be misleading, in terms of trends. ABC, the great imitator, tried to cash in on the "trend" with something called *Turn-On* which both premiered and vanished all in a night, like the ghost of Christmas Past, February 5th. It wasn't that it was a bad show, it was that it was an awkward show, and someone canceled it after the first commercial. The fastest death scene since Tammy Grimes gurgled her last, and *Championship Bowling Starring Milton Berle* rolled a gutterball.

ABC seems to be having better luck with *What's It All About, World?* which is a scarifying fact of life on which I'll comment shortly; but for now, I'll return to my reasons for not hyping *Laugh-In*. They're relatively simple, actually.

When all the squares on the streets of Tustin and La Mirada are socking it to one another, betting each other's bippies, offering to expose their Walnettos, intoning "werry inter-est-ink" in pseudo-Eichmann accents, and in general blowing in one another's ears to see if it'll follow them anywhere, I figure this column isn't needed for ersatz accolades.

But the Smothers Brothers, it has been pointed out to me, are not faring quite as well. Though the hip folk are watching the show religiously (or anti-religiously, depending on where your Valhalla is located), what the Smothers Sons are getting a potload of is letters of moral indignation and raw-throated outrage from the neatsy-clean tickytacky types out there in the Great American Heartland. The scuttlefish.

Well, the scuttlefish, it seems, don't like the Smothers Boys sticking up for integrity and daring and a little truth and a lotta commitment, not to mention some honest concern for this great, glorious country of ours, as long as it's being expressed by them long-haired, dope-puffing degenerates. And the networkers, heaven fore-fend, certainly don't want to unsettle anyone. (Which is another reason I don't stick up for *Laugh-In;* though it breaks me up with much of its humor, I think it's a cop-out, and never gets near the gut of anything genuinely controversial. A few scrotum references are not my idea of a dangerous vision, contrary to the belief of some literary critics.)

But the Smothers Guys do. I speak in particular of two items they've offered recently. The first was a scathing putdown of that saccharine Top 40 "hit" in which the mealymouth widower bemoans the fact that his coocoo-clock wife, Honey, has passed away. It was a cheap song, for openers, and I've got to hand it to the Smothers Types and their writers for doing it in royally, exposing the tawdry sentimentality of it for the shuck it was.

But the second item was the heavier of the two. It was the ensemble offering, three weeks ago, with Burl Ives doing a Thornton Wilder *Our Town* to the strains of Dylan's *The Times They Are A-Changin'*. If you saw it, you know what came down. If you didn't, I'll describe it briefly.

Ives comes back to his old home town. He is pleased to see that with all the rampage and riot running amuck in America Today, his old home town is still the same, still living by honest, simple values, unchanged from the turn of the century. And as he professes this belief, we are treated to blackout vignettes of what's *really* happening in the town:

A homicidal barber, cutting the hair of a hippie, rails about long-maned lunatics ruining his business, ruining the country, ruining everything. The hippie is terrified as the barber wields the razor, spouting endless violence. When the hippie gets out of the chair, the barber bids him goodbye, take it easy . . . and gives him the peace sign.

A spinster schoolmarm in a drug store, getting her

weekly supply of sleeping pills, diet pills, uppers, downers, sidewayers, and telling the druggist she'll need all the tranquilizers she can get because she's sitting on the jury trying the case of that terrible Jones boy. What's he being tried for? asks the druggist. "Drugs," says the teacher.

The local clergy rapping. One of them is a "traditional" prelate, who reveals himself as a venal, materialistic *schlepp,* and the other tries to tell him about getting out and working with the people in the streets. Ives encounters the latter, and says is it *all* in the streets? Isn't there anything sacred any more? Like the good old institution of marriage? The pastor says sure there is, why today he married a young couple in love . . . and we see them in silhouette. Ives beams . . . yes, love is still the same. And then the couple is lit up, and we see it's a black and white marriage.

Effective skit? You bet your ass it was. Simple, direct, eloquent, and enormously well-done because it was all underplayed, with just the right touches of comedy and not a cornball note in the entire production.

But the important thing about that bit was in what it means in terms of the reactionary tenor of the country. And as I've said before, if you haven't yet snapped to the reality that this is a hideously reactionary, scared little cloud-world, just consider the outrage letters of the middle-class viewers, who get hacked when they hear the Church, the Schools, the Home, the Sanctity of the Family Unit and Propriety maligned. Oh, sure, in the Thirty Cities Ratings, the Smothers Clan does well, but in the outlying regions, where most of the soap-suds are bought, they die. And the network notices this, make no mistake.

So I guess supporting Smothers et al becomes a holy chore. Because that was a devilishly clever, well-thought-out pastiche, intended to state some cases for the abolition of arteriosclerotic thinking, in terms best

113

conceived and semantically offered for winning over the scared squares.

Dig, this is somewhere near where it's at, I think: the majority of the people in this country really don't know what's happening. They can't be shot down like dogs for this lack of information . . . they haven't been given the opportunity for weighing one side against the other. The entrenched forces rule the mass media, in ways they deny because they don't conceive of them as being misused. But we all know that the primary job of those in power is to *stay* in power; and if concepts such as the Smothers Troupe suggest each week go into practice, a lot of old tigers gonna have their teeth pulled, gonna get gelded, gonna get sent out to pasture. And they can't have that.

So, inexorably, they will kill a show like *The Smothers Brothers Comedy Hour*. They have to. It threatens them too much. Courage and honesty such as Smothers II show us each week must be protected. And if a couple of hundred dingdongs can get something like *Star Trek* renewed, it would seem to behoove all of us who *care,* to start writing letters to CBS to counteract the potency of those assassin diatribes from Mashed Potato Falls, Wyoming. It's that, or watch the satire segment of prime-time get taken over by shows like *What's It All About, World?*, a horror of right-wing imbecility that is already in the process of catching on with the crewcut set.

A subject which I intend to eviscerate in this space next week. Watch the show tonight, so next week we can rap about it with mutual insights. There may even be a test.

The answer is: I haven't the foggiest damned idea!
The question is: *What's It All About, World?*

Now maybe I'm suffering from oxygen starvation,
maybe I'm dry-hallucinating (that's like dry-heaving
without the use of chemicals), maybe I'm getting spirit
messages from another continuum in the form of a TV
show no one else is seeing, but for the last three Thursdays, at 9:00, I've been tuning in Channel 7, the ABC
outlet, and I've been having the *damnedest* experience!

First comes the image of this awfully clean dude I
recall from Walt Disney movies. He's usually wearing a
turtleneck and a Nehru jacket; wearing them the way
the white-socks-and-brown-shoes guys wear them; awk-
wardly, as if he were trying to hook a corner of the identification image with "the young people"; makes me
want to stop wearing turtlenecks and Nehru jackets, if
he's the kinda cat wearing them. Then he starts singing.
But sincere, you know. Really sincere. How this land is
my land, how it's his land, from California to the New
York island. But quietly proud, y'know. Humble. Sincere as a gas station attendant telling you your oil filter
needs replacing.

Only thing is, he doesn't sing so good. Has this musical range from E to B#. I kinda blink, tap the heel of
my hand against the side of my head, maybe my hearing is impaired.

Then on comes this announcer who tells us this is a
sparkling, contemporary new show, *What's It All
About, World?* And it's filled—he tells us—with pun-
gent, scathing satire on the events of the day, the world
around us, the problems and turmoil of our times, all

done with rare good humor. So I sit back and wait to see this new entry in the satire sweepstakes, having been pleasured by *Laugh-In* and *The Smothers Brothers Comedy Hour.*

For openers, the show bares its muscles and shows us where its courage is at. It tackles one of the truly pressing topics of the day, fearlessly, satirically, pungently. How to save money when shopping.

Got to hand it to Ilson & Chambers, the producers: they sure as hell managed to avoid dealing with any of those stale, overworked topics of the day like rioting, racial upheaval, militancy in the suburbs, student dissent, police brutality, nuclear proliferation, the war in Viet Nam, the breakdown of law'n'order, the growth of organized crime, the horrors of chemical-bacteriological warfare, school dropouts, starvation in Appalachia, misuse of Federal land grants, the hazards of offshore oil drilling, censorship, the upheaval in the Church, black anti-Semitism, the generation gap or corruption in government. They struck directly to the heart of today's most pressing social problem: how to save money when shopping.

By this time I'd been hitting the side of my head with the heel of my hand so long, I had a headache. So I went out and got a couple of Empirin while these dancers did a few turns.

When I came back, the singer who couldn't sing—his name is Dean Jones—was saying that everybody loves a child star, and he had one for all of us who were panting with our need. (Looking around the room, I saw no other dirty young men with a penchant for nymphettes, and so settled back on the sofa with open admiration for Mr. Jones, who had somehow pierced the veil of respectability I wear, and prepared myself to slaver over some nubile little pre-groupie toddler who would satiate my naked lusts.)

"And here she is . . . Happy Hollywood!"

Imagine my surprise to be confronted with a five or six year old Shirley Temple surrogate with a face as evil

116

as one of the Borgias. (My instant reaction to this child was one of physical revulsion. I could not clear my mind of the scene in *Barbarella* where the depraved children turn life-sized dolls with razor-sharp teeth loose on the semi-naked Jane Fonda. It was a scene of singular horror, and snaggle-toothed Happy Hollywood looked for all the world like nothing but one of those knife-toothed dolls.)

She spoke in a high, quavery voice guaranteed to shatter goblets, and she dedicated her song—with all sincerity—to our great and wonderful United States of America astronauts ... and named them one by one ... going on to name the project heads at the Houston tracking center. I kept expecting someone to hit her in the face with a pie, but it never came to pass. She *actually* sang *It's Only A Paper Moon*, complete with vaudeville tap dancing and extravagant hand movements reminiscent of the Supremes in their formative days. Again, I found myself hitting my head.

It went on in this vein for several years. At least it *seemed* to be several years. It may only have been decades, who knows? And the big extravaganza ensemble number was a Paean of Praise to Richard Milhous Nixon. Everyone dressed in suits of American flags, prancing around, shooting off fireworks, waving banners, and singing we're all God's Chillun and Dickie is God. (A thought occurred to me: they arrested Abbie Hoffman on the steps of the Cannon House Office Building in Washington, D.C., on his way in to appear before the House Un-American Activities Committee, because he was wearing a shirt made from an American flag. They indicted him on charges of desecrating the symbol of *America Uber Alles*. Has anyone preferred charges against Dean Jones and his company of Merry Pranksters for doing the same on coast-to-coast television? No? I rather thought not. The rules work *for* you, when you espouse the party line, but God forbid you should be on the opposing team.)

They sang and danced this Ode to the Odious for an-

other decade or three, with one of their number bob-
bling blindly around the stage wearing an enormous *papier-mache* head of Nixon; the most hideous case of
hydrocephalicism I've ever seen.

And again, with little evil-faced Happy Hollywood
down on one knee, saying, "We luuuuuuv you, Mr.
President!" I kept expecting the wings to explode with
a barrage of cream pies. But it didn't happen. They
played it straight.

Either that, or all the head-hitting had given me a
concussion.

And when the show was over, I sat there, genuinely
stunned, trying to arrange my thoughts in some coher-
ent manner. Had I indeed seen what I'd seen? A right-
wing reactionary satire show? It was a contradiction in
terms; a defiance of the square-cube law; a ghoul
created of the spare parts of dead bodies, like a Frankenstein's Monster; an enormous put-on, so cleverly conceived even I could not penetrate its straight face; an
atavistic throwback, a creature neither fish nor fowl,
lying there flopping its flippers trying to stand up; a video thalidomide baby.

I decided to reserve judgment till the next week. But
they did it again. Happy Hollywood shucked us. Dean
Jones inspired us. And the high point of the show was
Ralph Williams selling one of his brannew 'conomy
carz quipped with heeder'n'five widewalls, finally
catching those pies I'd expected to down Happy and
Dean. And you want to know something, that poor
bald sonofabitch was the *only* noble creature on the
show. But do you get the message? They wouldn't pie
each *other*, but they'd pie Williams ... the only one in
the group who was secure in his own bag, doing his
own thing. *He* was *safe* to attack!

I watched again last night (as I write this) and it was
more of the same. Happy dedicated her song to Mr.
Nixon's wonderful new cabinet, Dean Jones sang a
song about the nobility of getting out there and sucking
up them bullets like a good American, and they man-

aged to even emasculate the Smothers Brothers, who "guest starred." I think they said "tell it like it is," a hundred and seventy-eight times, more than enough repetitions to convince me that if I *never* heard that ungrammatical phrase again, it would be entirely too soon. The ensemble number was dedicated to the philosophy that every wrong road is a boon because it tells us where not to go; a concept firmly in the tone of the American Theme.

So what do we have here?

As I see it, we have a response to *The Smothers Brothers Comedy Hour* and the ill-fated *Turn-On.* A sort of right-wing attempt to prove how good things are these days. It might more appropriately be titled *The Establishment Strikes Back.*

And it forces me to devise what will henceforth be known as Ellison's Theorem: the further right your position, the less telling your satire. A corollary of which is that you can't lampoon anywhere near where you stand, because you'd annihilate your own troops.

They've put together a "satire" show guaranteed to offend no one, espousing all the time-worn adages and cop-outs of the midwestern Judeo-Christian ethos. And it is going across big. (I was informed, and received the intelligence with unabashed incredulity that Happy Hollywood—that gross little no-neck monster—has received literally *thousands* of letters of awe and affection from the Great American Heartland. Glory be to Baby Leroy, we has us a new moppet star! Just what we needed!) (Like an extra set of elbows.)

So take heed, all ye out there on the barricades; it is a sign of the times. The Establishment is no longer going to leave the guerrilla warfare to the dissidents. They are going to use our own weapons against us— and we should've expected it. The cunning mothers are like the v.d. germ; it adapts and gets too strong for penicillin. The Young Republicans are waging war against the rioters on campus. The short-haired reactionaries are handing out red/white/blue badges showing you support the *status quo*, and now TV has taken up the cudgel.

What's it all about, world? I'll tell you what it's all about: we've got to get cunninger than them. Anyone for von Clausewitz?

21: 7 MARCH 69

Come with me now as I hew out of a mountain of Jell-O, a structure of cowardice. Observe, if you will, two men—Leonard Goldberg and Elton H. Rule—the former, head of programming at ABC-TV, the latter, president of that network, who crutch along on spines of rubber, trembling timorously from lack of any discernible courage, so motivated by lack of understanding as to what "serving the public good" means, that they crawl crablike across a terrain of fear and hypocrisy.

ABC, because it was the youngest network, and—like Avis—because it was not number one, had to try harder. In trying harder, ABC occasionally took one or two steps further into bold and original programming than either NBC or CBS, the two arteriosclerotic elders of the television pantheon. It didn't happen often; usually all we got from ABC was cheapjack imitation and a replacement of plot with violence. But from time to time ABC *did* take a hesitant step toward maturity and responsible programming. So we came to expect that if there was a series possessing some degree of clout, it would be scheduled on ABC, rather than its two doddering rivals.

But Elton Rule has shown he is no man for courage. And the great expectations for ABC were dashed when he knuckled-under instantly to the blue-nosed, hidebound minority out there in the Great American Heartland, who were offended by the relatively mild and innocuous *Turn-On* some Wednesdays ago, and canceled the poor mother after the first commercial. It was a sign of evils to come, and this week I detail one more

121

such. One that can be more debilitating than the loss of *Turn-On*.

Sevearl weeks ago, on Sunday, February 16th, I was invited to attend the live taping of the pilot segment of a new half-hour comedy series into which ABC had poured over two hundred and ten thousand dollars. The show was called *Those Were The Days* and was written and directed by Norman Lear and Bud Yorkin, both men of great skill.

Those Were The Days is the American version of an enormously popular English TV series, *Till Death Us Do Part*, that ran for three years in England and is now in constant rerun throughout the United Kingdom. In both its incarnations, the series is about a simple, everyday household in which a young married couple are living with the girl's parents. The family unit is a familiar one ... the mother is a sweet, solicitous homemaker, God-fearing and church-going ... the father is a solid consumer type, simple and direct, a working stiff, a trifle crusty, but charming ... the kids are sweet and wholesome, deeply in love, a little awkward about having to sponge off in-laws, but industrious, college-going, all American. Sounds dull, doesn't it? Safe? Inoffensive? A natural for ABC?

Then why is it that Goldberg and Rule chickened-out and refused to schedule the series for next season, even after they'd laid out over $200,000?

The reason is simple. The head of the household, good old Archie Justice, is a bigot. A common garden-variety, prejudiced against Jews/blacks/Italians/Mexicans/Everybody bigot. He isn't a KKKer, he isn't a member of the German-American Bund, he isn't a gun-carrying Bircher, he's simply like the bulk of us, a stupid man who sees no insult in calling Afro-Americans "them black beauties," or Jews "yids," or Irish "micks" or Italians "wops." And he will defend with all the lung-power at his command his right as a good American to express himself in that time-honored manner.

It wouldn't be so bad in the house if the kids weren't campus political activists who doubt the existence of God, self-consciously carry the banner of equality as do most "liberals," and who find themselves constantly at loggerheads with blustering Archie.

In company with something over two hundred other people, culled from supermarkets in Pacoima, street corners in Pasadena and bowling alleys in Tuston, I sat through a delightful half-hour taping of the pilot script. It was by no means offensive. When Archie, in a rage, says "God damn it," his sweet little wife calls him on it. Archie then explains how he was *not* swearing because, "God. That's a good word isn't it? And damn. You dam a river, don't you? It's in the bible. God was always damning this one, or that one, for committing 'insects' in the family. Now that ain't swearing, is it?" The racial references became not quite harmless, but certainly impotent, when taken in context with the character of Archie.

The point to be made, simply, is that the series dealt with a common American archetype, and did it with rare good humor and extraordinary good taste.

It would have made a dynamite series.

After the taping—in which Carroll O'Connor as Archie and Jean Stapleton as his wife were abetted by the brilliant D'Urville Martin as a black oddjob-man doing a calculated Steppin Fetchit to stay out of Archie's way—and were flawless in their performances—Norman Lear emerged on stage to ask the audience's opinion. He was greeted with unrestrained huzzahs and applause. The random sample audience loved it. They had laughed till tears rolled down their faces, and they knew they were seeing a winner.

Then Lear asked if anyone in the audience had been offended by anything he'd seen.

Three or four people raised their hands, and Lear gave them full time to express their unease. One man said he thought it was a terrible show because he wouldn't want his kids to hear swearing like that. Another woman said she thought it was disgraceful to portray such things on television. A wizened old man who was a dead ringer for The Hanging Judge opined that Lear and his cohorts were not only trying to subvert the American Ideal, but inferred that the series, if aired, would somehow mysteriously pollute the precious bodily fluids of all American Youth.

The bulk of the two hundred in the theater laughed them down. Yet I had a premonition, and asked Lear, from the floor, "Using ABC's reaction to *Turn-On* as a guide, do you think they'll have the guts to put this series on the air?" Lear shrugged and then smiled and said he had been in closest contact with Rule and Goldberg through all stages of the production, and they were solidly, courageously behind the project. He said he felt certain it would be on the 1969-70 ABC schedule.

Poor Lear. All these years in the Industry, and he still believed in Santa Claus. He believed, in fact, right up to Thursday night, the 27th of February. The pilot had been shot in a hurry, because ABC wanted to show it to top management at the last moment, as the *coup .de grace*. On that Thursday night Lear and Yorkin and all the actors and even CMA, Lear's agent, believed there was a Santa Claus, because it was on that Thursday night ABC showed it to their task force. The reports were glowing; everyone loved it. "Played like a baby doll, sweetheart!"

On Friday, the 28th, ABC announced its schedule for next year.

Is anyone surprised that *Those Were The Days* was not on it?

The only time I ever met Norman Lear was backstage at the taping, at which time I shook his hand and told him he was a good man, and had done a good thing. One of these days I'll run into him again, and I'll ask him if he still believes in Santa Claus.

And like all men in this business, who set out to tell something even remotely like the truth, to deal with something even remotely like reality, I suspect Lear will have the appearance of a man stunned by a hammer.

For make no mistake: This was a *good* show; it was adult, it was funny, it was presumptuous, and it would have been a success. Oh, of course it would have brought its share of outraged cries from that withering minority of backwater scuttlefish who cannot accept the fact that one pallid "God damn" on after-9:00 television means nothing to kids who hear "mother fucker" a hundred times a day in the streets and schoolyards ... it would have brought down the impotent wrath of the DAR and other blowhard patriotic nits who refuse to recognize that bigotry *does* exist in this country ... and it would raise shrieks from the vocal minority of Puritanical throwbacks who still live in Plymouth Bay Colony and could never understand that showing all the Archie Justices of this country for what they are, with a degree of affection and ridiculousness, pulls their teeth.

And like the ones who *would* have howled, had ABC had the balls to proceed with the project, Rule and Goldberg made an *a priori* decision, and faded to black before the battle was even engaged.

This column conceives of their act as naked cowardice. They may wear their facades of bold businessmen in a commercial arena, but they are like the Emperor with his new clothes. Everyone of us children on the sidelines see them naked, with their petards hanging out. And we cringe at having gutless wonders like that running *our* public airwaves.

I would suggest to Messrs. Goldberg and Rule, should a good elf somewhichway slip this column before their poached-egg eyes, that here is one newspaperman who was *not* offended by the show; there are undoubtedly others. If they wish to save some of that $210,000, why don't they set up a screening of the pilot for columnists and TV people from all over the country, and *then* make a decision? Is that too incomprehensible a move for them to make, in an effort to save a product that can enrich us—rather than merely continuing with series like *It Takes A Thief*, in which a crook is glorified, week after week?

How about it, gentlemen; the glove is dropped.

Santa Claus and I want to know if you can find the guts to act like responsible creators, rather than timid and flaccid cowards.

22: 14 MARCH 69

Where to start . . . where to start? For me, a heavy
column. Maybe not for you, but for me. I find myself
once more impelled to declare a position, as a result of
NBC's often-brilliant *First Tuesday* program. I caught
it last week, the installment for March, and saw an incredibly strong segment on racial intolerance in Ireland.
The Protestants against the Catholics. The Orangemen
against the wearers of the green. The Fundamentalist
fanatics of Rev. Ian Paisley against the Papists. And it
made me sick. Hundreds of memories of my own childhood flooded back on me. . . .

I was in Lathrop Grade School, in Painesville, Ohio.
Maybe third grade. I was the only Jewish kid my age,
as I recall. There were a few other Jewish families in
Painesville—a town thirty miles east of Cleveland—but
even so, I was quite alone as a Jew. They used to beat
the shit out of me, regularly. It got so I could wade into
the middle of them and let them pummel me, and not
even feel it. Have you ever been so inured to pain that
you actually *sought* their fists, as a defiance of them?
My mother used to have to come to school to pick me
up; not because I was afraid to walk home the few
short blocks from Lathrop, but because they ripped my
clothes, and we weren't terribly wealthy, and we couldn't
afford to have my clothes ruined. I got used to it. Weep
no tears for that little kid getting kicked unconscious in
the schoolyard by Jack Wheeldon, because he learned
defiance early, and it changed his life. No, he came out
of it okay. But weep for this other one:

The one who walked behind me all the way from

school one afternoon. This little girl. A nice one, she was. She wanted to help me.

You see, I was a Jew, and that meant that I was one of those who ground up babies to make matzohs for the High Holy Days. She believed that, and she wanted to save me. She followed me for several days, and then one day she caught up with me and tried to help.

"You've got to repent," she said, seriously.

I stared at her. I didn't know what she meant, but I was frightened.

"You're a heathen," she said. "You're damned to hell by God because you aren't baptized."

I wanted to run.

"Please, please"—she was almost crying—"you've got to believe in the Christ Child, because you're going to Hell, and you'll be burning, and you'll ask for water on your tongue, and I can't give you any, because you're a heathen . . ."

I turned and ran, terrified that she was right.

No, don't cry for me. Cry for her.

And for those Irish who hate and don't know.

Margaret Mead, the anthropologist, once observed that it is possible to judge the level of a civilization by the amount of religion it needs to sustain it. The closer to barbarism, the more religion the culture needs.

Father Coughlin and his Church of the Little Flower in Detroit, spreading anti-Semitic poison.

Sirhan Sirhan, murdering Bobby Kennedy because he supported the Israelis against the Arabs. The Hebraic faith versus the Mohammedans.

The Catholic Church saying give me your children for the first ten years, and they are mine forever.

Christian Scientists letting their children die rather than allowing a surgeon to operate.

The Spanish Inquisition. Torquemada torturing women and children for doubting. The Salem witch trials. The Dan Smoots and the Paul Harveys and the George Putnams . . . who coat their bigotry and evil with the sanctimonious jelly of religion. Pope Pius, allowing Hitler to gas the Jews and the Catholics, and turning his head away. All the martyrs who ever were. Christ, who would shrink in horror at what his faith and kindness has become.

My position: religion is an evil and debilitating force in the world.

In a time when men are separated by economic barriers, by social and political beliefs, by territorial and linguistic walls . . . religion keeps them stupid, keeps them intractable, keeps them locked within their fears.

It became hideously apparent, watching *First Tuesday*. A Protestant woman in Ulster, probably a good woman, a woman who would never intentionally hurt anyone else . . . saying, "They had that new housing project, and all the Roman Catholics moved in, and—a Roman Catholic coal man told me this—they wanted the coal dumped in the bathtubs. Now it's a slum. They're dirty. All they want to do is drink and lay around. And as long as they can go confess, they think it's all right. They breed like rabbits, you know . . ."

I could hear a White woman saying the same things about black men: "They move into a good neighborhood, into a new project, and the next thing you know, it's a slum. They'll live in filth and starve their kids, so long as they can drive a Cadillac. And they breed like rabbits, you know . . ."

I saw, on that program, militant students campaigning for civil and religious rights. And I saw the Irish cops using their truncheons the way Daley's pigs used theirs. And why shouldn't they? After all, weren't they fighting God's fight? Weren't they carrying out the word of the Lord?

How they do believe it, all of them, all of us.

That the Lord speaks only to *us*, in Yiddish or Latin or Arabic. That God is on our side. Holy Wars, each of them. And will they never realize what they do?

Is it any wonder that kids today reject God?

How can they believe in such a God, who brings ha-

129

tred and terror to his supplicants? Such a God must be totally mad. Living in a Heaven that is certainly Hell, and sending down messages of awfulness to be written in blood and treachery and bigotry.

Why do the churchmen wonder in confusion that their pews are empty Sunday after Sunday ... is it beyond their ken that the young people want no more of this insanity? Can they not see that holding jazz masses and sending their pseudo-hip men of the cloth into the drug scene and into the ghettos only reveals them for the hypocrites they are?

No, wait a minute, I've gone too far. My friend Philly makes a good point. It isn't religion, because religion is merely belief. If you believe in yourself, or you believe in people being kind to one another, or you believe in that fine chair over there, that's religion. Being part of the universe is lovely: you breathe out carbon dioxide for the plants, and the plants breathe out oxygen for you, and when you see a falling star you know God is the Natural Order of things, and if you are a part of that Natural Order, then you are God, and I am God, and even that sorrowful, hating woman in Ulster is God. And that's cool.

It's *organized* religion. It's religion with a label. That's what stinks. It's what keeps all those old Jewish men on Fairfax from having a nice bacon, lettuce and tomato sandwich. It's what sends all those young girls into the ghoulish lives of nuns. (And did you dig the Saturday night movie several weeks ago, of Audrey Hepburn in *The Nun's Story?*—without even *trying* to put down the nun game, it was a petrifying picture of women who have "married Christ." And if that isn't theological necrophilia, I don't know what is.) It's what twists men's minds.

If you ever had any doubts that was true, you only needed to see *First Tuesday* last week.

And having so positioned myself, I now await with clean hands and composure a bolt of lightning from Heaven to strike me in my atheistic spleen. If you find

130

a column under my byline next week, it will mean God didn't take too unkindly to my pulling the covers of those who say they serve him, but in fact serve another, more crimson master.

23: 21 MARCH 69

Darling, by the time you read this, I'll be in Rio. Phoenix? Galveston? No thanks. I'll take two lumps. I was once tossed up underneath the jail in Fort Worth. On a vag charge, hitchhiking with 17¢ in my kick. They whomped me. Twice. Two lumps. About seven years later, which was seven years ago, coming through Fort Worth again, I was in a car accident—fault of this snockered cowboy, one of the long-standing denizens of the Alcoholic Generation—and the local newspaper made a foofaraw about it. Seems I was a "c'lebrity" by that time. Ah-*HAH!* So, down comes the Sheriff of Fort Worth, big beautiful bull moose of a guy, name of Cato Hightower. Got me all squared away with a motel room, repaired my squashed typewriter, took me to dinner, lovely fellah. Never knew I was the same dude he'd tanked seven years before. That's about all with Fort Worth, to which I was led, here, by way of Glen Campbell and Phoenix/Houston, because I needed the line from the song to let you know that while you crouch there smog-snogged, I'm down in gorgeous Brazil canyoudigit, attending the 2nd International Film Festival of Rio de Janeiro, at which they're showing a TV segment of *The Outer Limits* for which I won a Writers Guild award a couple of years ago. They think it's some sorta classic of fantasy in films, and I ain't about to shatter their little bubble, because they paid all the expenses and do you have any *idea* how much loot it costs to go to Rio?

All of which bottom-lines to this: I'll watch a little Brazilian TV while I'm down there, and though I don't speak Portuguese, at least I can report on the Latin

Ralph Williams or how a Biz commercial looks in bossa novalese. But using that line from the Glen Campbell song brings to mind that I've been meaning to mention him and his *Good Time Hour* for several weeks.

Glen is so clean, it hurts.

Now I am a real cleanliness freak. Friends and lovers of mine will attest to the fact that I am so neatsie I border on anal retentiveness. But Glen Campbell is so soft and pink and succulent looking, I have visions of the makeup man dusting him with ZBT Baby Powder before he goes onstage. And his show is nothing if not clean. Clean, clean, clean! His banjo-plonking buddy, John Hartford, got off a mildly blue remark last Sunday, about as innocuous as you can get and still evoke a titter from the basically prurient loons who attend these tapings, and Campbell got uptight so fast I thought his E-string was gonna snap.

What an irony. Here is immaculate Glen Campbell, hearing spirit messages through the telephone wires, digging Galveston's sea-winds crashing, et al, a spinoff from *The Smothers Brothers Comedy Hour,* obviously "making it" for the scuttlefish in Kankakee, while his mentors, the Smothers, are being assassinated during the Ides of March.

I'm sure you heard about the caper. For the last year or so, the local CBS outlets around the country, responding to affronted letters by the Fundamentalists in their locales, have been demanding advance tapes of the Smothers shows, to see if there was anything in them that was "offensive." This, in effect, put censorship powers in the hands of timorous station executives. They had the clout to decide whether entire cities would or would not see the show. The odiousness of this cop-out on CBS's part—acceding to such a despicable demand—sat not at all well with Dick and Tom. But they sorta shrugged and went with it. For a year. Couple of weeks ago they decided they'd had it. No, we ain't gonna do it no more. So they didn't send the tapes out. And CBS blanked them. They put on a re-run. (Ironically, Canada got the new show.) When that went down, the Smothers Duo decided they weren't going to do the show next year. And at last report, CBS was still mumbling in its Ovaltine.

So if you haven't responded overwhelmingly with letters as I suggested several weeks ago, for Christ's sake, get off your ass and do it!

Otherwise we will have nothing to gaze upon but the baby-fat face of Glen Campbell. Clean. Clean. Clean.

On to other matters.

Many of you have written me letters, some demanding that I strike out against fluoridation, others suggesting I state just *which* political activist groups you should join, offering to service me sexually because we are apparently soulmates, enlisting my aid in placing your unfinished epic poem about the fall of the Great Wall of China with a publisher, and just a shitload of other etcetera.

Well, I don't intend this as a shock to anyone's nervous system, but honest, friends, I am a teevee critic. This column is intended to look at what's happening around us, culturally and politically and esthetically, but in terms of what television is saying, and how they're interpreting the passing scene. I frequently skitter off into the realm of serendipity, but that's only because I happen to rap that way. My own personal beliefs are pretty obvious in what I write about, and the way I write about it, but if you feel the need to mount the barricades, don't look to me to sound your specific clarion call. There are things that piss me off mightily, and I do what I can to bring them to the populace, but when it comes to individual activity, I am strictly a crawling-through-the-sewers-with-plastic-charges-strapped-to-my-back kind of guerrilla; and for that sort of scene, having True Believers underfoot is about as handy as being in a street fight with your girl friend pulling at your arm trying to stop the slaughter. A guy can get *killed* that way.

134

Final item for this week: several of you have asked when you'll see the next installment of my diary of the script on which I'm working for *The Name Of The Game*. Well, this is it.

I got well into the treatment (for those of you who missed the first thrilling installment of this chronical, a "treatment" is the story-line you write for the producer and the network, before they tell you to go ahead with the script) on dissent at the university, and made the grievous error of watching some television shows myself.

After seeing *Adam-12* and *Tuesday Night At The Movies* (a World Premiere done by Universal titled *The Whole World Is Watching*, a pilot movie for a next-season series) and *Ironside*, all of which dealt with dissent on campus, I realized that once again the gargoyles had taken over the cathedral.

They have now started to merchandise dissent, even as the fat burghars and the *tummelers* and the entrepreneurs merchandised the hippie culture when they moved into the Haight. And the effect is the same. They have killed the subject for any sensible and original attack. So I tore the twenty-five pages of unfinished treatment in half, tore it in fourths, threw it in the circular file, and called my producer, the beautiful George Eckstein—who is surely one of God's great creatures—and told him the way I felt about it. He agreed, and asked what else I'd like to write about. I said, "How about pornography?" He said, "For or against?" I said, "For, naturally." He said, "Starring Robert Stack?" There was a disbelieving quaver in his voice. I said, "Yeah." A little slowly, but with fear of his own trust in me, he said, "Okay, take a crack at it."

Friends, at the moment I am rushing to complete the treatment of a *Name Of The Game* segment I have titled *Smut*. It will be done before I go to Brazil, and by the time I flap back into town, both George and I—and you, shortly thereafter—will know whether I was

135

able to write it in such a way that I could tell some truth and not scare off both the network and Mr. Stack.

I'll keep you posted.

And if you don't see a column here by me next week, don't panic (he said, with faint hope). It'll only mean I had too much getting-together to write two columns ahead.

Oh, and incidentally, as a reply to the nice ladies who offered to share carnal pleasures with me because they fancy my writings, I am currently deeply involved with a dynamite redhead named Leigh Chapman, herself a film and TV writer, who keeps a Huck Finn smile on my face. But the offers were appreciated. It's a good life, sometimes, ain't it, folks?

24: 28 MARCH 69

As tax-time hurtles inexorably down on us, a hungry carrion bird we must annually feed with our own flesh, the Aesop that television can sometimes become offers a fable that points a strong moral: there are no more willing boobs than those who remain boobs willingly.

In a year when we are compelled to pay taxes so the police can purchase tanks, so student dissenters can be more effectively muzzled, so the rich can get richer and the poor get poorer, so the new Attorney General can go into wiretapping in a big way, so the oil companies and the nighthawk land developers can more comfortably rape the victim earth—we are told the infamous 10% surtax will not be dropped as promised, but maintained *another* year. There are no more willing boobs than those who remain boobs willingly.

How we detest that war in Viet Nam! How we despise the inertia that keeps it fed with men and materiel and money needed so desperately in this country (for instance to alleviate the incredible hunger and poverty the Florida land-owners railed at the McGovern Commission did not exist, despite all the starving workers the Commission saw). How we detest having to pay such an enormous chunk of our taxes to keep the inertia in effect, to keep up the evil of Viet Nam! And how gently we sit, with folded hands, as Johnson's Folly—a ten per cent overcharge on our taxes, earmarked *specifically* for napalm and low-yield defoliation—is not dropped in one year *as we were promised,* but is slyly retained by our new Commissar. By Tricky Dicky, who, now having hyped 42% of the scuttlefish into voting him the clout, drops even the clown mask of trickiness, and out-front calls us boobs to our faces.

Some months ago, when (with incredulity) I heard the surtax would not be dropped as we had been promised, I swore I would not pay it. I swore I would go to jail first. Perhaps it will come to that. (Though the silly futility of the gesture became obvious to me last week when my CPA did up my taxes. I told him there would be no surtax paid by Ellison. I told him had they kept their promise, myself being a usually law-abiding boob, I would have paid it this once, felt had, but say no more. But when they flout their own promises, when they take relish in calling me a boob by insisting they'll surtax me again *next* year, I draw the line. I make my stand here. I deny them the funds to kill. And my CPA shook his head sadly at my naïveté. Boob, he said politely you won't go to jail: they will attach your bank account. I will empty the bank account, I replied, knowing what hassles that would make for myself. Then they'll attach your wages, he responded. Then I'll—I stopped. It was hopeless. The marauders were everywhere. By the balls they had me. Not only a boob, but a helpless, futile, posturing boob.)

Yes, perhaps it will come to jail. Much as I hate the slammer, as ugly as the memories of jails are to me, I think I would much prefer incarceration to standing passively by as they grind away my ethics with a cheese grater.

And Aesop, the TV point-maker, showed me what boobs we *really* are:

Last Tuesday night, March the 18th, CBS presented its bi-monthly newsmagazine of the air, *60 Minutes,* with Mike Wallace and Harry Reasoner. They juxtaposed two fifteen-minute sections about life in these United States that at once sickened, horrified and frustrated me.

Beginning with a brief documentary about people on welfare relief in Baltimore, they succinctly presented a living statistic, visual documentation of the two million

Americans—mostly black—who live in a hell of deprivation and personal debasement amid the plenty of a nation that possesses 50% of the world's total wealth, *ten times* the per capita wealth of any other nation!

Eighty-two per cent of those on relief are women and children. Mainly mothers with children, who make so little from the public dole that they cannot leave their kids and find work, thereby *keeping* them on the welfare treadmill. A spokesman for these women, a marvelously articulate, honest black mother of seven in a Baltimore ghetto, let it all hang out when she snapped back at the interviewer's suggestion that she had had some of her kids merely to pick up an extra thirty-two dollars and change per month: "You crazy? You think I *like* goin' down there to that welfare office and gettin' treated like an animal the way they do? I want to get *off* the welfare. Ain't nobody can live decent on what they give you. I only get forty-five dollar a month for each child—up to five children, after that they don't give you no more noways—and that don't 'clude bus fare to school, or enough for supplies, nor nothin'!"

There was a personal strength in the woman that was difficult to ignore. Even in the ghastly plaster-falling cell where eight people crammed together for the barest essentials of a life devoid of sunshine or hope, she was determined to make for her brood the best life she could. And later in the segment, when Governor Charles Percy told of how he and his family had been on relief during the Depression, how humiliated he'd felt when the food parcels had arrived, how he *knew* all the canards of the reactionaries that those on welfare were *in toto* loafers and ne'er-do-wells was so much bullshit . . . then I felt genuinely lost. Why had we not nominated a man like Percy for President? Why could we not have set in office a man with some humanity in him, a man who could understand that we don't *like* being willing boobs?

The segment proceeded, and in fifteen brief minutes it made a case against the current outmoded welfare *apparat* and for the first time—that I know of—on television, told the mass of the American viewing public that those two million black faces wanted *off* the dole, wanted to regain their dignity, and a semblance of joyous living.

Then, from abject, pesk-crawling poverty, *60 Minutes* winged down to Palm Beach for fifteen minutes of examination of the Beautiful People. Palm Beach, where at times during "the season" there are more millionaires per square inch than anywhere else in the world.

Oh, it was a chi-chi segment all right.

Mrs. Woolworth-Birdseed plays a fine game of tennis. You really *must* play tennis on her courts to be "in" in Palm Beach. She had the begonias dyed to match the color of the swimming pool.

Mrs. Thorton-Twitchell plays tennis wearing a necklace. On occasion she scrubs her own floors, and on Wednesday afternoons she washes her porcelain birds.

One never goes anywhere in Palm Beach in a Rolls Royce that is filled. Two or three is the most the car should carry. If you have four or more, you take *two* Rolls's and go in a caravan.

Mrs. Grubber's party cost $50,000 but it was a tame evening for her. She only wore the ruby earrings, no necklace, bracelet or brooch.

And on ... and on ... and hideously on. ...

Fat bellies, wattled necks, liver spots from eating too well, too much, too often. Aging owners of the American Dream. The titled. The privileged. With their WASP clubs that don't admit Jews, and their Jewish clubs that discourage the *goyim*. Maintaining a level of society steeped in prejudice, conspicuous waste, arrogance, phony charity to assuage guilt, and insulating themselves from reality by erecting a wall of bland indifference to that black woman in Baltimore.

The parallel, the Aesop moral of the show, could not be ignored. *60 Minutes* did not need to editorialize verbally. By the chockablocking of the two extremes,

140

they stated the case for Life in Our Times with pellucid verve.

Well, we are by no means the ghetto-trapped black woman ... nor are we Mrs. Asshole-Moneyswine with her dyed blue begonias. But here we sit in a nation that will not tax the giant corporations as they should be, will not tax the Church as it should be, will not tax organized crime as it should be, will not tax the oil companies as they should be ... but has the audacity to *surtax* us again and again to pay for the war that will only help to enhance the fortunes of the Palm Beach habitues.

Here we sit, with Aesop the TV telling us we are certainly boobs. Telling us the rich get richer and the poor get poorer. And maybe worst of all, the mass of us, neither extremely rich nor extremely poor, but in the middle, will get more and more of our world chipped away from us ... whether we like it or not.

It makes one wonder: at what point does the boob despise himself enough to take up the club and smash to jelly the heads of those who exploit him?

25:   18 APRIL 69

For those of you out there who make a fetish of jotting down annual high and low tide figures, who fill in every box on a baseball scorecard, who save old newspapers and knot up twittles of twine till you have a giant ball—in short, for those of you who pay close attention to trivial matters—I am back from two weeks in Brazil and New York. For the rest of you, who could care less, the only benefit you will derive from my journey is a revelation of what TV is like in Rio de Janeiro, under the hand of a military dictator, with eighty per cent of the population stone illiterate. But that comes next week, or the week after, as soon as one of my spies back in Rio manages to smuggle out some statistics to me. And if you think I'm kidding about smuggling the information out, you should be in Rio at seven o'clock every night, when every station simultaneously broadcasts the same news, word for word, videotaped by the same announcer.

It suddenly makes you very warm and cuddly feeling about the good old US of A, despite all the nonsense going down. I can suddenly dig where all the superpatriots are at, when they say "America: Love it or Leave it." Shit, Jack, comes to one or the other, I'll love the ass off it . . . the coffee in Brazil can kill you!

But it isn't Brazil about which I choose to ramble this time. It is about the snake pit that was waiting for me when I got back to Los Angeles.

If you recall, in the last exciting chapter of "Harlan Ellison, Boy Scriptwriter," our hero had decided not to do his *Name Of The Game* script on student dissent because every Manny, Moe and Jack was doing the sub-

142

ject to death (there was another one on *Mod Squad* last week). Our intrepid hero, committed to integrity and T*R*U*T*H, had somewhichway flummoxed his producer, George Eckstein, into allowing him to write the script on pornography. Our Hero, you recall, had started out in deadly fashion by titling his epic *Smut*.

(One sure way of avoiding being bought-out by the Establishment is by setting a price they can't possibly meet.)

But, onward.

Our Hero thereafter sat down and wrote a splendid 24 page "treatment" of the script as he intended to develop it. As we all know, a script assignment for TV is divided into three parts: treatment, first draft, final draft. You can be "cut off" after the treatment, meaning they pay you only for what you have already written, and the assignment is dead. (There are two variations on the "cut off." In the first mode, they pay you x amount of dollars and they own the treatment or story idea. In the second manner, they pay you less money and *you* own the treatment; the latter method is more advantageous if it's the kind of idea you can rewrite and sell to another show, but let's face it, how many shows are there on the air with little people on a planet of giants? You getting the picture, troops?)

If the treatment passes muster with the producer, the studio and the network schlepps, then you are given a "go ahead" (oh! how they do use the English language!) and from that point on, win or lose, class or shit, you cannot be taken off the assignment. Until it's over, at which point they start rewriting you, but that's another horror story.

Okay, so I wrote the treatment, a contemporary action-adventure story loosely paralleling a Jack-the-Ripper theme, the main point of which was that Dan Farrell (played by Robert Stack), as editor of *Crime Magazine*, is trying once and for all to establish a direct casual link between crime and reading pornography. You know, that old saw about girlie magazines warping the minds of kids so they go out and rape their school teachers, or drag nine-year-old birds into the coal bins of church basements. You know.

(N.B. Only a real sickie, like the wizards who make these suggestions, could think there'd be any jollies in screwing a nine-year-old. You ever see the figure on a nine-year-old? Twelve-year-old, okay, that's a different matter . . . but *nine? Chickens?*)

In the writing, I had to face the inescapable problem that Mr. Stack is a highly conservative gentleman, and he would *never* give script approval to a show in which he came out for smut and filth. So I had to pose an intellectual problem, and let the answer be revealed to Stack as he went along. It was a tightrope act, I'll grant you, but because of the purity of my desire and the clean hands & composure which I brought to the project, I was able to accomplish this well-nigh-impossible feat of legerdemain.

Even George Eckstein was amazed.

I handed in the treatment before I left for Rio, and though George had some reservations about the number of hideous, ghastly, brutal murders committed in the segment (3), he was delighted with the manner in which I'd managed to make a case both pro and con for pornography. That is, I'd made a pro case for *good* pornography, such as the Alexander Trocchi and Hank Stine and Philip Jose Farmer novels being published by Brian Kirby out at Essex House, but had bummed the crotch magazines whose Brobdingnagian photos of moist pudenda are about as sexy as a closeup of Ausable Chasm guaranteed to turn-off all but righteous acne-fetishists.

When I returned, I found George Eckstein whimpering beneath his desk at Universal Studios. The man was a distant echo of his former magnificence. He needed eight scripts to shoot for next season, had had twelve in the works when I'd left, and now had six that the networks had thumbed-down.

He was incapable of speech. His secretary and I

helped him into the sofa, put a cold compress on his furrowed brow, and I went off around Universal to find out what had happened.

The answer was quick in coming. Senator John O. Pastore (D., R.I.) had happened.

All five foot four of him had happened to television. This latter-day Fredric Wertham had clouded up and rained all over TV. "Violence, smut, degradation!" he had shouted, in a voice acknowledged to be the loudest (by decibel-count) in the Senate.

And with their usual fortitude, the network mufti had stood their ground for artistic integrity and the merits of realism in television drama, and had started killing scripts left and right.

I discovered that one script in which there was *no* violence had been strangled a-borning because there was a suicide in it, and near the end someone calls a girl who has slept with countless hordes of men a "nymphomaniac." The word come from upstairs that if there was to be a suicide, it had to be an unsuccessful one, and that the word nymphomaniac could not be used. This was one of the more rational decisions. The others were straight out of chicken-licken the sky is falling.

Naturally, Eckstein had not even submitted my treatment, in which three luscious girls are done away with. By a deranged killer with a length of silk rope. Oh boy! Blood! Naked thighs! Insane chuckling in the dark!

When Eckstein had recovered somewhat, we talked over the possibilities of salvaging what had been written, and at last report George was going to propose to the network Gods that Our Hero rewrite the treatment to examine how and why pretty young girls wind up in stag movies.

For those of you who have been following this diary of a script in *The Glass Teat*, you will perceive that much ground has been covered since the assignment was first given. Yet no progress has been made.

I will keep you advised as this black comedy proceeds.

In the meantime, don't give up hope; the Kid has sold a series to NBC (in conjunction with his partner, Paramount) which the network seems to be exceedingly high on. I am at present scripting the pilot segment. It is a one-hour dramatic science fiction idea called *Man Without Time* and has considerable clout built into it. If the Gods be kind, in addition to the staggeringly obscene amounts of money I've made and *can* make from this series (I own 15%), we may be able to get something rewarding before your now-bleary eyes. I'll keep reporting on this one, too.

Oh, and by the way, as a public service announcement, they've pretty well established that color TV sets give off harmful radiations, so if you don't want your kids coming up with warped chromosomes or *their* kids being born with three heads, I suggest you not sit up close to the color box, and keep the viewing to a minimum.

Which, considering the clams currently being hacked onto the screen, shouldn't be too hard to manage.

26:   25 APRIL 69

If we can forget about white Stetsons for a while,
maybe we should talk about The Hero. The Good Guy.
What brings me to an examination of the phenomenon
of The Hero is a movie-for-TV-intended-as-a-2-hour-
pilot I caught on the 17th, on CBS's *Thursday Night
Movie*. The film was titled *U.M.C.*, which stands for
University Medical Center. It is coming on as a contin-
uous series in the Fall. There are few good things to
say about the film itself, for—like most medical shows
in particular, and most films-for-TV in general—it was
a crashing bore.

Correction: it was a plopping bore.

The nominal "star," a silver-haired gentleman named
Richard Bradford, is an iron-jawed type straight out of
the Richard Egan mold, and played his part as the noble healer with all the verve of a three-toed sloth. The
cameos were so tiny one might more accurately term
them intaglios ... Edward G. Robinson said seven
lines and spent the rest of the time in a coma; Maurice
Evans pontificated two or three times, reminding us
what the English language sounds like when spoken
properly; Kim Stanley gave her usual excellent but all
too brief performance; Kevin McCarthy allowed himself to perform as an attorney in the style of fustion
most memorable as having been proffered by Fredric
March in *Inherit The Wind*, a disservice to his considerable talent, and the easy way out insofar as interpretation is concerned. And that about says it.

For the film in particular. But not for the subject of
The Hero.

You see, we're re-entering (it would seem) the doctor

147

cycle. A few years back it was Kildare and Casey and *Breaking Point* and that other psychiatric series, whatever it was called. They ran their course, and we went through the traditional situation comedy, western and detective/cop cycles. But now, with the networks spasming with a serious case of the Pastores, hoping to cure themselves of the disease of violence by blood-letting and the use of leeches, occupations such as cowboy and cop become untenable on a medium pathologically dedicated to portraying a world in which violence does not exist. So alternate Heroes must be found. Non-violent heroes. Good guys who epitomize drama without ever really getting near the heartmeat of violence that lies at the core of our troubled today.

So what does TV come up with? Again? The doctor.

While I would be the last one to deny that there are bold and dedicated men in the medical profession—even as there must be bold and dedicated plumbers, cabinet-makers, telephone linemen and pharmacists—it strikes me as merely one more indication of television's paucity of inventiveness that the best they can do is offer us another spate of physicians.

Yeah, sure, doctors are generally considered to be Heroes. They deal in life and death, and I suppose in a network presentation that can read like "high drama"; and since they sweat and struggle for years toward the ultimate goal of saving lives, they are obviously on the side of the angels. One would be a cad to suggest, however obliquely, that medical men are merely more highly trained plumbers, cabinetmakers, pharmacists, as committed to coining a good buck as they are to the Hippocratic Oath. Yet a professional man is still a professional man, and aside from the inherent drama of dealing with life on the line, a doctor's life is usually no more compelling or fraught with danger than that of a high-steel construction worker. Physically, I would imagine considerably less.

(I realize this view is tantamount to heresy, not only to the AMA, which has a considerable stake in

148

maintaining the image of the doctor as holier than thou [I anticipate the burning of a Blue Cross on my lawn], but to the even hordier hordes of *yiddishe mamas,* not the least of whom is mine own, who conceive of no fate for their nubile daughters as glorious as marrying a "doctuh.")

Where I'm going with all of this is not to a conclusion that medicine men are quacks and should not be portrayed as Heroes. Hell, John Romm, *my* doctor, not only cured the tendonitis inflicted on me by an over-zealous cop, but he got me off cigarettes, a feat only slightly less miraculous than the mountain giving birth to the mouse. Where I'm going is that TV's conception of what it takes to be a Hero is slightly myopic. Jeezus, sometimes I have a gift for the ridiculously under-stated: myopic? Righteous tunnel vision is closer to the truth.

So what alternates do we have for the archetypal Hero? Let's go down the list, and see how many TV has considered.

Let's begin with the one I mentioned *en passant* a moment ago: the construction worker. Does anyone here recall a very groovy series that ran for one season in 1959, starring Keenan Wynn and Bob Mathias as *The Troubleshooters?* Despite some serious handicaps, not the least of which was Mathias (who, oddly enough, had much in common with "Dr." Richard Bradford, acting-wise), the show was filled with high adventure, danger, and managed to convey, within the parameters of hokey TV melodrama, the sheer wonder of men who literally go out to change the face of the earth. The old *Empire* series had a segment in which Frank Gorshin portrayed a "fire dancer," a troubleshooter called in to extinguish a wildcat oil well fire. *Naked City* did one of its most memorable shows about the AmerIndian high steel workers in Manhattan. Non-violent in the Pastore sense of the term, the lives of builders and shapers can be infinitely more compelling than those lives lived in sterile white corridors.

Or how about the men of the W.H.O., the World Health Organization, if we *must* have doctors. Treating patients in jungles and backward, emerging nations, with all the political and ethnic conflicts attendant, *must* provide more pathos than that in a University Medical Center.

What about cross-country truck drivers, à la *The Price of Tomatoes?* The men who push freight across this continent are heroes, too. They keep it all happening. What about Peace Corps volunteers? Or news photographers out on the line? Or men like Chuck Dederich, founder of Synanon ... Dr. Spock ... committed teachers in ghetto schools ... diplomatic couriers ... social workers. About this last: George C. Scott and Susskind had the right idea. *East Side*, *West Side* may have been depressing most of the time, may have turned off the scuttlefish out in the Great American Heartland, but by Christ they *dealt* with depressing realities, the kind of realities the scuttlefish choose to believe don't exist in their soft pink-and-white bunny rabbit world of *Green Acres*.

How about explorers? No one can deny that a series about Marco Polo or Lewis & Clark or Cortez is built-in with more heroics than that of a modern physician. And while I know I'm not only building dream castles, but trying to furnish them and move in first of the month, a series about a student militant, a series about a Congressional investigator, a series about a civil rights worker, or a series about a university psychiatrist experimenting with LSD, would be genuine stoppers. And if you choose to take any other position than that of the Center or the Right, these are Heroes in the truest sense of the world.

The bottom line, I suppose, is that TV's conception of what it takes to be a Hero is—like much of the posturing on television—intellectually fifty years out-of-date. TV, in declaring heroes only those who work at occupations considered noble by the mass, remain safe, and remain bland. Doctors, veterinarians, spies for the

U.S., cops, people in the world of show biz (*That Girl*), or just-plain-folks (*Mayberry, RFD, Beverly Hillbillies, The Good guys*) are certainly non-violent, inoffensive and safe, but they are also predictable, bland and rapidly boring.

The Hero is not the man who looks good while risking nothing. Which is why *Hogan's Heroes* has no Heroes in it. The Hero is the man who can stand to lose something heavy is he commits himself.

And what I suppose I'm getting at is that in these times of fence-sitters, hemmers and hawers, bet-hedgers, what we need to see on our TV screens are men and women who have something at stake, something to lose, something that can ennoble them for us. We need guidelines today, and those guidelines are hardly evident in fare such as *Here Come The Brides*.

A doctor is a good thing, I can dig it. But he sure as hell isn't my idea of a man in a position to become a Hero. His job isn't dangerous enough. Not nearly as dangerous as, say, that of a television critic.

27: 2 MAY 69

The only no-talent "second lead" in the history of television series programming who crossed them up and turned out to be a star was Bill Cosby. That was because Culp was a beautiful loving cat who shared what he knew about acting, and Cosby'd be the first to confirm that.

But can you dig all the bright young jocks bopping around the screen these days, who simply don't cut it, and never will, because they're overshadowed by name leads with more clout lost or strayed then these kids will *ever* show? The roster goes something like this:

Kent McCord runs second to Martin Milner. Richard Dawson places to Bob Crane. Gary Conway, Don Marshall and Don Matheson look sick next to Kurt Kasznar; William Reynolds loses (again), this time to Efrem Zimbalist, Jr.; James Stacy bulks tiny beside Andrew Duggan. David Soul and Bobby Sherman don't have a prayer next to Robert Brown. Don Mitchell grows faceless in the face of Raymond Burr. Ben Murphy (who?) and Robert Stack. Stephen Young and Carl Betz.

And every season they roll in more of these faceless devils who will wither in the television wasteland, hoping the "exposure" will catapault them, if not to stardom, at least to solvency. And every year they go the way of Don Quine. It would be sad, if it weren't so predictable.

The only one currently swinging (and off he goes with new year cancellation) is Otis Young, who gives Don Murray a helluva fight for center stage. (Does it strike anyone as fine and interesting that the two big new talents to emerge from the box in the last few years are both black?)

There's an obvious reason why these cats are doomed, of course. Aside from their general lack of charisma and/or talent. It is that their roles are superfluous. Like Ben Murphy on the Stack segments of *The Name Of The Game,* they are jacked-in by format writers as a sop to "the younger audience." They are supposed to be identification for the youth set who can't see themselves in Walter Brennan or Lorne Green. They are patent shucks like Luci and Desi Jr., brought in to revitalize saggers like Lucy, or they are calculated vote-getters like The Monkees (the single greatest hype of this decade). And they fail ninety-nine per cent of the time.

They fail to grab the younger viewer. They fail to up the ratings. They fail dramatically and they fail personally. Because they are like a second nose. They can sniff, but they don't really blow.

Instead of creating series ideas that require the services of younger actors who have the steam and the muscle to carry a series, the networks either slip us fading swordsmen like Mike Connors, Darren McGavin and Robert Wagner (who have some redeeming qualities but become embarrassing hustling teenie-boppers on-screen)—or they put all the meat of the shows on the Gene Barrys, the Robert Stacks, the James Whitmores, and let the Enzo Cerusicos flounder along behind playing straight men.

Writers are instructed that the subsidiary parts must not become dominant or the star will get uptight, directors instinctively shoot the two-shots so the star has the better angle, studio protocol forms itself so the star has a parking space beside the sound stage and the second lead parks outside with the secretaries and the guys in the payroll department.

If you get the impression I'm lamenting for these poor nameless ones, you have glommed the wrong impression. They get paid a helluva lot more than school teachers, postmen, sanitation truck workers and research chemists—occupations I consider substantially more noble than that of *poseur*—so no one should cry for them. Their greatest loss is that they will be denied the inordinate amounts of egoboo and adoration they often need to sustain them in lives of hapless shamming.

What I am lamenting is the crippling of often intelligently conceived series ideas by the addition of the second nose, the second lead.

They are unnecessary. But unlike the auk, the dodo and the passenger pigeon, though their time is long past as a species, they have not been allowed to slip quietly, like the saurians, into the primordial slime. Though their function is no longer valid, they have not been excised like the appendix of the vestigial tail.

I cannot conceive of the perpetuation of this archaic thinking as a result of inadequate acting talent on the star or potential star level. It would appear that the networks erroneously believe they must still offer the viewer a Doris Day or an Eve Arden or a Barbara Stanwyck to get the audience, when Patrick MacNee and Diana Rigg have shown this is clearly untrue.

For rather than opt for inventiveness and daring and fresh conceptualizations in their series proposals, the networks continue to choose the safe path, ignoring the lessons of Cosby, Otis Young, Leonard Nimoy and Martin Landau. And condemning more and more young actors every year to stunted careers that inevitably end in failure.

This is merely one more facet of a policy toward new programming that is so encysted with its own past, even the *possibility* of new directions seems impossible. It is a system whose existence is seemingly validated only by the inertia that keeps it running. A self-fulfilling prophecy, a laocoönian serpent swallowing its own tail, a moebius cliche of endless repetitions. Last week I dealt with another element of this problem in noting that we go from cycle to cycle—cops to westerns to medical shows to situation comedies and back to cops—and this week a look at all those second leads. Walking gravestone markers. Carrying the seeds of their own destruction in the roles they accept. Which are, I guess, better than no roles at all, but guaranteed to cut them off at the hips in mid-season.

The answer, of course, is an obvious one. In two parts. The first is selecting actors with undeniable talent, not merely Barbie and Ken dolls who look good in their Harry Cherry suits. Talent cannot be ignored. We've had too many TV actors pass on to other, larger areas, to ever accept the canard that TV is *solely* the province of the mediocre. Steve McQueen, Leonard Nimoy, James Garner, Robert Culp, Dick Van Dyke, Bill Cosby, Mia Farrow—all of them came from television and all of them proved their worth by using their special talent to surmount mediocre material handed to them.

But the second part of the answer is the more important. Conceptualization.

The new series must either be constructed so one heavyweight actor dominates and is allowed to expand himself artistically—à la Ben Gazzarra and David Janssen—or the format must be so constructed that an integrated "team" of actors is needed to carry any one story-line. The most obviously successful rendering of this last is *Mission: Impossible*, whereas *Here Come The Brides, The Big Valley, The Virginian* and even *Bonanza* seem to me to be artificial versions of the same.

Creators of TV series must be ready to acknowledge the truth that what is needed to hook a viewer, and hold him for thirty weeks, is not "something for everyone" (an old man filled with wisdom for the septuagenarians, a young stud for the Now Generation, a middle-aged ex-star for the matrons) but a clearly defined personality whose week-to-week growth and involvement with *people* and the issues of the day has some substantial meaning for *other* individuals.

155

The TV audience may be referred to as a "mass," even by me in my crankier moments, but when you pick it apart, the audience is still one-to-one, each person looking out of his own head for something to enrich and entertain him. Facelessness, homogeneity, a mass looking back at him can *never* provide an answer. Or enrichment.

N.B.: As you read this, I'll be winding up a week in Texas, lecturing at Texas A&M. Next week I'll tell you what the attitude toward TV is in the Lone Star State. Presupposing, of course, that someone doesn't pick me off from a bell tower. In expectation of same, I'm wearing my plastic head to Houston, Bryan and Dallas.

S'long, y'awl.

28: 9 MAY 69

Well-fed, decently talcumed, ex-Los Angeles Police Chief Tom Reddin made his show biz debut Tuesday evening. First at five o'clock, then again in reprise at 10:00, Reddin held center-stage on KTLA Channel 5's *The Tom Reddin News.*

How did he look? When I was very young, there was a popular song titled *Penguin at the Waldorf,* and all I remember of it is the line, "Penguin at the Waldorf, sitting in a big plus chair . . ." How strange that Reddin's demeanor brought back that song, that image. That's how he looked.

How did he sound? He sounded like the strident voice of the Establishment. But then, what did we expect: conscience compels admission that expectations were not high for Reddin in his new role as newscaster, but a desire to be fair forced at least this reviewer to compose himself before the set swearing honest reportage of Reddin's initial outing. The tip-off should have been the station-break billboard flashed just before Reddin made his appearance. It was a screaming American eagle, rampant on a lurid shield of stars and stripes. It was no mere call-card: it was an escutcheon, a standard, a presager of what was to come in the first Reddin hour. Lord, how that eagle shrieked.

Twenty-eight years a cop—and thus heir to all the questions one must ask about the sort of mentality that finds succor in badge, gun and uniform—Reddin was quite obviously, and quite understandably, self-conscious as a public performer. Though rarely nervous, he was stiff, pedantic, well-rehearsed but somehow resembled a latter-day Clark Kent in search of a broom

157

closet in which he could change to his alter-ego, Capt. Charisma.

He opened with a personal statement of position, heavily larded with the word truth, flanked on all sides by words like "balance," "candor" and "honesty." Yet even girded to be fair to Reddin, it became apparent, early in the presentation, that once a cop . . . always a cop. Though Reddin swore at length that he was not a voice for right or left, police or politicos, his personal views—expressed with plastic helmets and cans of mace in another incarnation—were so blatantly obvious that to call what he presented news would be as appropriate as calling what Eichmann did an attempt at solving the overpopulation problem.

Credentials for Reddin were presented at the outset in a fifteen-minute segment during which testimonials were hurrah'd by everyone from Supervisor Warren Dorn, who presented Reddin with a plaque, through Yorty and Bradley and George Murphy, to Councilman Gilbert Lindsay; Lindsay performed so handsomely in the role of "show nigger," declaring what a gentleman Reddin was, that his act could be termed with appropriateness, nothing less than a superlative Double Tom.

After the fifteen minutes of everyone vouchsafing what a joy and delight it was to have Capt. Charisma with us twice nightly, Tom actually got around to reporting some news: the overruling of the Navy court-martial in the case of the *Pueblo's* Cmdr. Lloyd Bucher.

Reddin mispronounced Bucher's name in at least three different ways.

Byew-ker. Boo-chur. Byew-chur.

In point of fact, Reddin didn't actually *report* too much news. Other than the Bucher/*Pueblo* item, some chit-chat about how thrilled he was to be on the air, and "The Reddin Report," an editorial about which more in a moment, Capt. Charisma was kept away from the heavyweight merchandise like Just Plain Bull

In A China Shop. Experienced Hal Fishman got all the goodies: the Viet Nam report, the Israeli-Arab troubles, the Paris gold reserve drop, and a *New York Times* newsbreak (suspiciously passed over for all its import) about Nixon's war plans on the occasion of the downing of the "flying *Pueblo*."

Cheap thrills, however, were achieved when a Channel 2 camera crew and reporter broke onto the set just as Reddin concluded his first news item ... and interviewed *him*. It was one of those rare moments in television when the viewer feels as though he has plunged down a rabbit hole: the interviewer who is merely a shadow image, being treated like an authentic happening, being interviewed by *other* shadows. It was the head of the snake swallowing its own tail.

But for all these wonders, we had not yet reached, nor been treated to, the heartmeat of the Reddin mystique. We had not yet had unveiled before us the special fillip that was to validate that screaming eagle and its declaration of naked patriotism. But it was not long in coming.

Again, the shield and bird; and with *voice over* in a tone usually reserved for announcements of the Second Coming, we were told we were next to be treated to an editorial on matters of pressing public concern ... T*H*E*R*E*D*D*I*N*R*E*P*O*R*T!

What followed was a potpourri of all the hackneyed cliches employed by right-wing doom-criers since Nat Turner took on the white power structure. Reddin spewed forth a hateful little posture-reinforcer with no more than a nickel's difference between it and a campaign speech on "law and order" by either George Wallace or Ronald Reagan. It was the party line, pure and exceedingly simple. After the obligatory nod to "righting wrongs" (none of which were mentioned in specific), Reddin went on to espouse the same hard line for "dissidents," "trouble makers," "anarchists" and "revolutionaries" that we have seen to work so charmingly

159

on college campuses across the nation. "No deals, no amnesty," Reddin declared.

(During the initial segment of laudits for Reddin, Robert Finch referred to Reddin as "compassionate." His first Reddin Report was many things, but it was hardly compassionate. More accurately, it was drenched with brutal and unfeeling jingoism.)

It was the Reddin stand on opposing voices we had seen in his reactions to dissent during his tenure as Police Chief, changed not one whit. It offered nothing new, it expressed no degree of understanding or humanity, it merely reflected the tenor of violence that marked Reddin's police rule of Los Angeles, and that of his predecessor, under whom he studied well.

It was "America: Love It or Leave it" without a warming or ameliorative trace of "America: Change It or Lose It." One's reaction to Reddin's editorializing, viewed through his glass darkly, could only be "Reddin: Pick It and Stick It." For it was George Putnam without genitalia. It was the same nauseous, superpatriotic baiting that has kept this nation divided and trembling for ten years. It was "I love America" without the wit or sense or decency to understand that there are terrors in men's hearts today that cannot be quieted by pointing to our own children and calling them the enemy.

We might have expected something lucid and rational and impressive for a first editorial, something heavy-weight ... but we were handed merely another Xerox copy of the standard voice-of-the-right platform. And God knows we have enough of that for one more to be the gas bubble that breaks the surface tension.

The editorial was reinforced by a patently rigged item from Long Beach State College, in which we were treated to riot scenes on the campus, as played for us by the hawk-faced *oburstleutnant* college security force. The item was introduced by an impartial, unslanted Reddin comment, "The militants usually have their way on campus, but I'm happy to report that today was an exception . . ." and it was epilogued by Reddin's equally unbiased, "Militants *have* overreached, and the good people are being heard from . . ." It was as unprejudiced a bit of reportage as Joe Pyne's displaying his hand-gun, on-camera, during the Watts Riots. And it proved to one and all the truth of Reddin's opening assurances that he was not the voice of left or right, revolutionaries or reactionaries, etcetera, etcetera.

As a tapesty of the American Scene, as seen from the blind right, it was total, with the proper counterpoint being played to Reddin's comments about American affluence by commercials that came in groups, clusters, hordes:

Use Bold to win points over your neighbors . . . use Listerine to get ahead in your job . . . use MacLean's to get laid . . . it was all a theremin background of corrupt values to Reddin's naked gloating over SDS opposition. It was the essence of cheapjack, slanted yellow journalism.

What a delight it was, just a little later, to catch Cronkite and Severeid. What a return to sanity.

Rather than editorializing about Nixon's instant reaction to the shooting down of our spy plane with *retaliation* . . . rather than commenting on the systematic building of a Nixon Dynasty with daughter Trish dating Barry Goldwater, Jr. and daughter Julie married to David Eisenhower . . . rather than trying to examine how and why our educational system is in the state it is . . . Reddin chose to indicate the thrust of his interests by further alarming the crazies who suspect every kid who wants a better education or voice in his own future, of Communist activity.

Well, we can take some small consolation in KTLA's scheduling Capt. Charisma at five, when most people are en route from one place to another . . . and at ten, while the network prime shows are still on. It will cut down the audience he reaches.

Though I suspect the bottom line on Reddin is that

he will genuinely speak only to those who heard his deadly message of mace in the streets and parks of Los Angeles. For a few days he will be a fad, like Shipwreck Kelly, like mah jongg, like hula hoops and Dagmar and the Twist. And like them, the boredom of repetition will drive him from public attention

Because, again bottom line, Reddin is a dreadful bore. His manner of newscasting is stiff, undramatic, amateurish. His pronunciation is typified by an inability to call the city that employed him anything but "Luss Ann-uh-luss." His gift for cliche is Promethean. (At one point he actually demonstrated his grasp of the nature of education by referring to universities as "think factories" and went on to insist that dissenters who keep throwing "monkey wrenches" into the factory machinery . . . but, you know what I mean.)

When Reddin began the telecast with his introductory comments, he asked the audience to bear with him as he adjusts to his new role. Why should we? Intellectually, he affronts us with second-hand, non-viable red-baiting and hate. Artistically, we expect professionalism in our TV viewing fare, and should be impatient with anything less. Why should we bear with a stiff amateur, mouthing the same platitudes and nonsense we've heard from other more articulate charlatans? Merely so KTLA, in an obvious bid for some weather-worn publicity, can reap the dubious benefits accruing to the metamorphosis of a toad into a toad prince? Zero chance.

Good night, Chet. Good night. David. Sleep easy; you have nothing to fear from Capt. Charisma. Who can worry about a super-hero who vanishes when you change channels?

29: 9 MAY 69

TEXAS: PART I

Hand over hand, head still whirling, I've returned from a week of lecturing at Texas A&M with some hell-visions to impart about TV-time, thoughts, frights, and passing scenes.

This will be the first of a two-part column about Texas. About living death in the Great American Heartland. About a week so inextricably intertwined with the reality of college life and preparing to enter the adult world ... and the unreality of television, the GOD TV, the great glowing glistening glass teat ... that it will take two columns merely to report what went down, and hope some sense and/or sensible conclusions emerge. Pay attention.

Under the guise of being a science fiction writer (working in a horde of genres has its advantages: totally divergent groups know my work in a compartmentalized way: one group knows me as a film and TV writer, another knows me as a speculative fiction writer, another knows me as a film or music critic, yet another knows only this column: and that's cool ... I get to cut across artificial barriers into allkinda other scenes), I was booked to give two one-hour lectures on succeeding nights. And to speak to an English class or two.

But Texas A&M is not UCLA. It is not Berkeley. It is not U. of Chicago. It is a grass roots school where, until a few years ago, there were no co-eds. (Until, oddly enough for this writer, the mother of the girl who heads up the A&M science fiction club sued the school,

163

and won women the right to attend.) Now there are a few females walking the campus.

And until a few years ago, everyone at the school was in ROTC, better known as "the Corps" by the fish (freshmen), the pissheads (sophomores) and zips (seniors). Now, out of a 13,000-student community, only 3,000 wear the khaki. Yet they, and their little newspaper *The Battalion*, are a force on the campus.

I knew none of this when I was asked to speak to a class on science-and-literature. Nor did I know that the President of the university—a gentleman named "General" Rudder—and his Trustees had decreed there would be no political speakers at A&M. Not merely no Cleaver or Rap Brown, but Ronald Reagan (our very own *wunderkind*) and George Wallace had been denied speaking privileges on the campus. I had no way of knowing I was walking into a crazy-quilt hodge-podge of Fundamentalist religiosos, mock army troopers, underground "liberals" and people who *believe* everything they see on the television screen.

I knew none of this as I stood before that 8:00 ayem class, and instead of boring them to death with talk of science fiction, suddenly starting rapping on student dissent, the military, Viet Nam, political activism, racial unrest, the evils of religion, the new morality, life in the big cities, the fucked-up educational system, and other topics of a similarly hilarious nature.

Within three hours, the word got out. The classes to which I spoke swelled, the students cut their classes to come listen. My lectures grew from an hour to two and then almost three. They drank at me. They looked out of their eyes and begged to know all the things we take for granted in the pages of the *Free Press*.

There I stood in my striped bells, my floral double-barreled cuff shirts, my silk scarves, before these students in their pima cotton shirts and goat-roper boots, a creature from *out there*, from a place none of them seemed able to grasp as being *real*. They stared at me like a thing that had fallen off the moon.

And I rapped. For endless hours, day after day. Not merely one or two classes, but almost *thirty* classes in four days. Their hunger to hear was unbelievable. Their lack of awareness was staggering. Their willingness to accept whatever they were told by the mass media, even when patently false, was disheartening. But as the days went by, I began to see a change: in them, and in me.

In an early class, one of the students asked me if I believed in God. I replied, "I don't think so." And then I proceeded to wail on the theme, using material from this column of some weeks ago, in which I observed the perpetuation of insanity on this planet through the mediums of Arabs-vs-Jews, Catholics-vs-Protestants, Southern Baptists-vs-Everyone. I said I felt if "God created man in his *own* image, in the image of God created he them," (Genesis 2:27, King James's italics, not mine) then *we* were God. And when Man (*my* cap, not King James's) in his most creative, his most loving, his most gentle and most human, then he is most Godlike.

The student said he would pray for my immortal soul. He also asked for my address, so he could send me some literature on the subject of God. I thanked him politely and told him I'd gotten all the literature I could handle on the subject from a certain Thomas Aquinas.

He then accused me of being one of those heathens who had been in favor of *The Smothers Brothers Comedy Hour*. I agreed that I was, indeed, one of those heathens. And I asked for a show of hands (which I repeated in many classes) of how many had felt the Smothers Brothers had been in bad taste, had been seditious, had felt delighted when they'd been canceled. He was not alone in raising his hand.

In all conscience I must report that the majority of the students I asked had been saddened to see SmoBro go, but the tiny minority that raised hands were the *vocal* ones. They were not Nixon's fabled Silent Majority, they were the Committed Few who *knew* there was a Heaven, there was a Hell, that God was a jealous people, and that the SmoBroShow was intended as a devious Communist plot to pollute the minds and precious bodily fluids of the Great American Viewing Public, which was not nearly mature enough to watch and make its own decisions.

I pointed out that if I—or any other viewer—did not dig the brand of pap being proffered by, say, *The Good Guys* or *Green Acres* or *Mayberry RFD*, we expressed our displeasure by turning that special knob. But *we* never mounted campaigns of outraged indignation to have those shows canceled. *We* were perfectly happy to let everyone watch or not watch as they chose. Yet *he*, and his ilk, not only wouldn't watch the shows themselves, but they wanted *no one* to watch. I asked him what he was afraid we might find out. He had no answer. Yet he knew he was on the side of the angels.

That led us to censorship.

Taking off from a local Texas news item, reported on TV during my stay there, I presented them with a situation: it seems a 63-year-old man in the Land Office in the Texas state capitol, Austin, had decided women's skirts were too short, and men's sideburns were too long. He *decreed*, unilaterally, that 188 employees of the Land Office had to conform with women's skirts to (or below) the knee, and men's sideburns to the middle of the ear lobe, and no longer. (I, in my madness, instantly pictured a man with twelve-foot-long earlobes and flowing sideburns, but that's another vision.) I asked the True Believer if he thought there was any parallel that could be drawn between the cancelation of SmoBro and that TV news item. He said yes, that the director of the Land Office had the right to do it, because the employees worked for him. He then said something that sounded suspiciously like, "America: Love It or Leave It." In other words, that pregnant woman who was beaten at Century City

166

deserved what she got, because she shouldn't have been there. If the employees wanted to defy the decree, they could go work somewhere else.

And I suddenly began to realize that I was now in direct confrontation, vis-a-vis, with the very people to whom I have referred as "scuttlefish" in these columns.

This was the TV viewing audience.

And I began to probe at all the places they ached.

I discovered some obvious but disheartening things.

This was not the arteriosclerotic generation, the heavy-lidded drinkers and haters who lay bloated before their television sets like wheezing whales in shoal ... these were the Hope of Tomorrow. These were the younger generation, the ones who couldn't trust me because I was on the verge of thirty-five. And they were content to allow themselves to be lock-stepped in khaki uniforms toward all the insane battlefields a misplaced patriotism would devise for them between now and age forty. They were content to be punched, stapled and cross-filed in readiness for the giant corporations. At A&M there would be no upset that Dow was recruiting. There would be no dissent that what they were getting in their classrooms—via the TV box visual aid— would be outdated and useless by the time they graduated. There would be no anger that they were being prepared not to lead outgoing lives of joy and grandeur, but were rather being processed like live meat to fit into the computer coding of great faceless business empires. I suggested this to them, and in one class a young girl justified the loss of her life by saying, "Well, somebody has to keep the wheels turning." And silently I felt a leap of smugness: yeah, baby, *you* do it; you and all the others like you. Because as long as you're willing to die through every day of your life, it leaves the world free for jokers like me. As long as you'll till the fields, I can sing my songs and run loose.

But then it followed in the next thought that I was no better than the line-trooper who is momentarily relieved that the next man caught the bullet, rather than

167

himself. And I started saying things like, "There has to be a better life for you. There has to be a way to taste all the pleasures and freedoms they tell you are yours, without consigning yourselves for half your waking hours to gray little boxes, doing the work of manufacturing death."

They did not understand.

They were the older generation.

Trapped in the Great American Heartland, cut off from knowledge—truly!—and cut off from flexibility. They were the next generation to support a Viet Nam. And they could not understand how an obvious Commie fink revolutionary such as myself could be allowed to write for television.

I assured them it was hardly easy.

For TV, the one all-seeing-eye of our time that could have hipped them, could have liberated them, had lied to them. Had systematically lulled them into bovine complacency, into tacit acceptance of all the hideous wrongnesses that leprously fester on the soul of our country.

Perhaps crossing the line from *here,* from this place where kids lay their lives and their college careers and their beliefs on the line, to free *them,* there in Texas ... into that other country, had made me paranoid.

But with a sickening lurch I realized that I was perhaps the one-eyed man in the kingdom of the blind.

30: 23 MAY 69

TEXAS PART II

In which your humble columnist, himself a man of peace, was pressed into unwitting service during a lecture tour at Texas A&M University as a spokesman for dissent, moral and intellectual freedom, awareness, and equality. You may recall some of this from part one of this two-part triptych through the Country of the TV Blinded.

After discussing the growing role of the black man in television—and noting *Julia* was only Julie Andrews with Man-Tan—I discussed some of the more blatant ways in which television had misrepresented the realities of the race/class struggle in America today. After I had done riffs all too familiar to readers of this newspaper, a young lady in the class raised her hand. All through the class lecture, this young woman had sat quietly, staring at me with that expressionless immobility night club comics fear. It means not only are you not hipping them, amusing them, stimulating them ... you are not even penetrating through the bone and flesh walls of their prejudices. When, earlier in the class, I'd asked her if she wanted to ask me anything, she informed me that she would listen, and then at the end of the period she would "make her comment." I somehow felt I was going to be asked to take a test, but I didn't know what notes to make.

So now, as I finished, she raised her hand, to make her summing-up comment. We all waited breathlessly. And this, approximately, is what she said:

"I live in Marion County, where there's a lot of nig-er-ahs; I ride my horse in the woods there. We had a white girl raped by a nig-er-ah out there. And the other nig-er-ahs came to our house and told my mother and father I shouldn't ride my horse there any more. *I* believe, that most nig-er-ahs are happy the way they are, that it's only a trouble-making few who are causing all this trouble."

I waited. Surely she would not fail to add that if the "nig-er-ahs" were given sufficient quantities of watermelon, were allowed to dance with their natural rhythm on "de lebee," and were not whipped by "massa," they would settle back into a pre-Confederacy happiness of idyllic cotton-plucking and baby-birthing.

There was no response possible to this gross theory. But I was overjoyed to hear the groans of disbelief from other members of the class, among whom this new-generation blind one had been sitting, without ever having previously revealed herself.

Yet how many others in that class, in that University, in that state, in this country, thought as she did? Were there still so many of them? Had we lulled ourselves, we who take black-as-noble as a matter of course? Or was the poison still being passed on by the dying old ones? As the dirt was being shoveled in over their faces, did they still reach up from the grave, in one final ghoulish act, and say, "Heah, mah child, take this heah wisdom with y'all . . . it's mah legacy . . ."?

Knowing this, as I sit here writing of that encounter, two weeks later, I am listening to Sly and the Family Stone singing *Stand* and *Don't Call Me Nigger, Whitey*, and I know as sure as God made black'n'white that if the black man ceases pushing, young girls like that one will slip back into control. And rather would I see a thousand Watts's than a return to that quiet, sinister evil. Can the inevitability of it be that unclear to the white power structure? Can it truly be beyond the grasp of a Reagan? Prayers won't help. Someone needs to *inform* the ones on top. Why hasn't television accepted this responsibility?

170

The why remains unanswered, but the manifestation of regional avoidance of the problem was demonstrated on a talk show I did from Bryan, Texas that same day. It was a "women's show" called *Town Talk,* hosted by a rather pleasant but uninformed woman named Fern Hammond.

It was the traditional chit-chat format every small town TV station offers. Miss Hammond began her program with an interminable reading of local flower shows, revival meetings, Kiwanis raffles and sodality picnics. Then she introduced me as a writer of scientific fiction, or fiction science, or somesuch. And within moments of that starting gambit, the troublemaker I had become since arriving in Texas asserted himself, and I was rapping about the lack of perceptivity of the people I'd met in Texas. The song was one of trust in the young, with a theme of being kind to one another, laced with melodies about not believing all the lies told nature of evil, and put forth the Pope's encyclical as a concrete example of same in a world rapidly strangling on the waste products of its overpopulation. We got into the subject of allowing people to (forgive the phrase) do their own thing, as long as they stayed off other people's toes. Fern opined that might not be such a hot idea.

I countered with an observation that she wore her skirt well above her knees, and that only a few years ago had she chosen to do so, she'd have been arrested for indecent exposure. I presented it as an example of how people fear to do what they want, until the mass accepts it. And that, I concluded, was denying one's own soul.

The discussion got a tot hairy, at least on my part, as I pointed out that girls matured earlier today than they did even twenty years ago, because of diet, assault of information through the visual media, because of the mobility provided by cars-for-everyone. And I said if teen-aged girls wanted to have sex, that was cool, as long as the responsible media, such as Miss Hammond's TV show, informed them The Pill was available. Miss Hammond was speechless (confidantes in the Bryan area informed me it was the first time they'd ever seen her so) and the cameraman got so nervous he let go of the elevation control on the camera, which proceeded to drift ceilingwards, giving everyone an unobstructed view of the lights and flies above us.

Now, mark this: what went down between Miss Hammond and myself was nothing startling, nor even terribly radical. By *our* standards. It was old hat in literature and even films ten years ago. But television, playing to some mythical audience of cretins and scuttle-fish, persists in maintaining lies and outdated postures that only serve to confuse and encyst the viewers.

Multiply Fern Hammond and the implicit lies of her chit-chat show by a thousand, for every TV station in every locality in America, and you understand, finally, why Richard Nixon won the Presidency; you understand why George Wallace cadged 14% of the vote; you understand why a large segment of the "straight" students on campuses band together—as they did at Long Beach State—to fight the very kids who are putting their educations, their futures and sometimes their lives on the line, to provide better facilities and more open discussion for *all*.

Fern Hammond is by no means an evil woman. Yet by her tacit acceptance of the *status quo,* by her abrogation of the responsibility of letting her viewers *know* what the real world is about, she serves the ends of evil in this country.

She is one with all the decaying corpses of bigotry who poured the poison into the ears of girls such as the one who rode her horse through Marion County. And until people as outspoken, passionate and *caring* as, say, Tom Smothers begin hosting shows like *Town Talk*, the greater portion of average citizens in this country will be kept in the dark. While their age-old prejudices and fears are played upon by craftsmen like

172

George Putnam and Tom Reddin and Paul Harvey and Joe Pyne, all the Fern Hammonds, of boondock TV will lull them into believing nothing is happening, that their world is merely a trifle dyspeptic, rather than helping to cure the cancer that will surely destroy us all without crystal awareness of just how imminent are the dangers.

It was that way all through the week in Texas. I found people who could by no stretch of the imagination be called evil, but who served the ends of the demons by having been lied to so engagingly by television, that anything outside the simple good-and-bad Disneyism of what they'd been programmed to understand, seemed destructive, seemed radical and deserving of death.

It was not difficult to understand how all those 13,-000 A&M students could be lock-stepped toward the gray cubicles of the military or giant corporations. It was the result of a cultural pattern set in motion many years ago, whose aim it was to produce a mindless, unfeeling, basically hostile and subservient *mass*, fit for no better than serving the financial ends of the corporate behemoths.

What did I find in Texas, gentle readers?

I found a cheerless, empty Stonehenge of complacency, stupidity, desperation and amenity. I felt compassion for all of them. They suspect the rest of the country of being engaged in a monstruous plot to corrupt and kill them. They have been lied to, seduced, bludgeoned and hypnotized by the monster eye of television.

And if there is any saving them, it will have to be through a long, passionate war of re-education and freedom. Before I went to Texas, my gut had been with revolution, but I'd had reservations. Now I have none.

For I've seen what happens to the mass when the Reddins, the Putnams, the Pynes and the Harveys are allowed to disseminate their hideous view of reality without being opposed.

I tell you straight, friends, the lingering death is a far

more hideous one than that postulated by those who fear fire and the storm.

The question thus becomes: who will send missionaries to underprivileged, emerging nations such as Texas?

31: 16 MAY 69

For my next number, friends, a genuine open suicide note. Watch Ellison kill himself, before your very eyes.

You see, it's like this. I'm a writer. That's not just what I *do,* it's what I *am.* Understanding *that,* you can perhaps understand why I am impatient with my fellow members of the Writers Guild of America who don't seem offended by their number who are crummy writers.

In an intelligent discussion of television, and the reasons why it is deficient in so many areas, the writer must come in for his share of *mea culpa.* While it is no secret that writers in the television arena are considered little more than chattel, to be used then excluded from any of the important artistic decisions between script stage and screening, still it cannot be denied that a share of the blame for bad TV can be laid to the writers.

This seems to me a fair statement, and one that should upset—least of all—the conscientious writers in the Guild. Yet, a statement I made in one of these columns, many months ago, was picked up by a fellow Guild member, and has been used as an example of my "disloyalty" to my chosen union.

The offending remark went as follows: "Most of them [my fellow scriptwriters] couldn't write their way out of a pay-toilet for openers, and they simply don't have the craft or the heart to write what matters, what counts, what we can feel and care about." The remark was part of an article on the abrogation of responsibility to those who *create,* to utilize their passion to present a more realistic portrait of the world today on

175

television. It was not a diatribe against writers solely, for it took to task actors, producers, directors and network mufti. It appeared in the October 18th *Free Press*, my third column to hit print. And yet, of all the matters I've discussed here, all the pressing topics with which TV has dealt or avoided, it was this lone sentence that caused a fellow Guild member, Mr. Mort R. Lewis, to speak out against me. His forum was a letter to the Writers Guild Newsletter just this month, and ...

But I get way ahead of myself.

If I'm going to commit suicide, at least let me do it in as neat a way as possible. It starts like so:

The Writers Guild has a Film Society.

We see advance screenings of new films twice a month. Several years ago, we had such a rash of unmannerly behavior at these screenings—booing and catcalling—that several studios refused to allow their films to be shown at our Film Society. At that time, strong outcries were heard from many responsible members of the Guild to try and quash this ungentlemanly behavior. The decorum was restored.

But two months ago, it started again. In specific, the rudeness was demonstrated at two films written by, or from the works of, members who happened to be present at the screenings. The display of bad manners was disgraceful, and made the more horrendous by the presence of the men who had created the films. One of them fled in embarrassment.

In my anger at this sorry display of intellectual inflexibility, I wrote a letter to the Newsletter addressed to "Writers Guild Swine," that is, the rude among our membership who demean their brother members. It was a quite loonie letter, written in the same tone of rudeness as the original demonstrations. It was printed.

A month went by, and in the current issue of the Newsletter are replies. Naive Tom Sawyer that I be, I rather thought my fellow Guild members would join in to condemn the rank gross-outs of the vocal few. But instead, every one of the letters printed condemned me for being a brash Neanderthal who would dare to tell anyone anything.

(Now understand something: I am against censorship of any kind, any time, anywhere. If a film, or a TV show, or a book, or an act of artistic creation of any kind offends or bores or insults you . . . put it down! I have been known to groan with undisguised nausea as my gorge became buoyant, at many a flick. But it seems to me a special kind of cruelty, to make a public display of gratuitous rudeness in the *presence* of the men who invested their craft and art in the presentation. I know they boo and hiss in theaters in Europe, and I cannot say this is a bummer . . . but we of the Writers Guild are *supposed* to be on a somewhat more elevated plane than "mere filmgoers." We are alleged to be men and women with some sensibilities where the craft is concerned, and a bad film should be an exercise in avoidance for us. We should take the lesson of failure as offered, and profit by it. Hooting and belching makes us no better than the fraternity crowds that attend the Saturday night AIP flicks, throwing popcorn and screaming cliches for the amusement of their dates.)

Well, to get on with it . . . whatever my motivations for writing the letter, the responses were unanimous in their affront and disgust with me; for speaking out.

And that, in a Guild where silence seems to prevail with all but a dedicated handful, was tantamount to heresy. I was obviously a smartass upstart telling his betters what to do, and bastioning my position with threats of violence—which *really* uptighted them.

Now, I suppose it wouldn't have much mattered, and would have soon been forgotten, but it seems that your humble columnist is also running for a position on the Council of the film branch of the Writers Guild of America, West.

Needless to say, my credentials were hopelessly compromised. Several days running, after the platform

177

statements of the candidates had been mailed out to the membership, I received unsigned hate letters with my statement torn in quarters, and enclosed as a notification that I would not be voted for. That's cool.

Better they should know where I'm at, in front, than think I'm running on a platform of silence and then be surprised to find me a viper at their breast.

All of which brings me to Mort R. Lewis's letter, in which he proves the hypocrisy of my being upset at the rudeness of the few, when I had the audacity to say most of my fellow screenwriters couldn't write their way out of a pay-toilet. And to my committing suicide in public. Because what I'm about to say will certainly insure my being passed-over by the voters.

I say it now, not out of any misplaced courage, but because it needs to be said, and if I safely waited till *after* the election, I would find myself wondering if I'd done it out of fear, or sick need to be elected.

What I have to say, Mr. Lewis, and all of you, is this:

Sturgeon's Law holds true, especially for writers. The Law says: 94% of *everything* is shit. Puddings, plays, poetry, parties, pistols, people. That is, ninety-four per cent of everything is merely average. Merely sufficient. There is only 6% grandeur in the universe anywhere!

That means ninety per cent of the writers in any given field are shit. Most screenwriters can't write their way out of pay-toilets. Sorry, Mr. Lewis. But if you doubt it, read their scripts.

Even mine. Often, they're shit. The only difference, I suppose, between them and me is that I never *set out* to write shit. (That is: merely sufficient, average.) And of all the crimes that may be attributed to me—numbering among them rudeness, lechery, viciousness, imprudence and disgusting egocentricity—the one that can *never* be laid on me is the one epitomized by the line, "I just write what they want, by Tuesday, take the money and run." I've heard too many of my fellow

178

Guild members say it to feel ashamed that I said they couldn't write their way out of pay-toilets.

They aren't even honest hacks, Mr. Lewis.

An honest hack writes entertainment, and has no pretensions to greatness, such as flawed scriveners like myself. Honest hacks like Melville and Dickens and Trocchi and Simenon and MacDonald and Sam Clemens. They only wanted to entertain, Mr. Lewis. But they at least did it in their own voices. They didn't sell out before they were asked to. They didn't bear the responsibility for a nation being lied-to and badly used. and corrupted by its best medium of information. They cared about what they wrote, Mr. Lewis, even as some members of the Guild care about what *they* write. Men like John D.F. Black, and George Clayton Johnson, and Lee Pogostin, and Christopher Knopf, and Bruce Geller, and Howard Rodman.

You see, Mr. Lewis, I'm a guttersnipe. I have no class. I don't know enough to stand shoulder to shoulder with fellow Guild members who don't give a damn. I take pride in my craft, Mr. Lewis. I think we *can* change the face of not only TV Land America . . . but the face of our times! And I'm more concerned, as a member of the Writers Guild, with getting some control over my scripts than getting a few bucks more per segment. Right now, most TV writers are hideously over-paid for the kind of idiocy they write. But then, so are directors, and grips, and everybody else concerned with the imbecilic business of slapping together cliches, so that faceless gray men out there somewhere can sell more rectal suppositories.

That's what I meant about the pay-toilets, Mr. Lewis. Look, it's like this: the Guild is a beautiful thing. It is responsible for more advances in working conditions in The Industry than any other Guild. It operates out of strength, because there is a fierce kind of pride in being a writer. And the Guild is a banding-together of individual, eccentric, non-conformist, *prideful* men and women. But a Guild is a union, and a union can

179

only stand when all stand together. Yet that does not mean that some of us cannot rail against the inept practitioners of our midst. Every time a bad script is flung out over the channelways, *all* writers suffer.

Joyce Miller, herself a TV writer, does a radio show called *Encounter* over KPFK. She asked me on as a guest a few weeks ago. We argued about the state of TV, and what could be done to better it. She suggested we should "starve it to death"; the creative talents should move off, do other things, till the medium got so bad they'd call for the talent, and *then* we'd take back control of our television. I told her she was wrong.

You know *why* she's wrong, Mr. Lewis? Because there will *always* be mediocre writers and directors and actors who will fill the empty hours that must be filled with product. Just as "W. Hermanos" wrote all those pseudonymous scripts during the writers' strike in 1960.

We can't starve them by running away. We can only beat them by staying and writing like such bloody beautiful motherfuckers that they can't *not* put our scripts on as we write them.

That's what I meant by pay-toilets, Mr. Lewis.

I'm a writer, not a carpenter or a plumber or a bricklayer. Writing is a holy chore. And I don't give a damn if I'm not elected, or if you bounce my ass out of the Guild, or if you shove a thermite bomb up my *tuchis* ... I'll *still* curse the lousy writers in our Guild who write the slop and the pap and the insulting, degraded Creative Typing they call scripts. Because they weaken us, they sell out in the cheapest, ugliest way to the forces that seek to own our souls and our thoughts.

Pride in craft, Mr. Lewis. Can you dig *that!* Or is all you've read in these pages the line you chose to remember for eight months? Are you that afraid our Guild is weak, that you refuse to admit most of us don't write very well? Come on, Mr. Lewis, who the hell is *writing* all that tripe if it isn't *us?* Do elves come in, during the night, and cobble up those inept teleplays?

Maybe it's just because I come out of the publishing

180

bag, Mr. Lewis, where—unlike films and TV—they don't pay you till after you're done and they like it. Maybe it's because I figure a writer should think of himself as something nobler than an employee, and what he writes as something more noble than bricks or puddings. Maybe it's because when I came out here and became, with pride, a member of our Guild—*our* Guild, Mr. Lewis—I thought I could write what hadn't been written before, say what others hadn't said, not merely to fill empty hours with emptier refuse, but *to change the face of our times*, Mr. Lewis! Maybe that is why I said pay-toilets.

Because . . . and you'd better dig *this*, Mr. Lewis . . . the times are too perilous, the stakes too high, the forces aligned against us too powerful . . . to permit second-rate, untalented ex-PR men and mailroom boys to write the words and form the thoughts that follow on the heels of that holiest of phrases . . .

"Written by . . ."

Vote NO on Ellison, Mr. Lewis. It's safer.

32: 30 MAY 69

Two weeks ago, as you read this, I went for a walk in the Imperial Valley with some other TV folk, in support of the Grape Pickers' Strike against the table-grape growers of Delano and the Coachella Valley. No one needs to be told how important and how noble this strike is, nor with what a sense of holy purpose and personal dignity it has been pursued by Cesar Chavez and his long-suffering, incredible people.

Yet how strange it is, to walk in 118-degree heat down a dusty road toward Calexico, in the company of bronzed farmworkers who trudged that road all the way from Indio—to find oneself confronted *again* with the mythic import and impact of television on every dark corner of the culture. For even though some of those dusty pilgrims had suffered and hobbled (one man was on crutches most of the way) over a hundred miles to reach the Mexican border, in an attempt to appeal to the "green card" workers who are trucked across late at night to work the struck vineyards, the radio and television interviewers fastened on our little band of "Hollywood celebrities" and spent an inordinate amount of time getting *our* reactions and opinions ... though we were to walk only seven miles.

In company with Leonard Nimoy, most recently of *Star Trek* fame, Antoinette Bower, Richard Forbes, Linda Marsh and Mario Alcalde, actors and actresses, Joel Kane, TV writer and producer, Joyce Miller and Robert Angus of KPFK, and led by the exquisite Leslie Parrish, Mr. & Mrs. Stan Bohrman and I, and another dozen show biz and political types, made the trek down south in an air conditioned bus, laughin' and scratchin' all the way. We didn't suffer the slightest deprivation (unless you could call a bus toilet that didn't work and smelled like something from Belsen a deprivating consideration), and when we finally hit that road, the discomfort we felt—if any—was due to having lived too soft, for too long.

All around us, in front and behind us, stoical, resigned farmworkers and their families marched. And when they passed us—in our gaily patterned clothes, our bell-bottoms and white cowboy suits—their faces split in grins, they flung up the peace sign with two-fingers, and shouted, "Viva huelga!" Yeah, they were pleased to see us. We had come from Cloud-CooCoo-Land to participate in their struggle; and that was cool.

(I'm sure each of us felt so fucking noble, had we died and come up for eternity assignment, right then and there, we'd have made book we were going to that special Heaven reserved for The Good Guys.)

Now this is by no means intended to demean any of us who went down to Calexico. I'm sure Len Nimoy and Leslie Parrish would have much rather sat home that Sunday, feet up, with a cold drink. But they *couldn't*. They *had* to go, and that puts them so many brownie points ahead of all you fat assholes sitting in your split-levels mouthing liberal doctrine. I don't even want to get into it. But the *attention* we drew, the emphasis put on us was—to use the word of one of the actresses in the line—obscene.

And it comes down to the silly reality of what incredible power showfolk have, in the eyes of the rest of society. Even in the eyes of those who should know better.

Sure, certainly, of course, it's groovy to have Burt Lancaster plumping for Tom Bradley on TV spots. But what about all those John Wayne spots we've heard for Los Angeles's own Toad Prince, Sam Yorty? What about all the simpering, sillyass political philosophizing of Jack Paar?

The question is certainly being asked, somewhere out

there: what would I have ... showfolk abstaining from political action and commitment? The answer is, obviously, no. Whether actor or plumber, if a man feels he must speak/act, then he should.

What I'm going toward is an examination of the kind and degree of power and value put into the mouths of people no more experienced (and frequently less) than the politicians who are allegedly running things. Because a man commits to coaxial cable an exemplary Hamlet does not mean he knows which of those gimlet-eyed politicos is worth voting for. Bertrand Russell is a groovy man, with his head and his heart in the right place, but let's face it, the old man is a political illiterate.

So instead of shoving those interview mikes under the noses of deprived and yet courageous farmworkers who have spoken from their hearts with the eloquent simplicity of those who have felt the boot and the tongue-lash, *we* were asked how we felt about the march, and the *causa*. And what could we say? We could say all the phony, party line nonsense we'd heard from others, and never, never get anywhere near the core of sincerity or heartbreak I heard in the words of Joe Serda, a little Mexican cat who is head of the LA boycott on Safeway.

Here's where it's at, I think. Mind you, I said: I think. One never really *knows*. (I've been bashed at Century City, threatened in Selma, clubbed in Chicago, tossed in jail in New Orleans and been shot at in North Carolina, and *still*—feeling in my gut that I've paid dues—I have these qualms.)

Ours is a society so immersed in the sea of video reactions that there are little old ladies out there who *know* Hoss Cartwright is more real than their next door neighbors. Everyone of value to them is an image. A totem. A phosphor-dot wraith whose hurts and triumphs are created from the magic of a scenarist's need to make the next payment on his Porsche. (I recommend a book titled *Bug Jack Barron* by Norman Spinrad, for

184

a more complete, and horrifying analysis of this phenomenon. It's an Avon paperback, so it shouldn't trouble you too much to pick it up.)

But because of this *acceptance* of the strangers who appear on the home screen, ours has become a society where shadow and reality intermix to the final elimination of any degree of rational selectivity on the part of those whose lives are manipulated: by the carnivores who flummox them, and the idols they choose to worship.

I don't know that there's any answer to this. If we luck out and we get a John Kennedy or a Leonard Nimoy (who, strangely enough, tie in to one another by the common demonimator of being *humane*), then we can't call it a bad thing. But if we wind up with a public image that governs us as Ronald Reagan and Joe Pyne govern us, then we are in such deep trouble the mind turns to aluminum thinking of it.

The abrogation of reality by the scuttlefish is now so complete that a silver-tongued George Lincoln Rockwell could easily arise from the slime-pits of necessity and run away with this country. And *then,* all the blind and self-serving politicians would find themselves helpless. Right now, they can put down the forces striving for a change to the better, because those forces are random, disorganized, in the main ludicrous. But let a determined and TV-primed hero step forward whose compulsions drive him toward oppression and repression . . . and we would have about as much of a chance for survival as a snail in a bucket of salt.

For the news media covering that march to Calexico, in great part it was Hollywood folk surrounded by insubstantial shadow-masses, trembling toward a social goal no more significant than a Trendex rating. And for those interviewers *we* were the reality; the ones who truly mattered, who genuinely *lived* that march . . . they were no more important than Central Casting extras.

Certainly, our being there drew a trifle more attention for the march than would have obtained had it only been hordes of sweating, non-English-speaking *peons* hiking for ten days in killing heat. Yeah, sure, we did our bit, we contributed to the commonweal . . .

But who the hell *were* we? What made us more noble than them? Why should *we* have been spotlighted? Why?

Because America needs its idols. It needs its gloss and its glamour. Because it denies the sweat and stink of what is *really* happening, and if it can have just a touch of pink garbage cans in *West Side Story,* just a whisper of Alan Arkin as the deprived Puerto Rican in the film *Popi,* if it can have some suitable TV-oriented lie that says, "None of this is really happening, it's only an extension of *Peyton Place,*" then America can continue to rock back and forward complacently as entropy settles it further and further into the slag-heaps of all dead cultures.

As a party to this genuinely evil contract, I feel my gut heave, even as it heaved from too many salt tablets on the march. But being ill at the understanding of what it is we've done to ourselves, what we *continue* to do to ourselves, does not eliminate the dichotomous nature of the evil.

We do good by being there and by allowing the teat-suckers in their living rooms to see us there; but we kill them a little bit by allowing it. We kill us, too.

But worst of all . . . so hideously much worse . . . we kill Joe Serda and his grape pickers, marching endlessly down a road that has no destination, save in oblivion.

A clean-up column, this week. Some new shows, some old facts, a few wrap-ups, some mail answered publicly, and even a sizeable retraction. Ah, stay tuned in, gentle readers. New horrors! New horrors!

First order of business is tying-off the bloody artery that was my *Name Of The Game* script. It has been many weeks now since George Eckstein, a lovely man, but an unfortunate prisoner of the gargoyles who run the networks, first hired me to write a segment for Robert Stack. We tried to do our thing, we gave it a fairly competent shot, and either through my own bull-headedness or a failure to accept the rigors of The System (which I consider a noble act), we got shot down in embers, if not flames. It ain't that big a thing, friends. *The Name Of The Game* will sail on, proffering 90 minutes of pseudo-marmalade; Universal's king of the black tower, Mr. Wasserman, will continue to make eighty million grupniks a year; George Eckstein will do the best he can to get some blood into the segments he has to produce, and your friendly scribe will write something else.

So that ends the journal of a script. It began nowhere, it went nowhere, and it ended nowhere. But that is, as I said, no big thing. It is in fact, the name of the game.

Next, we come to a little mail.

To the lady in the Valley, who wrote me after my anti-religion column several months ago, informing me that she agreed totally, that I was a clear-thinker because I'd bumrapped organized religion, and knew that I was hip to the International Zionist Conspiracy that was bent on taking over the world ... lady, you're a bigot. (Can you dig that, friends: when you pointedly describe what a bigot looks like, do an entire column on what evils are born out of hatred for other religious beliefs, and condemn them in the bluntest terms ... the very ones of whom you're speaking don't recognize themselves. The asses always think you're talking about somebody else. Can it be possible that people really *are* that blind to self? I suppose so. I don't imagine Eichmann really thought of himself as a mass murderer, and Capone probably never referred to himself as a "gangster." Jeezus, group, when will we stop shucking ourselves? A garbage collector is a garbage collector, not a Sanitation Disposal and Facilitation Executive.)

To the people who've asked me to review NET, the Channel 28 items particularly: okay. But not right now. Look, it's like this: KCET programs some of the finest hours television has to offer ... Fritz Weaver and Uta Hagen doing Sandburg's poetry, Lotte Lenya in an hour of Kurt Weill cabaret music, Dustin Hoffman in a brilliant production of *Journey of the Fifth Horse, Black Journal* ... but National Educational Television is not what is having an effect on this country today. Nine out of ten dial-twiddlers, given the option of three national channels and half a dozen locals, will opt for a re-re-run of *Dr. Ehrlich's Magic Bullet* before they'll tune in for a little smarts on Channel 28. Anyone not picking up on the joys NET is offering is a shmuck. No help for them. But it's not the intellectual fare on NET that is shaping and twisting and warping this country ... and so right now, with the smell of fire and destruction in the air, I've pretty much committed myself to examining *mass* programming. This does not mean your steadfast columnist will not, from time to time, do a fancy number on some item of NET grandeur. It just means the times are perilous, and there isn't a moment to be spared belaboring those who are *already* on the side of the angels.

To the lady who hit me with the fluoridation problem: I've done some research on your claims, and I'm forced to the conclusion that you're on to something. No, it isn't a heinous Communist Conspiracy, but there *is* some rational doubt about how good fluoridation can be for human beings. Unfortunately, as I said in my earlier response, this is a television column, and while I go pretty far afield each week—we got into *this* via the chemical/bacteriological warfare column I did a while back—I choose not to lift the banner on *every* cause. I mean, really, I hit 35 years of age on May 27th, darlin', and that makes me five years past being trustable, so who'd listen anyhow?

On the matter of new shows, I caught the debut of the nighttime *Dick Cavett Show* (Monday, Tuesday & Friday nights, 10:00, ABC), and I've got to report it is a ball. Cavett, who got bounced off daytime programming (I suspect because his brand of humor and simple honesty was too tough for the soaper-oriented *yentas* to handle with the sun shining), is genuinely inveigling, urbane, puckish, adroit at listening, and manages by dint of his gallows humor to work himself into syntactical cul-de-sacs that are rather more charming than the studiedly sniggering dead ends up which Carson and Joey Bishop usually thrash themselves. The show I caught had James Coburn, Candy Bergen, Liza Minnelli and Truman Capote as guests. It was the first time I was able to take Capote, a writer whose talents, to be Christian about it, are vastly overpraised. There was a strangely honest interchange between the Misses Bergen/Minnelli about being rich little kids in Beverly Hills and—again, in a strange way—Cavett silkily played interlocutor, drawing ease in repartee from them. What it is Cavett possesses, that makes him a runaway winner as a talk-show host, is something that seems pure and fresh; something that is sickly sour when exuded by Joey Bishop or Merv Griffin or Johnny Carson. It *appears* to be a depth of character that goes beyond the mere manipulation of charisma employed by these others. In any case, I suggest you catch Cavett. He may not be a replacement for the Smothers Brothers, but there is *something* happening there ... and I have this theory that (as with Lenny Bruce and SmoBro) the commitment of dissent is *forced* on certain men, because of the time and the place. Cavett may well be the next prophet in this regard.

Of course, if he's smart, he'll reject the mantle. Our society (and that includes *us,* fellow assassins) has a nasty tendency to kill its poets and prophets, or drive them inexorably to their personal madhouses (as I said in a literary essay somewhere). Whether Muhammad Ali or Lenny, Malcolm X or what was left of Dylan Thomas by the time the U.S. got to use him—genius affronts us. We chivvy and harass it, and slaughter it. So if Cavett doesn't want to wind up like Stan Bohrman or Les Crane or the Smothers Brothers, he'd better opt for the wise man's position—the show must go on, and leave the dissent to those who dig slashing their wrists.

And for my final item this week, I have to make a retraction. Thus proving flexibility is the watchword of this column, and if you can show me the error of my ways ... I'll get very uptight.

I bummed *Mod Squad* many months ago.

On the basis of only a few shows.

Those were shows produced in execrable taste with a minimum of articulation or inventiveness.

Last week I was dragooned into attending a special screening of two *Mod Squad* episodes produced by Harve Bennett. Mr. Bennett wrote one of them, and William Wood (who is about as golden a writer as this town has seen in many moons, WGAw please note) wrote the other. The first was about a draft resister whose father was a brigadier general in Viet Nam and how his refusal to not only not register, but to use violence of *any* kind, finally ends in triumph and tragedy. The other show was about a militant black priest who is drummed out of the Church for his activities. Neither show copped-out. The three undercover kids who work for the Laws were used eminently well in context; the acting was, in the main, superlative; the scripts were authentic and honest; and the series has developed into one of the heavier items in mainstream programming.

So I have to retract what I said earlier (though what I said about those early shows in particular still stands) when I recommended you avoid *Mod Squad* like the Dutch Elm Blight. Catch the shows produced by Mr. Bennett. I do not think you will be too upset by my urging.

Because it seems that Mr. Bennett and his new story editor, Rita Lakin, are keeping their promises to their writers: say what you want to say. And if this is the case, which it seems to be (because ABC backs off and lets the kids play when the ratings develop a thyroid condition), then *Mod Squad* is the place to watch for the good writing.

In this respect, Mr. Bennett and Miss Lakin have discussed script with your demon columnist. At the moment I'm still a bit gunshy from my *Name Of The Game* experience. But we shall see . . . we shall see. . . .

As you read this, the mayoral election will, by a week, be dead history. But as I write it, the thing has just happened. I spent my birthday surrounded by friends, watching the results come in, interspersed with snatches of *A Hard Day's Night*. It was a surrealist nightmare. One of the rare video experiences of my life, on a par for impact with the McCarthy-Army hearings and the JFK funeral. It was that unbelievable commingling of reality and fantasy that ends with the dragon devouring St. George. And now, as I sit here, woebegone, sunk in my flesh like a tired old man, I feel the anger rising out of my gut, and all I can say to that 53% of Los Angeles who sold themselves and their brothers out is, damn you. *Damn you!*

A few days ago, when I trotted my week's murmurings in to the offices of managing editor Jack Burgess, he put his cast-clad leg up on the desk, fixed me with an editorial stare of singular penetration, and said, "Say, Ellison, why don't you talk about some of the good things on television instead of always bitching?" Well, he didn't say it *quite* like that (he usually calls me "jerko" instead of "Ellison"), but he *did* precisely say, "We're trying to alter the thrust of the paper, make it a little more constructive, and well, why don't you talk about some of the good things on Channel 28, for instance?"

I could not be more delighted that at long last the volcanic powers of the *Free Press*, long used to disrupt our community and spread commiesymp pornographic dissension, will be employed to heal the running sores and knit up the raveled sleeve of our fractured city. Huzzah, I say.

But—aside from the understanding when I took on this column that I'd write what I darned well pleased—there are a number of reasons why I harp more on what's wrong than what's good. I'll get to that in a moment, but first let me list all the subjects on which I've said nice cute pretty things:

A rock group named The New Wave; *Laugh-In; The Smothers Brothers Comedy Hour; The Ghost and Mrs. Muir;* Edward Mulhare in particular; *Mission: Impossible; Adam-12* the sign-off sermon; Les Crane; Stan Bohrman; *He & She*; three different movies-for-TV; a dozen different Saturday morning cartoons; Diana Ross and the Supremes; Ivan Dixon; a *Name Of*

The Game segment and it's writer/producer/director Leslie Stevens; the ACLU; Ralph Williams; Universal producer George Eckstein; NBC's *First Tuesday* series; Doug McClure; Norman Lear & Bud Yorkin; their pilot of *Those Were The Days;* the ex-sheriff of Fort Worth, Cato Hightower; CBS's *60 Minutes* series; Gov. Charles Percy; the *Mod Squad* shows produced by Harve Bennett; a buncha old shows like *Naked City* and *The Troubleshooters;* Bob Culp; Bill Cosby; *some* of the writers in the Writers Guild; Cesar Chavez and the UFWOC; and not least, Dustin Hoffman, *Black Journal* and half a dozen other shows on Channel 28.

Now, for a cynical, bitter anthracite-hearted, asp-tongued guttersnipe such as myself—who doesn't like much of anything or anybody to begin with—that seemingly endless compendium of praiseworthy topics (hardly complete, merely a smattering from 35 weeks of this column) seems to me to indicate a definite bending over backward to be nice.

Not once have I said what a bore Red Skelton is. Never anywhere in these columns have I remarked on Ed Sullivan's mangling of the English language. Nowhere have I made sly references to how many times Arlene Francis has had her face lifted. I even refrain from bum-rapping Johnny Carson—the world's oldest Huckleberry Finn—or spending the vitriol necessary to demolishing Joey Bishop, as phony a flag-waver as ever touted motherhood, apple pie and the Amurrican Way!

So, though I look-with-alarm frequently, kind thoughts and cherry blossoms are not beyond my capabilities. It's just that they nauseate me.

And, as for Channel 28 . . .

I refer good old Jack Burgess to my last week's column, in which I explained why I didn't spend more time on NET and Channel 28, which should explain *that.*

But the reason I dwell more at length on the things wrong is that the good things take care of themselves.

193

Let's face it, even though there are an enormous number of bummers going down in the country today, this is still the number one place to live. (Which may not be saying much when you consider Brazil, Czechoslovakia, France or India.) For every stupid act committed by someone in authority, there is one that brings a smile to the face. Sure, cops are busting kids left and right for pot, but Leary got turned loose. Sure, we're still fighting in Viet Nam, but the dissent movement against ROTC has grown big and even partially successful. Sure, we're polluting the air, but even a clown like Nixon has laid the law down to the automobile manufacturers: find a replacement for the internal combustion engine. Sure, jazz died, but it got replaced by better pop music than we've ever known before.

It's the sound of the other hand clapping, gang.

But those good things will take care of themselves. They *will* happen. The good things we *need* to happen don't get enough press. They don't get talked about enough. That's what I'm about. You see, it's like this: doing a column on television, and moving around the country as I do, I get to make some direct linkages between what we are *really* like, and what *TV tells* us we're like. There is an enormous gap. My comments usually tend to fall into the foggy area of that gap. In the area where we need to know.

For me to spend a column telling you how good a rerun of Kubrick's *Paths of Glory* might be, is to waste your time, the Freep's space, and my brilliant way with words. I would much rather hip you to how they're using a blonde cupcake named Kam Nelson on *The Groovy Show* to sell a debased image of American femininity; or try to explain one of the reasons why the TV programming structure is corrupt in its use of "second leads" to hook the younger generations. This, it seems to me, is the kind of job that needs to be done, which I can do, that nobody else appears to be doing.

(Of course, it has its bizarre moments. F'rinstance, after my piece of Tom Reddin's debut, I received word that George Putnam was a big fan of this column. It gave me pause. If Putnam, whom I despise, likes me . . . then I'm in deep trouble.)

And the final reason why I don't simply report the good things that will be available on your screens in the weeks to come, is that the *TV Guide* listings handle that more than adequately. I tend to think of my readers as bright enough to know that television (at its best) is as worthwhile an art form as ballet, the opera, books, movies, and painting. Assuming that, I must then assume that my readers will cast through their weekly TV listings to spot the items that will enrich them, and watch accordingly. If I were to spend time commenting on good shows (usually already aired) that simple intelligence should prompt my readers to catch, I'd be carrying coals to Newcastle.

Which is not to say if something meritorious comes along that I'll ignore it. My aim in these columns is to present a fully rounded picture of what's happening on the glass teat.

Does that answer your question, Mr. Burgess?

And just so you won't think this entire column is an exercise in "What I shoulda said to him was . . .", I offer the following observation of the TV-season-to-come.

This year, on prime-time, there are nine series in which the lead character is a widow or widower, struggling manfully to bring up tots in a world generally no more threatening than an afternoon at Disneyland.

Next season, the total will jump to thirteen.

The Brady Bunch is tagged as: the romantic adventures of Robert Reed and Florence Henderson as a newly married couple who each bring three children to their second marriage.

The Courtship of Eddie's Father is Bill Bixby as a widower with a little boy and a Japanese nanny, Miyoshi Umeki.

The Governor and J.J. has Dan Dailey as the widowed governor of a midwestern state (wonder why they didn't make it a deep south state, hmmm?), his political activity and his relationship to his 24-year-old daughter, Julie Sommars. (Having seen Julie Sommars, were this not Blandsville TV, Inc., we might make some interesting conjectures as to their relationship, but, well . . .)

And . . .

On the press handout I received from Don Fedderson Productions, listing their two already established shows, *Family Affair* and *My Three Sons,* I found word of a new Fedderson project, a classic of originality, whose bold new directions can best be ascertained by reprinting *exactly* what is said of all three series:

FAMILY AFFAIR: CBS, 7:30 P.M., Thursdays; 30-minute episodic comedy (film); Bachelor and his English valet try to raise seven-year-old twins and a teen-age girl.

MY THREE SONS: CBS, 8:30 P.M., Saturdays; 30-minute episodic comedy (film); Fred MacMurray tries to raise three sons, aided by Bill Demarest, without the woman's touch.

TO ROME, WITH LOVE: CBS, 7:30 P.M., Sundays; 30-minute episode comedy (film); John Forsythe, a recent widower, takes his three young daughters to live in Rome to get away from the unhappy memories of their loss.

Now, I ask you, Jack Burgess, with 7½ hours of prime-time every week given over to this kind of horse-shit, what would you have me do? Turn my back and talk about NET's *Black Journal* and how it's helping to prove to America that the black man is a vital and important factor in our finally growing up? I should talk about a show that the intellectuals will watch and the scuttlefish won't (many can't even *get* the Channel 28 programs in their area), while prime time tells everyone that the only difference between

Hope Lange and Diahann Carroll is a little natural rhythm?

The network mufti who bought all of this drivel, from *The Doris Day Show* to *Here's Lucy,* in their paralyzing fear of portraying anything even remotely resembling the realities of life in These United States, have opted for crippled families of husbandless wives or wifeless husbands, all playing Pygmalion to raise their kids with a vested interest in "acceptable morality" and the beliefs of generations nudging the grave.

The trappings may be a bit different from show to show—one a governor, another the ruler of the Ponderosa—but the situations that can be devised for these hidebound, limited life styles are all so drearily familiar that we run the risk of *turning-off* the very young people who *need* to turn to television for contact with the outside world.

I can see decades of kids just now getting into the streets, who *never* watch TV, because they've been in that elevator again and again and again. And asses like Reagan wonder why there is a marked difference between what *his* world is supposed to be like, and the world of the kids who marched on People's Park.

The answer, Mr. Reagan, is that you were brought up to swallow, whole, the hack ideas of situation comedy writers, but the kids have seen those same dumb shows so many times they know the climaxes after the opening commercial.

They, and we, but certainly not you, Mr. Reagan, want a world that is something more than a situation comedy.

And if you don't get with *that* truth, friend, you may live to see the day when the option won't be picked up on this country. And unlike *Death Valley Days,* Reagan, when you get a country canceled, you get no reruns, no residuals.

35: 1 AUGUST 69

Don't ask. Just accept my apologies. Almost four solid months of traveling around, lecturing, getting in trouble, trying to beat short-story deadlines and the shrieking imprecations of NBC in my ears (they wanted the revised pilot segment treatment of my impending series, *Man Without Time*). I kept promising Burgess and the Freep Group I'd get a column in to them ... but before I could get to the typewriter there I was in Boulder, Colorado or Madeira Beach, Florida or Clarion, Pennsylvania, God, I'm weary.

But I'm back. For those of you who inquired of the *Free Press* what had happened to Ellison, and seemed saddened that the column was not forthcoming—bless you. It won't happen again; I solemnly promise. For those of you who were delighted I'd passed from human ken—eat your hearts out. I'm back.

And to pleasure those of you who went seven weeks without the cinnamon taste of Truth, here is a triple-length column. It is also triple-length to bug those of you who can't even stomach a regular-sized portion of these here now goodies. (It'll be a disjointed column, because it contains the beginnings of three other columns I started during the layoff, but I'll separate the sections with bullets and if the sterling typesetting department can figure it all out, we shouldn't run into too much confusion.) So ... onward!

*

I'm out on another foray into the Great American Heartland, reporting back in (as Irwin Shaw put it) "where I think I am ... and what this place looks like today."

As I write this, I'm 31,000 feet in the air (sans acid), or so Braniff tells me. In the seat in the front and to the left of me, a blonde cupcake with a Shirley Temple postiche is sleeping with her seat tilted back so that I get an unobstructed view down past her black bra, and onto the snowy slopes of her capacious bosom.

A little while ago this sensual maiden, in an attempt to establish a liaison my shy, retiring nature can only suppose was sexual in nature, asked me if I was with The Beach Boys. (On a flight midway between Tampa and Denver, surrounded by neat little junior executives and Peter Gunn-haircutted NASA space engineers, I reluctantly admit I stand out like a fresh plot-twist on a situation comedy, with my long hair and leather vest, but The BEACH Boys!?!)

I told her no, I wasn't a rock musician, though I do hum a lot, no, I am a TV WRITER. I could have said I was a television columnist or a science fiction novelist, but those occupations simply don't have the glamour of being heavy behind showbiz, and while I am not, strictly speaking, a sexual insatiable, a man would be a fool to pass up a chance to keep in practice, and there's always the chance ... well, the inflight potties on airliners are small, but where there's a will, there's always a way....

"Ah!" this fire-maiden says to me, "you write tee-and-vee! I watch it alla time!"

My heart leaps in my chest.

I have here an opportunity unparalleled in the history of this column, right at my fingertips, to plumb the mind of what seems to be a typical young female television viewer. To ascertain, from the grass roots, if you will, what is drawing approbation and denigration via the tastes of the Average American.

"Tell me, young lady," I say, with a disarming grin, exposing my dimples, "what do you watch—when you watch?"

199

She senses she is on trial, that her words may shape the designs of High-Echelon Programming, and without a pause she replies, "Oh, God, I *LOVE* Tom Jones!"

She repeats it. Love. Tom Jones. Her Graf Zeppelin breasts heave at mention of the magic name, causing to be born in me a moment's panic at fear of the already sorely tried black bra rending with a fearful shriek, sending those cannonball convexities hurtling into my face. Fortunately, she's turned around in the forward seat, and the trajectory would just miss my right ear.

"What is it about Mr. Jones that so delights you?" I inquire, shifting slightly further out of the line of fire.

"Why, the way he sings, prithee, good sirrah," she responds. "He sings like'a angel."

"Of course, of course," I stammer. She is looking at me in a manner I take to approximate that given to Cary Grant in *Gunga Din* when the *thugee* killers of Kali find him defiling their temple. "To be sure, the way he sings. An angel, of course. Nay, an *arch*angel! But what else?"

She subsides, willing to give me another chance. Then, palpitating handsomely, she rises once more. "He's *very* good-looking."

(So is a side of prime rib, I think. To myself.)

"And he dances so nice." (Nicely, I think. To myself.) (Have you ever stopped to consider the extent of the shit up with which a man will put when there is a possibility of getting laid? Lawd, what shabby creatures we are!)

"And when he teases the girls in the bleachers, I could just . . ." She doesn't complete the sentence, but suddenly, 31,000 feet in the air, there is the moist scent of female musk.

I crimson, blanch, and cough to cover my embarrassment. "Are you, perhaps, inveigled by the production values of the show?" I ask.

"The what?"

"The pro—" Then I stop. I suddenly recall a special moment when I went on a road tour with The Rolling

Stones, several years ago. We were in Sacramento, I believe (after three days of gigs-and-planes I couldn't tell San Jose from San Diego, except San Jose is where we had to go in and out of the stadium in an armored car because the crowds were so big and ruthless). It was a twitchy crowd that had filled the auditorium. Rows of cops up and down the aisles. The groupies and teeny-boppers were pitched at the fracture point. They'd run out of jellybeans to throw on the stage and had started tossing underpants, bras, kotex, jewelry, anything that wasn't hammered down. The preliminary acts had come and gone, and now the Stones were on. You couldn't even hear them. The crowd noise—from where I stood in the wings—was like the sound of waves washing up on a beach. Or maybe like that of a wounded animal. A riot broke out in back. Cops put it down. The manager was getting uptight. His auditorium was hung with tapestries and expensive drapes. He went from uptight to outright terrified when three young birds boiled out of the audience and tried to climb over the wheelchair cases in the front in an attempt to leap the orchestra pit and get on stage.

He came over to me, and whispered, "Are you with them?" I nodded that I was. "Look, tell this one nearest you"—he meant Bill Wyman, who was closest to the stage-right wing—"tell him I'm going to lower the fire curtain . . . and they should step back three paces so it doesn't hit them." I said okay, and when Bill caught my signal and moved close enough for me to howl the instructions over the music and the crowd noise, I gave the word. He nodded, and passed it down the line to Brian Jones, Keith Richards and Mick Jagger. Charlie Watts, the drummer, was already well back of the drop-point. Three paces back is what the manager wanted.

Mick and Brian Jones took three steps *forward*. It was now virtually impossible to seal off the stage . . . and the crowd was getting crazier. Then Mick started to tease the girls. He moved sinuously, getting them

201

even more turned-on, if that was possible. Then he slowly stripped off his jacket, wriggling out of it while holding the hand-mike. As they shrieked and moaned to be thrown the incredible souvenir of their love-idol, Mick folded the jacket into a little square, and held it out over the footlights. The girls tore their hair and cried and beat the arms of their seats. The sound climbed till you could hear nothing but the blood pounding in your temples. And just when the animal horde thought they were going to get the jacket, he spun neatly and dropped it onstage behind him.

Then they broke and ran. Hundreds of them. They came right through the cops, slamming them into the walls. They went over the seats, and hit that row of cripples in their wheelchairs like a Kansas twister. The first onslaught of young girls fell into the orchestra pit and the others went right over their backs like troops crossing barbed wire on the backs of their buddies. (I heard a report there were fifteen broken backs in that batch.)

It was crazy as sixteen battlefields. Screaming, sliding chicks, crawling on their bellies across the stage—and the Stones were already gone. They were by that time in the basement, going out a service door, into an unmarked little compact car (the kids would never suspect it was the getaway vehicle, because the decoy Continental was parked in front of the stage door), and were out of the area, on the way to the airfield where their private plane was already warming up. But back in the theater, a thousand mindless little hippie mommas were tearing that jacket to shreds, and themselves in the bargain.

I remember that now, listening to Miss Chest of '69 tell me how thrilling it was to see Tom Jones "tease" the girls in the bleachers on his show. I remember, and I have the insight (not for the first time) that there was nothing noble in Mick Jagger's "tease." He didn't take those three steps forward, rather than back, because he cared about his audience and wanted those kids to get their money's worth. He despised the kids. Traveling with the group for three days I could understand why. The fans were as filled with love and adoration as the cannibals who tore Sebastian to shreds and ate him in *Suddenly, Last Summer*. They were a mindless, slavering horde; individually they were lovely kids, but jammed together they were as terrifying as the *marapunta*, the army ants.

Jagger despised them, and he had goaded them purposely into wrecking his vengeance on themselves—as well as $160,000 worth of damage to the theater. It was a mind-croggling demonstration of the love/hate relationship between superstars and their insatiable fans.

And I had seen that same detestation in Tom Jones when he turned-on the girls in his audience.

And it tied in with the artificial "soul" of Tom Jones singing, with the Vegas-style trappings he employs to straddle the line between music the older generations can accept, and the younger dig. It was a keynote to the hypocrisy and shallowness of the Tom Jones scene, the Tom Jones show, and the ease with which people allow themselves to have their energy tapped and their emotions fucked-over.

I guess, in that moment, 31,000 feet in the air, I understood why I had always been vaguely repelled by Mr. Jones, who sings like a angel.

That he is a sensation among women of all ages from one corner of this country to the other—a phenomenon I'd glimpsed in New York, Texas and Florida—is a dead giveaway to the state of flux in which the sexual idiom of our times finds itself. In a society where everyone was getting it frequently and healthily and effectively, Tom Jones would probably appeal to an audience as large as the one that digs Mrs. Miller.

*

Hey, did I tell you I lost that Writers Guild election? Well, yeah, I did. Predictable, of course. They take unkindly to people who Speak Out. Might make waves and jeopardize the gravy train's journey to the sea. George Clayton Johnson and Joyce Geller and all the other young turks got defeated as well. With one or two exceptions they put back in office on the Guild Board the older, more stable, better-oriented gentlemen who know how to "talk to Lew Wasserman" and his crowd. And I've been told that the reason I'm considered *persona non grata* with my fellow Guild members is not so much that I'm a loudmouthed, obnoxious troglodyte, but because I did that column about the writers in these pages some months ago. They didn't like having it pointed out to them that it was, after all, *we writers* who do all those crummy scripts. To be honest, I love my Guild, and I would give almost anything to be back in the good graces of my fellow scriveners, but I have a hunch the price would be too high.

And besides, if my series goes on the air, alla sudden I'm going to be a very popular guy among my buddy writers, because I'll be the story editor, and doing the hiring of scripters. At which point my ugly penchant for revenge will manifest itself. A chick I know was surprised a while back that I still carried a grudge from the year before. I hipped her that that was nothing: "Baby," I said, "I'm still working on grudges from 1937."

*

Ambivalence, the curse of keeping your mind open and receptive to new ideas, assails me this week. The Apollo 11 went up, came down, went up again, and came down again. Like you, I sat Elmer'd (as in the glue) in front of various TV screens, watching us engaged in our first activity on alien soil: dropping litter. It scared the ass off me.

(A reader of this column sent along a copy of *I.F.*

Stone's Weekly, with the following circled for my attention, and I pass it on to you:

(PLAQUE FOR THE MOON LANDING

(Here Men First Set Foot Outside The Earth On Their Way To The Far Stars. They Speak Of Peace But Wherever They Go They Bring War. The Rockets On Which They Arrived Were Developed To Carry Instant Death And Can Within A Few Minutes Turn Their Green Planet Into Another Lifeless Moon. Their Destructive Ingenuity Knows No Limits And Their Wanton Pollution No Restraint. Let The Rest Of The Universe Beware.)

In the background, as I write this, Jeff Beck is singing, and all that nice stuff gives me hope that perhaps I'm grown too cynical, and there may be hope.

But . . . ambivalence!

You see, I'm a science fiction writer, among other things. I've been a reader of the form since I first came upon Jack Williamson's story *Twelve Hours To Live* in a 1946 issue of *Startling Stories.* I remember very well, back in 1952, when I was 17 and in high school in Cleveland, a reporter for the *Cleveland Press* coming to interview me and the other members of the fledgling Cleveland SF Society. I remember this clown's unrestrained laughter when I told him (and this was pre-Sputnik) that we would surely have men on the moon within fifteen years. He wrote an article that made us all look like morons, made us seem to be coocoos who probably believed in ghosts, elves, a flat Earth and other improbables like an actor becoming Presidential timber. A few years later, when Sputnik went up, I took my copy of that article and went to find the reporter, at the *Press* offices, to rub his porcine nose in it. But he'd died. It was a bitch of an anti-climax.

So you see, I've been dreaming—along with all the other sf fans—about that moment when the first men would get Lunar dust on their boots. Unfortunately, for me, it was another anti-climax.

I'll admit I was knocked out by Buzz Aldren bounding about the Moon like a kangaroo, but there were so many negative vibes attendant on the project that it really brought me down.

For instance, nitty-gritty, we did it like jerks. It cost us I can't remember how many billions to put all that scrap metal up there, merely to haul men, when a mechanical probe such as the Russians postulated could have done the same thing, and achieved the very same results. But the plain fact is that we wouldn't have gotten the appropriations for the project if it *hadn't* hauled the three astronauts. People just don't get excited about machines going to the Moon, but they do about other men. The Russians correctly bummed us for risking lives in a flamboyant publicity gig that could have been accomplished as easily by a robot.

But a robot wouldn't have been as inspiring for Nixon and his carnival. "Participation Day," indeed! And that simpering buffoon on board the *Hornet* when they splashed down. The insipid remarks he made were almost as stultifying as the dumb things the astronauts themselves said from space. (I, for one, am sick to the teeth of hearing the Bible quoted to me from Out There. It's bad enough we have to put up with so much outdated philosophy back here on the mudball. It would have pleasured me no end had they landed and come upon the First Church of Throgg the Omniscient, there in the Sea of Tranquility. Wow, can you see the seizure Bishop Sheen would have had!?!) (Or maybe, simply, God appearing in a burning bush and saying, "Okay, you guys, knock off that shit!")

You see, it just sorta killed all the adventure for me. Maybe because I'd taken that first journey so many times being led by Ray Bradbury and Robert Heinlein and Isaac Asimov and Arthur C. Clarke, who dreamed all these dreams twenty years ago. I can see why all the rest of you dug it . . . inherently it is the single most exciting thing that's happened since Christ splashed down on Calvary, but for the guys who knew without a doubt that it was coming—all the science fiction fans and writers—it was a letdown . . . I guess. At least a little.

But I understand there were some marvelous serendipitous benefits: such as the crime rate in the country dropping to almost nothing. All the crooks and heistmen and cat burglars were in front of *their* sets, too. Right up to the point where Nixon said the Apollo 11 flight had brought the world closer together than ever before.

After which point the crooks turned off their sets, and went out to mug old ladies for seventy-four cents.

*

It was my own fault, my error, and I deserved precisely what I got. Turning for the David Frost talk show on Channel 11, I hit 7, the phone rang, I turned around to answer it, and when I turned back, I was watching The King Family. Oh, my dear God. Can such things be!?!

There were a great many studiedly square-looking people of varying ages (slightly overweight suburban ladies with plastic hair dominated; the kind of chicks who tell their old men, no, I can't fuck tonight, Fred, I had my hair done today), and they sorta sang.

I guess that's what they were doing, when they weren't being homey and cute.

Hincty songs so devoid of even that mystical "blue-eyed soul" that I had to dash to my music and lay on about forty minutes of Shakey Jake, The Dells and Richie Havens.

What kind of people dig The King Family? Can anyone tell me? Aside from wanting to ball three or four of the King Kousins, there was such a dearth of meritorious reasons for watching that show, I cannot fathom why various syndicates and networks keep thrusting the Kings before our already squared eyeballs. For they seem to me to represent in totality a template of all that is fabricated, artificial, lowbrow and meretricious on the American Scene. They strive so massively to be cleancut that I suspect most of the men in the group have hernias.

How I would love to see a live King Family segment after someone had dumped specially made acid in the water cooler. "And now, all you friendly folks out there in the Great American Heartland, something special! Right here, tonight, on our show, you're going to see an authentic King Family orgy, with the King Kiddies and the King Kousins engaging in one hundred and thirty-five vile and noxious sexual perversions, all at once . . . and while the King Sisters make it with (respectively) a St. Bernard, a Tibetan Yak, a Sumatran black panther and a sex-crazed chicken, Alvino Rey will play accompaniment on his talking electric tissue-paper-and-comb; his selection for tonight is the Love Theme From Marat/Sade. And for a once in a lifetime showbiz thrill, we've even brought Granny King on tonight with her specialty number, wherein she machine-guns two hundred, assorted blackjack and slot machine losers from the six biggest casinos in Las Vegas! Okay, gang, everybody start rubbing on the Velveeta!"

The King Family is the Harold Robbins of music. More below the belt than that I cannot get.

*

One of the commitments that kept me from writing this column for seven weeks was a stint as Guest Lecturer at the University of Colorado Writers' Conference in the Rockies. I did two weeks in company with such eminent writers as Richard Gehman, George P. Elliott, Vance Bourjaily and Pulitzer Prize-winning poets Alan Dugan and Richard Eberhart.

On Friday, June 27th, I was hauled, along with Gehman and the incredible Dugan, into Denver, to do a talk show on KOA-TV.

The host of the show, a self-satisfied, rigid-minded

gentleman named Bill Barker, cozied with the three of us before we taped (the show was to be aired the following Sunday night). He stressed one point: this was a freewheeling interview show in which he most sought a level of depth-analysis that would enrich the subject. He was not after cheap sensationalism or the sort of "controversy" Joe Pyne seeks. We felt relieved; Gehman, as one of the premier non-fiction magazine writers of the past thirty years, had a store of anecdotes and opinions to impart ... and Dugan, who had won not only the Pulitzer for his brilliant poetry but also the National Book Award and the Prix de Rome, was an outspoken student of the passing scene. As for myself, I relished the opportunity to speak about the Writers' Conference and what it was doing to bring forth young talent.

Yet I should have known better. Though milder in his approach than Pyne, Barker was no better, no more noble than any other cheapjack interviewer on the boondock stations. The show opened with Barker asking us what he considered to be the responsibility of the writer. It was a strangely phrased question, foggy in its implications, but all three of us had done sufficient camera-time to re-parse it, knowing that to look confused or hesitant during an interview is to instantly invalidate anything you might say for a viewing audience. We began rapping about the writer's responsibility to tell the truth, to keep *au courant*, to be committed, to pursue every facet of a subject till he could present a fully rounded portrait.

Dugan—a tall, distinguished-looking, gentle man—made a side comment, nothing more than that, that it was also necessary to reproduce the *speech* of people almost phonographically, even if it meant using obscenity. It was a casual remark, but Barker pounced on it like a vulture finding carrion.

It led us into an ugly, circuitous argument about the necessity of the creator using whatever language he felt was most necessary to making his point. Barker started

209

laying that "why must you use filthy language" number on us. Dugan responded that if the word fuck appeared in the normal speech patterns of someone in a story or poem, to substitute copulate or a similar euphemism would be to corrupt the veracity of the image. Barker got uptight and started saying Dugan was a child with a foul mouth, using the words for shock value. This, to a man whose credentials as an artist are unimpeachable.

Things went from bad to horrendous. Barker baited Dugan, who rose to the bait only inasmuch as he used more fucks and damns and shits, just to drive Barker up the wall; thereby proving that the words were loaded for *Barker*, and caused *him* pain; it also allowed me to point out that it was the responsibility of the artist to de-fang those poisonous words so their meanings, not their emotional impacts were what counted.

Barker refused to listen. He raved and screeched, and when the show was finished, it looked like fine old Belgian lace, so filled was it with bleeps.

I'd confronted the stultifying provincialism before. You may recall my report on the TV talk show I did in Texas. But it keynoted for me one of the timorous areas of television programming, one of the disastrous hypocrisies that render so much of television impotent and valueless.

I recalled one of the major networks' broadcast of a filmed report on the President's Commission Analysis of Violence, some months ago. It was told through the medium of interviews with people on the streets who had been interviewed for the Report, and interspersed with charts and quotes from the Report itself. Every time someone used an obscenity, it was bleeped. It made for a curiously comic program. Not merely because the viewer would substitute something far more offensive for the bleep, but because it was a flagrant example of television trying to protect its audience from that which it already knew.

Is there anyone in America over the age of six months who is not familiar with the vagaries of the vulgar, all the way from shucky-darn to cunt? Is there anyone who will not admit that these are mere *words*, that they bear no more *de facto* power than a soap bubble?

Then precisely what is it that makes them taboo? From whom are we keeping these words? From the fringe coocoos who are offended when an astronaut says damn or shit when something unpleasant has happened onboard his rocket? Are we to remain a nation of hypocrites, lumbered by our most provincial and hidebound elements? It is as valid a concept as writing every book on the level of Dick and Jane in order not to corrupt the minds of the young.

It becomes readily obvious, if one extrapolates. that more and louder use of these words would rapidly render them as meaningless and powerless as "where it's at," "do your thing," "confrontation" and such similar jingoisms. And what would emerge from such a situation would be a need to speak better, more precise, more original and imaginative obscenities. Which could only enrich the language. So ... yours for bigger and better fucks ...

36:   15 AUGUST 69

Commencing the middle of September, stay away from restaurants on Tuesday nights.

Because, if I'm correct in my evaluation of the dangers, of provincialism in the thinking of network programming, Tuesday night television is going to be so gawd-awful on NBC that everyone will flock out to eat, and you won't be able to get seated for two hours.

I'll work from the specific to the general on this one: hang on, it gets hairy.

September 16th is the Tuesday night season premiere on NBC. Let us consider what the top television network in the country has prepared for us:

7:30 . . . *I Dream of Jeannie*
8:00 . . . *The Debbie Reynolds Show*
8:30 . . . *Julia*
9:00 . . . *Tuesday Night Movies,* debuting in this fresh, bright, innovative 1969-70 season with Doris Day in *The Ballad of Josie.*

(About this last: one of the genuinely horrendous gut experiences of my recent past was finding myself crossing and re-crossing the continent via airplane several years ago, and being "treated" to *The Ballad of Josie* not once, twice or thrice, but *four* times in a month. Common decency forbids my explicating quite how bad the film is. Suffice it to say that it was the first time I ever considered leaving a movie in the middle, when I was 31,000 feet in the air; but until I solved the problem by locking myself in the plane's toilet with a William Golding novel, death seemed a more desirable choice than sitting through Doris in the Wild West again.)

There is no need to dwell on the already established and potentially inevitable level of paucity proffered by these series. If it were not for the ingenuousness of Miss Barbara Eden—one of the surest comediennes going—and Larry Hagman's herculean efforts at bringing some dignity to what is essentially a mindless enterprise, Tuesday night on NBC would be totally without light. And having given praise in the only quarter where it is deserved, I reluctantly address myself to considerations of ghastliness.

Bearing in the back of the mind the many paradigms of NBC's other female-oriented shows, as well as those on other networks—Lucille Ball, Doris Day, *Petticoat Junction*, *Mothers-In-Law*, *Family Affair*, *That Girl*, *The Flying Nun*, *Bewitched* (the one superlatively intelligent exception is *The Ghost & Mrs. Muir*)—one comes to a realization that Someone Up There is not only thirty years behind the times in terms of the Female Liberation Movement, but is easily thirty years behind in accepting reality. Even as blacks despise stereotypes of themselves in the mass media (though even the square Network Programmers are hip to how laughable it would be to try and get away with a Steppin Fetchit character), so do intelligent women, I've found. Dithering fumblefoots as portrayed by Lucille Ball or Marlo Thomas are as repellent to women of dignity and pride as *Julia* is the black community as a whole. As I understand it, that is not precisely what Afro-Americans intend when they refer to "pride in black." But I digress. We were rapping about women.

The Female Liberation Movement—and I have this on the best authority: a seven-foot blonde who manages to combine sensual femininity with a don't-fuck-with-me-self-assurance—is most lumbered by its own fifth column. Subversion from within. So many women have been brainwashed by the image of the happy little homemaker, birthing babies and cooing over the wonders of pre-soak Axion that it is virtually impossible to convince the mass of chicks that they are really truly

213

emancipated, and don't have to stagger about wearing a subservient facade.

And because of this fifth column, Network Programmers—who are 99% male, and what is worse 100% male chauvinist—keep playing to that image. Every season sees its share of Blondie-*Doppelgängers*. This coming season, Tuesday night on NBC will be surfeited with them.

Tossing aside the terminally damning obviousness that what they are dealing in are hoary clichés, the more serious indictment that can be laid on this kind of thinking is that it helps perpetuate an unrealistic view of an entire segment of the population. It aids and abets the dangerous gapping between reality and image in our society. When the ideal held up for a modern American woman to revere and emulate is no more demanding than Debbie Reynolds (as she plays it on her series), what can we expect but another generation of simpering female Dagwood Bumsteads? The only out the contemporary chick is offered in terms of TV images is Samantha (a witch), Jeannie (a genie), or Sister Bertrille (who can fly). The message is painfully clear; if you can't wiggle your nose and make miracles, or hop into the sky and fly away, or flip your ponytail and change the world, girls, pack it in and settle for being some guy's unpaid slavey. Because all those other women you see cavorting in phosphor-dot reality are inept, hampered with children, prone to execrable involvements or simply accident prone.

Around us, we see women taking the reins more and more in a world seemingly bent on being cruel to itself. There is hope, we feel, in the more sensitive rationality of women—to stop wars, to give the underdog an even break, to clean up the messes we guys have made. Yet on TV if we see a Committed Woman, she is usually a housewife taking time off from making nesselrode pie to carry a placard for allowing school kids to put on their yearly musicale. And she'll probably wind up in the slammer for it. But with funny. How does this com-

214

pare with the women I've seen on protest marches and rallies, who've been beaten senseless by cops' riotsticks? How does this compare with the women who went for a walk in 118° heat in the Imperial Valley, to support the grape boycott? How does this compare with the genuinely incredible women who ramrodded the Bradley campaign or fight for free speech, or went to Chicago and Washington and Selma?

This year we're going to get doctors who are heroes, school teachers who are heroes, lawyers who are heroes, and of course cops who are heroes. None of them are female. (Peggy Lipton on *Mod Squad* doesn't count. She isn't strictly speaking a cop, she's a noble fink for the fuzz, and besides, Pete and Linc usually wind up saving her attractive fanny.)

It's another scintillant TV season of lies and unusually off-center representations of still one more social element. Except this time it's a social element that is composed of half the population.

One can only wonder how much longer the birds are going to allow themselves to be used as consumer machines for pimple-disguiser, hair-remover, smell-deadener and uplift bras. How much longer before they start demanding some authentic portrayals of themselves as human beings?

Because, frankly, it's about time they made their move. It shouldn't have to fall to guys like me to tell them their shackles have been struck off. Or will they wake up only when guys like me demand our ribs back?

37:   22 AUGUST 69

Oh my, no sooner am I back in town, back writing the column, promising it won't be skipped again (after which, promptly, the very next week, it's skipped, thereby doing a gaslight number on my poor head), than I'm in trouble once more. How do I seem to offend you all? It's really uncanny! There's no telling *what* casual comment will outrage some ethnic group. It's enough to make a guy clam up and stay out of the line of fire. In fact, I can dig why all the scuttlefish refuse to "get involved" and speak out; hell, without even *trying* to piss someone off, you can have an entire social strata down sucking the marrow out of your bones.

This time it's the WASPs in my readership who are properly annoyed, because with all the civil rights action going down, they're the only group a commentator can bum-rap, without having himself protest-marched. Two weeks ago it seems I made sort of an offhand crack about the "alleged" existence of something the communications media call "blue-eyed soul."

Sort of Ajax-clean nitty-gritty Fights Back. Or something.

It all seemed pretty funny to me—honkies trying to horn in on what is clearly a black product. I didn't think *any*one took it seriously. But here come de mail, here come de mail, and I get four letters from WASPs in Tuston, La Canada, Glendora and (this one I don't even *believe*, it's *gotta* be a made-up) the City of Industry, all of which accuse me of being a traitor to my pigmentation because I won't credit Whitey with having soul. (Man, I was blown away! I didn't even know

216

those people out there had gotten shoes yet, much less learned to read! I mean, if they could read, then they must have seen there were other names on the ballot than Reagan or Nixon.)

So I'm all ready to drop a fragmentation item in this week's edition about how those kindly folk out there should take not just this column, but the entire Freep—both sections—roll it into a tight funnel and jam it up their blue-eyed soul. Feeling very smug, was I. Until I bought Tony Joe White's album, hoping some of the other cuts would be as heavy as *Polk Salad Annie*, and found out that down home voice was coming out of a good old boy who looked like a Florida redneck. Second biggest aural shock of my life. The first was finding out, about ten years ago, that Mose Allison was white.

So already I'm reeling, right?

Then I turned on the Johnny Carson thing a couple of weeks ago, August 5th to be precise, right after the column with that remark was published, and had my smug mind crinkled like Alcoa-Wrap. (You probably didn't hear it, what with all the shrieking in the land from the NarkDepart moving ·its families here and there. Personally, I chuckle and gloat at the beautiful inhumanity of it. Let *them* know what it's like to be naked and harassed. Don't try and make me feel bad because the Freep pulled their covers and "inconvenienced" them. I can't work up any sad about undercover finks having to move to new lairs and eyries, maybe sweating out a freako phone call or two. Now they know how the rest of us feel. We get the freako phone calls all the time. And worse. The "inconvenience" to the narco squad and their families doesn't seem to me one one-millionth as inhumane as the years spent in reform schools, county jails, penitentiaries and other gaols by kids whose worst affront to their society was taking a toke of grass. When marijuana is legalized—as it most certainly will be when Liggett & Myers, et al, find they can't advertise traditional can-

217

cer-sticks on TV; a certainty I gauge as inescapable when considered in the light of the information that L&M has copyrighted the words "Acapulco Gold"— when the powerful tobacco lobby in Washington gets behind grass in a sort of "joint effort" yuk yuk—who will repay all those kids for their ruined lives? Who will take their fingerprints out of the FBI files? Who will erase from their minds the memories of the smell of piss and disinfectant from how many lockups and drunk tanks? Who will put them back in college and make up the years they lost on the way to their B.A. or M.A.? Who will lobotomize the crime data they picked up in the slammer? Who will apologize for witch-hunting them, and treating them like criminals for a "crime" no worse than that perpetrated by every member of our parent's generation who sipped a teacup of Cosa Nostra bourbon in a speakeasy, 37 years ago? Who will pay reparations when pot is legal? Who? *No one*, that's who the bloody hell who! So I conceive of the Freep's publishing that secret list of nark addresses and phone numbers a courageous and significant gut-punch in the dirty war for justice. Beside that, dirty trick though it may be, the renting of new apartments for the secret police seems like a mere bagatelle. None of which has to do with the main topic of this week's column, but I felt compelled to get on the record, particularly after I spoke to a student group at Cleveland High School, out in the Valley, last week, and was called to task for the Freep's "inhumane act." So now you know where it's at for me. Back to the Johnny Carson Show, and blue-eyed soul, and what I started to say a while ago.)

There before me was one of the mythical creatures of all time—akin to dryads, hobbits, smoke ghosts and leprechauns—a chick with blue-eyed soul. This kid was called Elyse Weinberg, and she went about three points further toward gut-level than either Janis Ian or Buffy Sainte-Marie. She isn't as funky as Janis Joplin, she isn't as gothic-moded or genius'd as Laura Nyro, she isn't as gravelly as Judy Henske, she isn't as heavy or as gorgeous as Lotti Golden, but would you believe she puts Joan Baez and Judy Collins away proper?

So I had to re-gear my thinking—which is happening much too frequently these days for any security at *all*—and I had to wonder how and why such blue-eyed sisters as this Elyse chick and Laura Nyro and Lotti Golden and all the others suddenly came trumpeting on the scene. And naturally, I blamed TV for even this largesse: what else would you blame, in the Age of McLuhan, for everything from smog and violence to Elyse and the Dutch Elm Blight?

Where has this chick *been?* I asked me. And from the slag-heaps at the rear of my skull, a voice screamed, "You shmuck! Don Shain at Tetragrammaton Records told you this broad was dynamite two months ago, and he even sent you her record, and you stuck it up on the shelf because you were going out of town, so why don't you take it down and listen to it?" So I did, and you know, high pressure Shain was right: she's even heavier on records than she was on the tube. (The reason for that will close out this column and lead into the next, so bear it in mind.)

Where this chick had been, of course, was getting born. She didn't spring full-blown with a voice like that out of nowhere, like Athena from the forehead of Zeus. She was twenty years of shit-pop-music in the making. She is a natural reaction to Patti Page and Doris Day and even Jeri Southern. She and Lotti Golden and Janis Joplin and Laura Nyro are the female equivalents (coming on the scene a little later than their male counterparts) of Mose Allison, Mick Jagger, Bob Dylan, and most recently Tony Joe White. They were the men who studied not Julius La Rosa or Buddy Greco or Tony Vale, they were the ones who listened to Lightnin' Hopkins and Blind Lemon Jefferson and B.B. King. They were the ones who understood that the true voice of American Music was not in the phony cabaret idiom, the big-cufflink-whiteonwhite-shirt idiom. It was the sound of the black man with passion and verve.

And they revolutionized the sound of today. Granted, they followed Otis Redding and James Brown and Wilson Pickett out of the ghetto into Motown and Staxmoney villas, but they laid down the highest tribute ... even the Britishers. They said *this is the real sound*. And now the women have done likewise.

Elyse Weinberg and her white sisters are paying the highest tribute to Big Maybelle and Billie Holiday and Mildred Bailey. They are singing with the voice of the land. And they are saying to television that twenty years of proffering Dinah Shore and Lawrence Welk and Dean Martin is all they're going to give. They are saying that the Lennon Sisters and the King Family don't get it no more. They are saying that if there's going to be truth in the land, it's going to come first, as an example to others, in the songs and the singing.

Yet somehow television cannot comprehend the simple reality of such a situation. They still program prime-time hours of (such upcoming wowsers as) Leslie Uggams, the Lennons (presented, God help us, by Jimmy Durante!), the King Family, Dean Martin's Goldiggers, all the Vegas lounge acts—though the supreme nadir was reached when Sandler & Young, two Mafia rejects with voices as compelling as fishmongers suffering Cheyne-Stokes breathing, were given their own summer hour. They manage to ignore the enormous purchasing power of the young, whose taste in music run more to Stevie Wonder than Glen Campbell; they still trot out those dyspeptic old firehorses, and wonder why they aren't selling the depilatory and now-beverages.

But Lotti and Elyse and Janis and Laura are making all the waves, and the day is rapidly approaching when they will be freed from the slums of TV, the afternoon lip-synch dance shows, and will even put Diana Ross and her glitter scene to shame.

They will dominate. But not if they are treated the

220

way Elyse Weinberg was treated on the Carson Show, hosted by Flip Wilson; which brings me to the lead-in for next week's column. I'll start with Wilson and the shameful manner in which Elyse was shunted on and offstage ... and while I'm starting with Wilson, I'll proceed onwards and downwards with some observations about, uh, er, nigger comedians. But you've gotta understand ... some of my best friends ...

38: 29 AUGUST 69

So we'll understand from the outset just where I
stand in this *terra incognita* of racial identity, paddies
and jigaboos being what they are, let me take you back
back back through the veil of time to Chicago, 1961.
Rainbow Beach. You probably never heard of it. Little
shit strip of land on the scungy Lake Michigan shore.
Landed gentry, all white, naturally, decided they were
not going to follow suit with all the other beaches in
Chicago, were not going to integrate. No black allowed.
So, also naturally, the blacks decided to stage a swim-
in. God only knows why *anyone*—black or white—
would want to swim in that crud-infested water, but
they did. (As a matter of fact, it might well have solved
the entire race thing; no matter what color you were
when you went in, you'd be green when you came out.)

The ancestors of the Blackstone Rangers came out
on a Sunday with weapons, and were met by white
street gangs. It was brutal. Nobody won. Lotta heads
got dented.

The following week, everyone in Chicago knew there
was going to be worse trouble on the Sunday coming.
The South Side ghetto was an armed camp. Spade cab
drivers rode around with loaded shotguns on their laps.
White cops went in threes. Nobody in Highland Park
wised-off to his Negro help. Lorraine Hansberry wrote
a poem. James Baldwin got sent in by *Time* to cover it.

I went out on the beach. My sentiments went with
black. I was there to aid and abet the swim-in. Riot
started. Oh boy. Got my skull fractured by a black with
a tire iron, got my rib cage sprung by a white with a
length of chain. You see, the trouble was: I was gray.

222

Now you know where I'm at? Good. Just so long as we understand that your faithful columnist stands four-square for Justice, Decency, Equal Rights and All That Good Stuff.

Because what I want to rap about this week is, mainly, nigger comedians.

(I can just hear Lenny Bruce back there, affronted, saying, "Nigger? Nigger? What kind of a cheap hook is that? Jesus Christ, does he need cheap sensationalism to get their attention? Nigger!?! God, what bad taste!"

Okay, so you'll call me a kike and we'll call it even, and we'll move on.)

What leads me into these observations is the tail-off from last week's column, wherein I commented on the abominable treatment afforded singer Elyse Weinberg on *The Johnny Carson Show,* hosted by black comedian Flip Wilson. (No, scratch that. Knowing what comes next, let's refer to Wilson as a mocha comedian. Black connotes strength, even in coffee. Mocha is diluted, weaker, softer, ameliorative. Yeah, that pins Wilson for me. A mocha comedian. Light tan, with three lumps.)

How it happened was this: Elyse had been scheduled for the week preceding, but Carson got to rapping with some banal ex-vaudevillian, and time ran out. So Elyse was promised for the next night. She never showed. They shunted her around like REA Express. The following week, with Carson on sabbatical, and Wilson doing the turn, Elyse was slotted.

On a show distinguished by its paucity of talent (even the incredible Joe Tex was gawdawful), Elyse was bucked back and back and back till they managed to squeeze her in between a couple of pimple commercials. She did one number, no backdrop, perched on a stool circa Andy Williams 1965, showed none of the fire or verve so handily available on her album, and with a smattering of applause (as much as due a trained seal act), she was blacked out. It was ruthless treatment of a skillful performer, and if anyone conceived of that shot as furthering a career—forget it. But, annoyed at having watched that entire dumbass show for three and a half hours, just to see Elyse, and having been short-shrifted, I *did* derive one benefit: it exposed Flip Wilson to my penetrating gaze for a protracted period.

And, Elyse now passed into obscurity and last week's column, let me deal with the estimable Mr. Wilson, as a manifestation of his times.

For openers, he's about as funny as a ruptured spleen. Now, I am by no means calling for a return to Amos n' Andy—though they had the saving grace of being genuinely funny—but I'm observing jaundicedly that aside from Cosby and Dick Gregory, the last ten years of struggling for equal rights for blacks has produced a strain of handkerchief-head shuffling comics of the Flip Wilson/Scoey Mitchell sort that demeans the dues paid by millions of their brothers.

The genre comedians—Redd Foxx, Pigmeat Markham, Moms Mabley and others—*still* get denied prime-time exposure (unless you call Pigmeat slapping the *Laugh-In* cast with his famous pig bladder exposure), while the mocha comics slurp up the gravy with weak-wristed routines that present to the Honkie Mass a picture of the black man as little better than the good-natured, kinds dumb Uncle Tom was all recognize as thirty years out of date. Oh sure, every once in a while Wilson or Mitchell will make some fairly safe social comment about the Detroit Riots or looting or bigotry, but they are de-fanged comments, bearing none of the genuine rage we know lies in the world-view of every rational black man. They are the *bought* comedians. They are neither black nor white, but a colorless, emasculated something else. They have opted for show biz, for the phony camaraderie of the klieg lights. They have copped-out on their people and their destiny.

I cannot watch Flip Wilson and his breed with anything but contempt, even though I understand the glittery appeal inherent in belonging to that select little circle of stars, superstars and semi-stars. Nonetheless, it's a cheap in-group reward, a mess of pottage exchanged for dignity and responsibility to one's own kind.

Hell, Lenny was white, and he took more risks with his material in defense of the black man than Wilson or Mitchell or even Nipsey Russell has ever taken.

How it must gall a guy like Dick Gregory, who can't get booked on a major TV show, to see a hankie-top like Wilson hosting the top night-time talk show, playing the biggest clubs, working the lounges in Vegas, copping top bread for routines as simpering and approbation-seeking as the worst shuffle ever displayed. What must Gregory think, a man who lays it on the line as he does—for instance—in a new two-record set called *Dick Gregory: The Light Side: The Dark Side?* We hear the genuine humor of the black man thereon; we also hear his rage, his hatred, his frenzy, his demand for a better life . . . not only for blacks, but for poor stupid rednecks and even the rest of us provincial, terrified scuttlefish who walk through Spanish Harlem after midnight.

What does Cosby think of these others? He seems to be a man who has not deserted his people, who pours time and money and effort back into the black community. What does he think about those routines Wilson twinkles, in which the *new* cliché of the black man is tendered?

In Mario Puzo's brilliant novel of the *mafiosi, The Godfather* (which I recommend to you unreservedly), the second- and third-generation Sicilian-Americans refer to the old-style caricature *capos* as "Moustache Petes." What do the new blacks, the Clarence Williams and the Hari Rhodes, call the Flip Wilsons? What name is Scoey Mitchell given by Greg Morris? Does Otis Young identify with his soul brother Nipsey Russell?

How nauseating it is to realize that the cunning racist society in which we move has once more manipulated its opposition. If you can't take the gun and the hate

225

away from the black man, then buy him. Give him prime-time shots, give him Harry Cherry suits and good living, and he'll prance around on the set telling the white community that the nigger is still impotent, kinda silly, and just downright grateful to be allowed to loot and pillage and burn every once in a while, in exchange for the amazing benefits of the Great Society.

Flip Wilson did a week on the Carson Show. I didn't watch him more than once more, just to see if my perceptions were consistent. He did it the next night, too.

During WWII they had a name for guys who sold out. The informers were called Quislings.

I wonder if Dick Gregory knows that word. He might mention it to his black, er, his mocha brother, Flip. We honkies haven't the right to say it. Shit, we haven't even got the right to be disgusted by shmucks like Wilson. All we have the *obligation* to do is go out on Rainbow Beach and get our ribs banged in. Even for jerks like Wilson.

I'm getting angry. Forget it.

Next week, at long last, my Rio contact has managed to smuggle out that dope on dictatorship-ruled TV in Brazil. Watch for it next week.

39: 19 SEPTEMBER 69

History refuses to allow me to keep my promises, which annoys not only me, but you readers as well. The promise: I wouldn't miss any more columns. How broken: last week, no column. Cause: history. Explanation: I'd promised at long last to do that column on the state of television in Brazil, a column I'd been planning since my trip to Rio many months ago. It took this long to get the information smuggled out. And no sooner had I written the column, a week ago Monday, than all hell broke out in Brazil, as your *other* newspapers told you, and I pulled back the column to rewrite it, to get it up to date. And missed my deadline. I'm sorry. And here, totally revised, and quite a bit longer, is the column.

After I returned from Rio, after I'd had the time to let what I'd seen there sink in, I included some thoughts about it all in an introduction I did for my most recent book of short stories. I'd like to excerpt those sections from the introduction and present them here, as something of a preamble.

THE WAVES IN RIO

Standing in the hotel window staring out at the Atlantic Ocean, nightcrashing onto the Copacabana beach. Down in Brazil on a fool's mission, talking to myself. Standing in the window of a stranger whom I suddenly know well, while down the Avenida Atlantica in another window, one I know well, who has suddenly become a stranger.

Watching the onyx waves rippling in toward shore,

227

suddenly facing-out like green bottle glass, cresting
white with lace, reaching, pawing toward shore, and
spasming once finally, before vanishing into the sponge
sand. I am a noble moron. I compose a poem.

My poem says, standing here, staring out across the
works of man, wondering what the hell I'm doing here,
an alien in a place he can never know . . . and there are
the waves. Boiling across two thousand miles of emp-
tiness in the terrible darkness, all alone, all the way
from Lagos like the Gold Coast blacks who came,
stacked belly-to-butt like spoons in the bellies and butts
of alien ships. All that way, racing so far, to hurl themselves up on this alien beach, like me.

Now why in the name of reason would anyone, anything, travel that far . . . just to be alone?

Christ on the mountain looks down over Rio de
Janeiro, arms spread, benediction silently flowing from
stone lips. He was sculpted by an Italian, and brought
to this mountain, staring off toward Sugar Loaf. There
are lights hidden in Christ. Once a year—you know
when—a remote switch is thrown at the other end of
those lights, in the Vatican, and the Pope lights *Cristo
Redentor*.

This is the Christ of the wealthy who live in the
bauhaus apartments out along Leblon; the Christ of the
blue carpet bettors at the Jockey Club; the Christ of
those who dine on *fondue orientale* at the Swiss Chalet;
the Christ of those who sail into Rio harbor on proud
white yachts so proud and so white the sun blinds anyone staring directly at them. This is the Christ on the
mountain.

Rio de Janeiro is a city of startling contrasts: from
the yachts and the Jockey Club and the bauhaus apartments . . . to the shanty villages glued to the sides of
the hills, where the poor scrabble for existence in their
tropic paradise. *Favellas* they are called. Down there
below the big Christ, but above even the wealthy, the

Gold Coast blacks have deposited their descendants, and the poor *mestizos* crowd one atop another in shanties built of corrugated shed roofing and wood slat that rots in the pulsing heat. They rise up in a crazy-quilt city above the city. And above them is a smaller hill. And on that hill they have erected another Christ. The Christ of the poor.

They are not noble morons. They are not writers who draw senseless parallels between the great white Christ on the mountain, and the little black Christ on the hill. They only know he is Christ the Redeemer. And though they have not enough *cruzeiros* to buy food for their rickety children, they have *centavos* to buy cheap tallow candles to set out on the altar of the street church. Christ will redeem them. They know it.

They are alone. In their own land, they are alone. Christ will never save them. Nor will men ever save them. They will spend their days like the waves from Africa, throwing themselves onto the beach of pitiless living.

They are no better than you or I.

It is only truth to tell you that as night approaches we are *all* aliens, down here on this alien Earth. To tell you that not Christ nor men nor the governments of men will save you. To tell you that we must all work and struggle and revolt against those who live in yesterday, before all our tomorrows are stolen away from us. To tell you no one will come down from the mountain to save your lily-white hide or your black ass. God is within you. Save yourselves.

Otherwise, why would you have traveled all this way ... just to be alone?

That was written in March. Two weeks ago, on Saturday, September 6th, the people of Brazil formalized their belief that God was, indeed, within them ... that no one was coming down from any mountain to save them from the unspeakable dictatorship that rules Brazil-as if it were a humid madhouse. Members of what the American establishment press call a "Castroite terrorist group" (the same kind of terrorist group to which Paul Revere belonged) kidnapped the U.S. Ambassador, C. Burke Elbrick. Two days later, with the release of fifteen political prisoners being held by the detestable military junta that had taken over Brazil, Elbrick was turned loose.

I will not go into any lengthy discussions of our part in the disgraceful treatment of an entire nation's people—we've done it too often, in too many other places. Suffice it to say, the poetic justice inherent in the kidnapping of the *Norteamericano* Ambassador is sufficiently pellucid to delight even a Thomas Hardy.

We supported the dictatorship, with money and arms and trade pacts. Even when the people of Rio could not pass unmolested in their own streets—littered with tanks and armed soldiers—we expressed no concern.

So when they decided to break out, the National Liberation Action organization and their militant arm, MR-8, went for pay dirt. They didn't kidnap Foreign Minister Jose Magalhaes Pinto or the Generals leading the First, Second or Third Armies—they copped Elbrick. They knew which side the bread was buttered on.

At long last, the Brazilians decided to take some concrete action against the level of poverty, illiteracy and degradation in which they'd been forced to exist. And they went for the money. They didn't bother with the puppets, they went for the puppet master. And won the day. Yeah!

But what has all this to do with television? Well, it had a lot more to do with it in the unrevised column you might have been reading had not MR-8 slapped chloroform over Elbrick's ambassadorial snout. Because, before September 6th, television (and to an even greater degree, radio) in Brazil was one of the most potent weapons used to keep the people happily mud-condemned. Before the Age of the Machine it was God

230

and Religion that kept the poor blacks in America hardly content but certainly befuddled. In Brazil, in the Age of the Machine, it is God and Religion and clowns like Silvio Santos from Sao Paulo and Chacrinha from Rio.

The latter is a grossly boorish television star, cavorting about like a Saturday morning kiddie show emcee, hosting one of the most popular shows in Brazil. The former is Chacrinha's counterpart from "more serious, sober Sao Paulo." Some serious; some sober. His program consists of selecting the ugliest man in Brazil, the fattest man, the longest moustache, the most ridiculous name of an individual, and something called City Against City, in which the insipid rivalries of the *cariocas* (Rio residents) and the *paulista* (from Sao Paulo) are exploited. Under the guise of an amusing inter-city contest, the TV medium manages to keep alive and fiery a sectional hatred no more sensible than that of Catholics and Protestants in North Ireland. The name of the game is divide and keep subservient.

Santos is a classic example of the bread-and-circuses Quisling whose lust for the buck (or in this case new *cruzeiros*) forces him into such public positions as the one expressed in a recent interview:

"But what do you want me to do? A certain publication criticizes me. It wants me to present programs of a higher level. But TV is a fierce battle to capture the audience. There's no middle ground, either you have an audience or you don't. Who doesn't, disappears.

"I was always crazy about money.

"There are certain programs which are bad for my image. For instance, the City Against City show. When one of the cities loses, all of the people from that city turn against me. Even though it's prejudicial to me, it can't be taken off the air because of its popularity with the viewers. Because of this, many shows which were considered horrible—and I agree that they were—couldn't be taken off.

"I'm the most optimistic guy in Brazil."

His optimism is based, probably, on his position as a 34-year-old millionaire (in Brazilian terms) with more side-interests than Senator Dodd.

Santos is only one of many manifestations of the corrupt and debased nature of Brazilian television. Even as the Roman arena and stock car races have kept the groundlings too busy being entertained to know their heads are being turned around by their governments, television has been turned to this most odious of uses.

Telethons on which physical deformities and terminal cases have been exhibited as *grand guignol* works of art.

News reports filtered, laundered, managed and castrated by such government agencies (horrifying object-lessons to those among you who think *Yanqui* TV ought to be government overseen) as the IBOPE, the Brazilian Institute of Public Opinion and Statistics. News reports that come on almost simultaneously on every radio station and TV channel, each one a carbon copy of the others.

Frequent news blackouts, when things get sticky ... such as now.

No documentaries, save travel talks.

The deification of the absurdly banal in such comedy soap operas as *The Trapp Family*. You think *our* daytime soapers are bad. They are as a cold sore to mouth cancer when compared to their Brazilian counterparts.

A level of programming guaranteed to provide no thought, no controversy, no enrichment.

By aiding and abetting the Brazilian Establishment in keeping the illiterate mass desensitized to the winds of revolution and change sweeping over the world, by substituting cheap slapstick for social involvement, by permitting the nationwide audience to believe it cannot rise above its station in life, television in Brazil has become a more effective riot control weapon than tanks or mace or troops.

232

It seems almost as though Brazilian video (divided between TV Globo and TV Tupi) is engaged in a program of barring the way to the twentieth century for the common man. The twentieth? Hell, consider the twenty-*first* century! And consider how Brazilian television handled the Apollo 11 moonflight:

No preparations were made to utilize the facilities of INTELSAT properly. Where almost every other nation in the world had been rigging its equipment and schedules for a month before the lunar landing, Brazilian television went on its imbecilic way with its usual belly-laugh programming, and on the day of the landing, beginning in the early afternoon, rather than showing what was happening at Houston, rather than relaying information as accurately as *every other televising country* was doing, Brazilian TV broadcast the microcephalic antics of Silvio Santos followed immediately by the loon Chacrinha.

Kindly note these were *special* programs, cut specifically for that day. It was as if on the day of JFK's funeral, CBS and NBC had prepared two special three-hour segments of *Green Acres* or *Queen For A Day* to be shown in lieu of the grim proceedings. Granted, it makes life a little more smiley, but it could hardly be construed as serving the needs of the viewing audience by keeping them in touch with the world around them.

And if it seems this is a gringo's carping about a state of affairs that does not bother the Brazilian people, I offer the following excerpt from the *Jornol Do Brasil* of 23 July:

"Instead of torturing the public with their foolish exuberance, Rio stations could have easily filled in the remaining time, while waiting for the heroic arrival of the first man on the moon, with really interesting news such as that sent minute by minute over the teletype.

"But ... it was necessary to give a little local color to the transmissions, and at the precise moment in which man was entering a new era, Rio TV viewers were informed that the presence of a man on the moon

233

would not alter the tides, nor would it change women's menstrual cycles. While everyone held his breath in expectation of the unequaled feat, the composers of Mangueira (a samba school were asked if they would agree to have a parade for the moon-men."

O Pasquim, in its July issue, related an even more incredible state-of-affairs during the moonshot. It seems that rather than having any intelligent and accredited commentators onscreen during the mission, the "keep the people uninformed" program was pursued by having an inept commentator named Hilton Gomes interview a "scientist" named Heron Domingues and a "philosopher" named Rubens Amaral, who opened their stint by shaking hands and taking credit for man's arrival on Luna.

(What follows is excerpted intact, translated from the Portuguese.)

"I want to give you my heartiest congratulations for this magnificent feat," Heron Domingues said smiling.

"But this would have been impossible without your collaboration," replied Rubens Amaral, with false modesty.

"The fact is," observed Heron, "that the public understands our efforts."

"And has been telephoning constantly," interrupted Amaral, "in a show of solidarity for our work."

(If you, gentle reader, are shaking your head in righteous confusion, don't feel like the Lone Ranger.)

(Then followed a fifteen-point resume of all the asinine and inept and downright scientifically inaccurate remarks made by these three ding-dongs. I'll only repeat a few here . . . they're sufficient to boggle the mind.)

(Remember: these are the two "experts" selected, presumably, from the cream of Brazilian intelligentsia, to inform the folk of what was going down. Or up.)

"The temperature at the moment is 150-degrees centigrade—we don't know if this is above or below zero." (Domingues)

"In the right leg of Armstrong's spacesuit is a sample of Lunar soil, which is different from ours." (Amaral)

"The man won't leave any footprints on the moon." (Domingues.)

"Armstrong is a cameraman, or shall we say, one of our television colleagues?" (Gomes)

"We've just gone to the window to check, and the moon really is a long way off." (Gomes and/or Amaral)

"There exists two hypotheses about the Luna-5: one ridiculous and the other absurd." (Domingues)

"Really . . . interesting." (Amaral in a rare moment of lucidity.)

"The respiration of the Americans is throbbing." (Amarel, brilliantly translating NASA's information that "the heartbeats had quickened.")

"Without the attention and kindness of our TV viewers, this great feat would have been impossible." *O Pasquim* commented on *this* one: "It's interesting to note that he didn't reveal the exact way in which TV viewers helped. According to reliable sources, it was by means of prayers.")

At last report, Santos, Chaerinha, Gomes, Amaral and Domingues were being sought by an outraged and finally uprisen Brazilian populace, to star in a new TV series called *Biggest Asshole On The Moon. Paulistas* and *cariocas* were placing bets in their respective cities to see which one of these estimable pawns of the establishment would make the loudest squeal as he was fired from a giant cannon at the moon. Which really is a long way off.

This week another shower of goodies. They ran the banned Smothers Brothers show on KTTV; I caught an even half-dozen of the new shows in debut performances; there were two important specials I want to gibber about—Woody Allen and *The Battered Child*—and it'll probably all slop over to next week's installment, but that's what I'm into, so don't wander too far.

The *Smothers Brothers Comedy Hour* that CBS censored into the relative oblivion of independent airing last April 6th was viewed on something over eighty stations nationally, Wednesday, September 10th.

After all the foofaraw about how obscene it was, after CBS, martinet position about "defending American morality," the show came as something of a letdown. Artistically, it was far from the best SmoBro product, and objectively, it was light-years away from their most controversial. The plain fact—horrifyingly obvious considered in the context of the total show—is that CBS was chickenshit frightened of Senator Pastore. There was nothing else on the show even *remotely* controversial. Oh sure, there was a pseudo-Nelson Eddy/Jeanette MacDonald duet between Tommy Smothers and Nancy Wilson, but it was in painfully good taste, and even accepting for an instant the shuck offered by CBS that their southern affiliates would have dropped the show for that duet, it would take someone who had been oblivious to the black/white things the southern stations *have* been showing, since *I Spy*, to believe it for a moment.

No, what that banned segment shows us, showed all

of the country, was that not only are the network po-
tentates a gaggle of cringing, petrified, spineless twerps,
they are ripe patsys for extortion and blackmail. Pastore is the blackmailer—a power-mad little Caesar with
the Monkey Trial morality of a troglodyte—and CBS
was his willing victim this time.

And just what element of the SmoBro show was it
that held CBS in such quivering thrall? Was it
Tommy's unclothed penis? Was it a full-face scene
from *Oh, Calcutta*? Was it Kate Smith going down on
a chacma baboon? Hell no, it was merely Dan Rowan
mealy mouthing whether or not to give the Fickle Fin-
ger of Fate Award to Senator John Pastore, that's what
it was.

As blatant and mind-croggling an example of personal censorship as we have ever witnessed on network
television. Whether Pastore actually saw the tape of the
show and blew heavy about it, or CBS just pre-cen-
sored itself, the crime was revolting, as gutless, as un-
ethical as even the dimmest, dumbest viewer could desire. CBS saying the show was censored for "moral"
reasons is about as valid as Lester Maddox refusing to
integrate on grounds of "states' rights." It is another example of the moral corruption of our politicians, not of
our television personalities.

Now that *we've* seen it—not just a few TV critics
and newspapermen, none of whom, incidentally, had the
balls to speak up since April 6th, but *all* of us—what
will CBS do? Knowing *we* know them for what they
are. Knowing their pat little up-the-line obfuscations
won't play any more. Knowing we have *proof* they
don't give a damn about serving the public interest.
Knowing we understand the contempt they have for us,
the ease with which they'll sell us out. What are they
going to do, those fatcat heroes, those shadow entrepreneurs, those lizard-blood killers of every truth, every
hope, every dream? Do we get mad, CBS? Do we want
to kill? Oh, babies, you'll never know. You'll never suspect, but let me tell you how deep it runs, what you're

237

building, where it's going to go, till the day they come after you at your tower in CBS Television City. Like this:

I had an uncle who fought in WWII. He was attached to an English commando unit in Europe. One time when he was sick with a fever, years later, I was tending him, and he thought he was going to die, and he told me the worst thing he'd ever done. It was bitter cold, one winter during the war, and his unit came crawling through the night, and they found a German battalion bivouacked in a forest. It was so numbing cold, the men had doubled up together, sleeping hugging each other in sleeping bags to keep from freezing to death. My uncle, and his unit, crawled in, moved among them, and carefully cut the throats of *one man per sleeping bag*. Not both of them ... only one. To leave all those poor fuckers to wake up the next morning hugging corpses with an extra mouth. It was a terrible thing; my uncle couldn't live with it; it killed him, butchered his soul.

That's how deep the hate runs, CBS. Keep fucking around.

Look, CBS, I'm talking to you like a Dutch Uncle. You see, what's happening is that we're building a psychopathic society. Everybody lies, everybody sells out, everybody stinks of hate. We're all being driven mad as mudflys, CBS. The hatreds are running deep, core-deep. How much longer do you think we can tolerate our guardians of the public trust, dudes like you, who corrupt and bastardize that trust? How much longer can we be expected to see you contributing to the creation of that mad world, without taking the lynch rope in our hands? The rope, or the razor. Mme. De-Farge lives in all of us, CBS, and you're summoning her forth. By your corrupt acts we see that only corruption pays off. By your dishonesty we see that only dishonesty—or the razor—offer hope of cessation to this madness, one way or the other.

I'm sorry I yelled at you, CBS. No . . . no, I'm not; not really. Perhaps I should have spoken softly, to win your mind, to convince you of the sincerity and immediacy of what the people are saying. Perhaps this time I should have spoken softly; I'm sorry. But tell me, CBS, at what point do all the soft voices stop and you begin to hear the terrible snick-snick of Mme. DeFarge's needles?

Now, if the typesetter left a two-line space between that last line and this one, indicating I want to change the subject, we can go on to what I hope (if I live long enough) will be an annual feature of this snake pit: ELLISON'S MINUTE CAPSULE REVIEWS OF NEW SHOWS!!!

The Bill Cosby Show: Missed it the first week, but caught it last Sunday. Seemed awfully situation-comedy to me, but funny. Cosby learned well from Culp, and brought the best of his standup stuff with him. I'm sorta disappointed to see it played so White (Cosby might as easily be Jim Nabors for all the difference in tone), with all that great specialized background Cosby has, but I'm willing to wait a few weeks and see of Cos can't work in a tot more soul.

The Bold Ones: The New Doctors on Sunday the 14th didn't show me much: John Saxon could have phoned in his part, E.G. Marshall wasn't onscreen enough to get his teeth into it, David Hartman tried his best but he lacks a certain charisma, and for the better part of the hour all we had to contend with was Pat Hingle doing something that resembled, in thespic terms, an AmerIndian rain dance. The script was a slightly slicker version of *Ben Casey* or *The Doctors* and, in all, it seemed as though I was watching TV 1963 again. On the 20th, NBC fired the second stage of their rocket with *The New Lawyers* and things perked up. James Farentino and Joe Campanella (aided as minimally as possible by Burl Ives) did their turn in a script that started out to say something important about the disregard of *some* police for the constitutional rights of those they arrest ... and went rapidly downhill into banality and cop-out à la Universal Studios' determined effort never to produce an honest drama. Steve Ihnat played well, as usual, and that, coupled with the verve of Campanella and Farentino, gave me some hope that perhaps this tripartite series might not be a total dud. Actually, I'm waiting to see Leslie Nielsen and Hari Rhodes in the law enforcement third of the project. Hari is a friend, see, and he knows I'll expect him to start pushing for some heavy scripts. Because if he doesn't, he knows he'll get the same shit from me that I get from him every time they run *The Oscar*.

My World—And Welcome To It: Don't miss it. A nice piece of work with William Windom playing James Thurber. Animation, shtick, good acting, genuine comedy, a real addition to the scrawny roster of worthwhile viewing. If only they'd scrap that bloody laugh track!

The Debbie Reynolds Show: As many points as I have to give Miss Reynolds for quitting the show when NBC crossed her and ran a cancerstick ad, I cannot tell a lie. I managed to watch that awful first show for four minutes and twenty seconds (by my Accutron) before I fled shrieking. One can only wonder if Miss Reynolds caught the show herself. One remembers the Tammy Grimes Graf Zeppelin of some years ago. It was too bad Tammy didn't hate cigarettes.

The Courtship of Eddie's Father: is also fine. Producer Jimmy Komack, despite his stated reluctance to even take a visible part in the proceedings (many months ago), steals any part of the show in which he appears. What *he* doesn't grab, this kid, Eddie, played by Brandon Cruz, manages to cop. And so my award for bravest man in the world goes to Bill Bixby, who plays the "lead." And man who'll toss himself onto a screen with leggy, foxy chicks, a tiny Japanese lady, Jimmy Komack *and* a kid actor, has got to be the most secure, bravest actor in town.

Bracken's World: Oh, *this* one, friends, I gotta do an entire column on. Suffice it to say that a man who wrote a movie as shitty as *The Oscar* is the only one in a position to comment on *Bracken's World*. I know it's going to be tough sitting through it, gang, but I recommend that you not miss it. It has the evil facination of rotting orchids. And smells about the same. More of *this* cesspool at a later date. I'm going to let them expose their running sores and pustules a while longer before I lance them proper.

Yeah, just as I thought. No room to tell you how good and groovy Woody Allen was, or how uptight *The Battered Child* put me, or even about the ABC News Special on *Ethics In Government*, which was *really* chilling. But I'll be here again next week, so maybe we can rap about them then.

Oh ... yeah ... I almost forgot. For those of you who might have caught your charismatic commentator on John Barbour's Sunday night show (KTTV, Channel 11) last week, who called to tell me they wished Mr. Barbour had spent more time with me and talked about something more important than Western movies, rest easily. Mr. Barbour and his producer have indicated they want me to return shortly, and I will take such an opportunity to say onscreen a few of the things I've been saying on your behalf in these columns.

One never knows. I might attract a following, become a "TV personality," talk about revolution and getting it all together ... and get shot in the head by a True American.

Stay tuned. History may swallow all of us as we hone our razors.

Is that the snick of needles I hear?

This is a special week for me. It's the first anniversary of this column. The 42nd installment. [Through a fluke of rearrangement to maintain continuity, it is the 41st column in this book; but it was the 42nd I *wrote*. —HE] And what grinds me most is that it isn't the 52nd. I missed ten weeks worth of columns; eight times my fault, twice the Freep's. In this year, since Art Kunkin collared me at that party and said write something for us, a great many things have gone down. For me, for you, for television, for the country, and for the world.

We're on the moon now, but we're still in Viet Nam. Julian Bond got elected, but so did Nixon. Kurt Vonnegut had a best-seller, but so did Jaqueline Susann. *60 Minutes* and *First Tuesday* got some things said, but we lost the Smothers Brothers. *Che* turned out a dud, but *Easy Rider* came out of nowhere. Reddin left the law, but we got him on the tiny screen. There were plenty of protests, but very few riots.

Don't ask me if things got better this last year, because I don't think so. I went down to the Valley, to a high school, to talk to some kids about . . . stuff, you know . . . what seems to be happening . . . trying to understand, and like that . . . and while I was inside the school, some other kids busted my car and swiped my tapes. What do you say? How pissed-off you get, how upset, how ironic? Very little of it makes any sense. The nits behind Operation Intercept actually think they're going to kill off marijuana, when everybody with a grain of sense knows all they're doing is setting up a Prohibition scene so grass becomes big enough business for the Cosa Nostra to add it to its roster of enterprises. How do you break through their fifty years of conditioning? How do you get them to tell a little truth, cop to the fact that *every*body's turning on, that maybe it's not devil-weed, but only as good or bad as booze? The military spend our money, kill our friends, fuck up our country, and all in the name of keeping us safe from the wrong bogey man. We've gone so far into the bag of killing trust and honesty among one another that we're like Cro-Magnons again. We have to approach one another with our hands outstretched, palms up. We have to show we're weaponless. And still it doesn't help. Why do we continue to hurt one another? Why do we persist in lying? And why do we stand by and let other men poison our world?

So don't ask me if the year has totaled out at profit or loss. I don't know. The only thing I know is that I'll be here this year, too, and I'll keep trying to make some sense out of it. Entertainment is only part of what I'm into here, and I have to thank those of you who loved or hated what I did last year sufficiently to comment on it. And I ask this of you: keep me honest. Copping out gets easier and easier, the higher the stakes get.

Now let's get to work this week.

ELLISON'S CAPSULE REVIEWS OF NEW SHOWS!!! (Part 2).

To Rome with Love: returns John Forsythe to the ranks of situation comedy half-hours. He's not a bachelor father in this incarnation, he's a widowed father, with three little girls, one of whom, played by Joyce Menges, is the nicest-looking chick to come on the tube since Anjanette Comer made it. But even Miss Menges' sensual face isn't enough to save this paucive little half hour from falling down the saccharine tube. There are so many poignant moments of Forsythe and his kids looking woebegone because "Mommy" is dead, one begins to suspect she croaked from familial diabetes. If this series were to fold tonight, it would have passed with no one's having known it was there.

The Bold Ones: The third section of Universal's acromegalic rotating-series (doctors, lawyers and police) was aired last Sunday, with Leslie Nielsen as a Deputy Police Chief and Hari Rhodes as the DA. Jesus, did it stink! The script had three names on it, and in case you need a rule of thumb, gentle readers, for knowing when a script is going to stink on ice, use that. More than two names (and usually only one) means it was hashed and re-hashed by every sticky-finger on the lot, and what you'll be getting is watered-down nothing. Instant vacuum.

The female lead was a lady named Lorraine Gary, whose marital relation to Universal's top attorney causes pause to wonder on what grounds she was tapped for the part, because she recited every sententious line of that gawdawful script in Capital Letters As Though They Should Have Been Carved On Mt. Rushmore. But she was only the foremost of many downers that show sported. Hari Rhodes was awkward, overacted and generally a talent wasted. Not to be undone, Nielsen, who is as competent and professional a stock artist as Universal has kicking around out there, leaned into his role with such affectated ferociousness that one expected him to have a coronary at any moment. The plot was straight out of 1939 *Black Mask* magazines, and I swear the shades of Hammett and Woolrich and Chandler must have been thrashing in their graves. I understand that this section, originally slated for eight productions, even as the Doctors and Lawyers were slated for eight, has been cut back to six. It's amazing how the Universal thugs will never cop to their own inadequacies, but cut off the field troops as if it was *their* fault the ambush failed.

Music Scene: is my pick as the best of the new. The tone and tempo of the potpourri is strongly reminiscent of Barry Shear's well-remembered *The Lively Ones* of some years ago. By pre-taping all sorts of people doing all sorts of pop numbers, and then selecting from the backlog as one or another talent hits the charts, *Music Scene* can roll with the on-the-moment top dogs, and provide a running compendium of the best in current music. There are six bright and funny young people—notable among them is David Steinberg, who grows more infectious with each appearance on TV—who fill the interstices between numbers with SmoBro-like one-liners and shticks that are so hip they *must* go over the heads of the septuagenarians in the Great American Heartland. The sets and innovative thinking used to showcase the groups and individuals are superlative. Three Dog Night did *Easy To Be Hard* against a background of wrecked automobiles, and the eerie feeling it produced made, that song (one I'm not especially fond of) seem, for the first time, meaningful. James Brown did a turn that was also incredibly effective and even the taped melange of John and Yoko (who has *got* to be the ugliest chick in the civilized world) moved at a pongy pace. The show is intelligent, lively, colorful, something meaty on which to chew. And it is a beautiful lead-in for young viewers to:

The New People: which got off on the right foot behind some bravura acting by Richard Kiley as the only adult left (temporarily) alive on a downed airliner full of young people. The show employed the very best tenets of dramatic writing to say what it had to say about Our Times while not sacrificing action. That it slipped, momentarily, into Preachment can be chalked up to Rod Serling's script, and it's a bad habit Mr. Serling has not yet learned to control. But one we can tolerate when he manages to perform his craft so well in all other particulars. This is a series to watch. It is potentially solid gold.

I missed *The Brady Bunch*, the Durante/Lennon Sisters Hour, *Bronson* again, *Room 222* and a few others, but I'll be falling in on them this week, so look for them next time.

I did manage to see a few minutes of the Bob Hope special, which was glutted with more unfunny comedians than the world has witnessed since Quantrell was working. It only served to convince me more strongly that any number of Grand Old Men (some of whom are younger than me) ought to be confined to Vegas or Friars dinners.

Understand Debbie is back with her show, and inside information has it that her leaving the program because they ran a cigarette ad was strictly a hype. It seems they cut her salary somewhere during the summer, and she just walked to get them to up her again. Be interesting to see what would happen if they Viceroy'd her again, at the new rate.

42: 10 OCTOBER 69

So early in the new season, and already we have a
name for it. Each year's heaviest tone has been discernible in the most prominent product. The year of
the hardcase cowpokes, the year of the doctors who
struggle for humanity, the year of the witless situation
comedies ... last year was the year of the widows,
white and black.

And this year is the Time of the Plastic People.

A parade of silly, coiffed and cuffed templates; a
smoothly performed pavane of slick, empty cliches; a
ghastly rigadoon of obstinately endless phoniness so
corrupt it climbs to a new video pinnacle.

Purple is as purple does.

The punishment fits the crime.

Purple plastic people push me to puce and paucive
pejoratives. They also make me puke.

But that's another vessel of vomit.

(You'll pardon me. Occasionally the Writer takes
over from the Critic and the sound of me own silver
words gets a tot too much. It usually happens in
columns wherein I am discussing the craft of writing.
Which is what this is.) (On second thought, make that
The Craft Of Writing. If I'm going to be pretentious, I
might as well go all the way.)

Anyhow, the problem is ...

(Hold it. Make that THE CRAFT OF WRITING.
I'm feeling festooned with power. It means I'll probably get actively abusive.)

The problem is *Bracken's World* and *Harold
Robbins' "The Survivors"* as an emerging species.
Bracken's World is still festering, as I indicated two

weeks ago, and I'm summoning up firepower. Gonna let'm run for another coupla weeks so all you folks can dig'm in their full flower. Then, when I flit them, you can't say I didn't give them a chance to mend their ways, even if it did mean scrapping the series and putting all those nice young kids back on unemployment.

In any case, the evil that *Bracken's World* manifests is also redolently obvious on ABC's *The Survivors,* a multi-million dollar gawdawful cobbled-up by the Albert Payson Terhune of the Garbage Novel, Harold Robbins. Since the one rivals the other for greasiness, I'll deal here with Robbins, with ABC, with *The Survivors* and with the taste of the American Scuttlefish. Those who survive may consider they've won a merit badge.

Mr. Robbins, one of the more artful dodgers of our time, pulled a little fast ramadoola on Elton Rule and the ABC brain dancers, and using the same technique he employed to hustle Trident Press into an enormous contract for *The Adventurers* on the basis of only a title, he angered his little pixie way into their exchequer with the title *The Survivors.*

There's no point going into the horrors and hectics that pursued this abomination on its pestiferous path from Robbins' skull to the tiny screen . . . the loss of one producer after another (until they settled on Walter Doniger, the whizzer who gave us *Peyton Place*) . . . the internecine warfare between the "stars" . . . the rewrites of the rewrites of the rewritten scripts . . . the money flushed down the gilded toilet . . . no point. Let's just dwell on the finished product that debuted on Monday night, September the 29th.

The product is the same old product. Soap opera.

Except Robbins' product has enzymes.

Newly activated, sparkling with green and blue and gold spots. Before your eyes. The green is from moral rot, the blue is the alleged better blood of the jet set, and the gold is fool's.

Advertised as a "television novel," *The Survivors* is

248

simply daytime tearjerking without even a nod toward verisimilitude. It's the downhome story of the Carlyle family: simple, good-hearted billionaires who lead lives like you or I. Septuageneric Daddy owns his own bank and is *shtupping* his thirtyish secretary on the side. Indolent playboy son races at Monaco, quits three laps short of winning to chase a piece of tail, and gets himself and his Lear jet hijacked to a Latin duchy in the throes of revolution. Daughter is a clotheshorse with an illegitimate son who's married to an elegant embezzler notable for having clipped Daddy to the tinkly tune of seven hundred grand.

Why go on? Add the dimension of thespic luminaries like Ralph Bellamy, Kevin McCarthy, George Hamilton and Lana Turner, and you have the total package. No better or worse than the general sling of slop we get? Is that what you think? Oh, come come, my friends. Just reconsider the cast: Bellamy, McCarthy ... Hamilton and Turner. Two fine actors and two gold lamé loxes whose "acting" ability is so scant it can only be termed amoebic. So why opt for glitterfolk like Hamilton and Turner, chockablocking them with genuine talents like Bellamy and McCarthy, when you have your choice of every fine actress and actor in town?

Because Lana Turner and George Hamilton are intrinsically involved in the myth world *The Survivors* tries to tell us is an actuality. Hamilton's spotty past is well-known, as is Miss Turner's. They are living, walking, talking symbols of the *recherché* mode of existence on which this series builds its rationale.

Which brings us to the rotten core of the matter.

Mr. Robbins, whose novels are ennobled by the words *dishonest* and *illiterate*, has made a not inconsiderable fortune by proffering to all the scuttlefish living lives of dreariness and encapsulation, a phantom image of a world in which the rich get richer and there are no poorer. A world in which black men do not exist, in which women are fit for little better than consumer consumption on the Tiffany/Cartier level—and having illegitimate babies. A world in which the pettiest problems become high drama merely because they occur in a red velvet snake pit.

Chromed and rhinestoned, Robbins has marketed a world where everyone is J. Paul Getty or Aristotle Onassis, and considering the lives and hopes of the Average Man would be as unthinkable as one of the Czar's cossacks worrying which peasant's cabbage patch he was galloping through. It is a view of the universe that was disgracefully irrational fifty years ago, and is totally out of place in the world of today.

The vapid, incestuous, self-concerned fools who people Robbins' series are the very people against whom every revolution in the world is directed. The Wall Street bankers who backed Batista against Castro, thereby assisting in driving Fidel into the waiting arms of Communism. The munitions men, the high-rollers, the wastrel playboys, the maudlin women with their overweening concern for their falling breasts and mansion peccadilloes. The blind and the precious. Those to whom creature comforts come before ethic. The emotionally and intellectually de-sensitized. The rhodium-plated ghouls who live off the masses, whose fortunes and perpetuations of fortunes can only be realized when field laborers are forced to work for 30¢ an hour. *These* are the contemporary nobility Harold Robbins and his bloated associates at ABC have chosen to offer us as idols. I would be willing to wager the much-belabored network jingoism of "viewer identification" was not mentioned with great frequency when this epic was being assembled. For there is no one in this series with whom *to* identify. The men are all crippled by their corruptions and intravenous tie-lines to the corrupt power structure; the women are all indolent leeches, living off that same corruption and merely offering their bodies to their men as payment. They are modern courtesans (albeit with that little piece of paper that makes it legal) and their men are little better than cheaphustle 42nd Street johns.

Once again ABC has proved that it will go with "name power" rather than quality. It has swallowed the Robbins shuck—as distasteful as it may be—and convinced itself that what it's digested is caviar, not guano. It has lied to itself in believing we can't see that Miss Turner has grown older and more lined without having improved one whit as an actress. (No amount of Lord & Taylor clothes will cover it.) It has lied to itself in believing that we will accept a paragon of moral and ethical turpitude like no-neck George Hamilton as a model of Concerned Humanity. (As an actor, he is the compleat gigolo.) It has lied to itself in believing that a world about to commit suicide is interested or enriched by a weekly viewing of the very societal elements *most responsible* for anguish in our times; and that by gilding them, we will accept their right to rule.

If the series was at least an accurate portrait of that materialistic, destructive coterie of thieves and killers, it would serve as an object lesson—perhaps to delineate the face of the enemy for the younger generation. But ABC has even shied away from *that* nitty-gritty, and has slapped together every cliche and hack theme of a hundred Robbins and Robbins-imitated novels. And what punishment will they be meted for it?

Mr. Robbins will make a billion megabucks, ABC will get it sponsored up the ass and out the gullet, and the peons in the Great American Heartland will accept this as just another affirmation of the impossibility of ever climbing out of the mud.

Troops, they come wearing white-on-white, with diamond cufflinks and plastic hair. And if this series inspires you to any feelings but a desire to tear down their towers, then you are already lost.

I do not think it mere chance that Robbins, in the fullness of his contempt for the true human condition, chose the name of this series. If he, and ABC, and the people whose shadow images are played by these actors, have their way, they indeed *will* be the only survivors.

43: 17 OCTOBER 69

"THE COMMON MAN": PART I

I cannot remember being more disturbed or depressed about something I'd seen on television than what concerns me this week. So unraveling and serious is it, I feel, that I don't think there'll be much ranting or pyrotechnics. You can usually tell when I'm genuinely bent out of shape; I get very quiet.

Helen McKenna, a reader of this column from San Diego, sent me a carbon of a "letter of concern" she'd written to ABC, NBC and CBS. Her concern stemmed from an article in the September 27 issue of *TV Guide*. The article, by Edith Efron, was titled *The "Silent Majority" Comes Into Focus*. It was another in *TV Guide*'s more or less continuing series of reassurances to the Common Man in its readership that all the unpleasant things happening in this country will pass, that this craziness stemming from longhairs and unruly adolescents is essentially unimportant, that the Common Man will prevail, as he always has in the past.

It was a lie, of course; an elaborate lie as distasteful to those of us who know it will *not* pass, who see those "America—Love It or Leave It" bumper stickers and fear their undercurrent inferences, as *TV Guide*'s wretched editorial vindication of the CBS cancellation of the Smothers Brothers. *TV Guide* is edited out of Radnor, Pennsylvania and that is a small town where the thunder of a world in upheaval reverberates back merely as a laugh track gone slightly out of synch.

Miss McKenna's letter, a small moan for nobility in a land sadly lacking in same, came three days after I'd seen the two hours of television which so frighten and shake me this installment. They seemed to tie in together so well, I would like to address this column to Miss McKenna and *all* the Helen McKennas who know our time is running out, that we have come to the brink of nightmare and must find new answers or perish in our own poisons.

I am glad she did not see the program I'm about to discuss, for had she, she would have known (as I now know) that Miss Efron and *TV Guide* well understood the audience they were addressing with their perpetuations of the lies that basically America is sound at the grass roots, that the Common Man, like the Fifth Cavalry in a late late show western, will rush to save us at the final desperate stroke of midnight.

The show aired over KCET Channel 28, the educational channel, on Friday, October 3rd. It was *The David Susskind Show* and it was titled "The White Middle Class." In two hours of gut-level conversation, Mr. Susskind gave a forum to five typical, average, middle class white Americans. Not rabid Birchers, not hysterical religious fanatics, not insensitive bigots . . . just five ordinary Common Men. And they revealed themselves to be typically American.

And—dear God, why am I so numb and resigned? —that was the horror of them.

The five men were:

Mike Giordano, 47 years old, from Newark, New Jersey; take-home pay $140 a week as a factory mechanic; net annual income, $8500; father of nine.

Frank Mrak, 44 years old, from Cleveland, Ohio; works in an employment agency and moonlights a second job selling life insurance for a total income of $10,000 annually; he was the subject of a *Life* piece on the working class.

Paul Corbett, 40 years old, a traveling salesman from Philadelphia; six children, and a net income of $9000 a year. Remember this man.

Vincent De Tanfilis, 41 years old, works for an insurance agency; married, with two children, he lives in Norwalk, Connecticut; he earns between nine and ten thousand dollars per year.

Peter Brady, 30 years old, with five children; a truck driver who lives in Freeport, Long Island, he works as a part-time bartender, and makes between eight and nine thousand dollars a year.

Five sensible men. Rational men who might easily and with no denigration be labeled "pillars of the community." I saw them as epitomizations of the Common Man. The basic fiber of the American way of life. And so I could set down with absolute accuracy what they said, how they felt, I asked KCET to run the show for me at a private screening. There could be no room for error in this column, and I wanted to set it down just right. So on Monday, October 6th, with a cassette recorder to capture their every word, I sat in a darkened viewing room and lived again that most terrifying two hours with five models of what the bulk of our country considers the Common Man ... the "good" man.

And this is what they said; their words, unedited.

On the subject of welfare: "The most colossal fraud ever perpetrated on this country." (Giordano) / "They are nothing but a bunch of thieves who want what I worked for. It is not Christian for me to do for people who won't do for themselves. Paul's admonition to the Apostles was, 'If you do not work, you do not eat.' " (Corbett) / "It's all going into the pockets of those who don't deserve it, malingerers, crooked politicians. Someone is lining his pockets." (De Tanfilis) / "They're stealing from us legally, and they call it welfare." (Corbett) / "The hard core unemployed can't cut it. They all want to start at the top. They don't want to start at the bottom the way I did, the way my father did. We can't all be bus drivers; some of us have to be passengers. We can't all be chiefs; we have to be Indians." (Giordano)

On the subject of Viet Nam, the arms race and

money spent by the Pentagon on weaponry: "Seventy seven billion for armaments? I'm in favor of it, because that's to support our nation, not to destroy it." (Corbett) / "I find it alarming that the Russians are expanding their forces while we are decreasing our." (Corbett) / "I have absolute faith in the Pentagon. I believe they are the only ones qualified to set their budget. I don't care if it's a hundred billion or a hundred and ten billion; I don't care." (Mrak) / "I'm against the Viet Nam war, but not as a dove. I'm against it because when was in World War II I learned that you fight a war to win it; and I'm against the way we've been fighting the war ... dragging it out." (Mrak) / "We should drop the atom bomb." (Corbett) / "You peaceniks have been around for centuries. The guy who yells peace is the guy who always gets war, but the guy who stands up and says you mess with me and I'll give you war ... he gets peace." (Giordano) / referring to a young man with long hair who spoke from the audience:) "Withdraw! Withdraw! *You* people ... what's the matter with winning? I know the people in Washington are continuing the war, so they can soak up the tax dollars ... and the war could have been won seven years ago ... by getting in there and *really* fighting!" (De Tanfilis) / "The ones that are prolonging this war are the long-haired brats. Because the government listens to 'em, and the more they scream the more the war gets on the front pages." (Brady) / (Corbett asked Susskind if he didn't think we should have won the war long ago. Susskind said no, he didn't think we should have been there in the first place. Corbett then said, "I suppose you think we shouldn't have gone to war against the Nazis, huh?" Susskind said they weren't comparable situations. And Corbett said:) "Oh, I see, you don't think Communists are as bad as Nazis." / (Susskind asked if it might not just be barely possible that the United States had been wrong in entering the war. All five shouted, "No!" as one. And then Corbett said:) "No, sir! If they're against Communism, they can't be wrong. You can't make a deal with the devil. J. Edgar Hoover says it's a conspiracy to destroy America, therefore it's evil. It must be stamped out at the roots, even if we have to stamp out all of Russia." / "There's too much weaponry. We all ought to sit down and say we're going to get rid of the super-weapons and just go back to safe weapons." (Giordano) / "It's the liberal Mafia that keeps this war from being won." (Corbett)

It is difficult to proceed, setting down so much jingoism and muddy thinking. On the one hand these men all deplore the high income tax that keeps them working six days a week and leaching all joy from their existences, they deplore the ten per cent surcharge that was instigated by a man *they* elected, and extended by a *second* man they elected . . . but on the other hand they find nothing wrong in the bulk of their tax dollar being spent on the Viet Nam war or on military hardware that has been proved either boondoggle or ineffectual *before* it's built.

They were, to a man, paranoid. There were conspiracies everywhere. The Black Militant conspiracy. The White Liberal Conspiracy. The Communist Conspiracy. The Bureaucratic Conspiracy. The Conspiracy of the Judiciary. All their troubles stem from poor people on welfare rolls and from "bleeding heart liberals" who steal from them.

These were the opinions, the very words, of the average citizens who make up the bulk of this nation's population. There were more. Many more statements about the law, about the protest movement, about blacks, about relief and welfare to the aged and infirm, about racial prejudice and integration. They are startling and baldly revealing statements.

They were the thoughts and fears of the Common Man.

My space this issue has run out. There is considerably more that needs to be said here, and more space needed, so I beg your indulgence, and ask that you return here next week for the second part of this study of Who We Are, Who They Are, and the problem of the Common Man.

"THE COMMON MAN": PART II

"Black people just can't cut it. They don't have the
intellectual ability. Now I know how the Liberal Mafia
can discredit somebody who speaks his mind like that.
They call him a bigot and a racist, and that makes you
no good. It means what you say is no good. But I'm no
bigot and I don't even know what a racist is. What is a
racist? Can somebody tell me what a racist is? If you
go to the Ivory Coast in Africa, kids of four and five
years old are making baskets and learning how to make
things. But if you go into North Philadelphia or Bed-
ford-Stuyvesant or Harlem you see the old man sitting
around with his bottle of wine, which is paid for by
me, the hard-working taxpayer."

That quotation is actually two men speaking. Paul
Corbett, 40, a traveling salesman . . . and Mike Giordano, 47, a factory mechanic. I've fused the two quotes
together because during the two hours of the Susskind
interview these two men were the most outspokenly
racist and bigoted, the most jingoistic and illogical.
What each said might easily have come from the
other's mouth, and during the period excerpted above,
their comments overlapped as they rushed to get their
gut-feelings out. I don't think either of them could
honestly fault me for melding them into one definitive
personality.

Because Messrs. Corbett and Giordano—and their
three compatriots—were speaking the words of contemporary middle-class America. They were expressing the
secret and frequently not-so-secret beliefs of The Common Man in our country today.

Giordano also said, a trifle hysterically, "All I want is to be left alone! I'm not asking anyone for anything! I just want to be left alone. Every time I turn on the TV someone is telling me how bad off the blacks are, how the little kids fight off rats in the slums. I don't want to feel guilty, I just wanna be left alone!"

It was a pathetic sight. A grown man very nearly on the verge of tears as he expressed his confusion and fear of the world around him. He's a working man, an average sort of joe who knows only that thousands of dollars for which he worked brutally hard (he says) are being stolen from him by the aged, the infirm, the destitute, those who have illegitimate babies, who lay up in their ghettos with wine he's buying ... while four-year-olds on the Ivory Coast are making good living wages at cottage industry.

These are the men who voted for Wallace. They insist they are not bigots and racists, yet they cannot define the terms and seem to have no awareness that it is *they* to whom we refer when we speak of these types.

Giordano owns guns. He bought them to protect his property. The way he put it, unedited: "I hope I never have to use the gun I bought, but I would be remiss in my duty if I did not protect my house ... I have to protect myself, I have to protect my house." Do you see something rather peculiar there? He doesn't say he has to protect his wife and his *nine* children ... he says he has to protect his *house*.

There is very little point in going on with the comments these five men made. They are hardly startling remarks; we've heard them endlessly for the past fourteen years. Yet they were so well capsulized, so concretized in their own slogan rigidity, that the conclusions they indicate—on the part of these five and *all* the Common Men—give us a primer of the fears and stupidities that will certainly kill us, and our planet, if they are not soon combated.

Such as:

"The two or three hundred years of injustice we

whites are supposed to've perpetrated on blacks is a fraud." (Giordano)

"All the federal money for relief is going into the pockets of crooked politicians." (Vincent de Tanfilis)

"The Liberal Mafia has coerced the decent colored man. They were happy the way they were till all this noise started." (Corbett)

"I live in an integrated community. There are 27,-000 whites and seventeen to thirty non-white families." (Frank Mrak) And non-white could mean Mexican-American, Japanese, anything. But *he* thinks he lives in an integrated community.

"Billy Graham says the protest movement on campus is due to the infiltration of dissident elements like Communists. This SDS sucks kids in on LSD and it's a conspiracy." (Frank Mrak) Not so incidentally, Mr. Mrak didn't know the difference between SDS and LSD. He confused them, called one the other, and in general exhibited that most fundamental tip-off that we were dealing with the Common Man: inability to tell fact from fancy, reliance on rumor, gossip and the slogan.

"Administrators on campuses have no backbone. They outta take a firm line with kids." (De Tanfilis)

"The only reason we got permissive sex in this country is that people are making money off it. They only reason the radicals talk so much about the war is because the politicians stand to make money off it." (Peter Brady, 30 years old)

(Yes, I know the last remark above is totally incomprehensible, unbelievable, makes no sense and is the sort of thing you might expect to hear from a brain damage case, but Peter Brady was the youngest of the bunch. Younger than me, younger than most of you, and ostensibly one of the ones still "trustable" by the under-30 generation. Does this tell us anything?)

There are ten or twelve more single-spaced pages of remarks, but why pursue it? Two weeks worth of columns is more than enough space to give these men their ups.

It's time to make a statement and take a position and try to formulate a generality that isn't just hot air. And if such can be whomped-up from these crude materials, it is this:

We have long been a country where nature imitates art. When Evan Hunter wrote *The Blackboard Jungle* with its wholly inaccurate portrait of what delinquency was like in the New York school system—and when the film was cobbled up from that once-removed fantasy, thereby making it a third-hand unreality image— the kids began imitating what they'd seen in the film and read in the book.

We have a tendency to let our art forms exploit us. In the Forties, we were deluged with pro-war movies in which Robert Taylor or John Hodiak or John Garfield gritted his teeth and fired into the endlessly advancing ranks of the Japanazis, thereby proving to us that even though (at first) we were losing the war, we'd pull it out of the fire and save the American Way of Life—if only we'd Buy Bonds.

So, similarly have we swallowed whole the myth of the Common Man. The Mr. Deeds or the Mr. Smith who, because of his homespun philosophy, common sense and garden variety decency, emerges just at the last moment, just before the town lynches the wrong man or sells its heritage to the international cartel or lets the bully finish off the town weakling—and he saves the day. We *believe* in the Common Man. The man who works with his hands. The man who makes up the labor unions and the merchant class and the middle-America homeowner. We believe in his good sense, in his perceptions of what is right or wrong.

No good. It won't work no more. The "common man" philosophy is based on simple truths, eternal verities, on black and white and right and wrong. But the world is not that kind of Giant Golden Book any longer. The world is an incredibly complex skein of interwoven potencies, of power in too many hands, of power corrupted and people used.

The Common Man is no longer merely as outdated as the passenger pigeon. He is a living menace.

He is the man who votes for Wallace because Wallace offers him easy cop-out solutions to the fears he feels. He is the man who thinks everybody can earn a living. He is the man who, because he *personally* never lynched a nigger, believes there is no such thing as prejudice.

He is the man who believes only what affects him, what he sees, or what is most consistent with the status quo that will keep him afloat.

The time for worshipping the Common Man is past. We can no longer tolerate him, or countenance his stupidity. He is the man who keeps our air polluted, our country at war, our schools infested with police state-ism, our lives on the brink of oppression and our futures sold out for oil leases.

The Common Man—the kind Susskind showed us with such sorry clarity—has to go. If we are to continue living in this doomed world, if we are to save ourselves, we must kill off the Common Man in us and bring forth the Renaissance Man.

After those last two blood-curdling columns about
The Common Man (and the attendant mail that's been
pouring in, both with huzzahs from those of us who are
scared shitless by TCM and with death-threats from
several Common Men—thus proving every once in a
while I hit a truth or two) this time I'd like to do a
happyhappy tippy-toe commentary that will leave you
with a smile on your lips and a song in your heart.
There are two ways to do same: 1) review a show that
has something going for it and talk nice about it or 2)
blast the crap out of a stinker in Menckenesque terms.

Either way is fun, so this week I'll do both.

(But first a small aside, having nothing to do with
TV. Last week's Freep featured an article by a chopper
thug named Mike Brown. Mr. Brown is against a lot of
things I think are very nice, but whereas I wouldn't
take up a .30-06 to stop him from hating Jews, Blacks,
gays, Communists, Catholics, Free Masons, hippies and
all the other species he cannot abide, as long as he
didn't get physical about it ... Mr. Brown—how his
own last name must *bug* him!—has banded together
with a number of other over-six-foot proto-beefy bikers
to DEFEND AMERICA BY VIOLENCE. Mr. Brown
ought to get hip to the simple core truth that his problem is based on his own insecurity about being an ade-
quate male. What you or I would do if we felt uptight
like that, is go find us a lady and give her some pleasure. What Mr. Brown does is use Molotov cocktails on
trucks. We'd use the penis, he uses the truncheon. Mr.
Brown has banded together in the typical homosexual-
fear unit and thrust between his legs not a loving

woman but a snarling chopper. If he wasn't so pitiable, he'd be ludicrous. All concerned folk who read Mr. Brown's shriek of sexual impotency and frustration should send their freeze-dried semen to his lair, in hopes he will either face his emotional problems by making love, not stupidity, or—failing that—drive his air-cooled courage off a cliff in Coldwater at 100 mph.)

Onward and upward with truth and/or beauty.

First, the decimation. Second, the praising.

Up for destruction, one 90 minute movie produced for ABC by Aaron Spelling's jellybean operation over at Paramount. It was on the network a week ago Tuesday, and it was called *The Monk*. When—as a potential writer of 90-minute movies for this series of "World Television Premieres"—I was called in several months ago to sit through a screening of this classic cheapie cornball abomination, I could not really believe ABC would go ahead and put it on the air.

It was *so* bad, so completely and thoroughly without redeeming value of *any* kind, I felt certain the ABC khans would varf, retch, rush for toilets, and then come back and possibly lynch Spelling; the director, George McCowan; the scenarist, Tony Barrett; and even the principal accomplices thespically speaking, George Maharis, Janet Leigh, Carl Betz, William Smithers and even Jack Albertson, who should have known better. But they didn't, the ding-dongs. They ran it. They even took out ads for it.

Gawd, now that's what I call a frenzy for suicide.

In case you are among the blissful millions who missed this epic of stupidity, allow me to describe what it was about the show that makes it the lowest point thus far in a low season.

The idea is a fresh one. It's about this private eye

. . .

The original idea was conceived (if that is the word . . . spawned might be more on-target) by Blake Edwards, who created *Peter Gunn* some ten years ago. I understand the *Monk* idea was an earlier one, and was drawered when *Peter Gunn* took off. Edwards never finished the original version. Spelling bought it (I suppose because it had Edwards' name on it; surely it had nothing else going for it). He assigned the script-writing chores to Tony Barrett, a very nice man who used to write extensively for the Gunn series and worked for Spelling on *Burke's Law*. But Tony Barrett opted for cliche, and what he wrote would have looked pale on the *Gunn* series itself. It's the hack detective story about the big-time mob attorney who's afraid he's gonna be bumped off unless Gus Monk protects him, and Monk says fuck off you hood, and the attorney gets bumped, naturally, only it wasn't the attorney in that flaming car it was . . . well, you know the rest.

I'll tell you about the level of originality of this dog: during the screening, Maharis is leaving Miss Leigh to go off on a mission of spectacular (ho hum) danger and as he reaches the door, Janet says, "Gus . . ." and he turns around and looks at her, and me, sitting in the darkened viewing room, I say, "Be careful," a second before Janet says, ". . . be careful." At which point I *got* up and went out and got a pint of orange drink and a burrito from the studio coffee wagon. When I came back, not much had happened that I didn't remember happening in *77 Sunset Strip* back in 1959.

Maharis acted with all the wizard skill and animation of a poison dart-victim weighted down by anvils, trying to walk across the Bay of Biscayne on the bottom. Miss Leigh, who was cute and sensitive and fine to watch in this kind of role in *The Manchurian Candidate* and *Psycho* and even as far back as Orson Welles's *Touch Of Evil*, has allowed herself to either grow hard and brittle and leathery looking—like a dyke who ain't happy about being a dyke—or wasn't hip to the way they were shooting her. Everybody else mugged and overacted and slimed up the premises, thus telling us all we need to know about Mr. McCowan's directorial strengths, and in all it was marked n.g. from the git-go.

At some point along the way—and this is the point

265

of reviewing such an obstinately shitty flick—the powers that khan ... should. They *should* get hip to the fact that old men who wrote Raymond Chandler-fashion twenty years ago can't retool for contemporary drama. They *should* stop letting themselves get whip-sawed by fast talking Executive Producers like Danny Thomas and Aaron Spelling, who sell them meadow muffins which are called chocolate eclairs. They *should* begin to realize that they have a nice, viable form in the 90-minute movie, and stop castrating it by buying safe, hackneyed, cliché stories resuscitated from moldering issues of the pulp *Argosy*, vintage 1934. They *should* finally throw up their hands and admit that crud won't get it (if you haven't checked lately, ABC, you're trailing in the Ratings Race) and see if they could get somewhere with quality.

Like the guy who died on stage, and it was suggested from the audience that they give him an enema, it might not help ... but it couldn't hurt.

Taaaa-daaaaah!!

It also couldn't hurt to watch a lovely show called *My World—And Welcome To It* that NBC brings us every monday night at 7:30. It's a half-hour sitcom, but many marks above the Lucy level. Based on drawings and anecdotes and short pieces by James Thurber, it has a charming cynicism and unabashed joy in life that no series since the ill-fated *It's A Man's World* of 1962 has managed to capture.

William Windom, as the Thurberesque cartoonist chivvied by his sensible wife, his elderly (before her time) girl-child, and a random pack of dogs, editors, dream fantasies, plights of our time and garden variety horrors of contemporary society, runs the gamut from staunch nobility in the face of madness to bemused resignation that They Are Out To Get Him. He is Everyman with a green eyeshade.

The really great thing about this series, though, is that it attempts to use video as a *medium*. There is animation and cartoon backdrop and stop-action and all kindsa groovy things. It's visually very interesting. And using the Thurber material inventively (they've played with such famous bits as *The Unicorn In The Garden, If Grant Had Been Drinking at Appomatox* and the legendary anecdote about Harold Ross of the *New Yorker* insisting on knowing which of two hippos in a cartoon was the one delivering the punchline) they seem hellbent intent on singlehandedly raising the quality of TV situation comedy.

And so I shouldn't get stoned by agents for neglecting their clients, let me hasten to add that as inept an acting job Janet Leigh and Raymond St. Jacques and William Smithers and Maharis did in *The Monk*, that's how *good* the acting of Joan Hotchkis (as the wife) and Lisa Gerritsen (as the aging toddler) is in *My World—And Welcome To It*.

It ain't often I recommend anything as unreservedly as this show. And to the guy who wrote in to *TV Guide* saying the show wasn't doing appropriate honor to the work and memory of the God Thurber ... well, sir, you are hereby consigned to an eternity watching *Gilligan's Island* reruns.

Trouble with people, Clem, is that they don't know when they's well off.

46: 7 NOVEMBER 69

INTRODUCTORY NOTE TO A SPECIAL
COLUMN: The premier publication of the "new wave"
in speculative fiction is an English magazine titled *New
Worlds*. Recently, one of its editors, Charles Platt,
wrote me a letter in which he solicited a contribution
for an offbeat symposium on the theme of "1980." He
did not want the usual sort of predictive piece on what
the effects of over-population or atomic energy would
mean to the world of 1980, but rather (as he put it) "a
writer's personal, subjective, idiosyncratic reactions to
the 1980's—how they see the general idea of there
being a future, themselves in it, aging, progress in the
various arts . . ." Charles spoke very specifically of this
column—having read it on a recent trip to the
States—and he suggested I try something like it for
New Worlds. Yes, why not. So . . . postulating I don't
pick up a .45 slug in the head before that time, here is
a sample of *The Glass Teat* from the *Los Angeles Free
Press*, dateline Thursday November 13th, 1980. Res
ipsa loquitor.

THE GLASS TEAT

I've run out of pipe tobacco and I'm getting nervous.
Maybe tomorrow or the next day I'll have one of the
kids try to slip into Pasadena and rob a pipe store.
Maybe I'll do it myself. For those of you who may be
reading this—if the printing press hasn't broken down
again—you may gather that my wounds have healed
sufficiently well for me to consider a smash&grab raid.
Yes, your faithful columnist didn't buy it last time out.

But things here in the "underground" (if you'll pardon the pretensions) are nct good. The goddamed Good Folks are stepping up their activities. Christ only knows how they can find the extra money to finance stronger tac/squads . . . the way their taxes bleed them. But I suppose it's money well spent, from their viewpoint: cleaning out the dissidents. As far as I know, we're one of the last three or four pockets left in Southern California. And they almost brought down Chester Anderson's chopper last week when he made his run to drop the *Free Press* on LA. But I suppose we're still a pain in the ass, if hardly effective, because Mishkin came back on Sunday with the new wanted posters. My faithful readers will be delighted to know the price on this columnist has gone up to a full ten grand, plus a year's meat-and-sweet ration points. Now that's what I call critical acceptance.

However, enough personal chit-chat.

My subject for this week is the President's speech on The War, carried over the four major networks. For those of you reading this column in shelters and the outback, it won't provide anything more than another taste of the bitter gall we've grown to know as a steady diet. But for those of you Good Folks—true patriotic Americans—who find one of these newspapers lodged in your eucalyptus or missed being washed down the sewers by the watersweepers, it may offer a moment of doubt in your unshakeable faith. At worst, it can proffer a moment of humor, and God knows you poor fuckers don't have many of *those* these days.

He's wearing makeup better these days. They've managed to disguise the insincerity of the jaw, the deviousness of the eye-pouches, the corruption of the jowls, the thug-like stippling of unshaved follicles, the cornball widow's peak.

They've even managed to exquisitely cover the plastic surgery scars and the discoloration left by last December's assassination attempt on him. (I still contend if Krassner had used a thermite jug instead of that

269

damned Molotov cocktail, he'd have bagged the snake. But, if at first you don't succeed . . .)

But nothing serves to conceal his dissembling. Nothing works to cover his mealymouth. Nothing manages to fill in with substance the empty spaces of his endless promises. He used all the time-honored phrases—my fellow Americans, this Administration, the Search for Peace, let us turn our faces away from conflict, grave concern, you are entitled to your minority opinion—all of them. They were all there—arrayed in shabby tediousness. The War has been going on for seventeen years, my fellow Good Folk: how many times have you heard the Man mouth the words "peace with honor"?

And he's still wiping his nose publicly, on-camera.

He revealed a secret letter he had sent to Premier Mbutu, offering nothing new or conclusive, merely babbling that the United States is anxious to make some progress at the Trobriand Island Conferences. Well, hell yes, gentle readers, he wants to make some progress at the talks. Now that Tanzania and Zambia have joined the "menace" of Black Communism the President tells us is washing its tide over all the civilized world, he's scared out of his mind that his own American Black States—Kentucky, Georgia and Illinois—will get more out of hand. He hasn't forgotten (or by any means forgiven) Governor Gregory; offering sanctuary to Dennis 3X and his militants after what they did in Washington was enough to make the Man declare Chicago ripe for low-yield H-bombs.

Of course he wants peace, the snake! He wants peace on terms no one will give him. He wants more mindless flag-waving. He wants us to believe that there is some incredible nobility in our interfering in the internal affairs of *seventeen* Asiatic and African nations! He wants it all to go back the way it was, when he was a whey-faced lad in a small Florida town, forty years ago. He wants the death toll that now stands at 855,-000 to rise to a nice even million. And he wants you to swallow higher taxes so the Pentagon can raise its budget and build the spacedrop platform without worrying where its next billion is coming from. Won't that be a charmer, gentle readers: your sons and husbands and brothers dropping straight down from deep space into India and Rhodesia.

The Man gibbered you, friends. He said nothing new. He merely tried to pull the fangs of the December Offensive you know we dissidents will be mounting next month. He doesn't want a repetition of last year's Grade School Uprising.

He wants to make certain that the last few of us out here scrounging for canned goods to stave off scurvy don't get any help or succor from "confused, misled Americans who fail to realize that by aiding the dissident elements in our society you are helping to prolong the war." Well, he needn't worry. It's been seventeen years, and those of us who long ago committed ourselves to saving you poor scuttlefish from your own gullibility, we know we won't get any help. We've had our examples. Bobby Seale died in a Federal Penitentiary six weeks ago. Pneumonia. Sure, it was pneumonia. How many of you remember Bobby Seale?

You want some straight talk, gentle readers ... you want to know how we *really* feel about it?

Most of the spark has gone out of us. We can afford to tell you truths like that. We aren't on the same wavelength as those of you who lie publicly to keep up "morale" and buy "public support" with lies. We can tell the truth because *nothing* can stop us from doing what we have to do. We know we can't win, we know we can't change the course of history. But we do it because it's reflex now. We're resigned to living like animals in these sections of the Great United States you've come to call the outback. We're secure in the knowledge that one after another, we'll be picked off and killed. The tac/squads don't even take prisoners any more. They got their new orders last year: flatten them.

You don't know, you'll never know. You've let

271

yourselves be lied to so often and so ineptly, you're willing accomplices to your own destruction.

How do we feel about it? We feel that if there is a God he'll hasten the ecological debacle you've permitted to spread. He'll kill off the diatoms in the ocean faster, and he'll deplete the oxygen supply, and we'll all go under at the same time, gasping for air like iron lung rejects.

But if that doesn't come to pass, here's how we figure it: the Man and "Confucius" Ta Ch'ing and Mbutu will one day say fuck it, and turn loose the Doomsday Machines. And if—as predicted—it kills off ninety-six per cent of the population of the Earth, that'll be cool. Because you deserve no better.

And as for me, I personally look at it like this: if I'm in the ninety-six per cent that gets zapped, then I'm dead and I'm sleeping and I'm at peace at last and I don't have to fight a fight you scuttlefish never wanted me to fight. If I'm in the four per cent that manages to escape alive, well, I've learned how to live in a rabbit warren, and I'll survive.

Either way, I'll be delivered from ever again having to sit and be bored by the TV appearances of a man whose obvious disregard for humanity puts him solidly at the front of a nation that is notable for self-loathing.

My only regret is that I'm out of pipe tobacco. It's funny how little things come to mean so much at the final extreme.

Goodbye, gentle readers. I always end my columns these days with those words. Chances are very good that by this time next week one or the other of us won't be around.

This week, painful reappraisal and viewing-with alarm. The former is something I do only when irrevocably pressed to the wall by the realization that my godhood is fraying at the edges and the latter I do so often it has become the systole and diastole of my routine existence. Nonetheless, painful though they may be, they must be done this week.

Reconsideration of ABC's *The New People* is definitely in order, because after the first show—the airing of the pilot segment by Rod Serling—I recommended this sixty-minute's hype. Well, friends, they sucked me in, too. I will confess that much of my feeling of having been impressed by *The New People* was due to Richard Kiley's bravura performance as the last adult left alive when a planeload of peregrinating teen-agers gets downed on an uninhabited island in the Pacific. Kiley brought to the situation of a melting-pot of young minds forced to create a new society in their own image, a strength and order that catalytically forced the weaker characters of the kids to react in some positive and impressive ways. But Kiley's character was only in the pilot segment, used to set the scene. Then he was killed off. Now the shows rest heavily on the shoulders of unknowns like Peter Ratray, David Moses, Zooey Hall, Tiffany Bolling, Dennis Olivieri and Jill Jaress. And occasionally on the backs of semi-knowns like Rick Dreyfus and Brenda Scott.

But, surprisingly, the blame for this show's having gone instantly and disastrously downhill does not lie with the kids. They are quantum-jumps below even McQueen, Garner, Farrow or Barbara Hershey (all of whom were doing comparable TV parts at approximately the same ages) in talent, but they are game, and they do the best they can with the shabby material they get for scripts. For therein lies the reason *The New People* is mired down in the horse latitudes of the ratings. The basic concept of the show is a viable one; while not entirely fresh (they've been doing the old "how will people react in a microcosm of society" shtick since *Outward Bound*), it *is* workable. The production values are more than satisfactory, having managed to squeak by in establishing an entire AEC-abandoned test site city—a bit that does not bear too close examination before it becomes patently ridiculous, yet one we are willing to accept if the rest of the show functions logically. The direction and photography are hardly distinguished, but in a field where second-rate talent is the best one can hope to get when your real talents all flee to theatrical films, it is acceptable.

So all that remains on which to rationally dump the blame for the increasing failure of this show, is the script work. And there it takes no great depths of perceptivity to recognize why *The New People* has come a cropper.

The second week's plot was an impossible farrago of cliches harkening back all the way to Paul de Kruif's *Microbe Hunters* or the discovery that the anopheles mosquito causes malaria; one of those insane dumbplots in which people begin keeling over from The Dreaded Plague and some kid who had a semester of Pharmacology 101 brews-up the antidote from Brillo pad squeezings and the memory of his Granny's faithful spiderweb poultice chest-rub.

I can't tell you much about the third week's plot because the teaser and six minutes of act one were all I could stomach of acting so porcine and dialogue so pretentious that they instantly buried the story of one of the castaways who was either pushed or fell off a cliff. If you've ever watched a show that telegraphed itself as being unviewable a few minutes into the story, you'll

274

know what it was that impelled me to switch over to *Laugh-In*. (And while I'm at it, may I point out to the manufacturers of *The New People* that of all the ridiculous, insipid, insulting and generally all-around moronic theme songs jammed up the noses of the viewing public—dating all the way back to such classics as *77 Sunset Strip* snap! snap! and *Hawaiian Eye*— *The New People* is far and away the most offensive. Not merely because of its lack of musical value, but because of its cheap attempt to "reach the younger viewer" with what the old farts who created it think is a contemporary sound. Not only is it a far cry from even *kitsch* value as a contemporary sound, but it is a tieline into understanding why hypocrisy is spotted instantly by today's TV viewer. Particularly the younger ones. They *know* this is a young idea, written and produced by *old* people, trying to *sound* young. And they won't go for it. And that's why *The New People* has not pulled the core of viewers it needed to succeed. Older viewers can't identify with a bunch of young snots, and the young people won't be a party to being hustled.)

The fourth segment had hold of a marvelous idea, but once more opted for the obvious, cliché treatment, thereby emasculating the basic concept. Take a Suth'rin kid whose big love is automobiles, and stick him on an island where there are no cars, and how does he go about getting himself wheels; and further, once he has them, what does he do with them? It was a nice idea, synched-in with the theme of how much individual responsibility does a man have in a society where you can't really be made to pay for your acts? It was enough to hold one's attention, but it was hardly the heavyweight drama this series promised.

Fifth week, turn off again. Dulls the senses. Bludgeons the spirit. Twitches the fingers toward knob-turn. *Laugh-In* got my business. Again.

Sixth week, Brenda Scott played a hysteric to Peter Ratray's strong, semi-silent type. The kids get a little stir-crazy and some of them decide to build a raft to float off the island. Plotted as tightly as one of those see-through knit dresses, it was pedestrian, predictable, riddled with improbabilities and coincidences, and re-sembled for logic the attempt of Shipwreck Kelly to go over Niagara Falls in a Dixie Cup.

I've reappraised at such length a series that is obviously a bummer, for the sole reason of trying to save it. The basic idea, I repeat for the fourth time, is a solid one. There is something of consequence inherent in the plight of forty kids trying to create a workable society on an island unaffected by the world their elders made—save in the corruptions passed on to them *by* their elders.

But the producers of *The New People* are traveling down the road to cancellation tread by so many other series: the road that is paved with the hack scripts of old men and/or weary writers. There are young writers in town who know how to mirror the attitudes of the young, who know how to present problems that concern all of us *now*, who have a sense and a feel and a compassion for what's going down today. These are the writers who should be employed on *The New People*. They should be given their head, should have the reins let out on them, should be allowed to run with their ideas. Not hobbled and held in by arbitrary ideas of "what is so" by producers and networkers whose closest approach to the minds of the young is when they ride down the Strip of a Saturday night with their windows and their minds closed.

It should not fall to a television critic to point out to a show's creative personnel the insanity of having a show about the minds and hearts of young people— being written by old people. If I want an authority on how to chop-and-channel a Mercury, I don't hire the lady who won second place in the Betty Crocker Bake-Off.

And as for viewing-with-alarm, I am alarmed that the wonderful *Music Scene* show (which, unfortunately, comes on not only directly opposite *My World—And Welcome To It* but just before *The New People*, thereby laying two heavy strikes on it for openers) is down near the bottom in ABC ratings. This is a program that deserves to continue. It is wryly cynical, has sparkle and dash and originality, and even manages to make some scalpel slashes at the current scene.

David Steinberg and his compatriots are the most ebullient and compelling hosts we have been offered in many moons, and to see them back on the bread lines would be a shame.

Regularly, they showcase talent we don't see nearly enough of: Janis Joplin, Johnny Cash, Three Dog Night, Isaac Hayes, Richie Havens and Buffy Sainte-Marie. And they do it with innovation and sincerity.

I urge those of you who have not yet caught on to *Music Scene* to do so at once. It's so good the scythe-wielder of TV attrition will certainly mow it down forthwith. Or perhaps, having sounded the alarum, we can do something to prevent this winner going the way of the Smothers Bros.

Television and its occult machinations have finally produced their first genuinely tragic figure. How odd: we might have thought Senator Joseph McCarthy the proper one to be so recognized. TV stripped him raw—aided by the US Army and old Joe Welch—and in the last days of the now-famous McCarthy-Army hearings we saw that paragon of despotism bludgeoned from his position as a destroyer of lives, from his position as a disseminator of fear and hatred, from his position as the antichrist of Democracy ... to a sobbing, hysterical mass of ruined flesh. Soon after, he died. Destroyed by television. Surely McCarthy was the front-runner for the title. Then came William Talman, whose career was thrown up for grabs on the *Perry Mason* series because of bad publicity attendant on some minor dope-&-sex peccadillo; cancer added to his tragic stature. But his friends stood by him, to their everlasting credit, and he remained with the show. Yet he was a candidate. And then we saw Lyndon Johnson creamed by TV. By dissent and the rising gorge of American disgust at the way he manhandled the highest office in the land. If not McCarthy or Talman, then certainly weary old LBJ.

But no. None of them hold a candle to the man who emerges as the sorriest creature ever to flash across the land in phosphor-dot reality.

Art Linkletter is the most tragic figure.

It is difficult to bring myself to club a man when he's down, and make no mistake (as that incipiently tragic wager of war, Mr. Nixon, would say), Art Linkletter is down. So what you read here is carefully considered and even more carefully written.

Because the deadly irony of what has happened to Art Linkletter forces one to pause and consider just how uncaring the universe really is. For here is a man who helped build a multi-million dollar show business career in large part from the cute sayings of children, who never managed to glean from all those years kneeling beside tots with their directness and simple truth, enough perceptivity or perspective to help his own daughter as she crawled inexorably toward her own death. It is a universe that allows stupidity to exist, and so we must conclude the universe simply doesn't give a damn.

Diane Linkletter, twenty years old and quite pretty, threw herself from a sixth-floor window in West Hollywood on Saturday, October 4th of this year. She was on a bad trip with acid. (Dear God, how silly and futile resound the hip terminology of the in-group: "bad trip." What must she have been seeing, thinking, feeling as the LSD drove her down six floors to end the worst possible, short trip anyone can imagine?)

And she left behind Art Linkletter, who comes, too late, to a concern for young people.

Remorse, guilt, sorrow. He has no corner on the market, and saying other parents have experienced similar tragedies makes no mark. Life is not a comparison of other people's chamber of horrors. Yet Art Linkletter's purgatory is a very special one, for it was fashioned on network television and furnished by his persistent refusal to *understand*.

As the story is told, immediately after he learned of his daughter's death, Linkletter tried to quash the item. It would have been ugly for the world to know the daughter of such a man—a man so immediately identified with children—had been so alienated that she had taken her life in such a hideous fashion. But for whatever reasons, he verified the report that, yes, it had been acid. And weeks later he appeared on television

(TV again), having appeared before Nixon's committee on drug use. Now he was cast in the tragic role of grieving father, and emerged as a fighter in the war against drugs.

Well, fine. Not being a doper, I can't get very worked up about marijuana, but I've had enough friends and friends of friends blacked-out by heavier stuff to welcome *anybody* as an ally. But Art Linkletter seems *still* to fail to understand.

He fails to recognize the simple truth that when drugs were confined solely to the black ghetto, and hundreds of thousands of minority kids were getting their lives fucked-up, no one cared. Oh, the "authorities" made their token raids and arrests, but the great white world didn't care, didn't really think it mattered. But now that a Jesse Unruh's son gets busted for pot, now that an Art Linkletter's daughter dies behind drug use ... now, *now* the white community in the person of Art Linkletter cries out in anguish.

Too late, Mr. Linkletter! Too goddamed little and too goddamned late! Because you *still* don't know that your Diane's death was only symptomatically caused by LSD. It was caused by the world you, in great part, helped create for all the Dianes. It was caused by you and all the righteous "good folk" who continue to believe the hoary cliches of your own youth. That *anyone* can make it in America if he has the will and determination. That authority is always right, that children should respect their parents whether they've earned the respect or not, that hard work brings its just reward, that nice girls don't do this or that, that good little boys don't do that or the other. It was caused by all the people like yourself who've allowed the police to turn loose the hoses and the dogs and the tear gas and the cattle prods on "the enemy" in our streets.

Who *is* the enemy, Mr. Linkletter?

Is it the dreaded Communist Menace?

Is it the anarchist rabble?

Is it the drug-crazed dissenters?

No, Mr. Linkletter, it's your own kids.

How many parents will end their days sorrowing for their kids like you, because they fail to recognize the insanity of turning hate and prison and death against an "enemy" who is simply *your kids?*

Do you yet understand the nature of your tragedy, Linkletter, all of you? Do you understand that your tragedy is in what happened to the college dissenters convicted last week, in police photographing twelve and sixteen-year-old kids in the Valley as "subversives" because they wanted to join the Moratorium Day marching, in the trial of the Chicago Conspiracy 8, in the gagging of Bobby Seale. Can you dig it, Mr. Linkletter—Bobby Seale is *your* son!

Diane's death grew logically out of her disillusionment. I never knew her, I don't know you, but I know what was in her gut, because it comes from the guts of hundreds of other Dianes and Bobby Seales with whom I've come in contact. Disillusionment at Art Linkletter for helping to preserve a hypocritical and repressive *laissez-faire* society in which Diane and her contemporaries were lied-to every day of their lives. Lied to by TV (and that's *you*, Art), lied to by authority, lied to by the dichotomy between what you told her the world was like and what she found it to be for herself.

Jingo-ism! Dammit, jingo-ism. "Generation gap," "silent majority," "the American way," "the menace of Communism," "student radicals," "the drug culture." All of it is bullshit! It's death, Mr. Linkletter. Death and blood and suicide and stupidity.

I bought your record, Mr. Linkletter. The one made with Diane before she died. *We Love You, Call Collect* it's called, and there're photos of you and Diane on the cover. I'm not going to be gross and suggest you take any delight in this 45 rpm item. I suppose you've continued to let it sell in hopes some kid or parent may learn a lesson from it. I hear your voice break and tears in your words on this record, and I hope I'm not being hustled; I hope that was something more than theatrical histrionics. It would be too horrible to consider it anything else.

But the record is another part of your on-camera guilt, Mr. Linkletter. Because it proffers the same weary cliches to the young people that your generation has always proffered. It resounds with the helpless confusion and sorrow of people who have found the world in which they grew up totally different from the world of today. Well, what did you expect? You've allowed that world to poison itself with war for fifty years, you've permitted corruption and racism to flourish, you've sacrificed everything beautiful and meaningful to the building of bigger and better military establishments, political machines, television careers . . .

I understand also that Art Linkletter is going down to Synanon, to find out about drug use. It's a step in the right direction. But it's only a tool to be used in finally prying open that locked skull-box of set ideas and rigid beliefs. I'm not exactly sure how I came to be addressing Mr. Linkletter directly in this column, but I've switched back to the impersonal to prevent any of you who might pass it off as one man's anguish, from wriggling free.

For Art Linkletter has made his bed and now he'll have to sleep in it. What happened to him can happen to all of us. Unless we act now to stop the senseless stupidity and hatred that seem destined to rule this country. I can summon very little pity for Art Linkletter; for Diane, yes, quite a lot. Because I know how lost and helpless she must have felt. How lost and helpless all those kids in their real or mental prisons now feel.

You are TV, Mr. Linkletter. *You* have the power to go to school again, to understand *all* the reasons why Diane died. And once having learned, to speak up. To go to the council chambers of Nixons and Agnews and cry to them as you cry to us on your record.

Because you're only the first. The first major figure in the TV pantheon to discover that what you shot across the tube for so many years was waste and frippery and lies. In the council chambers of the networks, several weeks ago, the heads of the big three joined to establish a "youth" liaison with the younger generation, to find out what they are thinking, what they are about, what they want. They picked a kid named Waxman, I believe, to be the voice of youth.

You might speak to them about that, Mr. Linkletter. And tell them you'd like to spend some time going to school, and then assisting in forging that link between the generations. And the first step is not to lie, and the second is to try to understand.

There's no help for Art Linkletter. He's lost his, and I would certainly find it impossible to pack the guilt he'll have to pack. But guilt and sorrow can be softened by making sure what has happened to oneself happens to no one else.

It will take a strong and intelligent and very probably selfless man to carry such a load. Only time will tell if Art Linkletter packs the gear. Until then, he is merely the most tragic figure produced by the TV Generation.

49:   5 DECEMBER 69

I swear to Christ, sometimes I feel as though I've tumbled assoverteakettle down a rabbit hole. What I mean, maybe *you* aren't getting the same stuff over *your* TV set I'm getting on *mine*. Because the stuff on mine is crazy as a neon doughnut and I refuse to believe I'm seeing straight. Maybe all those Zonk-rays from the color set are turning my brains to cottage cheese. With chives.

On the Frank Reynolds ABC news I see where a US Marine has copped to the rumors of a Vietnamese massacre being true. And I see photographs that were taken on the spot, genuinely horrendous photographs. They look like replays of Bergen-Belsen or Buchenwald. Piles of emaciated bodies. Children with their faces blown off by riflefire. Mothers with bullet holes through their heads, stilled in the act of trying to hurl their babies from them. And the babies, lying twisted as Raggedy Ann dolls, as dead as their mothers. Somewhere between 170 and 700 people. Civilians. The total has not yet been agreed upon. Maybe VC-supporters, maybe not. But *civilians,* either way. Dead; all of them dead.

It happened 20 months ago, at My Lai, and we're just now finding out about it. When the first photos appeared in the *Cleveland Plain Dealer,* there was instant snarling from the Pentagon. It wasn't true. It didn't happen. The first Marine to talk about it was a psychopathic liar. And every day the Tom Reddin News on Channel 5 began with a map of Southeast Asia behind The Man, and he smiled and said triumphantly, "Today, further proof that the 'alleged' massacre of

Viet Namese civilians never happened! Pinkville is a calloused lie!"

And then the dam broke. And one after another the men who had participated in the crime came forward and extended their hands like Lady Macbeth and said they were finding it difficult to wash away the damned spot.

So now the Army has "taken steps" to set things to rights. They've initiated court-martial proceedings against the Lieutenant who ordered the massacre. And some twenty-odd others. (I won't even comment on the military position of letting the mass murderers wander around on their own recognizance. All I'll say is that Sirhan Sirhan only bumped *one* man, and he was indicted *without* bail.. But then, he killed an Amurrican, not them little slant-eyed devils.)

Now I don't know how you feel about this whole thing, there's an entire range of emotions one can experience, I suppose, but I'd suspect they have to weigh heavily on the side of revulsion, shame and horror. Yet *my* TV set showed me a gentleman in the House of Representatives who got up and deplored the military's preferring charges, on the grounds that it would make any soldier who committed (what he called) an "error in judgment" liable to prosecution as a "common criminal." Well, I'll agree with the rep; that Lieutenant is hardly a "common" criminal. I cannot conceive of the sort of mind that can butcher a hundred and seventy unarmed men, women and children—but it is unquestionably not "common."

So, you see what I mean about nutsy things coming in on my tube? Here is this shameful disgrace blotched on the escutcheon of the United States, and some ding-dong asshole in the House of Representatives is uptight because it might force *other* potential slaughterers to pause and consider abiding by the terms of the Geneva Convention.

But that's hardly an isolated dichotomy. Reagan finally gets around to having an ecological conference, to discuss how much longer we'll be polluting the state (not to mention the entire planet), and for two days we are bombarded with much high-flown political-sounding rhetoric intended to convince us that The Gipper is finally hip to the peril. He'll *do* things, he says. He'll take steps. And the very next day *my* TV set shows me the resumption of oil drilling in the Santa Barbara channel. Those poor slobs living out there dash out in fishing boats to prevent the oil company from hauling in their platform, and Reagan is still mulching about saying he's going to save the land. Because oil leases mean heavy sugar to the state and federal governments, and you *know* the oil lobby isn't going to let death and destruction get in the way of their showing a profit on their ledgers.

And the bill to double the income tax deduction for individuals is defeated soundly, but the oil men get another oil depletion allowance.

And TV news is primarily Establishment-oriented, but Spiro attacks them for being in *any* way fair to the dissent movement. To the resounding support of the Great American Masses.

And a soldier goes AWOL and finds sanctuary in a Unitarian church, and the Army brands the guy a traitor because he puked on the bayonet range when one of his buddies was told to "Kill Kill Kill" and he said he didn't believe in killing, and they beat the shit out of him.

Oh, lemme tell ya. Crazy stuff.

The interesting thing about all this, of course, is that—among other serendipitous side-effects—almost every deep-rooted belief of Americana is being exploded into lies and confusion. So with everything they've ever accepted as rockbed fact being proved a fraud, television viewers are flocking in ever greater numbers to situation comedies, where the ideals and beliefs of their youths thirty and forty years ago are still maintained. They can watch Lucy and *Petticoat* and *Green Acres* and continue to believe that *that* life still exists. In some mythical *terra incognita*, they know not where.

But how do they react to the massacre, the good folk who have always believed that Our Fighting Men are good and decent and honorable? How do they shiver and quake to the explosion of the Jack Armstrong myth? Do they rationalize it as the act of an isolated kill-crazy Lieutenant? If so, what about all the other guys in that outfit who joined in, dragging people to the edge of the ravine as their victims pleaded to be left alive, as they turned their weapons on them? Do they think about the conditioning that permits a man to murder children and hold his tongue about it for twenty months?

If ever there was an apocalyptic incident that speaks to the death of the past in this country, this week we have it. We can ignore the pollution, we can permit the political corruption, we can deny the paranoia and racism of our culture, we can substitute personal experiences with shitty Jews or blacks or Catholics or young people or old people for a careful, reasoned understanding of the human condition—but we cannot ignore this massacre.

In discussing this matter with friends, I've been reminded of the Viet Cong Massacre during the Tet Offensive, in which four thousand men, women and children were dumped into shallow graves and then clubbed or shot to death. Understand something: I do not carry VC flags. I am no lover of killers, be they Oriental or Caucasoid or Negroid. Hell, yes, they are vermin for the act. And not even saying they were murdering their own people is an excuse. What makes you think I have an answer? Love thy neighbor? That doesn't work either. History certainly gives us enough proof of it. But these are *our* guys. These are the direct lineal descendants of Robert Taylor and John Garfield and Victor McLaglin and Humphrey Bogart on Bataan and Corregidor and Iwo Jima and Kiska and Attu. These are *our* guys, godammit! Not those evil little yellow men with the sibilant hisses and the

287

bamboo shoots under the fingernails. These are Johnny and Billy and Gus from Trenton and Denver and Cleveland. They aren't *supposed* to be infanticides.

So now we learn the truth we always knew. *We* are as rotten as *them*. Violence knows no color barrier. Those who ball their fists keep going until they slaughter children. Now America has to face it.

No, Spiro, we can't let you silence the news media. We *need* to know the truth. Unpleasant as it may be, we have to have the truth now.

There isn't enough blood or time left in the world to permit your kind of dissembling, Spiro.

Hey ... Spiro ... you know what you are, man? You're the guy who greased that Lieutenant's trigger-finger.

POISONED BY THE FANGS OF SPIRO: PART I

Ugly, baby. Just righteously ugly. Dayton, Ohio, I mean. (Yeah, that's why my column's been absent for the last few weeks. I went to Dayton to deliver a lecture, and what happened there was such a bummer, such a downer, such a shitter, that I didn't even have the stuff to write a column. I'll tell you all about it. Might take three columns, but I'll lay it all on you, because it has to do with the power of fear generated by one of the great TV stars of our times, Spiro T. Agnew.)

I come to you, bloody and slightly bowed. To be perfectly honest, friends, I feel like Peter Fonda, AKA Captain America, living a real-life version of *Easy Rider*.

The hero of *Easy Rider* comes up against the violent fear and insanity of midcentury America, and gets his head blown off for his trouble. I didn't get my head blown off, merely got my mouth closed, but the background is much the same, and from the encounter I've drawn some inescapable conclusions, the first of which is:

AMERICA IS ENTERING A PERIOD OF REPRESSION AND WITCH-HUNTING THAT WILL MAKE THE TERROR TIMES OF THE McCARTHY ERA SEEM LIKE THE AGE OF ENLIGHTENMENT.

I will now proceed, through the fascinating relating of my travails, to document my thesis. Pax.

Early in September, I was contacted by the Dayton

Living Arts Center, in the person of Barbara Benham, its Creative Writing Director. She wanted me to come to Ohio in the capacity of a "Guest Artist" to both work with the students in the science fiction writing course, and to deliver an evening lecture to adults and college level students. We started negotiations.

(The Living Arts Center itself is a groove. It is a federally funded operational Project to Advance Creativity in Education—PACE—financed under Title III of the Elementary and Secondary Education Act of 1965. Its purposes are to "identify, nurture, and evaluate the creative potential of youngsters whose interests lie in the Fine Arts—creative writing, dance, drama, music and the visual arts." The participating students number from eight to twelve hundred, in grades 5 to 12, who show up at the Center after school and on weekends. The programs are varied and the faculty is top level. I lay all of this in, in front, in an effort to establish that the *Center* itself, and the faculty, are dynamite. Whatever horrors came down, they were by no means the fault of the Center and its instructors. Administration is another matter, and we'll get to that shortly. But if you see parallels between the Center and what has happened at colleges all across America, you will understand that it is not necessarily the faculty or the institution *itself* that is repressive, it is almost always the politicians, the "educators" in their little suits and ties, the Administration that takes its stand for censorship, control, rules&regs, guidelines, and a brutal maintaining of the no-waves status quo ... usually at the expense of the very kids they prattle about "serving.")

Through Barbara Benham, negotiations for my three days attendance (December 15, 16 and 17) were completed on the 22nd of October, and contracts were signed by myself and the Administrative Director, Jack A. DeVelbiss. His is not the name most properly to bear in mind. The name with which we will deal is Glenn Ray, a dude I will not soon forget.

Nor, if I have my way, will he soon forget me.

Now understand something: Dayton was my 152nd speaking appearance in the last five years. I've spoken to all levels of audience, from junior high school crowds through college level groups to adult audiences. With the exception of a horrendous situation that arose last Labor Day at the World Science Fiction Convention in St. Louis, I've never had any trouble. In fact, I've been asked back to speak second and even third times at some of the universities. I did not anticipate any trouble in Dayton, though my encounters in the Great American Heartland these last two years have hipped me to the growing tensions and tendencies to shy away from anyone bearing news of unrest from the outside world.

In a letter dated September 25th, Miss Benham tried—in a delicate way—to forewarn me of the tenor of Dayton thinking. She wrote, in part:

"As the Center depends on public support for its continuation, deliberate provocation is dangerous for us. I hope that, without being untrue to yourself, you can focus mainly on literature (from any angle, including its role in revolution) as opposed to politics."

I replied, on September 29th, "It is my intention to *win* them, not alienate them. I will not, repeat *NOT* provoke anyone. If you want a rabble-rouser, get someone else. I try to tell some truth in the course of my discussions of writing and the place of the *committed* writer in our society, and that occasionally upsets a few people who are locked into socio-economic or religious boxes, but in the main it is my intention to bring light, not darkness.

"As to my subject matter—you seem concerned I'll deliver a Julian Bond/Rap Brown diatribe—being literature rather than politics, yes, of course. I'm a writer. That's what I do, and it's what I know. But since I conceive of the role of the creator in our Times as inextricably involved with the world through which he moves, it is inevitable that my discourses will slop over

291

into human behavior, the state of the world, the effect of committed writing on the tenor of the Times, honesty and ethic in writing, et cetera.

"If any or all of these unnerve you, or lead you to believe I'll be doing your program more harm than good, I suggest again that you reconsider hiring me. The only guarantees I can offer are predicated on my past experiences with groups similar to the one for which I presume I'll be speaking (straight, middle-class, white mid-America folk who seem disturbed at the changes happening around them): they seem to relate to me, seem to appreciate someone telling them things straight out, and the leavening of humor I include inclines them to hang in there for the entire set. I've never had a riot or an insurrection."

Not till Dayton, that is.

We pause at this point to refresh your memories about the philosophical line all this history is taking: Spiro Agnew, the first vice-president of the United States to suffer from terminal foot-in-mouth disease; the power of TV in mass communicating *instantly* to an entire nation a gagging fear and horror of change; the use of the mass media to convince a middle-class white population that too much knowledge in the hands of longhaired freaks and natural-haired niggers is a deadly thing; the reassurances of dangerous slayers like Spiro that the final grasp for repressive power by the old order is, in reality, a rallying around the flag by a mythical "silent majority" of God-Fearing Good Solid Americans. And outside, peace on earth . . .

That's what we're talking about here, not a minor incident in Dayton, Ohio . . . good will to men . . .

Meanwhile, back at the story . . .

My duties during the three days at the Living Arts Center were as follows: four meetings with the science fiction workshop, under the direction of John Baskin, who turned out to be a hero in more ways than one; an adult lecture; three lectures for specially selected students of local high schools, brought to the Center for

292

that purpose. The tab for the three days was fourteen hundred dollars, including expenses.

I arrived by TWA on the evening of Sunday, December 14th. Dayton looked like all the rest of Ohio ... a state in which I'd been born ... a state I'd left many years before, perhaps with that sense of premonition known only to the young who sense this land in which they stand will never change, will never yield up treasures great enough for them. I had left and gone other places and found now, upon returning, that my heart and mind retained images of mid-America that were part childhood pains and joys, part cultural myth, part sadness at seeing smog and pollution and Big Boy hamburger stands ... and part triumph at returning to execute AN EVENING WITH HARLAN ELLISON.

It was a dream. If you basket-case a dream, it flops over as nightmare. Peace on earth ...

John Baskin and Barbara Benham picked me up at the airport and took me to the apartment she had vacated for my use while in town. She was staying elsewhere. It was a gesture of considerable hospitality, intended to save me the cost and loneliness of a hotel room. It was to be used later, against her, by the Administration, to whose eyes propriety is easily set awry.

The next morning they came for me, and I was taken to the Center. It was a converted warehouse, the facility having been handsomely renovated to accommodate work shops and a large theater and a dance studio and talk areas and God knows what all else. It was very impressive, very real, and held within its walls (even early in the day, childless) the sense and scent of life. Young minds came here to find direction, came here to taste joy and beauty. It looked lived in. I wanted very much to *do* for them.

What I did not know was that the following had occurred in Dayton:

1) There was a concerted program afoot to quash "freaks" in the city.

2) The school finance levy had been soundly de-

feated a few days before I'd arrived. This forced the Center to have to scramble for a quarter of a million dollars to keep running. So the Center could not afford to offend anyone. (Why Mr. DeVelbiss had not used the three years gravy time, during which the Center had been running on Federal funds, to make provisions for such an eventuality, was a question I heard asked many times during my brief stay in Dayton.)

3) A black educator named Art Thomas was in the process of losing his job because, in the course of averting a riot, he had used the word "pig" when speaking to a cop. It was a railroad kangaroo court scene, with every "liberal" in Dayton up-in-arms because his hearing was being held before the very people who had relieved him of his position—and everyone knew he was going to be set down. The case was big news and promised to go to the Supreme Court.

4) The Center had had mild troubles with other "Guest Artists" in the recent past. Pianist Lorin Hollander (who had charmed everyone during his first appearance at the Center) upset the Administration by returning with long hair and sideburns, hip clothing, and a program that was divided between music and political opinion. Square, suited and silent his first time there, Hollander had become "involved" in the world in the interim, and his frankly expressed concern for America and the world unsettled the Program Director, Glenn Ray. I was given to believe, in no uncertain terms, that Mr. Hollander would not be invited to return.

5) An appearance of a puppet theater at the Center had brought—for some inexplicable reason—shrieks of protest from parents who had attended an evening performance. Something about, "What are you liberals teaching our kids down there at that freak palace?"

6) Fear of "making waves" was high in the Administration of the Center, in the school board, in the city.

And here came I.

Innocent, starry-eyed, dew-bedazzled little me. Set to be cast in the role of insurgent dissident revolutionary. Ready to be typed outside agitator, corrupter of the young, *agent provocateur*, trouble-making wave-creator.

This has been the background. The cast of characters, the action, the incredible denouement—all of this in the next two week's blistering, scathing, uncompromising installments.

Can you bear to wait!?! The suspense is killing!

You know, sometimes my life flashes before my eyes ... and frankly, it ain't worth living a second time.

POISONED BY THE FANGS OF SPIRO: PART II

If you think the hope for tomorrow lies solely in the young—as did I—be advised the poison has seeped down through the veins of the society to them as well. If you keep reassuring yourself that as soon as the present generation of bigots, morons, haters and blue star mothers (who take open pride in having sent their sons off to die) kick off things will be better . . . start worrying again. Because they've already gotten to the mass of kids, out there in the Great American Heartland. Even as they've been planted, those good mommies and daddies have reached skeletal hands out of the graves to clutch their children and intone, "If you want to honor my memory, if you don't want me to have died in vain, remember: niggers are evil, they all want to rape your women; Jews secretly run the world and they'll steal everything you have; Communists roam everywhere; sex is dirty; don't let them Ivory Tower liberals corrupt you; trust in hate!" And then the dirt is shoveled in on them and they go to that big Klavern in the sky, leaving behind them the butchered minds and closed-off potentialities of the next generation.

I went to Dayton to talk writing, to talk science fiction, to talk about what I felt should be the role of the *committe*d writer in Our Times, what he could do to reshape the world through his writing. My first encounter was with a class of seniors from Wilbur Wright High School. I'd been briefed that they were "white Appalachian kids." Whatever *that* was supposed to mean, or to tell me. I figured they were like San Fernando Valley kids, middle-class, somewhat sleepy but wake-able if you prodded them and started them question-ing. I was wrong. Lord, I was wrong. They were touched by the grave-bone hands of their parents. And they had been poisoned by the fangs of Spiro.

They were marched in by two pleasant-enough-look-ing little old ladies with white hair tightly iron-curled (they looked like an advertisement out of a 1930's issue of *Liberty Magazine*, reading time: 1 minute 32 sec-onds).

It was cold in Dayton, in the mid-twenties, and they were bundled in heavy jackets or overcoats. Perhaps thirty of them, sitting terribly erect in four rows of straight-back chairs. Barbara Benham introduced me, and against a backdrop of two enormous posters (one of me, the other of the Eniwetok mushroom) I climbed up onto a tall stool. I grinned at them and said, "My name's Ellison. I'm a writer. How many of you have ever read anything I've written?"

Glen Ray sat in the back of the room, arms folded, watching me carefully.

There was silence from the audience.

It wasn't unusual. I'm under no illusions about the minority of Americans who read *anything*, much less me. But it's a hook with which to begin.

"Okay," I said, "let's try it this way: how many of you are interested in writing, about a career in writing, about what it's like to be a writer, his life . . . that sort of thing?"

Nothing. An oil painting. Mount Rushmore. Jeffer-son, Washington, Lincoln. Dead eyes. Slack jaws. Not a flicker. Not a twitch. Not a tremble.

"Oh boy," I murmured *sotto voce*, "I really *am* in the Great American Heartland, aren't I?" Glenn Ray crossed his legs uncomfortably. Big Brother was watching. "Well look, troops, you got hauled out of your class and drug over here to listen to some dude you never met before rap about a lot of dull stuff. So

297

what should we talk about? The world situation? How about the Art Thomas case?"

Nothing. But off to the left, in the rear, someone said, "Art *Who?*" (In the first installment of this Dayton Diatribe I mentioned that Art Thomas had been making headlines in Dayton. A black educator who had been railroaded out of his job because he had avoided a cops-and-kids confrontation by relating to the kids and getting them to back off, but in the process he had called a cop a pig.)

I couldn't believe they didn't know about it. "You've got to be kidding!" I said. "This is the biggest thing to happen in Dayton in years. It may go to the Supreme Court as a test case ... and you people haven't even *heard* about it? Okay, how about the My Lai massacre? You've been reading about *that*, haven't you?"

Television faces stared back at me. No, gentle readers, they had *not* heard about it. Or if they had, they didn't remember. Or if they remembered, they weren't sufficiently involved to even nod a yes at me. I was looking at the result of hours before the glass teat, passively suckling the distant images of dead bodies piled on top each other.

What do you do?

I did something.

What I did was wrong or right, depending on what you conceive to be the role of a guest artist brought in to impart information about a scene of the world different from that through which they move. I freely cop to culpability in what I did next. I could have accepted my intuition about those kids and where they were at. I could have said to myself, Ellison ... back off. Let them continue the way they're going. Let them think it's all somewhere off in the distance, has nothing to do with them. Let them think you're a sweet guy, kind of dumb, and kind of boring, and let them go back at the end of the hour to Wilbur Wright High School, having heard nothing more visceral than the nonsense those

298

two little old ladies feed them every day. I *could* have said that.

But I didn't.

Instead, I raised my tone of voice considerably and demanded, "What the hell is with you, people? What are you learning in school? My generation and all the ones that went before have left you a garbage dump, a cesspool: *you're* the ones who have to clean it up. Do you want another fifty years of war? Do you want the land and the air and the water to become so intolerably polluted they won't support life of any kind? Not just for your great-grandchildren, but for you and me? Chances are good if they don't slaughter us all first, we won't *live* for another fifty years. You see, there are these things in the ocean called diatoms, and they produce seventy per cent of our oxygen, and we've polluted the water so much the plankton that feeds on the diatoms is vanishing, and that means—"

And I was off. Running fast. Up and down and around. "What the hell are you people training yourselves to be? Redemption stamp center clerks?"

Then I read them one of my stories, *Shattered Like A Glass Goblin*, which—depending where your head is at—is either a pro- or an anti-dope story. I wrote it as an anti. And when I got finished, Glenn Ray was even unhappier. It had some sex in it, and some cursing, and some dope, and some violence.

Then one of the kids raised his hand. It was the first sign of mobility in the crowd. I wanted to rush over and play Monte Hall: for raising your hand, sir, I will make a deal with you! You can have your choice of a revolution, an all-expense-paid rejuvenated America, or a six-pack of groupies. But I'd forgotten for a moment that I was in Dayton.

"Are you telling us to smoke marijuana?" he asked. "Don't you know that it's against God's Covenant? Don't you know that marijuana leads to Hard Stuff that makes people want to go out and rob and kill to get the Hard Stuff?"

"Hold it, hold it," I said, dazed. "That was an *anti-*dope story I just read to you. But I think you're old enough to know the difference between Hard Stuff and marijuana. Either way, it's *your* life. I don't use, and if anyone asks me *my* opinion, I'd say forget it. But it's *your* life, baby, and if you want to mess it over with drugs, that's your prerogative. Kindly don't try and push me into a corner where I have to defend pot, because that doesn't happen to be my crusade."

It went on that way for the better part of an hour. Punching, punching, trying to get through, trying to tell them they were our last, best hope, and if *they* sat there with prognathous jaws and Little Orphan Annie eyeballs the whole *country* was doomed.

I'm afraid I said Spiro Agnew was an asshole.

And when the hour was up, the two little old ladies rose, and said, in their best Louisa May Alcott manner, "We'd like to thank you, Mr. Ellison, for your—uh—enthusiasm. But our bus driver is waiting for us to hurry back to school, so—uh—thank you and goodbye."

The kids, a mite dazed by the mixmaster into which they'd stumbled, were led docilely back to the Halls of Academe where they would be told to ignore that strangely garbed hippie with the decadent ideas and the inexcusable profanity.

They were given "evaluation sheets" on which they were to record their opinions of the hour.

Glenn Ray looked like a man who has just learned Santa Claus takes bribes.

Barbara Benham looked disturbed. She didn't say anything. But an hour later, we got word Mr. Ray wanted to see us. He came down to Miss Benham's classroom, and he said, "You'd better stick to talking about writing."

I asked him pointedly if that meant I was not allowed to talk about the world or politics or any of the other subjects on which I'd dwelled in the Wilbur Wright class. He hurriedly assured me he meant no such thing . . . just that I was a writer and should deal with these topics from that position. It seemed a reasonable request, and I said I would. When he left, Barbara Benham looked even *more* disturbed.

"Anything wrong?" I asked.

"I'm not sure," she said, and bit her thumb.

Later that day I had a get-together with students from the Living Arts Center itself, rather than a specially bussed-in crowd. It was called the "Let's Talk" session, and these were an entirely different breed of kids than the Wilbur Wright zombies. These kids— ages 12 to 17—were sharp, inquisitive, irreverent, uncompromising, alert. We got to rapping about all sorts of things love/hate, war/peace, truth/shucks, power/subservience—and the only bad moment I can recall was when a boy in the back asked, *non sequitur*, "What's Barbra Streisand like?" Everyone did a take. It had absolutely nothing to do with anything that had gone down in the dialogue, but I said simply that I didn't know her, but from what I'd heard around the studios, she was a royal pain in the ass to work with. The kid burst into tears later, I learned, telling Mr. Ray and others, "Why'd he have to say that about a *great* star like Miss Streisand?"

I won't say it was the greatest rapport in the history of Western Man, that afternoon session, but there is a photo on page 23 of the December 16th edition of the *Dayton Daily News* showing me surrounded by kids, laying an anecdote on them, and their heads are thrown back in laughter, their mouths open with joy; they are having a good time.

You see, we *related*. Remember that . . . it comes up later.

But: in the back of the group, Glenn Ray sat watching. This is a Watchbird watching you. He particularly didn't like my reading of the two *Glass Teat* columns dealing with The Common Man—a hobby horse I'm currently riding. He didn't like me saying the greatest danger to freedom and liberty in our country

301

was the stupidity of the masses, the passive acceptance of all the poison spurted from the fangs of Spiro.

Later that night I had my first meeting with the science fiction workshop kids. And we grooved. They were like the other Living Arts kids: bright, into it, curious.

Things were going well. I thought.

(What I did not know was that calls were coming in from the parents of those Wilbur Wright students. One man showed up at the Center and wanted to "look around" and see what this here now Center was all about. Glenn Ray was being drawn uptight. Waves were appearing on the placid surface of his little frog pond.)

Next morning came the pivotal scene, I feel. I was to meet my second bussed-in group. Black journalism students from Paul Lawrence Dunbar High School.

The instant I walked into the classroom, I felt it. A difference. The biggest difference. Life surged in that room. Thirty-some kids, all black, with a male, white teacher. They were slumped in the seats, eyes watching. Yeah. That's where it's at, friends. None of that "here I sit, docilely waiting for your effulgent intelligence, great white teacher" jive. These kids had had all the shit thrown at them. They were wide awake and wanted the dude up in front to *prove* he was worth listening to.

And *that*, Establishment, is the attitude all school kids should have. They should *demand* their teachers be interesting and on top of it and stimulating.

The difference was like, uh, black and white.

Glenn Ray sat in the back, watching.

We started out, and for the first ten minutes I was being tested. There was no hype possible with these kids. I was white, and that was a strike or two right there. And I was fancied-up with what looked (to them) like new clothes, and that was another couple of strikes. And I was in a position of authority, and that was strikes five and six. So I proceeded to put what I had in front of them. And that entailed doing precisely

302

what Art Thomas had done: talk to them the way they talked to each other. And that meant the words motherfucker and dumbshit and pile of crap were exchanged. Broke through. Read them a fantasy I'd written about an extraterrestrial who was passing as a human to illuminate the arid emotionalism of a black girl passing as white. They dug it. And we got to really rapping. Good things. Truths and fears and humor and some mutual affection were passed around. ("You know," I said to one black kid who'd asked a dumb question, "you are a dumb shit, man." And he replied, "Thass okay. You just an envious Jew, baby.")

When the hour was over, they didn't want to leave. The bus driver had to come in and practically drag them to the bus. Their teacher shook my hand and said it was a fine hour. He said he wished the time had been longer. Three of the students hung back. They wanted to have their picture taken with me. I dug it. One of their buddies cranked off a few snaps of us all together, and we made nice on each other and they split. I wasn't worried about *their* evaluation sheets.

I looked at Glenn Ray.

I've grown sensitive to the look of hate these last few years. I looked at Glenn Ray. He hated me.

The Program Director of the Dayton Living Arts Center hated me. I didn't know why, but later, talking to a member of the faculty (and for the benefit of Mr. Ray and Mr. DeVelbiss, who insist they don't want to fire Miss Benham for having had the wretched judgment to bring me in as a guest artist, despite the prevalent fears of everyone at the Center that that was *precisely* what they wanted to do, it is not Miss Benham to whom I refer here), I was told that Mr. Ray, even though he is the man most directly responsible for what happens to the kids, relates poorly to them. I was also told I made Ray angry, and that I'd capped it by getting along so well with the black kids. Though a Negro himself, it seems Mr. Ray can't talk to blacks the way I did.

303

I didn't think it mattered. Not till later that day, only a few hours before I was to deliver the public lecture for adults and college students that had been advertised for weeks. It was at that point that Glenn Ray's fear of "wave making" melded with his hatred of your gentle columnist, and he pulled the plug. Spiro Agnew bit Glenn Ray and . . .

He canceled my speech.

And that's when it hit the fan, friends.

POISONED BY THE FANGS OF SPIRO: CONCLUSION

A wound neither as deep as a Chicago Conspiracy Trial nor as wide as two US Army sergeants being removed from their Armed Forces Radio posts when they told their audience that they were being censored and could not tell the troops what was *really* happening in the War. Neither as final as the silencing of Lenny Bruce ... nor as significant as the attempted whitewash of My Lai before the evidence piled up so high it *couldn't* be denied (though *Time* reported last week that 54% of the American people *still* refuse to believe it happened); neither as painful as the police moving in on a recent Allen Ginsburg reading and first cutting off his mike, then putting on Muzak so he could not be heard ... nor as destructive as a Century City Riot; neither as debilitating as canceling Joyce Miller's *Encounter* from KPFK because she was sniping at the Administration ... nor as horrendous as the Smothers Brothers being flushed out of sight; neither as permanent as the silencing of Seale, Cleaver, King, Malcolm X, JFK, RFK or George Lincoln Rockwell ... nor as ghastly as court-martialing soldiers who protest. But when Glenn Ray panicked at the two or three phone calls he'd gotten from parents of students to whom I'd spoken, parents who didn't want their kids to hear any opinions but ones approved by the *Good Housekeeping* seal ... when he grew terrified that his petty sinecure at the Center was in danger ... when he realized that after the defeat of the school bond levy he was in a vulnerable position ... when push came to shove and he had to suddenly stand behind the free speech and dissent he had so liberally championed to all those kids ... the poison from the fangs of Spiro took effect, and he canceled me out.

What happened next happened so fast, some of it may have been rumor, some of it may have been nightmare, some of it may have been reality, and some of it will stick with those kids for the rest of their lives.

I was in a workshop session with John Baskin's science fiction writing class when Barbara Benham—the creative writing director who'd hired me—stuck her head in and asked me to step into the hall. "Glenn Ray canceled your speech for tonight," she said.

I grew very calm. Two thousand years of racial memory of pogroms took over and I grew very calm.

"Well, let's just go talk to Mr. Ray and see what's happening," I said.

The kids spilled out into the hall behind us. "What's happening?" they asked. "What's going on?"

"Go on back inside," I said. "Glenn Ray canceled the lecture tonight. We're going to go to his office and see if we can straighten it out. I'll come back and tell you what went down." They looked startled, uncertain and—unless you've seen it in the eyes of kids 12 to 16 years old you won't know how it can chew on your heart—frightened.

"He can't do that?!" yelled one girl.

I smiled my best Robert-Culp-going-into-combat smile. Little baby, you have no *idea* how easily he can do that.

We went to Ray's office, Miss Benham and myself.

He was sitting behind his desk. Jack DeVelbiss, the Administrative Director, was conveniently out of town or hiding out or comatose, God only knew what. So this was Ray's play, all by his lonesome. There was no love lost between us (and all this in *two* days). He had openly implied to other faculty members that despite the fact that Miss Benham was living elsewhere while I used her apartment for my stay in Dayton, there was something seedy and clandestine about it. Mr. Ray was lucky he never said that in front of her boy friend, John Baskin, who could separate Mr. Ray's tibia and fibula like a chicken leg without too much effort. He had evinced dislike for me that stemmed—I was told by another faculty member—from my "weird" clothes, my constant talk of sex, my seeming refusal to deal with him as an authority figure, and because of that strange class (strange to him, that is) in which I'd been able to relate to, and communicate with, black kids though Ray, nominally Negro, could not. So there we were, nose to nose.

What he said and what he meant were studies in the art of lying rationally, justifying evil in the name of good, and otherwise burning down the *Reichstag* himself so Spiro Hitler could acquire the reins of power.

"What seems to be the trouble?" I asked him.

"I'm canceling the balance of your contract here."

"Oh, really? How come?"

"I've decided you don't have the best interests of the Center at heart," is what he said. *I've decided you are making waves, saying things that will get the parents looking at us more closely,* is what he thought.

"You aren't relating to the children," is what he said. *You're getting through to them and they're going back home and asking questions and I'm getting phone calls,* is what he thought.

"You're turning a lot of them off," is what he said. *You're turning* me *off,* is what he thought.

"You're not fulfilling the role of a guest artist here," is what he said. *You weren't supposed to talk politics or start trouble,* is what he thought.

"I can't take a chance on your delivering a talk tonight that will cause the Center trouble. Our position is very uncertain right now," is what he said. *I'm scared shitless you'll offend the Middle Americans and I'll lose my job,* is what he thought.

"Anything else?" I asked.

"Yes; frankly, you have a foul mouth. It doesn't of-

307

fend *me*, you understand, but it has turned off some of the children."

I quote to you now from an article in the *Dayton Journal Herald* dated 17 December 69, headlined ARTS CENTER CANCELS WRITER (pars. 8 & 9). "Students who were with Ellison at the center yesterday said his blunt language might have been interpreted by Ray as offensive.

" 'He used a couple of beauties,' " a student said regarding Ellison's speech, "but it didn't bother anyone.' "

What Ray *said* to me, and what he *meant*, were light-years apart.

"We'll pay you the balance of your fee," Ray said. He had to. We had a contract. "Thank you, but I don't think I'll accept it," I answered. "Just my expenses will do."

"Great," grinned Ray. "We can use the money."

I suddenly had the feeling my ethics had made me a patsy. Even so, I suggested to him that he was being hasty, and that if he felt the night's lecture was going to be a debacle, I'd show him the material I'd prepared: an essay on creativity, a short story in the form of a fantasy about returning to one's childhood, and some anecdotes. "My mind is made up," he said.

"You don't want any facts to get in the way, is that it?" I asked.

"You're turning the children off," he said.

It was the one thing that could stop me cold. I bit on it, despite that photo in the *Dayton Daily News* of the session at which the kids were rocking with laughter. What I didn't know was that in the Evaluation Sheets that had been given out to the black students from Dunbar High School and their teacher, I'd been lauded as having delivered a wild, groovy hour talk, and they wanted to come back again. Had I known that, I would not have acquiesced so quietly.

But after all, he *was* the Director, wasn't he? He knew what went down with the kids. Didn't he? *Sure* he did.

So I went back to John Baskin's class, and told him and the kids what had happened.

The next thing I knew, there was a children's crusade.

(Bear in mind, these are not seasoned dissenters of whom I write. They are kids from twelve years old on up to maybe sixteen, middle-class mid-American, never been in a protest scene, never been beaten on by police clubs.)

They stormed Glenn Ray's office.

"You can't talk like a liberal and then cop out!" one girl shrieked.

"If this is the way you're gonna live up to what you tell us, you can take your Center and shove it up your ass!" howled a boy of fifteen, then he turned so we wouldn't see him crying, and stormed out of the building.

Little Nancy Henry, not yet in her teens, daughter of a Dayton policeman, began weeping, trying to get her voice high enough to yell, "You can't *do* this! You can't! We won't let you!"

One black kid summed it up, to Ray. "Man, you talk the talk, but you don't walk the walk."

I didn't want a bad scene, and I heard Barbara Benham urging them to go back to the classroom, to wait for their protest. Some did, some didn't. Many hung around outside Glenn Ray's office. At this point my mind went away, and so did my lust for reportorial accuracy.

Did they throw Glenn Ray out of his office and take it over? Did Ray call the police on the little kids? I've got three different stories, all of them culminating in a riot. I went back to Benham's apartment and later that night a mass of people who had come in from Antioch and Columbus and other cities came and sat around on the floor and looked woebegone. They all kept telling me, "This isn't what Dayton's like . . . honest!"

But it is, friends. It is also what College Station, Texas's like and Altoona, Pennsylvania and Madeira

Beach, Florida and Seattle, Washington and Wheatland, Wyoming. It is the time of the Middle Americans, friends. It is the day of the Silent Majority.

And we are moving into a period of repression that will make the McCarthy era seem like the Age of Enlightenment. I said that was the theme of this three-parter way back at the beginning of this outpouring, and as soon as I give you a few more loose ends on Dayton I'll deal with Spiro, TV, the wave of fear that's backlashing us, and try to pry some sense out of the rubble.

That night, after the mourners left, John Baskin, Barbara Benham and I sat and talked. We talked about John's fury at what had happened, and how he had used the riotous scene to make some strong points with the kids about liberalism meaning nothing if you fold when the pressure's on. We talked about Ray's intentions of getting Barbara fired, and how it had been that, more than anything, that had kept me from putting Ray against the wall. We talked about the sudden appearance at the evening's wake of Hugh McDiarmid, City Editor of the *Journal Herald*, and his amazing remark: "I wanted to meet you, Ellison. My God, you're awfully small to have caused all this trouble." We talked about my speaking to the final session of the science fiction workshop the next day ... in the Benham apartment.

The next day there was even more talk. But it all went on at the Center, with DeVelbiss and Ray talking to the faculty, talking to Barbara Benham, talking to the newspapers (the headline reads LIVING ARTS GUEST 'DIDN'T FULFILL ROLE'), talking to each other and very probably talking to themselves.

Finally, I got a delayed case of being pissed-off. Here were these two "administrators," down there at the Center, bumrapping me and telling the world their idiotic position was justified because I was a moral leper. I decided to *really* make waves. But when I finally confronted Ray and DeVelbiss in the Center, it was ap-

310

parent if I pursued my plan—to insist they pay me the full fourteen hundred dollar fee, and use it to hire Asher Bogen, Dayton's best attorney, and sue them for defamation of character and anything else I could think of—they would fire Barbara Benham out of serendipitous vengefulness. I backed off. In fact, I offered to stay on, at my own expense, and provide them with an opportunity to get off the hook by doing the evening lecture two days later, from material I would submit for their scrutiny.

But their position was so inflexible, they were unable to back off; thereby demonstrating the most debilitating aspect of educational confrontations: inability to mediate, refusal to deal, concretization of posture because of a need to preserve ego and authority.

So we made a deal, of sorts, after the following conversation:

ELLISON: I'll take my money.

DeVELBISS: You turned it down when it was offered.

ELLISON: I changed my mind. I have a use for it now.

DeVELBISS: I don't have to pay someone fourteen hundred dollars to come in here and curse and cause trouble. If I want to do that, I can do it myself, for free.

ELLISON: Yeah, but you were dumb enough to hire me to do it.

There was quite a lot more, and some threats, and some Raymond Chandler hardnosing, in which Mr. Ray understood that *after* I broke every bone in his body (though on reappraisal I realize if I'd broken him open, all I'd have gotten would have been jelly on my hands) I would sue him. Not the Center, but *him*, personally, so he'd have no Board of Education money behind him. And after that I'd speak to a friend of mine quite high in the Health, Education and Welfare Department, and I'd make sure that they cut back the funds of the Center just enough to have to dispense with *him* . . . nothing else, just him. So they paid me.

And they promised they wouldn't fire Barbara Benham.

And, of course, they are honorable men. "So are they all, all honourable men—"

And so, I left Dayton.

Neither as significant as the mass of current attempts to stifle dissent . . . nor as permanent as the crimes committed against those who *have* spoken out, my Dayton foray was one with the terrors of these new times. What came out of those three days in mid-December? Only this:

John Baskin, who taught the sf class, who stood up and told the administration they were wrong, who tried to pursue the matter in articles for his newspaper, the *Dayton Daily News*, who inspired his class kids with discussions of just what freedom of expression means—John Baskin was fired from the newspaper. Perhaps there's no connection. But . . .

Barbara Benham, who taught classes on revolution and the joys of being a "free spirit"—Barbara Benham has been cowed. Something has been stolen from her, at the precise moment it fell to her (as it falls to each of us) to discover whether she had enough courage to lose everything for that in which she believed . . . she found she did not.

The kids no longer trust Glenn Ray or the administration of the Center. They have been blunted once again with the knowledge that those who prattle about serving them, opening them, helping them—are merely exploiting them for their own personal aggrandizement. Those kids will be a trifle more cynical and bitter now.

What came out of those three days was ugliness, cupidity, irrationality and, in microcosm, provide a key to the days into which we are moving.

Time picked the Middle Americans as their man and

woman of the year. It picked them because Spiro Agnew and television have forged out of the fears and prejudices and know-nothing provincialism of the mass of middle-class Americans an army of dupes, to be used to destroy the very freedoms those people say they most respect. Repression, in the name of platitudes, is what destroyed half of Europe in the Thirties and Forties. It is what gave Joseph McCarthy his power. It is what has kept us fighting a senseless war for half a decade. It is the systematic terrorization of those who—like Barbara Benham—have found it is easier to be a little bit frightened all the time, to acquiesce, to *survive,* than to ask the right questions, take the right chances, and discover for themselves that *they* are stronger than their puppet masters.

I watched William Buckley last Sunday, talking to three bright young men concerned with Our Times. He was glib, he was clever, and he made them look silly. But he dealt only with words. To hear him tell it, everything they chose to worry about—pollution, prejudice, repression, duplicity on the part of governments, censorship—all these were in their minds. It was merely a matter of using the right words. Even as Glenn Ray and Jack DeVelbiss and the man who fired John Baskin use words. They say we are "not doing the job," or we are "foul mouthed," or we "don't have the best interests of the Center at heart," but these are just syntax. They are obfuscations. They are the eyewash used by men of weak will and frightened demeanor to keep the *status quo* free of waves.

And through the use of the greatest propaganda medium the world has ever known, television, the puppet masters are duping an entire nation. The thousands of letters in support of Spiro Agnew and his denunciation of newscasters who report any news but that which the Administration finds balming to its ego is eloquent testimony to the success of the hoodwinking.

It is significant, I think, that on December 3rd the

313

Writers Guild took a gutsy stand against Agnew and his pronouncements. Their press release said, in part:

"The Writers Guild of America, West, viewed with abhorrence the attacks of Vice President Agnew on the right of news and editorial media freely to analyze and criticize statements and policies of the administration.

"We found it shocking that the second officer of the nation dared to suggest that the Constitutional guarantee of the First Amendment, embodying the fundamental right of free speech, may not apply to TV commentators and should perhaps be abridged in the press as well.

"We are concerned that the President himself has not repudiated this assault on spoken and written opinion.

"We are aware of the curiously coordinated chorus of support for these attacks by three cabinet officers, the chairman of the Federal Communications Commission, and other office-holders. This kind of concerted pressure by Government on organs of public expression, and against individuals singled out by name, is exactly what we have condemned in our enemies.

"As writers who have faced censorship in many forms, we are not lulled by disclaimers that no censorship was implied, and condemn as repugnant and sinister any attack on the basic right of free expression. That right was meant to be exercised by Americans at any and all times, for or against any administration, policy or issue. That right was not meant to be altered or suspended following a particular speech, nor is it subject to any delays or qualifications imposed from above."

I find the above curiously parallel to my situation in Dayton. And I find it significant that it was the writers who said it.

When I began writing this column, little over a year ago, my first column dealt with what I called "the illiterate conspiracy against dissent." The war on counter-opinion. At that time I conceded that the attack was an unarticulated one, that no cabal of men actually sat down in a room and said this week we silence this one, and next week we get that one.

But even in one year the times have changed drastically. Faster than I'd thought possible. The conspiracy is open now. It comes down from the top. And because of its blatancy, men who were middle of the road have been pushed to their left, have become Liberals. Liberals have been jammed over into being Activists. The Activists have, against their will, become Militants ... and the Militants, who saw what this year would become, have now hideously, horribly, without their wanting it ... been crammed all the way over into the Revolutionary Blood and Death position.

Television has given Agnew and his ilk the platform from which to martial the fear and stupidity of the masses. And those of us who began the year with sanity and hope for change, now see the Middle Americans totemized as the epitome of rationality and patriotism. Now we find ourselves on the edge of a darkling plain, looking out across a time in this country when weak men like Glenn Ray and Jack DeVelbiss will conscience *any* degradation of their ethics and morality in the name of not being singled-out as The Enemy.

And the strong men will be picked off, one by one.

They will be gagged and tried and salted away. And the darkness will creep across this land.

Friends, you may not know it, but the war is on. The big war, and possibly the last war. It had a tiny skirmish in Dayton, and we lost it.

The puppet masters in Dayton are not evil men, they are merely weak men. And it is that weakness that will kill us. The fangs of Spiro bite deep.

AFTERWORD: 30 JANUARY 70

ADDENDUM TO DAYTON

I was wrong. At least in one very important matter. After almost 10,000 words of copy relating what went on down in Dayton, Ohio during my two-day lecture/lynching, I'd thought I'd said it all.

But there is one more final fillip to be added to the confection. One that humbles me. Because, if you recall, I began part two of "Poisoned By The Fangs of "Spiro" with the comment that even the kids might not be able to save this country, because the poison of repression had seeped down into *them*, too. Whew! That's what happens, friends. It gets so damned depressing, coming up against the cultural hari-kiri we keep committing, that cynicism becomes the only supportable attitude. And then the kids prove they've got it. Even I, anxious to give them every possible point, begin to suspect the rot goes from top to bottom, young and old alike. And then the kids do me in. They come up with solid gold, and make me feel like the idiot I certainly am, on occasion.

What I'm talking about is this: you recall I spoke to two high school groups in Dayton. One was a class of kids from Dunbar High. All black. They were hip, into it, really exciting kids to rap with. The other group was all white, middle to lower-middle-class Appalachian kids. I reported they were deadheads, were offended by my manner and my language and my choice of lecture material. I reported they were responsible for inflaming their parents sufficiently at the "freak" who'd talked to them, to get those parents on the muscle against the

316

Dayton Living Arts Center, which resulted in my being canceled.

That was incorrect reportage.

Barbara Benham of the Center has sent me a salient bit of information. Straight from the mouths of the kids.

Each of the classes was presented with "Student Evaluation Sheets" which were to be filled in with a) whether or not they enjoyed the presentation, b) whether or not they'd care to see similar presentations in the future and c) remarks on the lecturer's performance.

I expected the Dunbar kids to rate me high. We'd done okay together. We'd related. But I also expected the kids from Wilbur Wright High School, the ones with whom I'd gotten nowhere, to really put me down. I present here the results of the two Evaluations.

DUNBAR STUDENTS: 17 evaluations received.

ENJOYED THE PROGRAM: 17

DID NOT ENJOY THE PROGRAM: 0

WOULD LIKE TO SEE A SIMILAR PROGRAM AGAIN: 17

WOULD NOT LIKE TO SEE A SIMILAR PROGRAM: 0

SOME REMARKS: "It's something refreshing for the mind." "He talked the same talk we talk." "With him we could really get down and express our feelings." "I enjoyed it because he told what he thought and because he showed you don't have to go to college to learn things." "Liked it because he talked on my level and tried to get everyone to talk."

Yeah, great. But what about those Wilbur Wright kids whom I knew despised me and refused to even speak? How *about* them?

WILBUR WRIGHT STUDENTS: 22 evaluations received.

ENJOYED THE PROGRAM: 21

DID NOT ENJOY THE PROGRAM: 1

WOULD LIKE TO SEE A SIMILAR PROGRAM
AGAIN: 22

WOULD NOT LIKE TO SEE A SIMILAR PRO-
GRAM: 0

SOME REMARKS: "Enables one to meet someone
from another walk of life. A few moments with an interesting person like him is worth a lifetime with a dull
one." ". . . He made all students think about the institutions . . ." "I enjoyed the program from the aspect of
Mr. Ellison's ideas, but I believe many of his thoughts
were of a Utopian essence and I think the world the
way he wishes it is somewhat hard to imagine. I was
surprised that an association joined with the Board of
Education would bring a person like Mr. Ellison to the
Living Arts Center. His profanity during the program
was uncalled for. To me, it seems that he was . . . con-
tradicting himself." "I think that he was a good
speaker, not because of his language but for his knowledge and experience." "It really wasn't long enough
and each person could not talk to him privately." "The
speaker was certainly different from most. He was
much freer, easy to speak with, and very frank . . ."
"He was very open with us which I liked." "I liked Ellison's approach. He tried to get everyone involved.
We didn't talk anything about writing and that was our
main objective. He did convey good ideas to me,
though." "Ellison told it like it was." "He was frank
and outspoken, but was an intelligent man who told
things from experience. I could have listened to him all
day! A marvelous person with a fantastic outlook on
life." "I liked it because it was not formal and the talking was open. There was nothing I didn't like about the
performance." ". . . Programs like this are very valu-
able to high schoolers because we are preparing to take
our place in society and we must realize what society is
really like." "If Mr. Ellison is going to be the speaker I
wouldn't care to attend any other program concerning
any topic . . ."

You know, I actually went for the okeydoke Glenn

Ray laid on me, that I'd turned the kids off and hadn't related to them. Which—added to my thoroughly misjudging and ignorantly putting down those kids—goes to prove how muddied grow one's perceptions, the longer on the firing line. And it even seems I managed to convey in my ham-handed fashion that Barbara Benham was a culprit. Not so. A victim, like all of us, yeah sure; and frightened, like all of us, yeah that too. But a bad guy . . . no.

I owe apologies, herewith tendered. To Miss Benham, and to the kids of Wilbur Wright, who are infinitely wiser and groovier than any California mushhead come to tell them "where it's at." Once again, troops, you have showed me there is still hope, and you make it easier to fight the battles, big and small. Jesus, I feel good today.